BURMESE DAYS

GEORGE ORWELL

SANAGE
PUBLISHING HOUSE

Paperback: 978-819596174-0

Printed by: Manipal Technologies Limited, Manipal

Sanage Publishing House LLP
Mumbai, India

sanagepublishing@gmail.com

Eric Arthur Blair (25 June 1903 – 21 January 1950), better known by his pen name **George Orwell**, was an English novelist and essayist, journalist and critic. His works are characterized by lucid prose, biting social criticism, opposition to totalitarianism, and outspoken support of democratic socialism.

George Orwell is best known for the allegorical novella **Animal Farm** and the **dystopian novel Nineteen Eighty-Four**.

CONTENTS

CHAPTER 1

U Po Kyin, Sub-divisional Magistrate of Kyauktada, in Upper Burma, was sitting in his veranda. It was only half past eight, but the month was April, and there was a closeness in the air, a threat of the long, stifling midday hours. Occasional faint breaths of wind, seeming cool by contrast, stirred the newly drenched orchids that hung from the eaves. Beyond the orchids one could see the dusty, curved trunk of a palm tree, and then the blazing ultramarine sky. Up in the zenith, so high that it dazzled one to look at them, a few vultures circled without the quiver of a wing.

Unblinking, rather like a great porcelain idol, U Po Kyin gazed out into the fierce sunlight. He was a man of fifty, so fat that for years he had not risen from his chair without help, and yet shapely and even beautiful in his grossness; for the Burmese do not sag and bulge like white men, but grow fat symmetrically, like fruits swelling. His face was vast, yellow and quite unwrinkled, and his eyes were tawny. His feet—squat, high-arched feet with the toes all the same length—were bare, and so was his cropped head, and he wore one of those vivid Arakanese longyis with green and magenta checks which the Burmese wear on informal occasions. He was chewing betel from a lacquered box on the table, and thinking about his past life.

It had been a brilliantly successful life. U Po Kyin's earliest memory, back in the eighties, was of standing, a naked pot-bellied child, watching the British troops march victorious into Mandalay. He remembered the terror he had felt of those columns of great beef-fed men, red-faced and red-coated; and the long rifles over their shoulders, and the heavy, rhythmic tramp of their boots. He had taken to his heels after watching them for a few minutes. In his childish way he had grasped that his own people were no match for this race of giants. To fight on the side of the British, to become a parasite upon them, had been his ruling ambition, even as a child.

At seventeen he had tried for a Government appointment, but he had failed to get it, being poor and friendless, and for three years he had worked in the stinking labyrinth of the Mandalay bazaars, clerking for the rice merchants and sometimes stealing. Then when he was twenty a lucky stroke of blackmail put him in possession of four hundred rupees, and he went at once to Rangoon and bought his way into a Government clerkship. The job was a lucrative one though the salary was small. At that time a ring of clerks were making a steady income by misappropriating Government stores, and Po Kyin (he was plain Po Kyin then: the honorific U came years later) took naturally to this kind of thing. However, he had too much talent to spend his life in a clerkship, stealing miserably in annas and pice. One day he discovered that the Government, being short of minor officials, were going to make some appointments from among the clerks. The news would have become public in another week, but it was one of Po Kyin's qualities that his information was always a week ahead of everyone else's. He saw his chance and denounced all his confederates before they could take alarm. Most of them were sent to prison, and Po

Kyin was made an Assistant Township Officer as the reward of his honesty. Since then he had risen steadily. Now, at fifty-six, he was a Sub-divisional Magistrate, and he would probably be promoted still further and made an acting Deputy Commissioner, with Englishmen as his equals and even his subordinates.

As a magistrate his methods were simple. Even for the vastest bribe he would never sell the decision of a case, because he knew that a magistrate who gives wrong judgments is caught sooner or later. His practice, a much safer one, was to take bribes from both sides and then decide the case on strictly legal grounds. This won him a useful reputation for impartiality. Besides his revenue from litigants, U Po Kyin levied a ceaseless toll, a sort of private taxation scheme, from all the villages under his jurisdiction. If any village failed in its tribute U Po Kyin took punitive measures—gangs of dacoits attacked the village, leading villagers were arrested on false charges, and so forth—and it was never long before the amount was paid up. He also shared the proceeds of all the larger-sized robberies that took place in the district. Most of this, of course, was known to everyone except U Po Kyin's official superiors (no British officer will ever believe anything against his own men) but the attempts to expose him invariably failed; his supporters, kept loyal by their share of the loot, were too numerous. When any accusation was brought against him, U Po Kyin simply discredited it with strings of suborned witnesses, following this up by counter-accusations which left him in a stronger position than ever. He was practically invulnerable, because he was too fine a judge of men ever to choose a wrong instrument, and also because he was too absorbed in intrigue ever to fail through carelessness or ignorance. One could say with practical certainty that he would never be found out, that he would go from success to success, and would finally die full of honour, worth several lakhs of rupees.

And even beyond the grave his success would continue. According to Buddhist belief, those who have done evil in their lives will spend the next incarnation in the shape of a rat, a frog or some other low animal. U Po Kyin was a good Buddhist and intended to provide against this danger. He would devote his closing years to good works, which would pile up enough merit to outweigh the rest of his life. Probably his good works would take the form of building pagodas. Four pagodas, five, six, seven—the priests would tell him how many—with carved stonework, gilt umbrellas and little bells that tinkled in the wind, every tinkle a prayer. And he would return to the earth in male human shape—for a woman ranks at about the same level as a rat or a frog—or at best as some dignified beast such as an elephant.

All these thoughts flowed through U Po Kyin's mind swiftly and for the most part in pictures. His brain, though cunning, was quite barbaric, and it never worked except for some definite end; mere meditation was beyond him. He had now reached the point to which his thoughts had been tending. Putting his smallish, triangular hands on the arms of his chair, he turned himself a little way round and called, rather wheezily:

'Ba Taik! Hey, Ba Taik!'

Ba Taik, U Po Kyin's servant, appeared through the beaded curtain of the veranda. He was an under-sized, pock-marked man with a timid and rather hungry expression. U Po Kyin paid him no wages, for he was a convicted thief whom a word would send to prison. As Ba Taik advanced he shikoed, so low as to give the impression that he was stepping backwards.

'Most holy god?' he said.

'Is anyone waiting to see me, Ba Taik?'

Ba Taik enumerated the visitors upon his fingers: 'There is the headman of Thitpingyi village, your honour, who has brought presents, and two villagers who have an assault case that is to be tried by your honour, and they too have brought presents. Ko Ba Sein, the head clerk of the Deputy Commissioner s office, wishes to see you, and there is Ali Shah, the police constable, and a dacoit whose name I do not know. I think they have quarrelled about some gold bangles they have stolen. And there is also a young village girl with a baby.'

'What does she want?' said U Po Kyin.

'She says that the baby is yours, most holy one.'

'Ah. And how much has the headman brought?'

Ba Taik thought it was only ten rupees and a basket of mangoes.

'Tell the headman,' said U Po Kyin, 'that it should be twenty rupees, and there will be trouble for him and his village if the money is not here tomorrow. I will see the others presently. Ask Ko Ba Sein to come to me here.'

Ba Sein appeared in a moment. He was an erect, narrow-shouldered man, very tall for a Burman, with a curiously smooth face that recalled a coffee blancmange. U Po Kyin found him a useful tool. Unimaginative and hardworking, he was an excellent clerk, and Mr Macgregor, the Deputy Commissioner, trusted him with most of his official secrets. U Po Kyin, put in a good temper by his thoughts, greeted Ba Sein with a laugh and waved to the betel box.

'Well, Ko Ba Sein, how does our affair progress? I hope that, as dear Mr Macgregor would say'—U Po Kyin broke into English—'"eet ees making perceptible progress"?'

Ba Sein did not smile at the small joke. Sitting down stiff and long-backed in the vacant chair, he answered:

'Excellently, sir. Our copy of the paper arrived this morning. Kindly observe.'

He produced a copy of a bilingual paper called the Burmese Patriot. It was a miserable eight-page rag, villainously printed on paper as bad as blotting paper, and composed partly of news stolen from the Rangoon Gazette, partly of weak Nationalist heroics. On the last page the type had slipped and left the entire sheet jet black, as though in mourning for the smallness of the paper's circulation. The article to which U Po Kyin turned was of a rather different stamp from the rest. It ran:

In these happy times, when we poor blacks are being uplifted by the mighty western civilization, with its manifold blessings such as the cinematograph, machine-guns, syphilis, etc., what subject could be more inspiring than the private lives of our European benefactors? We think therefore that it may interest our readers to hear something of events in the up-country district of Kyauktada. And especially of Mr Macgregor, honoured Deputy Commissioner of said district.

Mr Macgregor is of the type of the Fine Old English Gentleman, such as, in these happy days, we have so many examples before our eyes. He is 'a family man' as our dear English cousins say. Very much a family man is Mr Macgregor. So much so that he has already three children in the district of Kyauktada, where he has been a year, and in his last district of Shwemyo he left six young progenies behind him. Perhaps it is an oversight on Mr Macgregor's part that he has left these young infants quite unprovided for, and that some of their mothers are in danger of starvation, etc., etc., etc.

There was a column of similar stuff, and wretched as it was, it was well above the level of the rest of the paper. U Po Kyin read the article carefully through, holding it at arm's length—he was long-sighted—and drawing his lips meditatively back, exposing great numbers of small, perfect teeth, blood-red from betel juice.

'The editor will get six months' imprisonment for this,' he said finally.

'He does not mind. He says that the only time when his creditors leave him alone is when he is in prison.'

'And you say that your little apprentice clerk Hla Pe wrote this article all by himself? That is a very clever boy—a most promising boy! Never tell me again that these Government High Schools are a waste of time. Hla Pe shall certainly have his clerkship.'

'You think then, sir, that this article will be enough?'

U Po Kyin did not answer immediately. A puffing, labouring noise began to proceed from him; he was trying to rise from his chair. Ba Taik was familiar with this sound. He appeared from behind the beaded curtain, and he and Ba Sein put a hand under each of U Po Kyin's armpits and hoisted him to his feet. U Po Kyin stood for a moment balancing the weight of his belly upon his legs, with the movement of a fish porter adjusting his load. Then he waved Ba Taik away.

'Not enough,' he said, answering Ba Sein's question, 'not enough by any means. There is a lot to be done yet. But this is the right beginning. Listen.'

He went to the rail to spit out a scarlet mouthful of betel, and then began to quarter the veranda with short steps, his hands behind his back. The friction of his vast thighs made him waddle slightly. As he walked he talked, in the base jargon of the Government offices—a patchwork of Burmese verbs and English abstract phrases:

'Now, let us go into this affair from the beginning. We are going to make a concerted attack on Dr Veraswami, who is the Civil Surgeon and Superintendent of the jail. We are going to slander him, destroy his reputation and finally ruin him for ever. It will be rather a delicate operation.'

'Yes, sir.'

'There will be no risk, but we have got to go slowly. We are not proceeding against a miserable clerk or police constable. We are proceeding against a high official, and with a high official, even when he is an Indian, it is not the same as with a clerk. How does one ruin a clerk? Easy; an accusation, two dozen witnesses, dismissal and imprisonment. But that will not do here. Softly, softly, softly is my way. No scandal, and above all no official inquiry. There must be no accusations that can be answered, and yet within three months I must fix it in the head of every European in Kyauktada that the doctor is a villain. What shall I accuse him of? Bribes will not do, a doctor does not get bribes to any extent. What then?'

'We could perhaps arrange a mutiny in the jail,' said Ba Sein. 'As superintendent, the doctor would be blamed.'

'No, it is too dangerous. I do not want the jail warders firing their rifles in all directions. Besides, it would be expensive. Clearly, then, it must be disloyalty—Nationalism, seditious propaganda. We must persuade the Europeans that the doctor holds disloyal, anti-British opinions. That is far worse than bribery; they expect a native official to take bribes. But let them suspect his loyalty even for a moment, and he is ruined.'

'It would be a hard thing to prove,' objected Ba Sein. 'The doctor is very loyal to the Europeans. He grows angry when anything is said against them. They will know that, do you not think?'

‘Nonsense, nonsense,’ said U Po Kyin comfortably. ‘No European cares anything about proofs. When a man has a black face, suspicion IS proof. A few anonymous letters will work wonders. It is only a question of persisting; accuse, accuse, go on accusing— that is the way with Europeans. One anonymous letter after another, to every European in turn. And then, when their suspicions are thoroughly aroused—’ U Po Kyin brought one short arm from behind his back and clicked his thumb and finger. He added: ‘We begin with this article in the Burmese Patriot. The Europeans will shout with rage when they see it. Well, the next move is to persuade them that it was the doctor who wrote it.’

‘It will be difficult while he has friends among the Europeans. All of them go to him when they are ill. He cured Mr Macgregor of his flatulence this cold weather. They consider him a very clever doctor, I believe.’

‘How little you understand the European mind, Ko Ba Sein! If the Europeans go to Veraswami it is only because there is no other doctor in Kyauktada. No European has any faith in a man with a black face. No, with anonymous letters it is only a question of sending enough. I shall soon see to it that he has no friends left.’

‘There is Mr Flory, the timber merchant,’ said Ba Sein. (He pronounced it ‘Mr Porley’.) ‘He is a close friend of the doctor. I see him go to his house every morning when he is in Kyauktada. Twice he has even invited the doctor to dinner.’

‘Ah, now there you are right. If Flory were a friend of the doctor it could do us harm. You cannot hurt an Indian when he has a European friend. It gives him—what is that word they are so fond of?—prestige. But Flory will desert his friend quickly enough when the trouble begins. These people have no feeling of loyalty towards a native. Besides, I happen to know that Flory is a coward. I can deal with him. Your part, Ko Ba Sein, is to watch

Mr Macgregor's movements. Has he written to the Commissioner lately—written confidentially, I mean?'

'He wrote two days ago, but when we steamed the letter open we found it was nothing of importance.'

'Ah well, we will give him something to write about. And as soon as he suspects the doctor, then is the time for that other affair I spoke to you of. Thus we shall—what does Mr Macgregor say? Ah yes, "kill two birds with one stone". A whole flock of birds—ha, ha!'

U Po Kyin's laugh was a disgusting bubbling sound deep down in his belly, like the preparation for a cough; yet it was merry, even childlike. He did not say any more about the 'other affair', which was too private to be discussed even upon the veranda. Ba Sein, seeing the interview at an end, stood up and bowed, angular as a jointed ruler.

'Is there anything else your honour wishes done?' he said.

'Make sure that Mr Macgregor has his copy of the Burmese Patriot. You had better tell Hla Pe to have an attack of dysentery and stay away from the office. I shall want him for the writing of the anonymous letters. That is all for the present.'

'Then I may go, sir?'

'God go with you,' said U Po Kyin rather abstractedly, and at once shouted again for Ba Taik. He never wasted a moment of his day. It did not take him long to deal with the other visitors and to send the village girl away unrewarded, having examined her face and said that he did not recognize her. It was now his breakfast time. Violent pangs of hunger, which attacked him punctually at this hour every morning, began to torment his belly. He shouted urgently:

'Ba Taik! Hey, Ba Taik! Kin Kin! My breakfast! Be quick, I am starving.'

In the living-room behind the curtain a table was already set out with a huge bowl of rice and a dozen plates containing curries, dried prawns and sliced green mangoes. U Po Kyin waddled to the table, sat down with a grunt and at once threw himself on the food. Ma Kin, his wife, stood behind him and served him. She was a thin woman of five and forty, with a kindly, pale brown, simian face. U Po Kyin took no notice of her while he was eating. With the bowl close to his nose he stuffed the food into himself with swift, greasy fingers, breathing fast. All his meals were swift, passionate and enormous; they were not meals so much as orgies, debauches of curry and rice. When he had finished he sat back, belched several times and told Ma Kin to fetch him a green Burmese cigar. He never smoked English tobacco, which he declared had no taste in it.

Presently, with Ba Taik's help, U Po Kyin dressed in his office clothes, and stood for a while admiring himself in the long mirror in the living-room. It was a wooden-walled room with two pillars, still recognizable as teak-trunks, supporting the roof-tree, and it was dark and sluttish as all Burmese rooms are, though U Po Kyin had furnished it 'Ingaleik fashion' with a veneered sideboard and chairs, some lithographs of the Royal Family and a fire-extinguisher. The floor was covered with bamboo mats, much splashed by lime and betel juice.

Ma Kin was sitting on a mat in the corner, stitching an ingyi. U Po Kyin turned slowly before the mirror, trying to get a glimpse of his back view. He was dressed in a gaungbaung of pale pink silk, an ingyi of starched muslin, and a paso of Mandalay silk, a gorgeous salmon-pink brocaded with yellow. With an effort he turned his head round and looked, pleased, at the paso tight and shining on his enormous buttocks. He was proud of his fatness, because he saw the accumulated flesh as the symbol of his greatness. He who had once been obscure and hungry was now fat, rich and feared. He was swollen with the bodies of his enemies; a thought from which he extracted something very near poetry.

'My new paso was cheap at twenty-two rupees, hey, Kin Kin?' he said.

Ma Kin bent her head over her sewing. She was a simple, old-fashioned woman, who had learned even less of European habits than U Po Kyin. She could not sit on a chair without discomfort. Every morning she went to the bazaar with a basket on her head, like a village woman, and in the evenings she could be seen kneeling in the garden, praying to the white spire of the pagoda that crowned the town. She had been the confidante of U Po Kyin's intrigues for twenty years and more.

'Ko Po Kyin,' she said, 'you have done very much evil in your life.'

U Po Kyin waved his hand. 'What does it matter? My pagodas will atone for everything. There is plenty of time.'

Ma Kin bent her head over her sewing again, in an obstinate way she had when she disapproved of something that U Po Kyin was doing.

'But, Ko Po Kyin, where is the need for all this scheming and intriguing? I heard you talking with Ko Ba Sein on the veranda. You are planning some evil against Dr Veraswami. Why do you wish to harm that Indian doctor? He is a good man.'

'What do you know of these official matters, woman? The doctor stands in my way. In the first place he refuses to take bribes, which makes it difficult for the rest of us. And besides—well, there is something else which you would never have the brains to understand.'

'Ko Po Kyin, you have grown rich and powerful, and what good has it ever done you? We were happier when we were poor. Ah, I remember so well when you were only a Township Officer, the first time we had a house of our own. How proud we were of our new wicker furniture, and your fountain-pen with the gold clip! And when the young English police-officer came to our house and sat in the best chair and drank a bottle of beer, how honoured we thought ourselves! Happiness is not in money. What can you want with more money now?'

'Nonsense, woman, nonsense! Attend to your cooking and sewing and leave official matters to those who understand them.'

'Well, I do not know. I am your wife and have always obeyed you. But at least it is never too soon to acquire merit. Strive to acquire more merit, Ko Po Kyin! Will you not, for instance, buy some live fish and set them free in the river? One can acquire much merit in that way. Also, this morning when the priests came for their rice they told me that there are two new priests at the monastery, and they are hungry. Will you not give them something, Ko Po Kyin? I did not give them anything myself, so that you might acquire the merit of doing it.'

U Po Kyin turned away from the mirror. The appeal touched him a little. He never, when it could be done without inconvenience, missed a chance of acquiring merit. In his eyes his pile of merit was a kind of bank deposit, everlastingly growing. Every fish set free in the river, every gift to a priest, was a step nearer Nirvana. It was a reassuring thought. He directed that the basket of mangoes brought by the village headman should be sent down to the monastery.

Presently he left the house and started down the road, with Ba Taik behind him carrying a file of papers. He walked slowly, very upright to balance his vast belly, and holding a yellow silk umbrella over his head. His pink paso glittered in the sun like a satin praline. He was going to the court, to try his day's cases.

Chapter 2

At about the time when U Po Kyin began his morning's business, 'Mr Porley' the timber merchant and friend of Dr Veraswami, was leaving his house for the Club.

Flory was a man of about thirty-five, of middle height, not ill made. He had very black, stiff hair growing low on his head, and a cropped black moustache, and his skin, naturally sallow, was discoloured by the sun. Not having grown fat or bald he did not look older than his age, but his face was very haggard in spite of the sunburn, with lank cheeks and a sunken, withered look round the eyes. He had obviously not shaved this morning. He was dressed in the usual white shirt, khaki drill shorts and stockings, but instead of a topi he wore a battered Terai hat, cocked over one eye. He carried a bamboo stick with a wrist-thong, and a black cocker spaniel named Flo was ambling after him.

All these were secondary expressions, however. The first thing that one noticed in Flory was a hideous birthmark stretching in a ragged crescent down his left cheek, from the eye to the corner of the mouth. Seen from the left side his face had a battered, woebegone look, as though the birthmark had been a bruise—for it was a dark blue in colour. He was quite aware of its hideousness. And at all times, when he was not alone, there was a sidelongness about his movements, as he manoeuvred constantly to keep the birthmark out of sight.

Flory's house was at the top of the maidan, close to the edge of the jungle. From the gate the maidan sloped sharply down, scorched and khaki-coloured, with half a dozen dazzling white bungalows scattered round it. All quaked, shivered in the hot air. There was an English cemetery within a white wall half-way down the hill, and near by a tiny tin-roofed church. Beyond that was the European Club, and when one looked at the Club—a dumpy one-storey wooden building—one looked at the real centre of the town. In any town in India the European Club is the spiritual citadel, the real seat of the British power, the Nirvana for which native officials and millionaires pine in vain. It was doubly so in this case, for it was the proud boast of Kyauktada Club that, almost alone of Clubs in Burma, it had never admitted an Oriental to membership. Beyond the Club, the Irrawaddy flowed huge and ochreous glittering like diamonds in the patches that caught the sun; and beyond the river stretched great wastes of paddy fields, ending at the horizon in a range of blackish hills.

The native town, and the courts and the jail, were over to the right, mostly hidden in green groves of peepul trees. The spire of the pagoda rose from the trees like a slender spear tipped with gold. Kyauktada was a fairly typical Upper Burma town, that had not changed greatly between the days of Marco Polo and 1910, and might have slept in the Middle Ages for a century more if it had not proved a convenient spot for a railway terminus. In 1910 the Government made it the headquarters of a district and a seat of Progress—interpretable as a block of law courts, with their army of fat but ravenous pleaders, a hospital, a school and one of those huge, durable jails which the English have built everywhere between Gibraltar and Hong Kong. The population was about four thousand, including a couple of hundred Indians, a few score Chinese and seven Europeans. There were also two Eurasians named Mr Francis and Mr Samuel, the sons of an American Baptist missionary and a Roman Catholic missionary respectively. The town contained no curiosities of any kind, except an Indian fakir who had lived for twenty years in a tree near the bazaar, drawing his food up in a basket every morning.

Flory yawned as he came out of the gate. He had been half drunk the night before, and the glare made him feel liverish. 'Bloody, bloody hole!' he thought, looking down the hill. And, no one except the dog being near, he began to sing aloud, 'Bloody, bloody, bloody, oh, how thou art bloody' to the tune of 'Holy, holy, holy, oh how Thou art holy ' as he walked down the hot red road, swishing at the dried-up grasses with his stick. It was nearly nine o'clock and the sun was fiercer every minute. The heat throbbed down on one's head with a steady, rhythmic thumping, like blows from an enormous bolster. Flory stopped at the Club gate, wondering whether to go in or to go farther down the road and see Dr Veraswami. Then he remembered that it was 'English mail day' and the newspapers would have arrived. He went in, past the big tennis screen, which was overgrown by a creeper with starlike mauve flowers.

In the borders beside the path swaths of English flowers—phlox and larkspur, hollyhock and petunia—not yet slain by the sun, rioted in vast size and richness. The petunias were huge, like trees almost. There was no lawn, but instead a shrubbery of native trees and bushes—gold mohur trees like vast umbrellas of blood-red bloom, frangipanis with creamy, stalkless flowers, purple bougainvillea, scarlet hibiscus and the pink Chinese rose, bilious-green crotons, feathery fronds of tamarind. The clash of colours hurt one's eyes in the glare. A nearly naked mali, watering-can in hand, was moving in the jungle of flowers like some large nectar-sucking bird.

On the Club steps a sandy-haired Englishman, with a prickly moustache, pale grey eyes too far apart, and abnormally thin calves to his legs, was standing with his hands in the pockets of his shorts. This was Mr Westfield, the District Superintendent of Police. With a very bored air he was rocking himself backwards and forwards on his heels and pouting his upper lip so that his moustache tickled his nose. He greeted Flory with a slight sideways movement of his head. His way of speaking was clipped and soldierly, missing out every word that well could be missed out. Nearly everything he said was intended for a joke, but the tone of his voice was hollow and melancholy.

'Hullo, Flory me lad. Bloody awful morning, what?'

'We must expect it at this time of year, I suppose,' Flory said. He had turned himself a little sideways, so that his birthmarked cheek was away from Westfield.

'Yes, dammit. Couple of months of this coming. Last year we didn't have a spot of rain till June. Look at that bloody sky, not a cloud in it. Like one of those damned great blue enamel saucepans. God! What'd you give to be in Piccadilly now, eh?'

'Have the English papers come?'

'Yes. Dear old Punch, Pink'un and Vie Parisienne. Makes you homesick to read 'em, what? Let's come in and have a drink before the ice all goes. Old Lackersteen's been fairly bathing in it. Half pickled already.'

They went in, Westfield remarking in his gloomy voice, 'Lead on, Macduff.' Inside, the Club was a teak-walled place smelling of earth-oil, and consisting of only four rooms, one of which contained a forlorn 'library' of five hundred mildewed novels, and another an old and mangy billiard-table—this, however, seldom used, for during most of the year hordes of flying beetles came buzzing round the lamps and littered themselves over the cloth. There were also a card-room and a 'lounge' which looked towards the river, over a wide veranda; but at this time of day all the verandas were curtained with green bamboo chicks. The lounge was an unhomelike room, with coco-nut matting on the floor, and wicker chairs and tables which were littered with shiny illustrated papers. For ornament there were a number of 'Bonzo' pictures, and the dusty skulls of sambhur. A punkah, lazily flapping, shook dust into the tepid air.

There were three men in the room. Under the punkah a florid, fine-looking, slightly bloated man of forty was sprawling across the table with his head in his hands, groaning in pain. This was Mr Lackersteen, the local manager of a timber firm. He had been badly drunk the night before, and he was suffering for it. Ellis, local manager of yet another company, was standing before the notice-board studying some notice with a look of bitter concentration. He was a tiny wiry-haired fellow with a pale, sharp-featured face and restless movements. Maxwell, the acting Divisional Forest Officer, was lying in one of the long chairs reading the Field, and invisible except for two large-boned legs and thick downy forearms.

'Look at this naughty old man,' said Westfield, taking Mr Lackersteen half affectionately by the shoulders and shaking him. 'Example to the young, what? There but for the grace of God and all that. Gives you an idea what you'll be like at forty.'

Mr Lackersteen gave a groan which sounded like 'brandy'.

'Poor old chap,' said Westfield, 'regular martyr to booze, eh? Look at it oozing out of his pores. Reminds me of the old colonel who used to sleep without a mosquito net. They asked his servant why and the servant said: "At night, master too drunk to notice mosquitoes; in the morning, mosquitoes too drunk to notice master." Look at him— boozed last night and then asking for more. Got a little niece coming to stay with him, too. Due tonight, isn't she, Lackersteen?'

'Oh, leave that drunken sot alone,' said Ellis without turning round. He had a spiteful Cockney voice. Mr Lackersteen groaned again, '—— the niece! Get me some brandy, for Christ's sake.'

'Good education for the niece, eh? Seeing uncle under the table seven times a week. Hey, butler! Bringing brandy for Lackersteen master!'

The butler, a dark, stout Dravidian with liquid, yellow-irised eyes like those of a dog, brought the brandy on a brass tray. Flory and Westfield ordered gin. Mr Lackersteen swallowed a few spoonfuls of brandy and sat back in his chair, groaning in a more resigned way. He had a beefy, ingenuous face, with a toothbrush moustache. He was really a very simple-minded man, with no ambitions beyond having what he called 'a good time'. His wife governed him by the only possible method, namely, by never letting him out of her sight for more than an hour or two. Only once, a year after they were married, she had left him for a fortnight, and had returned unexpectedly a day before her time, to find Mr Lackersteen, drunk, supported on either side by a naked Burmese girl, while a third up-ended a whisky bottle into his mouth. Since then she had watched him, as he used to complain, 'like a cat over a bloody mousehole'. However, he managed to enjoy quite a number of 'good times', though they were usually rather hurried ones.

'My Christ, what a head I've got on me this morning,' he said. 'Call that butler again, Westfield. I've got to have another brandy before my missus gets here. She says she's going to cut my booze down to four pegs a day when our niece gets here. God rot them both!' he added gloomily.

'Stop playing the fool, all of you, and listen to this,' said Ellis sourly. He had a queer wounding way of speaking, hardly ever opening his mouth without insulting somebody. He deliberately exaggerated his Cockney accent, because of the sardonic tone it gave to his words. 'Have you seen this notice of old Macgregor's? A little nosegay for everyone. Maxwell, wake up and listen!'

Maxwell lowered the Field. He was a fresh-coloured blond youth of not more than twenty-five or six—very young for the post he held. With his heavy limbs and thick white eyelashes he reminded one of a cart-horse colt. Ellis nipped the notice from the board with a neat, spiteful little movement and began reading it aloud. It had been posted by Mr Macgregor, who, besides being Deputy Commissioner, was secretary of the Club.

'Just listen to this. "It has been suggested that as there are as yet no Oriental members of this club, and as it is now usual to admit officials of gazetted rank, whether native or European, to membership of most European Clubs, we should consider the question of following this practice in Kyauktada. The matter will be open for discussion at the next general meeting. On the one hand it may be pointed out"—oh, well, no need to wade through the rest of it. He can't even write a notice without an attack of literary diarrhoea. Anyway, the point's this. He's asking us to break all our rules and take a dear little nigger-boy into this Club. DEAR Dr Veraswami, for instance. Dr Very-slimy, I call him. That WOULD be a treat, wouldn't it? Little pot-bellied niggers breathing garlic in your face over the bridge-table. Christ, to think of it! We've got to hang together and put our foot down on this at once. What do you say, Westfield? Flory?'

Westfield shrugged his thin shoulders philosophically. He had sat down at the table and lighted a black, stinking Burma cheroot.

'Got to put up with it, I suppose,' he said. 'B—s of natives are getting into all the Clubs nowadays. Even the Pegu Club, I'm told. Way this country's going, you know. We're about the last Club in Burma to hold out against 'em.'

'We are; and what's more, we're damn well going to go on holding out. I'll die in the ditch before I'll see a nigger in here.' Ellis had produced a stump of pencil. With the curious air of spite that some men can put into their tiniest action, he re-pinned the notice on the board and pencilled a tiny, neat 'B. F.' against Mr Macgregor's signature—'There, that's what I think of his idea. I'll tell him so when he comes down. What do YOU say, Flory?'

Flory had not spoken all this time. Though by nature anything but a silent man, he seldom found much to say in Club conversations. He had sat down at the table and was reading G. K. Chesterton's article in the London News, at the same time caressing Flo's head with his left hand. Ellis, however, was one of those people who constantly nag others to echo their own opinions. He repeated his question, and Flory looked up, and their eyes met. The skin round Ellis's nose suddenly turned so pale that it was almost grey. In him it was a sign of anger. Without any prelude he burst into a stream of abuse that would have been startling, if the others had not been used to hearing something like it every morning.

'My God, I should have thought in a case like this, when it's a question of keeping those black, stinking swine out of the only place where we can enjoy ourselves, you'd have the decency to back me up. Even if that pot-bellied greasy little sod of a nigger doctor IS your best pal. *I* don't care if you choose to pal up with the scum of the bazaar. If it pleases you to go to Veraswami's house and drink whisky with all his nigger pals, that's your look-out. Do what you like outside the Club. But, by God, it's a different matter when you talk of bringing niggers in here. I suppose you'd like little Veraswami for a Club member, eh? Chipping into our conversation and pawing everyone with his sweaty hands and breathing his filthy garlic breath in our faces. By god, he'd go out with my boot behind him if ever I saw his black snout inside that door. Greasy, pot-bellied little— !' etc.

This went on for several minutes. It was curiously impressive, because it was so completely sincere. Ellis really did hate Orientals—hated them with a bitter, restless loathing as of something evil or unclean. Living and working, as the assistant of a timber firm must, in perpetual contact with the Burmese, he had never grown used to the sight of a black face. Any hint of friendly feeling towards an Oriental seemed to him a horrible perversity. He was an intelligent man and an able servant of his firm, but he was one of those Englishmen—common, unfortunately— who should never be allowed to set foot in the East.

Flory sat nursing Flo's head in his lap, unable to meet Ellis's eyes. At the best of times his birthmark made it difficult for him to look people straight in the face. And when he made ready to speak, he could feel his voice trembling—for it had a way of trembling when it should have been firm; his features, too, sometimes twitched uncontrollably.

'Steady on,' he said at last, sullenly and rather feebly. 'Steady on. There's no need to get so excited. *I* never suggested having any native members in here.'

'Oh, didn't you? We all know bloody well you'd like to, though. Why else do you go to that oily little babu's house every morning, then? Sitting down at table with him as though he was a white man, and drinking out of glasses his filthy black lips have slobbered over—it makes me spew to think of it.'

'Sit down, old chap, sit down,' Westfield said. 'Forget it. Have a drink on it. Not worth while quarrelling. Too hot.'

'My God,' said Ellis a little more calmly, taking a pace or two up and down, 'my God, I don't understand you chaps. I simply don't. Here's that old fool Macgregor wanting to bring a nigger into this Club for no reason whatever, and you all sit down under it without a word. Good God, what are we supposed to be doing in this country? If we aren't going to rule, why the devil don't we clear out? Here we are, supposed to be governing a set of damn black swine who've been slaves since the beginning of history, and instead of ruling them in the only way they understand, we go and treat them as equals. And you silly b—s take it for granted. There's Flory, makes his best pal a black babu who calls himself a doctor because he's done two years at an Indian so-called university. And you, Westfield, proud as Punch of your knock-kneed, bribe-taking cowards of policemen. And there's Maxwell, spends his time running after Eurasian tarts. Yes, you do, Maxwell; I heard about your goings-on in Mandalay with some smelly little bitch called Molly Pereira. I suppose you'd have gone and married her if they hadn't transferred you up here? You all seem to LIKE the dirty black brutes. Christ, I don't know what's come over us all. I really don't.'

'Come on, have another drink,' said Westfield. 'Hey, butler! Spot of beer before the ice goes, eh? Beer, butler!'

The butler brought some bottles of Munich beer. Ellis presently sat down at the table with the others, and he nursed one of the cool bottles between his small hands. His forehead was sweating. He was sulky, but not in a rage any longer. At all times he was spiteful and perverse, but his violent fits of rage were soon over, and were never apologized for. Quarrels were a regular part of the routine of Club life. Mr Lackersteen was feeling better and was studying the illustrations in La Vie Parisienne.

It was after nine now, and the room, scented with the acrid smoke of Westfield's cheroot, was stifling hot. Everyone's shirt stuck to his back with the first sweat of the day. The invisible chokra who pulled the punkah rope outside was falling asleep in the glare.

'Butler!' yelled Ellis, and as the butler appeared, 'go and wake that bloody chokra up!'

'Yes, master.'

'And butler!'

'Yes, master?'

'How much ice have we got left?'

''Bout twenty pounds, master. Will only last today, I think. I find it very difficult to keep ice cool now.'

'Don't talk like that, damn you—"I find it very difficult!" Have you swallowed a dictionary? "Please, master, can't keeping ice cool"—that's how you ought to talk. We shall have to sack this fellow if he gets to talk English too well. I can't stick servants who talk English. D'you hear, butler?'

'Yes, master,' said the butler, and retired.

'God! No ice till Monday,' Westfield said. 'You going back to the jungle, Flory?'

'Yes. I ought to be there now. I only came in because of the English mail.'

'Go on tour myself, I think. Knock up a spot of Travelling Allowance. I can't stick my bloody office at this time of year. Sitting there under the damned punkah, signing one chit after another. Paper-chewing. God, how I wish the war was on again!'

‘I’m going out the day after tomorrow,’ Ellis said. ‘Isn’t that damned padre coming to hold his service this Sunday? I’ll take care not to be in for that, anyway. Bloody knee-drill.’

‘Next Sunday,’ said Westfield. ‘Promised to be in for it myself. So’s Macgregor. Bit hard on the poor devil of a padre, I must say. Only gets here once in six weeks. Might as well get up a congregation when he does come.’

‘Oh, hell! I’d snivel psalms to oblige the padre, but I can’t stick the way these damned native Christians come shoving into our church. A pack of Madrassi servants and Karen school-teachers. And then those two yellow-bellies, Francis and Samuel—they call themselves Christians too. Last time the padre was here they had the nerve to come up and sit on the front pews with the white men. Someone ought to speak to the padre about that. What bloody fools we were ever to let those missionaries loose in this country!

Teaching bazaar sweepers they’re as good as we are. “Please, sir, me Christian same like master.” Damned cheek.’

‘How about that for a pair of legs?’ said Mr Lackersteen, passing La Vie Parisienne across. ‘You know French, Flory; what’s that mean underneath? Christ, it reminds me of when I was in Paris, my first leave, before I married. Christ, I wish I was there again!’

‘Did you hear that one about “There was a young lady of Woking”?’ Maxwell said. He was rather a silent youth, but, like other youths, he had an affection for a good smutty rhyme. He completed the biography of the young lady of Woking, and there was a laugh. Westfield replied with the young lady of Ealing who had a peculiar feeling, and Flory came in with the young curate of Horsham who always took every precaution. There was more laughter. Even Ellis thawed and produced several rhymes; Ellis's jokes were always genuinely witty, and yet filthy beyond measure. Everyone cheered up and felt more friendly in spite of the heat. They had finished the beer and were just going to call for another drink, when shoes creaked on the steps outside. A booming voice, which made the floorboards tingle, was saying jocosely:

'Yes, most distinctly humorous. I incorporated it in one of those little articles of mine in Blackwood's, you know. I remember, too, when I was stationed at Prome, another quite—ah—diverting incident which—'

Evidently Mr Macgregor had arrived at the Club. Mr Lackersteen exclaimed, 'Hell! My wife's there,' and pushed his empty glass as far away from him as it would go. Mr Macgregor and Mrs Lackersteen entered the lounge together.

Mr Macgregor was a large, heavy man, rather past forty, with a kindly, puggy face, wearing gold-rimmed spectacles. His bulky shoulders, and a trick he had of thrusting his head forward, reminded one curiously of a turtle—the Burmans, in fact, nicknamed him 'the tortoise'. He was dressed in a clean silk suit, which already showed patches of sweat beneath the armpits. He greeted the others with a humorous mock-salute, and then planted himself before the notice-board, beaming, in the attitude of a schoolmaster twiddling a cane behind his back. The good nature in his face was quite genuine, and yet there was such a wilful geniality about him, such a strenuous air of being off duty and forgetting his official rank, that no one was ever quite at ease in his presence. His conversation was evidently modelled on that of some facetious schoolmaster or clergyman whom he had known in early life. Any long word, any quotation, any proverbial expression figured in his mind as a joke, and was introduced with a bumbling noise like 'er' or 'ah', to make it clear that there was a joke coming. Mrs Lackersteen was a woman of about thirty-five, handsome in a contourless, elongated way, like a fashion plate. She had a sighing, discontented voice. The others had all stood up when she entered, and Mrs Lackersteen sank exhaustedly into the best chair under the punkah, fanning herself with a slender hand like that of a newt.

'Oh dear, this heat, this heat! Mr Macgregor came and fetched me in his car. SO kind of him. Tom, that wretch of a rickshaw-man is pretending to be ill again. Really, I think you ought to give him a good thrashing and bring him to his senses. It's too terrible to have to walk about in this sun every day.'

Mrs Lackersteen, unequal to the quarter-mile walk between her house and the Club, had imported a rickshaw from Rangoon. Except for bullock-carts and Mr Macgregor's car it was the only wheeled vehicle in Kyauktada, for the whole district did not possess ten miles of road. In the jungle, rather than leave her husband alone, Mrs Lackersteen endured all the horrors of dripping tents, mosquitoes and tinned food; but she made up for it by complaining over trifles while in headquarters.

'Really I think the laziness of these servants is getting too shocking,' she sighed. 'Don't you agree, Mr Macgregor? We seem to have no AUTHORITY over the natives nowadays, with all these dreadful Reforms, and the insolence they learn from the newspapers. In some ways they are getting almost as bad as the lower classes at home.'

'Oh, hardly as bad as that, I trust. Still, I am afraid there is no doubt that the democratic spirit is creeping in, even here.'

'And such a short time ago, even just before the war, they were so NICE and respectful! The way they salaamed when you passed them on the road—it was really quite charming. I remember when we paid our butler only twelve rupees a month, and really that man loved us like a dog. And now they are demanding forty and fifty rupees, and I find that the only way I can even KEEP a servant is to pay their wages several months in arrears.'

'The old type of servant is disappearing,' agreed Mr Macgregor. 'In my young days, when one's butler was disrespectful, one sent him along to the jail with a chit saying "Please give the bearer fifteen lashes". Ah well, eheu fugaces! Those days are gone for ever, I am afraid.'

'Ah, you're about right there,' said Westfield in his gloomy way. 'This country'll never be fit to live in again. British Raj is finished if you ask me. Lost Dominion and all that. Time we cleared out of it.'

Whereat there was a murmur of agreement from everyone in the room, even from Flory, notoriously a Bolshie in his opinions, even from young Maxwell, who had been barely three years in the country. No Anglo-Indian will ever deny that India is going to the dogs, or ever has denied it—for India, like Punch, never was what it was.

Ellis had meanwhile unpinned the offending notice from behind Mr Macgregor's back, and he now held it out to him, saying in his sour way:

'Here, Macgregor, we've read this notice, and we all think this idea of electing a native to the Club is absolute—' Ellis was going to have said 'absolute balls', but he remembered Mrs Lackersteen's presence and checked himself—'is absolutely uncalled for. After all, this Club is a place where we come to enjoy ourselves, and we don't want natives poking about in here. We like to think there's still one place where we're free of them. The others all agree with me absolutely.'

He looked round at the others. 'Hear, hear!' said Mr Lackersteen gruffly. He knew that his wife would guess that he had been drinking, and he felt that a display of sound sentiment would excuse him.

Mr Macgregor took the notice with a smile. He saw the 'B. F.' pencilled against his name, and privately he thought Ellis's manner very disrespectful, but he turned the matter off with a joke. He took as great pains to be a good fellow at the Club as he did to keep up his dignity during office hours. 'I gather,' he said, 'that our friend Ellis does not welcome the society of—ah—his Aryan brother?'

'No, I do not,' said Ellis tartly. 'Nor my Mongolian brother. I don't like niggers, to put it in one word.'

Mr Macgregor stiffened at the word 'nigger', which is discountenanced in India. He had no prejudice against Orientals; indeed, he was deeply fond of them. Provided they were given no freedom he thought them the most charming people alive. It always pained him to see them wantonly insulted.

'Is it quite playing the game,' he said stiffly, 'to call these people niggers—a term they very naturally resent—when they are obviously nothing of the kind? The Burmese are Mongolians, the Indians are Aryans or Dravidians, and all of them are quite distinct—'

'Oh, rot that!' said Ellis, who was not at all awed by Mr Macgregor's official status. 'Call them niggers or Aryans or what you like. What I'm saying is that we don't want to see any black hides in this Club. If you put it to the vote you'll find we're against it to a man—unless Flory wants his DEAR pal Veraswami,' he added.

'Hear, hear!' repeated Mr Lackersteen. 'Count on me to blackball the lot of 'em.'

Mr Macgregor pursed his lips whimsically. He was in an awkward position, for the idea of electing a native member was not his own, but had been passed on to him by the Commissioner. However, he disliked making excuses, so he said in a more conciliatory tone:

'Shall we postpone discussing it till the next general meeting? In the meantime we can give it our mature consideration. And now,' he added, moving towards the table, 'who will join me in a little—ah— liquid refreshment?'

The butler was called and the 'liquid refreshment' ordered. It was hotter than ever now, and everyone was thirsty. Mr Lackersteen was on the point of ordering a drink when he caught his wife's eye, shrank up and said sulkily 'No.' He sat with his hands on his knees, with a rather pathetic expression, watching Mrs Lackersteen swallow a glass of lemonade with gin in it. Mr Macgregor, though he signed the chit for drinks, drank plain lemonade. Alone of the Europeans in Kyauktada, he kept the rule of not drinking before sunset.

'It's all very well,' grumbled Ellis, with his forearms on the table, fidgeting with his glass. The dispute with Mr Macgregor had made him restless again. 'It's all very well, but I stick to what I said. No natives in this Club! It's by constantly giving way over small things like that that we've ruined the Empire. The country's only rotten with sedition because we've been too soft with them. The only possible policy is to treat 'em like the dirt they are. This is a critical moment, and we want every bit of prestige we can get. We've got to hang together and say, "WE ARE THE MASTERS, and you beggars— "' Ellis pressed his small thumb down as though flattening a grub—'"you beggars keep your place!"'

'Hopeless, old chap,' said Westfield. 'Quite hopeless. What can you do with all this red tape tying your hands? Beggars of natives know the law better than we do. Insult you to your face and then run you in the moment you hit 'em. Can't do anything unless you put your foot down firmly. And how can you, if they haven't the guts to show fight?'

'Our burra sahib at Mandalay always said,' put in Mrs Lackersteen, 'that in the end we shall simply LEAVE India. Young men will not come out here any longer to work all their lives for insults and ingratitude. We shall just GO. When the natives come to us begging us to stay, we shall say, "No, you have had your chance, you wouldn't take it. Very well, we shall leave you to govern yourselves." And then, what a lesson that will teach them!'

'It's all this law and order that's done for us,' said Westfield gloomily. The ruin of the Indian Empire through too much legality was a recurrent theme with Westfield. According to him, nothing save a full-sized rebellion, and the consequent reign of martial law, could save the Empire from decay. 'All this paper-chewing and chit-passing. Office babus are the real rulers of this country now. Our number's up. Best thing we can do is to shut up shop and let 'em stew in their own juice.'

'I don't agree, I simply don't agree,' Ellis said. 'We could put things right in a month if we chose. It only needs a pennyworth of pluck. Look at Amritsar. Look how they caved in after that. Dyer knew the stuff to give them. Poor old Dyer! That was a dirty job. Those cowards in England have got something to answer for.'

There was a kind of sigh from the others, the same sigh that a gathering of Roman Catholics will give at the mention of Bloody Mary. Even Mr Macgregor, who detested bloodshed and martial law, shook his head at the name of Dyer.

'Ah, poor man! Sacrificed to the Paget M.P.s. Well, perhaps they will discover their mistake when it is too late.'

'My old governor used to tell a story about that,' said Westfield. 'There was an old havildar in a native regiment—someone asked him what'd happen if the British left India. The old chap said—'

Flory pushed back his chair and stood up. It must not, it could not—no, it simply should not go on any longer! He must get out of this room quickly, before something happened inside his head and he began to smash the furniture and throw bottles at the pictures. Dull boozing witless porkers! Was it possible that they could go on week after week, year after year, repeating word for word the same evil-minded drivel, like a parody of a fifth-rate story in Blackwood's? Would none of them EVER think of anything new to say? Oh, what a place, what people! What a civilization is this of ours—this godless civilization founded on whisky, Blackwood's and the 'Bonzo' pictures! God have mercy on us, for all of us are part of it.

Flory did not say any of this, and he was at some pains not to show it in his face. He was standing by his chair, a little sidelong to the others, with the half-smile of a man who is never sure of his popularity.

'I'm afraid I shall have to be off,' he said. 'I've got some things to see to before breakfast, unfortunately.'

'Stay and have another spot, old man,' said Westfield. 'Morning's young. Have a gin. Give you an appetite.'

'No, thanks, I must be going. Come on, Flo. Good-bye, Mrs Lackersteen. Good-bye, everybody.'

'Exit Booker Washington, the niggers' pal,' said Ellis as Flory disappeared. Ellis could always be counted on to say something disagreeable about anyone who had just left the room. 'Gone to see Very-slimy, I suppose. Or else sloped off to avoid paying a round of drinks.'

'Oh, he's not a bad chap,' Westfield said. 'Says some Bolshie things sometimes. Don't suppose he means half of them.'

'Oh, a very good fellow, of course,' said Mr Macgregor. Every European in India is ex-officio, or rather ex-colore, a good fellow, until he has done something quite outrageous. It is an honorary rank.

'He's a bit TOO Bolshie for my taste. I can't bear a fellow who pals up with the natives. I shouldn't wonder if he's got a lick of the tar-brush himself. It might explain that black mark on his face. Piebald. And he looks like a yellow-belly, with that black hair, and skin the colour of a lemon.'

There was some desultory scandal about Flory, but not much, because Mr Macgregor did not like scandal. The Europeans stayed in the Club long enough for one more round of drinks. Mr Macgregor told his anecdote about Prome, which could be produced in almost any context. And then the conversation veered back to the old, never-palling subject—the insolence of the natives, the supineness of the Government, the dear dead days when the British Raj WAS the British Raj and please give the bearer fifteen lashes. This topic was never let alone for long, partly because of Ellis's obsession. Besides, you could forgive the Europeans a great deal of their bitterness. Living and working among Orientals would try the temper of a saint. And all of them, the officials particularly, knew what it was to be baited and insulted. Almost every day, when Westfield or Mr Macgregor or even Maxwell went down the street, the High School boys, with their young, yellow faces— faces smooth as gold coins, full of that maddening contempt that sits so naturally on the Mongolian face—sneered at them as they went past, sometimes hooted after them with hyena-like laughter. The life of the Anglo-Indian officials is not all jam. In comfortless camps, in sweltering offices, in gloomy dakbungalows smelling of dust and earth-oil, they earn, perhaps, the right to be a little disagreeable.

It was getting on for ten now, and hot beyond bearing. Flat, clear drops of sweat gathered on everyone's face, and on the men's bare forearms. A damp patch was growing larger and larger in the back of Mr Macgregor's silk coat. The glare outside seemed to soak somehow through the green-chicked windows, making one's eyes ache and filling one's head with stuffiness. Everyone thought with malaise of his stodgy breakfast, and of the long, deadly hours that were coming. Mr Macgregor stood up with a sigh and adjusted his spectacles, which had slipped down his sweating nose.

'Alas that such a festive gathering should end,' he said. 'I must get home to breakfast. The cares of Empire. Is anybody coming my way? My man is waiting with the car.'

'Oh, thank you,' said Mrs Lackersteen; 'if you'd take Tom and me. What a relief not to have to walk in this heat!'

The others stood up. Westfield stretched his arms and yawned through his nose. 'Better get a move on, I suppose. Go to sleep if I sit here any longer. Think of stewing in that office all day! Baskets of papers. Oh Lord!'

'Don't forget tennis this evening, everyone,' said Ellis. 'Maxwell, you lazy devil, don't you skulk out of it again. Down here with your racquet at four-thirty sharp.'

'Apres vous, madame,' said Mr Macgregor gallantly, at the door.

'Lead on, Macduff,' said Westfield.

They went out into the glaring white sunlight. The heat rolled from the earth like the breath of an oven. The flowers, oppressive to the eyes, blazed with not a petal stirring, in a debauch of sun. The glare sent a weariness through one's bones. There was something horrible in it—horrible to think of that blue, blinding sky, stretching on and on over Burma and India, over Siam, Cambodia, China, cloudless and interminable.

The plates of Mr Macgregor's waiting car were too hot to touch. The evil time of day was beginning, the time, as the Burmese say, 'when feet are silent'. Hardly a living creature stirred, except men, and the black columns of ants, stimulated by the heat, which marched ribbon-like across the path, and the tail-less vultures which soared on the currents of the air.

CHAPTER 3

Flory turned to the left outside the Club gate and started down the bazaar road, under the shade of the peepul trees. A hundred yards away there was a swirl of music, where a squad of Military Policemen, lank Indians in greenish khaki, were marching back to their lines with a Gurkha boy playing the bagpipes ahead of them. Flory was going to see Dr Veraswami. The doctor's house was a long bungalow of earth-oiled wood, standing on piles, with a large unkempt garden which adjoined that of the Club. The back of the house was towards the road, for it faced the hospital, which lay between it and the river.

As Flory entered the compound there was a frightened squawk of women and a scurrying within the house. Evidently he had narrowly missed seeing the doctor's wife. He went round to the front of the house and called up to the veranda:

'Doctor! Are you busy? May I come up?'

The doctor, a little black and white figure, popped from within the house like a jack-in-the-box. He hurried to the veranda rail, exclaimed effusively:

‘If you may come up! Of course, of course, come up this instant! Ah, Mr Flory, how very delightful to see you! Come up, come up. What drink will you have? I have whisky, beer, vermouth and other European liquors. Ah, my dear friend, how I have been pining for some cultured conversation!’

The doctor was a small, black, plump man with fuzzy hair and round, credulous eyes. He wore steel-rimmed spectacles, and he was dressed in a badly fitting white drill suit, with trousers bagging concertina-like over clumsy black boots. His voice was eager and bubbling, with a hissing of the s’s. As Flory came up the steps the doctor popped back to the end of the veranda and rummaged in a big tin ice-chest, rapidly pulling out bottles of all descriptions. The veranda was wide and dark, with low eaves from which baskets of fern hung, making it seem like a cave behind a waterfall of sunlight. It was furnished with long, cane-bottomed chairs made in the jail, and at one end there was a book-case containing a rather unappetizing little library, mainly books of essays, of the Emerson-Carlyle-Stevenson type. The doctor, a great reader, liked his books to have what he called a ‘moral meaning’.

‘Well, doctor,’ said Flory—the doctor had meanwhile thrust him into a long chair, pulled out the leg-rests so that he could lie down, and put cigarettes and beer within reach. ‘Well, doctor, and how are things? How’s the British Empire? Sick of the palsy as usual?’

‘Aha, Mr Flory, she iss very low, very low! Grave complications setting in. Septicaemia, peritonitis and paralysis of the ganglia. We shall have to call in the specialists, I fear. Aha!’

It was a joke between the two men to pretend that the British Empire was an aged female patient of the doctor’s. The doctor had enjoyed this joke for two years without growing tired of it.

'Ah, doctor,' said Flory, supine in the long chair, 'what a joy to be here after that bloody Club. When I come to your house I feel like a Nonconformist minister dodging up to town and going home with a tart. Such a glorious holiday from THEM'—he motioned with one heel in the direction of the Club—'from my beloved fellow Empire-builders. British prestige, the white man's burden, the pukka sahib sans peur et sans reproche— you know. Such a relief to be out of the stink of it for a little while.'

'My friend, my friend, now come, come, please! That iss outrageous. You must not say such things of honourable English gentlemen!'

'You don't have to listen to the honourable gentlemen talking, doctor. I stood it as long as I could this morning. Ellis with his "dirty nigger", Westfield with his jokes, Macgregor with his Latin tags and please give the bearer fifteen lashes. But when they got on to that story about the old havildar—you know, the dear old havildar who said that if the British left India there wouldn't be a rupee or a virgin between—you know; well, I couldn't stand it any longer. It's time that old havildar was put on the retired list. He's been saying the same thing ever since the Jubilee in 'eighty-seven.'

The doctor grew agitated, as he always did when Flory criticized the Club members. He was standing with his plump white-clad behind balanced against the veranda rail, and sometimes gesticulating. When searching for a word he would nip his black thumb and forefinger together, as though to capture an idea floating in the air.

'But truly, truly, Mr Flory, you must not speak so! Why iss it that always you are abusing the pukka sahibs, ass you call them? They are the salt of the earth. Consider the great things they have done—consider the great administrators who have made British India what it iss. Consider Clive,

Warren Hastings, Dalhousie, Curzon. They were such men—I quote your immortal Shakespeare— ass, take them for all in all, we shall not look upon their like again!'

'Well, do you want to look upon their like again? I don't.'

'And consider how noble a type iss the English gentleman! Their glorious loyalty to one another! The public school spirit! Even those of them whose manner iss unfortunate— some Englishmen are arrogant, I concede— have the great, sterling qualities that we Orientals lack. Beneath their rough exterior, their hearts are of gold.'

'Of gilt, shall we say? There's a kind of spurious good-fellowship between the English and this country. It's a tradition to booze together and swap meals and pretend to be friends, though we all hate each other like poison. Hanging together, we call it. It's a political necessity. Of course drink is what keeps the machine going. We should all go mad and kill one another in a week if it weren't for that. There's a subject for one of your uplift essayists, doctor. Booze as the cement of empire.'

The doctor shook his head. 'Really, Mr Flory, I know not what it iss that hass made you so cynical. It iss so most unsuitable! You—an English gentleman of high gifts and character—to be uttering seditious opinions that are worthy of the Burmese Patriot!'

'Seditious?' Flory said. 'I'M not seditious. I don't want the Burmans to drive us out of this country. God forbid! I'm here to make money, like everyone else. All I object to is the slimy white man's burden humbug. The pukka sahib pose. It's so boring. Even those bloody fools at the Club might be better company if we weren't all of us living a lie the whole time.'

'But, my dear friend, what lie are you living?'

'Why, of course, the lie that we're here to uplift our poor black brothers instead of to rob them. I suppose it's a natural enough lie. But it corrupts us, it corrupts us in ways you can't imagine. There's an everlasting sense of being a sneak and a liar that torments us and drives us to justify ourselves night and day. It's at the bottom of half our beastliness to the natives. We Anglo-Indians could be almost bearable if we'd only admit that we're thieves and go on thieving without any humbug.'

The doctor, very pleased, nipped his thumb and forefinger together. 'The weakness of your argument, my dear friend,' he said, beaming at his own irony, 'the weakness appears to be, that you are NOT thieves.'

'Now, my dear doctor—'

Flory sat up in the long chair, partly because his prickly heat had just stabbed him in the back like a thousand needles, partly because his favourite argument with the doctor was about to begin. This argument, vaguely political in nature, took place as often as the two men met. It was a topsy-turvy affair, for the Englishman was bitterly anti-English and the Indian fanatically loyal. Dr Veraswami had a passionate admiration for the English, which a thousand snubs from Englishmen had not shaken. He would maintain with positive eagerness that he, as an Indian, belonged to an inferior and degenerate race. His faith in British justice was so great that even when, at the jail, he had to superintend a flogging or a hanging, and would come home with his black face faded grey and dose himself with whisky, his zeal did not falter. Flory's seditious opinions shocked him, but they also gave him a certain shuddering pleasure, such as a pious believer will take in hearing the Lord's Prayer repeated backwards.

'My dear doctor,' said Flory, 'how can you make out that we are in this country for any purpose except to steal? It's so simple. The official holds the Burman down while the businessman goes through his pockets. Do you suppose my firm, for instance, could get its timber contracts if the country weren't in the hands of the British? Or the other timber firms, or the oil companies, or the miners and planters and traders? How could the Rice Ring go on skinning the unfortunate peasant if it hadn't the Government behind it? The British Empire is simply a device for giving trade monopolies to the English—or rather to gangs of Jews and Scotchmen.'

'My friend, it iss pathetic to me to hear you talk so. It iss truly pathetic. You say you are here to trade? Of course you are. Could the Burmese trade for themselves? Can they make machinery, ships, railways, roads? They are helpless without you. What would happen to the Burmese forests if the English were not here? They would be sold immediately to the Japanese, who would gut them and ruin them. Instead of which, in your hands, actually they are improved. And while your businessmen develop the resources of our country, your officials are civilizing us, elevating us to their level, from pure public spirit. It is a magnificent record of self-sacrifice.'

'Bosh, my dear doctor. We teach the young men to drink whisky and play football, I admit, but precious little else. Look at our schools—factories for cheap clerks. We've never taught a single useful manual trade to the Indians. We daren't; frightened of the competition in industry. We've even crushed various industries. Where are the Indian muslins now? Back in the forties or thereabouts they were building sea-going ships in India, and manning them as well. Now you couldn't build a seaworthy fishing boat there. In the eighteenth century the Indians cast guns that were at any rate up to the European standard. Now, after we've been in India a hundred and fifty years, you can't make so much as a brass cartridge-case in the whole continent. The only Eastern races that have developed at all quickly are the independent ones. I won't instance Japan, but take the case of Siam—'

The doctor waved his hand excitedly. He always interrupted the argument at this point (for as a rule it followed the same course, almost word for word), finding that the case of Siam hampered him.

'My friend, my friend, you are forgetting the Oriental character. How iss it possible to have developed us, with our apathy and superstition? At least you have brought to us law and order. The unswerving British Justice and the Pax Britannica.'

'Pox Britannica, doctor, Pox Britannica is its proper name. And in any case, whom is it pax for? The money-lender and the lawyer. Of course we keep the peace in India, in our own interest, but what does all this law and order business boil down to? More banks and more prisons—that's all it means.'

'What monstrous misrepresentations!' cried the doctor. 'Are not prissons necessary? And have you brought us nothing but prissons? Consider Burma in the days of Thibaw, with dirt and torture and ignorance, and then look around you. Look merely out of this veranda—look at that hospital, and over to the right at that school and that police station. Look at the whole uprush of modern progress!'

'Of course I don't deny,' Flory said, 'that we modernize this country in certain ways. We can't help doing so. In fact, before we've finished we'll have wrecked the whole Burmese national culture. But we're not civilizing them, we're only rubbing our dirt on to them. Where's it going to lead, this uprush of modern progress, as you call it? Just to our own dear old swinery of gramophones and billycock hats. Sometimes I think that in two hundred years all this—' he waved a foot towards the horizon—'all this will be gone— forests, villages, monasteries, pagodas all vanished. And instead, pink villas fifty yards apart; all over those hills, as far as you can see, villa after villa, with all the gramophones playing the same tune.

And all the forests shaved flat—chewed into wood-pulp for the News of the World, or sawn up into gramophone cases. But the trees avenge themselves, as the old chap says in The Wild Duck. You've read Ibsen, of course?'

'Ah, no, Mr Flory, alas! That mighty master-mind, your inspired Bernard Shaw hass called him. It iss a pleasure to come. But, my friend, what you do not see iss that your civilization at its very worst iss for us an advance. Gramophones, billycock hats, the News of the World—all iss better than the horrible sloth of the Oriental. I see the British, even the least inspired of them, ass—ass—' the doctor searched for a phrase, and found one that probably came from Stevenson—'ass torchbearers upon the path of progress.'

'I don't. I see them as a kind of up-to-date, hygienic, self-satisfied louse. Creeping round the world building prisons. They build a prison and call it progress,' he added rather regretfully— for the doctor would not recognize the allusion.

'My friend, positively you are harping upon the subject of prissons! Consider that there are also other achievements of your countrymen. They construct roads, they irrigate deserts, they conquer famines, they build schools, they set up hospitals, they combat plague, cholera, leprosy, smallpox, venereal disease—'

'Having brought it themselves,' put in Flory.

'No, sir!' returned the doctor, eager to claim this distinction for his own countrymen. 'No, sir, it wass the Indians who introduced venereal disease into this country. The Indians introduce diseases, and the English cure them. THERE iss the answer to all your pessimism and seditiousness.'

'Well, doctor, we shall never agree. The fact is that you like all this modern progress business, whereas I'd rather see things a little bit septic. Burma in the days of Thibaw would have suited me better, I think. And as I said before, if we are a civilizing influence, it's only to grab on a larger scale. We should chuck it quickly enough if it didn't pay.'

'My friend, you do not think that. If truly you disapprove of the British Empire, you would not be talking of it privately here. You would be proclaiming from the house-tops. I know your character, Mr Flory, better than you know it yourself.'

'Sorry, doctor; I don't go in for proclaiming from the housetops. I haven't the guts. I "counsel ignoble ease", like old Belial in Paradise Lost. It's safer. You've got to be a pukka sahib or die, in this country. In fifteen years I've never talked honestly to anyone except you. My talks here are a safety-valve; a little Black Mass on the sly, if you understand me.'

At this moment there was a desolate wailing noise outside. Old Mattu, the Hindu durwan who looked after the European church, was standing in the sunlight below the veranda. He was an old fever-stricken creature, more like a grasshopper than a human being, and dressed in a few square inches of dingy rag. He lived near the church in a hut made of flattened kerosene tins, from which he would sometimes hurry forth at the appearance of a European, to salaam deeply and wail something about his 'talab', which was eighteen rupees a month. Looking piteously up at the veranda, he massaged the earth-coloured skin of his belly with one hand, and with the other made the motion of putting food into his mouth. The doctor felt in his pocket and dropped a four-anna piece over the veranda rail. He was notorious for his soft-heartedness, and all the beggars in Kyauktada made him their target.

'Behold there the degeneracy of the East,' said the doctor, pointing to Mattu, who was doubling himself up like a caterpillar and uttering grateful whines. 'Look at the wretchedness of hiss limbs. The calves of hiss legs are not so thick ass an Englishman's wrists. Look at hiss abjectness and servility. Look at hiss ignorance—such ignorance ass iss not known in Europe outside a home for mental defectives. Once I asked Mattu to tell me hiss age. "Sahib," he said, "I believe that I am ten years old." How can you pretend, Mr Flory, that you are not the natural superior of such creatures?'

'Poor old Mattu, the uprush of modern progress seems to have missed him somehow,' Flory said, throwing another four-anna piece over the rail. 'Go on, Mattu, spend that on booze. Be as degenerate as you can. It all postpones Utopia.'

'Aha, Mr Flory, sometimes I think that all you say iss but to—what iss the expression?— pull my leg. The English sense of humour. We Orientals have no humour, ass iss well known.'

'Lucky devils. It's been the ruin of us, our bloody sense of humour.' He yawned with his hands behind his head. Mattu had shambled away after further grateful noises. 'I suppose I ought to be going before this cursed sun gets too high. The heat's going to be devilish this year, I feel it in my bones. Well, doctor, we've been arguing so much that I haven't asked for your news. I only got in from the jungle yesterday. I ought to go back the day after tomorrow—don't know whether I shall. Has anything been happening in Kyauktada? Any scandals?'

The doctor looked suddenly serious. He had taken off his spectacles, and his face, with dark liquid eyes, recalled that of a black retriever dog. He looked away, and spoke in a slightly more hesitant tone than before.

'That fact iss, my friend, there iss a most unpleasant business afoot. You will perhaps laugh—it sounds nothing—but I am in serious trouble. Or rather, I am in danger of trouble. It iss an underground business. You

Europeans will never hear of it directly. In this place'—he waved a hand towards the bazaar— 'there iss perpetual conspiracies and plottings of which you do not hear. But to us they mean much.'

'What's been happening, then?'

'It iss this. An intrigue iss brewing against me. A most serious intrigue which iss intended to blacken my character and ruin my official career. Ass an Englishman you will not understand these things. I have incurred the enmity of a man you probably do not know, U Po Kyin, the Sub-divisional Magistrate. He iss a most dangerous man. The damage that he can do to me iss incalculable.'

'U Po Kyin? Which one is that?'

'The great fat man with many teeth. Hiss house iss down the road there, a hundred yards away.'

'Oh, that fat scoundrel? I know him well.'

'No, no, my friend, no, no!' exclaimed the doctor quite eagerly; 'it cannot be that you know him. Only an Oriental could know him. You, an English gentleman, cannot sink your mind to the depth of such ass U Po Kyin. He iss more than a scoundrel, he iss— what shall I say? Words fail me. He recalls to me a crocodile in human shape. He hass the cunning of the crocodile, its cruelty, its bestiality. If you knew the record of that man! The outrages he hass committed! The extortions, the briberies! The girls he hass ruined, raping them before the very eyes of their mothers! Ah, an English gentleman cannot imagine such a character. And thiss iss the man who hass taken hiss oath to ruin me.'

'I've heard a good deal about U Po Kyin from various sources,' Flory said. 'He seems a fair sample of a Burmese magistrate. A Burman told me that during the war U Po Kyin was at work recruiting, and he raised a battalion from his own illegitimate sons. Is that true?'

'It could hardly be so,' said the doctor, 'for they would not have been old enough. But of hiss villainy there iss no doubt. And now he iss determined upon ruining me. In the first place he hates me because I know too much about him; and besides, he iss the enemy of any reasonably honest man. He will proceed—such iss the practice of such men—by calumny. He will spread reports about me—reports of the most appalling and untrue descriptions. Already he iss beginning them.'

'But would anyone believe a fellow like that against you? He's only a lowdown magistrate. You're a high official.'

'Ah, Mr Flory, you do not understand Oriental cunning. U Po Kyin hass ruined higher officials than I. He will know ways to make himself believed. And therefore—ah, it iss a difficult business!'

The doctor took a step or two up and down the veranda, polishing his glasses with his handkerchief. It was clear that there was something more which delicacy prevented him from saying. For a moment his manner was so troubled that Flory would have liked to ask whether he could not help in some way, but he did not, for he knew the uselessness of interfering in Oriental quarrels. No European ever gets to the bottom of these quarrels; there is always something impervious to the European mind, a conspiracy behind the conspiracy, a plot within the plot. Besides, to keep out of 'native' quarrels is one of the Ten Precepts of the pukka sahib. He said doubtfully:

'What is a difficult business?'

'It iss, if only—ah, my friend, you will laugh at me, I fear. But it iss this: if only I were a member of your European Club! If only! How different would my position be!'

'The Club? Why? How would that help you?'

'My friend, in these matters prestige iss everything. It iss not that U Po Kyin will attack me openly; he would never dare; it iss that he will libel me and backbite me. And whether he iss believed or not depends entirely upon my standing with the Europeans. It iss so that things happen in India. If our prestige iss good, we rise; if bad, we fall. A nod and a wink will accomplish more than a thousand official reports. And you do not know what prestige it gives to an Indian to be a member of the European Club. In the Club, practically he ISS a European. No calumny can touch him. A Club member iss sacrosanct.'

Flory looked away over the veranda rail. He had got up as though to go. It always made him ashamed and uncomfortable when it had to be admitted between them that the doctor, because of his black skin, could not be received in the Club. It is a disagreeable thing when one's close friend is not one's social equal; but it is a thing native to the very air of India.

'They might elect you at the next general meeting,' he said. 'I don't say they will, but it's not impossible.'

'I trust, Mr Flory, that you do not think I am asking you to propose me for the Club? Heaven forbid! I know that that iss impossible for you. Simply I wass remarking that if I were a member of the Club, I should be forthwith invulnerable—'

Flory cocked his Terai hat loosely on his head and stirred Flo up with his stick. She was asleep under the chair. Flory felt very uncomfortable. He knew that in all probability, if he had the courage to face a few rows with Ellis, he could secure Dr Veraswami's election to the Club. And the doctor, after all, was his friend, indeed, almost the sole friend he had in Burma.

They had talked and argued together a hundred times, the doctor had dined at his house, he had even proposed to introduce Flory to his wife—but she, a pious Hindu, had refused with horror. They had made shooting trips together—the doctor, equipped with bandoliers and hunting knives, panting up hillsides slippery with bamboo leaves and blazing his gun at nothing. In common decency it was his duty to support the doctor. But he knew also that the doctor would never ask for any support, and that there would be an ugly row before an Oriental was got into the Club. No, he could not face that row! It was not worth it. He said:

'To tell you the truth, there's been talk about this already. They were discussing it this morning, and that little beast Ellis was preaching his usual "dirty nigger" sermon. Macgregor has suggested electing one native member. He's had orders to do so, I imagine.'

'Yes, I heard that. We hear all these things. It wass that that put the idea into my head.'

'It's to come up at the general meeting in June. I don't know what'll happen—it depends on Macgregor, I think. I'll give you my vote, but I can't do more than that. I'm sorry, but I simply can't. You don't know the row there'll be. Very likely they will elect you, but they'll do it as an unpleasant duty, under protest. They've made a perfect fetish of keeping this Club all-white, as they call it.'

'Of course, of course, my friend! I understand perfectly. Heaven forbid that you should get into trouble with your European friends on my behalf. Please, please, never to embroil yourself! The mere fact that you are known to be my friend benefits me more than you can imagine. Prestige, Mr Flory, iss like a barometer. Every time you are seen to enter my house the mercury rises half a degree.'

‘Well, we must try and keep it at “Set Fair”. That’s about all I can do for you, I’m afraid.’

‘Even that iss much, my friend. And for that, there iss another thing of which I would warn you, though you will laugh, I fear. It iss that you yourself should beware of U Po Kyin. Beware of the crocodile! For sure he will strike at you when he knows that you are befriending me.’

‘All right, doctor, I’ll beware of the crocodile. I don’t fancy he can do me much harm, though.’

‘At least he will try. I know him. It will be hiss policy to detach my friends from me. Possibly he would even dare to spread hiss libels about you also.’

‘About me? Good gracious, no one would believe anything against ME. Civis Romanus sum. I’m an Englishman—quite above suspicion.’

‘Nevertheless, beware of hiss calumnies, my friend. Do not underrate him. He will know how to strike at you. He iss a crocodile. And like the crocodile’—the doctor nipped his thumb and finger impressively; his images became mixed sometimes—‘like the crocodile, he strikes always at the weakest spot!’

‘Do crocodiles always strike at the weakest spot, doctor?’

Both men laughed. They were intimate enough to laugh over the doctor’s queer English occasionally. Perhaps, at the bottom of his heart, the doctor was a little disappointed that Flory had not promised to propose him for the Club, but he would have perished rather than say so. And Flory was glad to drop the subject, an uncomfortable one which he wished had never been raised.

'Well, I really must be going, doctor. Good-bye in case I don't see you again. I hope it'll be all right at the general meeting. Macgregor's not a bad old stick. I dare say he'll insist on their electing you.'

'Let us hope so, my friend. With that I can defy a hundred U Po Kyins. A thousand! Good-bye, my friend, good-bye.'

Then Flory settled his Terai hat on his head and went home across the glaring maidan, to his breakfast, for which the long morning of drinking, smoking and talking had left him no appetite.

Chapter 4

Flory lay asleep, naked except for black Shan trousers, upon his sweat-damp bed. He had been idling all day. He spent approximately three weeks of every month in camp, coming into Kyauktada for a few days at a time, chiefly in order to idle, for he had very little clerical work to do.

The bedroom was a large square room with white plaster walls, open doorways and no ceiling, but only rafters in which sparrows nested. There was no furniture except the big four-poster bed, with its furled mosquito net like a canopy, and a wicker table and chair and a small mirror; also some rough bookshelves, containing several hundred books, all mildewed by many rainy seasons and riddled by silver fish. A tuktoo clung to the wall, flat and motionless like a heraldic dragon. Beyond the veranda eaves the light rained down like glistening white oil. Some doves in a bamboo thicket kept up a dull droning noise, curiously appropriate to the heat—a sleepy sound, but with the sleepiness of chloroform rather than a lullaby.

Down at Mr Macgregor's bungalow, two hundred yards away, a durwan, like a living clock, hammered four strokes on a section of iron rail.

Ko S'la, Flory's servant, awakened by the sound, went into the cookhouse, blew up the embers of the woodfire and boiled the kettle for tea. Then he put on his pink gaungbaung and muslin ingyi and brought the tea-tray to his master's bedside.

Ko S'la (his real name was Maung San Hla; Ko S'la was an abbreviation) was a short, square-shouldered, rustic-looking Burman with a very dark skin and a harassed expression. He wore a black moustache which curved downwards round his mouth, but like most Burmans he was quite beardless. He had been Flory's servant since his first day in Burma. The two men were within a month of one another's age. They had been boys together, had tramped side by side after snipe and duck, sat together in machans waiting for tigers that never came, shared the discomforts of a thousand camps and marches; and Ko S'la had pimped for Flory and borrowed money for him from the Chinese money-lenders, carried him to bed when he was drunk, tended him through bouts of fever. In Ko S'la's eyes Flory, because a bachelor, was a boy still; whereas Ko S'la had married, begotten five children, married again and become one of the obscure martyrs of bigamy. Like all bachelors' servants, Ko S'la was lazy and dirty, and yet he was devoted to Flory. He would never let anyone else serve Flory at table, or carry his gun or hold his pony's head while he mounted. On the march, if they came to a stream, he would carry Flory across on his back. He was inclined to pity Flory, partly because he thought him childish and easily deceived, and partly because of the birthmark, which he considered a dreadful thing.

Ko S'la put the tea-tray down on the table very quietly, and then went round to the end of the bed and tickled Flory's toes. He knew by experience that this was the only way of waking Flory without putting him in a bad temper. Flory rolled over, swore, and pressed his forehead into the pillow.

‘Four o’clock has struck, most holy god,’ Ko S’la said. ‘I have brought two teacups, because THE WOMAN said that she was coming.’

THE WOMAN was Ma Hla May, Flory’s mistress. Ko S’la always called her THE WOMAN, to show his disapproval—not that he disapproved of Flory for keeping a mistress, but he was jealous of Ma Hla May’s influence in the house.

‘Will the holy one play tinnis this evening?’ Ko S’la asked.

‘No, it’s too hot,’ said Flory in English. ‘I don’t want anything to eat. Take this muck away and bring some whisky.’

Ko S’la understood English very well, though he could not speak it. He brought a bottle of whisky, and also Flory’s tennis racquet, which he laid in a meaning manner against the wall opposite the bed. Tennis, according to his notions, was a mysterious ritual incumbent on all Englishmen, and he did not like to see his master idling in the evenings.

Flory pushed away in disgust the toast and butter that Ko S’la had brought, but he mixed some whisky in a cup of tea and felt better after drinking it. He had slept since noon, and his head and all his bones ached, and there was a taste like burnt paper in his mouth. It was years since he had enjoyed a meal. All European food in Burma is more or less disgusting—the bread is spongy stuff leavened with palm-toddy and tasting like a penny bun gone wrong, the butter comes out of a tin, and so does the milk, unless it is the grey watery catlap of the dudh-wallah. As Ko S’la left the room there was a scraping of sandals outside, and a Burmese girl’s high-pitched voice said, ‘Is my master awake?’

‘Come in,’ said Flory rather bad temperedly.

Ma Hla May came in, kicking off red-lacquered sandals in the doorway.

She was allowed to come to tea, as a special privilege, but not to other meals, nor to wear her sandals in her master's presence.

Ma Hla May was a woman of twenty-two or —three, and perhaps five feet tall. She was dressed in a longyi of pale blue embroidered Chinese satin, and a starched white muslin ingyi on which several gold lockets hung. Her hair was coiled in a tight black cylinder like ebony, and decorated with jasmine flowers. Her tiny, straight, slender body was a contourless as a bas-relief carved upon a tree. She was like a doll, with her oval, still face the colour of new copper, and her narrow eyes; an outlandish doll and yet a grotesquely beautiful one. A scent of sandalwood and coco-nut oil came into the room with her.

Ma Hla May came across to the bed, sat down on the edge and put her arms rather abruptly round Flory. She smelled at his cheek with her flat nose, in the Burmese fashion.

'Why did my master not send for me this afternoon?' she said.

'I was sleeping. It is too hot for that kind of thing.'

'So you would rather sleep alone than with Ma Hla May? How ugly you must think me, then! Am I ugly, master?'

'Go away,' he said, pushing her back. 'I don't want you at this time of day.'

'At least touch me with your lips, then. (There is no Burmese word for to kiss.) All white men do that to their women.'

'There you are, then. Now leave me alone. Fetch some cigarettes and give me one.'

'Why is it that nowadays you never want to make love to me? Ah, two years ago it was so different! You loved me in those days. You gave me presents of gold bangles and silk longyis from Mandalay. And now look'—Ma Hla May held out one tiny muslin-clad arm—'not a single bangle. Last month I had thirty, and now all of them are pawned. How can I go to the bazaar without my bangles, and wearing the same longyi over and over again? I am ashamed before the other women.'

'Is it my fault if you pawn your bangles?'

'Two years ago you would have redeemed them for me. Ah, you do not love Ma Hla May any longer!'

She put her arms round him again and kissed him, a European habit which he had taught her. A mingled scent of sandalwood, garlic, coco-nut oil and the jasmine in her hair floated from her. It was a scent that always made his teeth tingle. Rather abstractedly he pressed her head back upon the pillow and looked down at her queer, youthful face, with its high cheekbones, stretched eyelids and short, shapely lips. She had rather nice teeth, like the teeth of a kitten. He had bought her from her parents two years ago, for three hundred rupees. He began to stroke her brown throat, rising like a smooth, slender stalk from the collarless ingyi.

'You only like me because I am a white man and have money,' he said.

'Master, I love you, I love you more than anything in the world. Why do you say that? Have I not always been faithful to you?'

'You have a Burmese lover.'

'Ugh!' Ma Hla May affected to shudder at the thought. 'To think of their horrible brown hands, touching me! I should die if a Burman touched me!'

'Liar.'

He put his hand on her breast. Privately, Ma Hla May did not like this, for it reminded her that her breasts existed—the ideal of a Burmese woman being to have no breasts. She lay and let him do as he wished with her, quite passive yet pleased and faintly smiling, like a cat which allows one to stroke it. Flory's embraces meant nothing to her (Ba Pe, Ko S'la's younger brother, was secretly her lover), yet she was bitterly hurt when he neglected them. Sometimes she had even put love-philtres in his food. It was the idle concubine's life that she loved, and the visits to her village dressed in all her finery, when she could boast of her position as a 'bo-kadaw'—a white man's wife; for she had persuaded everyone, herself included, that she was Flory's legal wife.

When Flory had done with her he turned away, jaded and ashamed, and lay silent with his left hand covering his birthmark. He always remembered the birthmark when he had done something to be ashamed of. He buried his face disgustedly in the pillow, which was damp and smelt of coco-nut oil. It was horribly hot, and the doves outside were still droning. Ma Hla May, naked, reclined beside Flory, fanning him gently with a wicker fan she had taken from the table.

Presently she got up and dressed herself, and lighted a cigarette. Then, coming back to the bed, she sat down and began stroking Flory's bare shoulder. The whiteness of his skin had a fascination for her, because of its strangeness and the sense of power it gave her. But Flory twitched his shoulder to shake her hand away. At these times she was nauseating and dreadful to him. His sole wish was to get her out of his sight.

'Get out,' he said.

Ma Hla May took her cigarette from her mouth and tried to offer it to Flory. 'Why is master always so angry with me when he has made love to me?' she said.

'Get out,' he repeated.

Ma Hla May continued to stroke Flory's shoulder. She had never learned the wisdom of leaving him alone at these times. She believed that lechery was a form of witchcraft, giving a woman magical powers over a man, until in the end she could weaken him to a half-idiotic slave. Each successive embrace sapped Flory's will and made the spell stronger—this was her belief. She began tormenting him to begin over again. She laid down her cigarette and put her arms round him, trying to turn him towards her and kiss his averted face, reproaching him for his coldness.

'Go away, go away!' he said angrily. 'Look in the pocket of my shorts. There is money there. Take five rupees and go.'

Ma Hla May found the five-rupee note and stuffed it into the bosom of her ingyi, but she still would not go. She hovered about the bed, worrying Flory until at last he grew angry and jumped up.

'Get out of this room! I told you to go. I don't want you in here after I've done with you.'

'That is a nice way to speak to me! You treat me as though I were a prostitute.'

'So you are. Out you go,' he said, pushing her out of the room by her shoulders. He kicked her sandals after her. Their encounters often ended in this way.

Flory stood in the middle of the room, yawning. Should he go down to the Club for tennis after all? No, it meant shaving, and he could not face the effort of shaving until he had a few drinks inside him. He felt his scrubby chin and lounged across to the mirror to examine it, but then turned away. He did not want to see the yellow, sunken face that would look back at him. For several minutes he stood slack-limbed, watching the tuktoo stalk a moth above the bookshelves. The cigarette that Ma Hla May had dropped burned down with an acrid smell, browning the paper. Flory took a book from the shelves, opened it and then threw it away in distaste. He had not even the energy to read. Oh God, God, what to do with the rest of this bloody evening?

Flo waddled into the room, wagging her tail and asking to be taken for a walk. Flory went sulkily into the little stone-floored bathroom that gave on to the bedroom, splashed himself with lukewarm water and put on his shirt and shorts. He must take some kind of exercise before the sun went down. In India it is in some way evil to spend a day without being once in a muck-sweat. It gives one a deeper sense of sin than a thousand lecheries. In the dark evening, after a quite idle day, one's ennui reaches a pitch that is frantic, suicidal. Work, prayer, books, drinking, talking— they are all powerless against it; it can only be sweated out through the pores of the skin.

Flory went out and followed the road uphill into the jungle. It was scrub jungle at first, with dense stunted bushes, and the only trees were half-wild mangoes, bearing little turpentiny fruits the size of plums. Then the road struck among taller trees. The jungle was dried-up and lifeless at this time of year. The trees lined the road in close, dusty ranks, with leaves a dull olive-green. No birds were visible except some ragged brown creatures like disreputable thrushes, which hopped clumsily under the bushes; in the distance some other bird uttered a cry of 'AH ha ha! AH ha ha!'—a lonely, hollow sound like the echo of a laugh. There was a poisonous, ivy-like smell of crushed leaves. It was still hot, though the sun was losing its glare and the slanting light was yellow.

After two miles the road ended at the ford of a shallow stream. The jungle grew greener here, because of the water, and the trees were taller. At the edge of the stream there was a huge dead pyinkado tree festooned with spidery orchids, and there were some wild lime bushes with white waxen flowers. They had a sharp scent like bergamot. Flory had walked fast and the sweat had drenched his shirt and dribbled, stinging, into his eyes. He had sweated himself into a better mood. Also, the sight of this stream always heartened him; its water was quite clear, rarest of sights in a miry country. He crossed the stream by the stepping stones, Flo splashing after him, and turned into a narrow track he knew, which led through the bushes. It was a track that cattle had made, coming to the stream to drink, and few human beings ever followed it. It led to a pool fifty yards upstream. Here a peepul tree grew, a great buttressed thing six feet thick, woven of innumerable strands of wood, like a wooden cable twisted by a giant. The roots of the tree made a natural cavern, under which the clear greenish water bubbled. Above and all around dense foliage shut out the light, turning the place into a green grotto walled with leaves.

Flory threw off his clothes and stepped into the water. It was a shade cooler than the air, and it came up to his neck when he sat down. Shoals of silvery mahseer, no bigger than sardines, came nosing and nibbling at his body. Flo had also flopped into the water, and she swam round silently, otter-like, with her webbed feet. She knew the pool well, for they often came here when Flory was at Kyauktada.

There was a stirring high up in the peepul tree, and a bubbling noise like pots boiling. A flock of green pigeons were up there, eating the berries. Flory gazed up into the great green dome of the tree, trying to distinguish the birds; they were invisible, they matched the leaves so perfectly, and yet the whole tree was alive with them, shimmering, as though the ghosts of birds were shaking it. Flo rested herself against the roots and growled up at the invisible creatures. Then a single green pigeon fluttered down and perched on a lower branch. It did not know that it was being watched. It was a tender thing, smaller than a tame dove, with jade-green back as smooth as velvet, and neck and breast of iridescent colours. Its legs were like the pink wax that dentists use.

The pigeon rocked itself backwards and forwards on the bough, swelling out its breast feathers and laying its coralline beak upon them. A pang went through Flory. Alone, alone, the bitterness of being alone! So often like this, in lonely places in the forest, he would come upon something—bird, flower, tree—beautiful beyond all words, if there had been a soul with whom to share it. Beauty is meaningless until it is shared. If he had one person, just one, to halve his loneliness! Suddenly the pigeon saw the man and dog below, sprang into the air and dashed away swift as a bullet, with a rattle of wings. One does not often see green pigeons so closely when they are alive. They are high-flying birds, living in the treetops, and they do not come to the ground, or only to drink. When one shoots them, if they are not killed outright, they cling to the branch until they die, and drop long after one has given up waiting and gone away.

Flory got out of the water, put on his clothes and recrossed the stream. He did not go home by the road, but followed a foot-track southward into the jungle, intending to make a detour and pass through a village that lay in the fringe of the jungle not far from his house. Flo frisked in and out of the undergrowth, yelping sometimes when her long ears caught in the thorns. She had once turned up a hare near here. Flory walked slowly. The smoke of his pipe floated straight upwards in still plumes. He was happy and at peace after the walk and the clear water. It was cooler now, except for patches of heat lingering under the thicker trees, and the light was gentle. Bullock-cart wheels were screaming peacefully in the distance.

Soon they had lost their way in the jungle, and were wandering in a maze of dead trees and tangled bushes. They came to an impasse where the path was blocked by large ugly plants like magnified aspidistras, whose leaves terminated in long lashes armed with thorns. A firefly glowed greenish at the bottom of a bush; it was getting twilight in the thicker places. Presently the bullock-cart wheels screamed nearer, taking a parallel course.

'Hey, saya gyi, saya gyi!' Flory shouted, taking Flo by the collar to prevent her running away.

'Ba le-de?' the Burman shouted back. There was the sound of plunging hooves and of yells to the bullocks.

'Come here, if you please, O venerable and learned sir! We have lost our way. Stop a moment, O great builder of pagodas!'

The Burman left his cart and pushed through the jungle, slicing the creepers with his dah. He was a squat middle-aged man with one eye. He led the way back to the track, and Flory climbed on to the flat, uncomfortable bullock cart. The Burman took up the string reins, yelled to the bullocks, prodded the roots of their tails with his short stick, and the cart jolted on with a shriek of wheels. The Burmese bullock-cart drivers seldom grease their axles, probably because they believe that the screaming keeps away evil spirits, though when questioned they will say that it is because they are too poor to buy grease.

They passed a whitewashed wooden pagoda, no taller than a man and half hidden by the tendrils of creeping plants. Then the track wound into the village, which consisted of twenty ruinous, wooden huts roofed with thatch, and a well beneath some barren date-palms. The egrets that roosted in the palms were streaming homewards over the treetops like white flights of arrows. A fat yellow woman with her longyi hitched under her armpits was chasing a dog round a hut, smacking at it with a bamboo and laughing, and the dog was also laughing in its fashion. The village was called Nyaunglebin—'the four peepul trees'; there were no peepul trees there now, probably they had been cut down and forgotten a century ago. The villagers cultivated a narrow strip of fields that lay between the town and the jungle, and they also made bullock carts which they sold in Kyauktada.

Bullock-cart wheels were littered everywhere under the houses; massive things five feet across, with spokes roughly but strongly carved.

Flory got off the cart and gave the driver a present of four annas. Some brindled curs hurried from beneath the houses to sniff at Flo, and a flock of pot-bellied, naked children, with their hair tied in top-knots, also appeared, curious about the white man but keeping their distance. The village headman, a wizened, leaf-brown old man, came out of his house, and there were shikoings. Flory sat down on the steps of the headman's house and relighted his pipe. He was thirsty.

'Is the water in your well good to drink, thugyi-min?'

The headman reflected, scratching the calf of his left leg with his right big toenail. 'Those who drink it, drink it, thakin. And those who do not drink it, do not drink it.'

'Ah. That is wisdom.'

The fat woman who had chased the pariah brought a blackened earthenware teapot and a handleless bowl, and gave Flory some pale green tea, tasting of wood-smoke.

'I must be going, thugyi-min. Thank you for the tea.'

'God go with you, thakin.'

Flory went home by a path that led out on to the maidan. It was dark now. Ko S'la had put on a clean ingyi and was waiting in the bedroom. He had heated two kerosene tins of bath-water, lighted the petrol lamps and laid out a clean suit and shirt for Flory. The clean clothes were intended as a hint that Flory should shave, dress himself and go down to the Club after dinner. Occasionally he spent the evening in Shan trousers, loafing in a chair with a book, and Ko S'la disapproved of this habit. He hated to see his master behaving differently from other white men. The fact that Flory often came back from the Club drunk, whereas he remained sober when he stayed at home, did not alter Ko S'la's opinion, because getting drunk was normal and pardonable in a white man.

'The woman has gone down to the bazaar,' he announced, pleased, as he always was when Ma Hla May left the house. 'Ba Pe has gone with a lantern, to look after her when she comes back.'

'Good,' Flory said.

She had gone to spend her five rupees—gambling, no doubt. 'The holy one's bath-water is ready.'

'Wait, we must attend to the dog first. Bring the comb,' Flory said.

The two men squatted on the floor together and combed Flo's silky coat and felt between her toes, picking out the ticks. It had to be done every evening. She picked up vast numbers of ticks during the day, horrible grey things that were the size of pin-heads when they got on to her, and gorged themselves till they were as large as peas. As each tick was detached Ko S'la put it on the floor and carefully crushed it with his big toe.

Then Flory shaved, bathed, dressed, and sat down to dinner. Ko S'la stood behind his chair, handing him the dishes and fanning him with the wicker fan. He had arranged a bowl of scarlet hibiscus flowers in the middle of the little table. The meal was pretentious and filthy. The clever 'Mug' cooks, descendants of servants trained by Frenchmen in India centuries ago, can do anything with food except make it eatable. After dinner Flory walked down to the Club, to play bridge and get three parts drunk, as he did most evenings when he was in Kyauktada.

Chapter 5

In spite of the whisky he had drunk at the Club, Flory had little sleep that night. The pariah curs were baying the moon—it was only a quarter full and nearly down by midnight, but the dogs slept all day in the heat, and they had begun their moon-choruses already. One dog had taken a dislike to Flory's house, and had settled down to bay at it systematically. Sitting on its bottom fifty yards from the gate, it let out sharp, angry yelps, one to half a minute, as regularly as a clock. It would keep this up for two or three hours, until the cocks began crowing.

Flory lay turning from side to side, his head aching. Some fool has said that one cannot hate an animal; he should try a few nights in India, when the dogs are baying the moon. In the end Flory could stand it no longer. He got up, rummaged in the tin uniform case under his bed for a rifle and a couple of cartridges, and went out on to the veranda.

It was fairly light in the quarter moon. He could see the dog, and he could see his foresight. He rested himself against the wooden pillar of the veranda and took aim carefully; then, as he felt the hard vulcanite butt against his bare shoulder, he flinched. The rifle had a heavy kick, and it left a bruise when one fired it. The soft flesh of his shoulder quailed. He lowered the rifle. He had not the nerve to fire it in cold blood.

It was no use trying to sleep. Flory got his jacket and some cigarettes, and began to stroll up and down the garden path, between the ghostly flowers. It was hot, and the mosquitoes found him out and came droning after him. Phantoms of dogs were chasing one another on the maidan. Over to the left the gravestones of the English cemetery glittered whitish, rather sinister, and one could see the mounds near by, that were the remains of old Chinese tombs. The hillside was said to be haunted, and the Club chokras cried when they were sent up the road at night.

'Cur, spineless cur,' Flory was thinking to himself; without heat, however, for he was too accustomed to the thought. 'Sneaking, idling, boozing, fornicating, soul-examining, self-pitying cur. All those fools at the Club, those dull louts to whom you are so pleased to think yourself superior—they are all better than you, every man of them. At least they are men in their oafish way. Not cowards, not liars. Not half-dead and rotting. But you—'

He had reason to call himself names. There had been a nasty, dirty affair at the Club that evening. Something quite ordinary, quite according to precedent; but still dingy, cowardly, dishonouring.

When Flory had arrived at the Club only Ellis and Maxwell were there. The Lackersteens had gone to the station with the loan of Mr Macgregor's car, to meet their niece, who was

to arrive by the night train. The three men were playing three-handed bridge fairly amicably when Westfield came in, his sandy face quite pink with rage, bringing a copy of a Burmese paper called the Burmese Patriot.

There was a libellous article in it, attacking Mr Macgregor. The rage of Ellis and Westfield was devilish. They were so angry that Flory had the greatest difficulty in pretending to be angry enough to satisfy them. Ellis spent five minutes in cursing and then, by some extraordinary process, made up his mind that Dr Veraswami was responsible for the article. And he had thought of a counterstroke already. They would put a notice on the board—a notice answering and contradicting the one Mr Macgregor had posted the day before. Ellis wrote it out immediately, in his tiny, clear handwriting:

'In view of the cowardly insult recently offered to our Deputy commissioner, we the undersigned wish to give it as our opinion that this is the worst possible moment to consider the election of niggers to this Club,' etc ,etc.

Westfield demurred to 'niggers'. It was crossed out by a single thin line and 'natives' substituted. The notice was signed 'R. Westfield, P. W. Ellis, C. W. Maxwell, J. Flory.'

Ellis was so pleased with his idea that quite half of his anger evaporated. The notice would accomplish nothing in itself, but the news of it would travel swiftly round the town, and would reach Dr Veraswami tomorrow. In effect, the doctor would have been publicly called a nigger by the European community. This delighted Ellis. For the rest of the evening he could hardly keep his eyes from the notice-board, and every few minutes he exclaimed in glee, 'That'll give little fat-belly something to think about, eh? Teach the little sod what we think of him. That's the way to put 'em in their place, eh?' etc.

Meanwhile, Flory had signed a public insult to his friend. He had done it for the same reason as he had done a thousand such things in his life; because he lacked the small spark of courage that was needed to refuse.

For, of course, he could have refused if he had chosen; and, equally of course, refusal would have meant a row with Ellis and Westfield. And oh, how he loathed a row! The nagging, the jeers! At the very thought of it he flinched; he could feel his birthmark palpable on his cheek, and something happening in his throat that made his voice go flat and guilty. Not that! It was easier to insult his friend, knowing that his friend must hear of it.

Flory had been fifteen years in Burma, and in Burma one learns not to set oneself up against public opinion. But his trouble was older than that. It had begun in his mother's womb, when chance put the blue birthmark on his cheek. He thought of some of the early effects of his birthmark. His first arrival at school, aged nine; the stares and, after a few days, shouts of the other boys; the nickname Blueface, which lasted until the school poet (now, Flory remembered, a critic who wrote rather good articles in the Nation) came out with the couplet:

New-tick Flory does look rum, Got a face like a monkey's bum, whereupon the nickname was changed to Monkey-bum. And the subsequent years. On Saturday nights the older boys used to have what they called a Spanish Inquisition. The favourite torture was for someone to hold you in a very painful grip known only to a few illuminati and called Special Togo, while someone else beat you with a conker on a piece of string. But Flory had lived down 'Monkey-bum' in time. He was a liar, and a good footballer, the two things absolutely necessary for success at school. In his last term he and another boy held the school poet in Special Togo while the captain of the eleven gave him six with a spiked running shoe for being caught writing a sonnet. It was a formative period.

From that school he went to a cheap, third-rate public school. It was a poor, spurious place. It aped the great public schools with their traditions of High Anglicanism, cricket and Latin verses, and it had a school song called 'The Scrum of Life' in which God figured as the Great Referee. But it lacked the chief virtue of the great public schools, their atmosphere of literary scholarship. The boys learned as nearly as possible nothing. There was not enough caning to make them swallow the dreary rubbish of the curriculum, and the wretched, underpaid masters were not the kind from whom one absorbs wisdom unawares. Flory left school a barbarous young lout. And yet even then there were, and he knew it, certain possibilities in him; possibilities that would lead to trouble as likely as not. But, of course, he had suppressed them. A boy does not start his career nicknamed Monkey-bum without learning his lesson.

He was not quite twenty when he came to Burma. His parents, good people and devoted to him, had found him a place in a timber firm. They had had great difficulty in getting him the job, had paid a premium they could not afford; later, he had rewarded them by answering their letters with careless scrawls at intervals of months. His first six months in Burma he had spent in Rangoon, where he was supposed to be learning the office side of his business. He had lived in a 'chummery' with four other youths who devoted their entire energies to debauchery. And what debauchery! They swilled whisky which they privately hated, they stood round the piano bawling songs of insane filthiness and silliness, they squandered rupees by the hundred on aged Jewish whores with the faces of crocodiles. That too had been a formative period.

From Rangoon he had gone to a camp in the jungle, north of Mandalay, extracting teak. The jungle life was not a bad one, in spite of the discomfort, the loneliness, and what is almost the worst thing in Burma, the filthy, monotonous food. He was very young then, young enough for hero-worship, and he had friends among the men in his firm. There were also shooting, fishing, and perhaps once in a year a hurried trip to Rangoon— pretext, a visit to the dentist. Oh, the joy of those Rangoon trips! The rush to Smart and Mookerdum's bookshop for the new novels out from England, the dinner at Anderson's with beefsteaks and butter that had travelled eight thousand miles on ice, the glorious drinking-bout! He was too young to realize what this life was preparing for him. He did not see the years stretching out ahead, lonely, eventless, corrupting.

He acclimatized himself to Burma. His body grew attuned to the strange rhythms of the tropical seasons. Every year from February to May the sun glared in the sky like an angry god, then suddenly the monsoon blew westward, first in sharp squalls, then in a heavy ceaseless downpour that drenched everything until neither one's clothes, one's bed nor even one's food ever seemed to be dry. It was still hot, with a stuffy, vaporous heat. The lower jungle paths turned into morasses, and the paddy-fields were wastes of stagnant water with a stale, mousy smell. Books and boots were mildewed. Naked Burmans in yard-wide hats of palm-leaf ploughed the paddy-fields, driving their buffaloes through knee-deep water. Later, the women and children planted the green seedlings of paddy, dabbing each plant into the mud with little three-pronged forks. Through July and August there was hardly a pause in the rain. Then one night, high overhead, one heard a squawking of invisible birds. The snipe were flying southward from Central Asia. The rains tailed off, ending in October. The fields dried up, the paddy ripened, the Burmese children played hop-scotch with gonyin seeds and flew kites in the cool winds. It was the beginning of the short winter, when Upper Burma seemed haunted by the ghost of England. Wild flowers sprang into bloom everywhere, not quite the same as the English ones, but very like them—honeysuckle in thick bushes, field roses smelling of pear-drops, even violets in dark places of the forest. The sun circled low in the sky, and the nights and early mornings were bitterly cold, with white mists that poured through the valleys like the steam of enormous kettles. One went shooting after duck and snipe. There were snipe in countless myriads, and wild geese in flocks that rose from the jeel with a roar like a goods train crossing an iron bridge. The ripening paddy, breast-high and yellow, looked like wheat. The Burmans went to their work with muffled heads and their arms clasped across their breasts, their faces yellow and pinched with the cold. In the morning one marched through misty, incongruous wilderness, clearings of drenched, almost English grass and naked trees where monkeys squatted in the upper branches, waiting for the sun. At night, coming back to camp through the cold lanes, one met herds of buffaloes which the boys were driving home, with their huge horns looming through the mist like crescents. One had three blankets on one's bed, and game pies instead of the eternal chicken. After dinner one sat on a log by the vast camp-fire, drinking beer and talking about shooting. The flames danced like red holly, casting a circle of light at the edge of which servants and coolies squatted, too shy to intrude on the white men and yet edging up to the fire like dogs. As one lay in bed one could hear the dew dripping from the trees like large but gentle rain. It was a good life while one was young and need not think about the future or the past.

Flory was twenty-four, and due for home leave, when the War broke out. He had dodged military service, which was easy to do and seemed natural at the time. The civilians in Burma had a comforting theory that 'sticking by one's job' (wonderful language, English! 'Sticking BY'—how different from 'sticking TO') was the truest patriotism; there was even a covert hostility towards the men who threw up their jobs in order to join the Army. In reality, Flory had dodged the War because the East already corrupted him, and he did not want to exchange his whisky, his servants and his Burmese girls for the boredom of the parade ground and the strain of cruel marches. The War rolled on, like a storm beyond the horizon. The hot, blowsy country, remote from danger, had a lonely, forgotten feeling.

Flory took to reading voraciously, and learned to live in books when life was tiresome. He was growing adult, tiring of boyish pleasures, learning to think for himself, almost willy-nilly.

He celebrated his twenty-seventh birthday in hospital, covered from head to foot with hideous sores which were called mud-sores, but were probably caused by whisky and bad food. They left little pits in his skin which did not disappear for two years. Quite suddenly he had begun to look and feel very much older. His youth was finished. Eight years of Eastern life, fever, loneliness and intermittent drinking, had set their mark on him.

Since then, each year had been lonelier and more bitter than the last. What was at the centre of all his thoughts now, and what poisoned everything, was the ever bitterer hatred of the atmosphere of imperialism in which he lived. For as his brain developed—you cannot stop your brain developing, and it is one of the tragedies of the half-educated that they develop late, when they are already committed to some wrong way of life—he had grasped the truth about the English and their Empire. The Indian Empire is a despotism— benevolent, no doubt, but still a despotism with theft as its final object. And as to the English of the East, the sahiblog, Flory had come so to hate them from living in their society, that he was quite incapable of being fair to them. For after all, the poor devils are no worse than anybody else. They lead unenviable lives; it is a poor bargain to spend thirty years, ill-paid, in an alien country, and then come home with a wrecked liver and a pine-apple backside from sitting in cane chairs, to settle down as the bore of some second-rate Club. On the other hand, the sahiblog are not to be idealized. There is a prevalent idea that the men at the 'outposts of Empire' are at least able and hardworking. It is a delusion. Outside the scientific services—the Forest Department, the Public Works Department and the like—there is no particular need for a

British official in India to do his job competently. Few of them work as hard or as intelligently as the postmaster of a provincial town in England. The real work of administration is done mainly by native subordinates; and the real backbone of the despotism is not the officials but the Army. Given the Army, the officials and the businessmen can rub along safely enough even if they are fools. And most of them ARE fools. A dull, decent people, cherishing and fortifying their dullness behind a quarter of a million bayonets.

It is a stifling, stultifying world in which to live. It is a world in which every word and every thought is censored. In England it is hard even to imagine such an atmosphere. Everyone is free in England; we sell our souls in public and buy them back in private, among our friends. But even friendship can hardly exist when every white man is a cog in the wheels of despotism. Free speech is unthinkable. All other kinds of freedom are permitted. You are free to be a drunkard, an idler, a coward, a backbiter, a fornicator; but you are not free to think for yourself. Your opinion on every subject of any conceivable importance is dictated for you by the pukka sahibs' code.

In the end the secrecy of your revolt poisons you like a secret disease. Your whole life is a life of lies. Year after year you sit in Kipling-haunted little Clubs, whisky to right of you, Pink'un to left of you, listening and eagerly agreeing while Colonel Bodger develops his theory that these bloody Nationalists should be boiled in oil. You hear your Oriental friends called 'greasy little babus', and you admit, dutifully, that they ARE greasy little babus. You see louts fresh from school kicking grey-haired servants. The time comes when you burn with hatred of your own countrymen, when you long for a native rising to drown their Empire in blood. And in this there is nothing honourable, hardly even any sincerity. For, au fond, what do you care if the Indian Empire is a despotism, if Indians are bullied and exploited? You only care because the right of free speech is denied you. You are a creature of the despotism, a pukka sahib, tied tighter than a monk or a savage by an unbreakable system of tabus.

Time passed and each year Flory found himself less at home in the world of the sahibs, more liable to get into trouble when he talked seriously on any subject whatever. So he had learned to live inwardly, secretly, in books and secret thoughts that could not be uttered. Even his talks with the doctor were a kind of talking to himself; for the doctor, good man, understood little of what was said to him. But it is a corrupting thing to live one's real life in secret. One should live with the stream of life, not against it. It would be better to be the thickest-skulled pukka sahib who ever hiccuped over 'Forty years on', than to live silent, alone, consoling oneself in secret, sterile worlds.

Flory had never been home to England. Why, he could not have explained, though he knew well enough. In the beginning accidents had prevented him. First there was the War, and after the War his firm were so short of trained assistants that they would not let him go for two years more. Then at last he had set out. He was pining for England, though he dreaded facing it, as one dreads facing a pretty girl when one is collarless and unshaven. When he left home he had been a boy, a promising boy and handsome in spite of his birthmark; now, only ten years later, he was yellow, thin, drunken, almost middle-aged in habits and appearance. Still, he was pining for England. The ship rolled westward over wastes of sea like rough-beaten silver, with the winter trade wind behind her. Flory's thin blood quickened with the good food and the smell of the sea. And it occurred to him—a thing he had actually forgotten in the stagnant air of Burma—that he was still young enough to begin over again. He would live a year in a civilized society, he would find some girl who did not mind his birthmark— a civilized girl, not a pukka memsahib—and he would marry her and endure ten, fifteen more years of Burma. Then they would retire— he would be worth twelve or fifteen thousand pounds on retirement, perhaps. They would buy a cottage in the country, surround themselves with friends, books, their children, animals. They would be free for ever of the smell of pukka sahibdom. He would forget Burma, the horrible country that had come near ruining him.

When he reached Colombo he found a cable waiting for him. Three men in his firm had died suddenly of black-water fever. The firm were sorry, but would he please return to Rangoon at once? He should have his leave at the earliest possible opportunity.

Flory boarded the next boat for Rangoon, cursing his luck, and took the train back to his headquarters. He was not at Kyauktada then, but at another Upper Burma town. All the servants were waiting for him on the platform. He had handed them over en bloc to his successor, who had died. It was so queer to see their familiar faces again! Only ten days ago he had been speeding for England, almost thinking himself in England already; and now back in the old stale scene, with the naked black coolies squabbling over the luggage and a Burman shouting at his bullocks down the road.

The servants came crowding round him, a ring of kindly brown faces, offering presents. Ko S'la had brought a sambhur skin, the Indians some sweetmeats and a garland of marigolds, Ba Pe, a young boy then, a squirrel in a wicker cage. There were bullock carts waiting for the luggage. Flory walked up to the house, looking ridiculous with the big garland dangling from his neck. The light of the cold-weather evening was yellow and kind. At the gate an old Indian, the colour of earth, was cropping grass with a tiny sickle. The wives of the cook and the mali were kneeling in front of the servants' quarters, grinding curry paste on the stone slab.

Something turned over in Flory's heart. It was one of those moments when one becomes conscious of a vast change and deterioration in one's life. For he had realized, suddenly, that in his heart he was glad to be coming back. This country which he hated was now his native country, his home. He had lived here ten years, and every particle of his body was compounded of Burmese soil. Scenes like these—the sallow evening light, the old Indian cropping grass, the creak of the cartwheels, the streaming egrets—were more native to him than England. He had sent deep roots, perhaps his deepest, into a foreign country.

Since then he had not even applied for home leave. His father had died, then his mother, and his sisters, disagreeable horse-faced women whom he had never liked, had married and he had almost lost touch with them. He had no tie with Europe now, except the tie of books. For he had realized that merely to go back to England was no remedy for loneliness; he had grasped the special nature of the hell that is reserved for Anglo-Indians. Ah, those poor prosing old wrecks in Bath and Cheltenham! Those tomb-like boarding-houses with Anglo-Indians littered about in all stages of decomposition, all talking and talking about what happened in Boggleywalah in '88! Poor devils, they know what it means to have left one's heart in an alien and hated country. There was, he saw clearly, only one way out. To find someone who would share his life in Burma—but really share it, share his inner, secret life, carry away from Burma the same memories as he carried. Someone who would love Burma as he loved it and hate it as he hated it. Who would help him to live with nothing hidden, nothing unexpressed. Someone who understood him: a friend, that was what it came down to.

A friend. Or a wife? That quite impossible she. Someone like Mrs Lackersteen, for instance? Some damned memsahib, yellow and thin, scandalmongering over cocktails, making kit-kit with the servants, living twenty years in the country without learning a word of the language. Not one of those, please God.

Flory leaned over the gate. The moon was vanishing behind the dark wall of the jungle, but the dogs were still howling. Some lines from Gilbert came into his mind, a vulgar silly jingle but appropriate—something about 'discoursing on your complicated state of mind'. Gilbert was a gifted little skunk. Did all his trouble, then, simply boil down to that? Just complicated, unmanly whinings; poor-little-rich-girl stuff? Was he no more than a loafer using his idleness to invent imaginary woes? A spiritual Mrs Wititterly? A Hamlet without poetry? Perhaps. And if so, did that make it any more bearable? It is not the less bitter because it is perhaps one's own fault, to see oneself drifting, rotting, in dishonour and horrible futility, and all the while knowing that somewhere within one there is the possibility of a decent human being.

Oh well, God save us from self-pity! Flory went back to the veranda, took up the rifle, and wincing slightly, let drive at the pariah dog. There was an echoing roar, and the bullet buried itself in the maidan, wide of the mark. A mulberry-coloured bruise sprang out on Flory's shoulder. The dog gave a yell of fright, took to its heels, and then, sitting down fifty yards farther away, once more began rhythmically baying.

Chapter 6

The morning sunlight slanted up the maidan and struck, yellow as goldleaf, against the white face of the bungalow. Four black-purple crows swooped down and perched on the veranda rail, waiting their chance to dart in and steal the bread and butter that Ko S'la had set down beside Flory's bed. Flory crawled through the mosquito net, shouted to Ko S'la to bring him some gin, and then went into the bathroom and sat for a while in a zinc tub of water that was supposed to be cold. Feeling better after the gin, he shaved himself. As a rule he put off shaving until the evening, for his beard was black and grew quickly.

While Flory was sitting morosely in his bath, Mr Macgregor, in shorts and singlet on the bamboo mat laid for the purpose in his bedroom, was struggling with Numbers 5, 6, 7, 8 and 9 of Nordenflycht's 'Physical Jerks for the Sedentary'. Mr Macgregor never, or hardly ever, missed his morning exercises. Number 8 (flat on the back, raise legs to the perpendicular without bending knees) was downright painful for a man of forty-three; Number 9 (flat on the back, rise to a sitting posture and touch toes with tips of fingers) was even worse. No matter, one must keep fit!

As Mr Macgregor lunged painfully in the direction of his toes, a brick-red shade flowed upwards from his neck and congested his face with a threat of apoplexy. The sweat gleamed on his large, tallowy breasts. Stick it out, stick it out! At all costs one must keep fit. Mohammed Ali, the bearer, with Mr Macgregor's clean clothes across his arm, watched through the half-open door. His narrow, yellow, Arabian face expressed neither comprehension nor curiosity. He had watched these contortions—a sacrifice, he dimly imagined, to some mysterious and exacting god—every morning for five years.

At the same time, too, Westfield, who had gone out early, was leaning against the notched and ink-stained table of the police station, while the fat Sub-inspector interrogated a suspect whom two constables were guarding. The suspect was a man of forty, with a grey, timorous face, dressed only in a ragged longyi kilted to the knee, beneath which his lank, curved shins were speckled with tick-bites.

'Who is this fellow?' said Westfield.

'Thief, sir. We catch him in possession of this ring with two emeralds very-dear. No explanation. How could he—poor coolie— own a emerald ring? He have stole it.'

He turned ferociously upon the suspect, advanced his face tomcat-fashion till it was almost touching the other's, and roared in an enormous voice:

'You stole the ring!'

'No.'

'You are an old offender!'

'No.'

'You have been in prison!'

'No.'

'Turn round!' bellowed the Sub-inspector on an inspiration. 'Bend over!'

The suspect turned his grey face in agony towards Westfield, who looked away. The two constables seized him, twisted him round and bent him over; the Sub-inspector tore off his longyi, exposing his buttocks.

'Look at this, sir!' He pointed to some scars. 'He have been flogged with bamboos. He is an old offender. THEREFORE he stole the ring!'

'All right, put him in the clink,' said Westfield moodily, as he lounged away from the table with his hands in his pockets. At the bottom of his heart he loathed running in these poor devils of common thieves. Dacoits, rebels—yes; but not these poor cringing rats! 'How many have you got in the clink now, Maung Ba?' he said.

'Three, sir.'

The lock-up was upstairs, a cage surrounded by six-inch wooden bars, guarded by a constable armed with a carbine. It was very dark, stifling hot, and quite unfurnished, except for an earth latrine that stank to heaven. Two prisoners were squatting at the bars, keeping their distance from a third, an Indian coolie, who was covered from head to foot with ringworm like a coat of mail. A stout Burmese woman, wife of a constable, was kneeling outside the cage ladling rice and watery dahl into tin pannikins.

'Is the food good?' said Westfield.

'It is good, most holy one,' chorused the prisoners.

The Government provided for the prisoners' food at the rate of two annas and a half per meal per man, out of which the constable's wife looked to make a profit of one anna.

Flory went outside and loitered down the compound, poking weeds into the ground with his stick. At that hour there were beautiful faint colours in everything—tender green of leaves, pinkish brown of earth and tree-trunks—like aquarelle washes that would vanish in the later glare. Down on the maidan flights of small, low-flying brown doves chased one another to and fro, and bee-eaters, emerald-green, curvetted like slow swallows. A file of sweepers, each with his load half hidden beneath his garment, were marching to some dreadful dumping-hole that existed on the edge of the jungle. Starveling wretches, with stick-like limbs and knees too feeble to be straightened, draped in earth-coloured rags, they were like a procession of shrouded skeletons walking.

The mali was breaking ground for a new flower-bed, down by the pigeon-cote that stood near the gate. He was a lymphatic, half-witted Hindu youth, who lived his life in almost complete silence, because he spoke some Manipur dialect which nobody else understood, not even his Zerbadi wife. His tongue was also a size too large for his mouth. He salaamed low to Flory, covering his face with his hand, then swung his mamootie aloft again and hacked at the dry ground with heavy, clumsy strokes, his tender back-muscles quivering.

A sharp grating scream that sounded like 'Kwaaa!' came from the servants quarters. Ko S'la's wives had begun their morning quarrel. The tame fighting cock, called Nero, strutted zigzag down the path, nervous of Flo, and Ba Pe came out with a bowl of paddy and they fed Nero and the pigeons. There were more yells from the servants' quarters, and the gruffer voices of men trying to stop the quarrel. Ko S'la suffered a great deal from his wives. Ma Pu, the first wife, was a gaunt hard-faced woman, stringy from much child-bearing, and Ma Yi, the 'little wife', was a fat, lazy cat some years younger. The two women fought incessantly when Flory was in headquarters and they were together. Once when Ma Pu was chasing Ko S'la with a bamboo, he had dodged behind Flory for protection, and Flory had received a nasty blow on the leg.

Mr Macgregor was coming up the road, striding briskly and swinging a thick walking-stick. He was dressed in khaki pagri-cloth shirt, drill shorts and a pigsticker topi. Besides his exercises, he took a brisk two-mile walk every morning when he could spare the time.

'Top o' the mornin' to ye!' he called to Flory in a hearty matutinal voice, putting on an Irish accent. He cultivated a brisk, invigorating, cold-bath demeanour at this hour of the morning. Moreover, the libellous article in the Burmese Patriot, which he had read overnight, had hurt him, and he was affecting a special cheeriness to conceal this.

'Morning!' Flory called back as heartily as he could manage.

Nasty old bladder of lard! he thought, watching Mr Macgregor up the road. How his bottom did stick out in those tight khaki shorts. Like one of those beastly middle-aged scoutmasters, homosexuals almost to a man, that you see photographs of in the illustrated papers. Dressing himself up in those ridiculous clothes and exposing his pudgy, dimpled knees, because it is the pukka sahib thing to take exercise before breakfast—disgusting!

A Burman came up the hill, a splash of white and magenta. It was Flory's clerk, coming from the tiny office, which was not far from the church. Reaching the gate, he shikoed and presented a grimy envelope, stamped Burmese-fashion on the point of the flap.

'Good morning, sir.'

'Good morning. What's this thing?'

'Local letter, your honour. Come this morning's post. Anonymous letter, I think, sir.'

'Oh bother. All right, I'll be down to the office about eleven.'

Flory opened the letter. It was written on a sheet of foolscap, and it ran:

MR JOHN FLORY,

SIR,—I the undersigned beg to suggest and WARN to your honour certain useful pieces of information whereby your honour will be much profited, sir.

Sir, it has been remarked in Kyauktada your honour's great friendship and intimacy with Dr Veraswami, the Civil Surgeon, frequenting with him, inviting him to your house, etc. Sir, we beg to inform you that the said Dr Veraswami is NOT A GOOD MAN and in no ways a worthy friend of European gentlemen. The doctor is eminently dishonest, disloyal and corrupt public servant. Coloured water is he providing to patients at the hospital and selling drugs for own profit, besides many bribes, extortions, etc. Two prisoners has he flogged with bamboos, afterwards rubbing chilis into the place if relatives do not send money. Besides this he is implicated with the Nationalist Party and lately provided material for a very evil article which appeared in the Burmese Patriot attacking Mr Macgregor, the honoured Deputy Commissioner.

He is also sleeping by force with female patients at the hospital.

Wherefore we are much hoping that your honour will ESCHEW same Dr Veraswami and not consort with persons who can bring nothing but evil upon your honour.

And shall ever pray for your honour's long health and prosperity.

(Signed) A FRIEND.

The letter was written in the shaky round hand of the bazaar letter-writer, which resembled a copybook exercise written by a drunkard. The letter-writer, however, would never have risen to such a word as 'eschew'. The letter must have been dictated by a clerk, and no doubt it came ultimately from U Po Kyin. From 'the crocodile', Flory reflected.

He did not like the tone of the letter. Under its appearance of servility it was obviously a covert threat. 'Drop the doctor or we will make it hot for you', was what it said in effect. Not that that mattered greatly; no Englishman ever feels himself in real danger from an Oriental.

Flory hesitated with the letter in his hands. There are two things one can do with an anonymous letter. One can say nothing about it, or one can show it to the person whom it concerns. The obvious, the decent course was to give the letter to Dr Veraswami and let him take what action he chose.

And yet—it was safer to keep out of this business altogether. It is so important (perhaps the most important of all the Ten Precepts of the pukka sahib) not to entangle oneself in 'native' quarrels. With Indians there must be no loyalty, no real friendship. Affection, even love—yes. Englishmen do often love Indians— native officers, forest rangers, hunters, clerks, servants. Sepoys will weep like children when their colonel retires. Even intimacy is allowable, at the right moments. But alliance, partisanship, never! Even to know the rights and wrongs of a 'native' quarrel is a loss of prestige.

If he published the letter there would be a row and an official inquiry, and, in effect, he would have thrown in his lot with the doctor against U

Po Kyin. U Po Kyin did not matter, but there were the Europeans; if he, Flory, were too conspicuously the doctor's partisan, there might be hell to pay. Much better to pretend that the letter had never reached him. The doctor was a good fellow, but as to championing him against the full fury of pukka sahibdom— ah, no, no! What shall it profit a man if he save his own soul and lose the whole world? Flory began to tear the letter across. The danger of making it public was very slight, very nebulous. But one must beware of the nebulous dangers in India. Prestige, the breath of life, is itself nebulous. He carefully tore the letter into small pieces and threw them over the gate.

At this moment there was a terrified scream, quite different from the voices of Ko S'la's wives. The mali lowered his mamootie and gaped in the direction of the sound, and Ko S'la, who had also heard it, came running bareheaded from the servants' quarters, while Flo sprang to her feet and yapped sharply. The scream was repeated. It came from the jungle behind the house, and it was an English voice, a woman's, crying out in terror.

There was no way out of the compound by the back. Flory scrambled over the gate and came down with his knee bleeding from a splinter. He ran round the compound fence and into the jungle, Flo following. Just behind the house, beyond the first fringe of bushes, there was a small hollow, which, as there was a pool of stagnant water in it, was frequented by buffaloes from Nyaunglebin. Flory pushed his way through the bushes. In the hollow an English girl, chalk-faced, was cowering against a bush, while a huge buffalo menaced her with its crescent-shaped horns. A hairy calf, no doubt the cause of the trouble, stood behind. Another buffalo, neck-deep in the slime of the pool, looked on with mild prehistoric face, wondering what was the matter.

The girl turned an agonized face to Flory as he appeared. 'Oh, do be quick!' she cried, in the angry, urgent tone of people who are frightened. 'Please! Help me! Help me!'

Flory was too astonished to ask any questions. He hastened towards her, and, in default of a stick, smacked the buffalo sharply on the nose. With a timid, loutish movement the great beast turned aside, then lumbered off followed by the calf. The other buffalo also extricated itself from the slime and lolloped away. The girl threw herself against Flory, almost into his arms, quite overcome by her fright.

'Oh, thank you, thank you! Oh, those dreadful things! What ARE they? I thought they were going to kill me. What horrible creatures! What ARE they?'

They're only water-buffaloes. They come from the village up there.'

'Buffaloes?'

'Not wild buffaloes—bison, we call those. They're just a kind of cattle the Burmans keep. I say, they've given you a nasty shock. I'm sorry.'

She was still clinging closely to his arm, and he could feel her shaking. He looked down, but he could not see her face, only the top of her head, hatless, with yellow hair as short as a boy's. And he could see one of the hands on his arm. It was long, slender, youthful, with the mottled wrist of a schoolgirl. It was several years since he had seen such a hand. He became conscious of the soft, youthful body pressed against his own, and the warmth breathing out of it; whereat something seemed to thaw and grow warm within him.

'It's all right, they're gone,' he said. 'There's nothing to be frightened of.'

The girl was recovering from her fright, and she stood a little away from him, with one hand still on his arm. 'I'm all right,' she said. 'It's nothing. I'm not hurt. They didn't touch me. It was only their looking so awful.'

'They're quite harmless really. Their horns are set so far back that they can't gore you. They're very stupid brutes. They only pretend to show fight when they've got calves.'

They had stood apart now, and a slight embarrassment came over them both immediately.

Flory had already turned himself sidelong to keep his birthmarked cheek away from her.

He said:

'I say, this is a queer sort of introduction! I haven't asked yet how you got here. Wherever did you come from—if it's not rude to ask?'

'I just came out of my uncle's garden. It seemed such a nice morning, I thought I'd go for a walk. And then those dreadful things came after me. I'm quite new to this country, you see.'

'Your uncle? Oh, of course! You're Mr Lackersteen's niece. We heard you were coming. I say, shall we get out on to the maidan? There'll be a path somewhere. What a start for your first morning in Kyauktada! This'll give you rather a bad impression of Burma, I'm afraid.'

'Oh no; only it's all rather strange. How thick these bushes grow! All kind of twisted together and foreign-looking. You could get lost here in a moment. Is that what they call jungle?'

'Scrub jungle. Burma's mostly jungle—a green, unpleasant land, I call it. I wouldn't walk through that grass if I were you. The seeds get into your stockings and work their way into your skin.'

He let the girl walk ahead of him, feeling easier when she could not see his face. She was tallish for a girl, slender, and wearing a lilac-coloured cotton frock. From the way she moved her limbs he did not think she could be much past twenty. He had not noticed her face yet, except to see that she wore round tortoise-shell spectacles, and that her hair was as short as his own. He had never seen a woman with cropped hair before, except in the illustrated papers.

As they emerged on to the maidan he stepped level with her, and she turned to face him. Her face was oval, with delicate, regular features; not beautiful, perhaps, but it seemed so there, in Burma, where all Englishwomen are yellow and thin. He turned his head sharply aside, though the birthmark was away from her. He could not bear her to see his worn face too closely. He seemed to feel the withered skin round his eyes as though it had been a wound. But he remembered that he had shaved that morning, and it gave him courage. He said:

'I say, you must be a bit shaken up after this business. Would you like to come into my place and rest a few minutes before you go home? It's rather late to be out of doors without a hat, too.'

'Oh, thank you, I would,' the girl said. She could not, he thought, know anything about Indian notions of propriety. 'Is this your house here?'

'Yes. We must go round the front way. I'll have the servants get a sunshade for you. This sun's dangerous for you, with your short hair.'

They walked up the garden path. Flo was frisking round them and trying to draw attention to herself. She always barked at strange Orientals, but she liked the smell of a European. The sun was growing stronger. A wave of blackcurrant scent flowed from the petunias beside the path, and one of the pigeons fluttered to the earth, to spring immediately into the air again as Flo made a grab at it. Flory and the girl stopped with one consent, to look at the flowers. A pang of unreasonable happiness had gone through them both.

'You really mustn't go out in this sun without a hat on,' he repeated, and somehow there was an intimacy in saying it. He could not help referring to her short hair somehow, it seemed to him so beautiful. To speak of it was like touching it with his hand.

'Look, your knee's bleeding,' the girl said. 'Did you do that when you were coming to help me?'

There was a slight trickle of blood, which was drying, purple, on his khaki stocking. 'It's nothing,' he said, but neither of them felt at that moment that it was nothing. They began chattering with extraordinary eagerness about the flowers. The girl 'adored' flowers, she said. And Flory led her up the path, talking garrulously about one plant and another.

'Look how these phloxes grow. They go on blooming for six months in this country. They can't get too much sun. I think those yellow ones must be almost the colour of primroses. I haven't seen a primrose for fifteen years, nor a wallflower, either. Those zinnias are fine, aren't they?—like painted flowers, with those wonderful dead colours. These are African marigolds. They're coarse things, weeds almost, but you can't help liking them, they're so vivid and strong. Indians have an extraordinary affection for them; wherever Indians have been you find marigolds growing, even years afterwards when the jungle has buried every other trace of them. But I wish you'd come into the veranda and see the orchids. I've some I must show that are just like bells of gold—but literally like gold. And they smell of honey, almost overpoweringly. That's about the only merit of this beastly country, it's good for flowers. I hope you're fond of gardening? It's our greatest consolation, in this country.'

‘Oh, I simply adore gardening,’ the girl said.

They went into the veranda. Ko S’la had hurriedly put on his ingyi and his best pink silk gaungbaung, and he appeared from within the house with a tray on which were a decanter of gin, glasses and a box of cigarettes. He laid them on the table, and, eyeing the girl half apprehensively, put his hands flat together and shikoed.

‘I expect it’s no use offering you a drink at this hour of the morning?’ Flory said. ‘I can never get it into my servant’s head that SOME people can exist without gin before breakfast.’

He added himself to the number by waving away the drink Ko S’la offered him. The girl had sat down in the wicker chair that Ko S’la had set out for her at the end of the veranda. The dark-leaved orchids hung behind her head, with gold trusses of blossom, breathing out warm honey-scent. Flory was standing against the veranda rail, half facing the girl, but keeping his birthmarked cheek hidden.

‘What a perfectly divine view you have from here,’ she said as she looked down the hillside.

‘Yes, isn’t it? Splendid, in this yellow light, before the sun gets going. I love that sombre yellow colour the maidan has, and those gold mohur trees, like blobs of crimson. And those hills at the horizon, almost black. My camp is on the other side of those hills,’ he added.

The girl, who was long-sighted, took off her spectacles to look into the distance. He noticed that her eyes were very clear pale blue, paler than a harebell. And he noticed the smoothness of the skin round her eyes, like a petal, almost. It reminded him of his age and his haggard face again, so that he turned a little more away from her. But he said on impulse:

'I say, what a bit of luck you coming to Kyauktada! You can't imagine the difference it makes to us to see a new face in these places. After months of our own miserable society, and an occasional official on his rounds and American globe-trotters skipping up the Irrawaddy with cameras. I suppose you've come straight from England?'

'Well, not England exactly. I was living in Paris before I came out here. My mother was an artist, you see.'

'Paris! Have you really lived in Paris? By Jove, just fancy coming from Paris to Kyauktada! Do you know, it's positively difficult, in a hole like this, to believe that there ARE such places as Paris.'

'Do you like Paris?' she said.

'I've never even seen it. But, good Lord, how I've imagined it! Paris—it's all a kind of jumble of pictures in my mind; cafes and boulevards and artists' studios and Villon and Baudelaire and Maupassant all mixed up together. You don't know how the names of those European towns sound to us, out here. And did you really live in Paris? Sitting in cafes with foreign art students, drinking white wine and talking about Marcel Proust?'

'Oh, that kind of thing, I suppose,' said the girl, laughing.

'What differences you'll find here! It's not white wine and Marcel Proust here. Whisky and Edgar Wallace more likely. But if you ever want books, you might find something you liked among mine. There's nothing but tripe in the Club library. But of course I'm hopelessly behind the times with my books. I expect you'll have read everything under the sun.'

'Oh no. But of course I simply adore reading,' the girl said.

'What it means to meet somebody who cares for books! I mean books worth reading, not that garbage in the Club libraries. I do hope you'll forgive me if I overwhelm you with talk. When I meet somebody who's heard that books exist, I'm afraid I go off like a bottle of warm beer. It's a fault you have to pardon in these countries.'

'Oh, but I love talking about books. I think reading is so wonderful. I mean, what would life be without it? It's such a— such a—'

'Such a private Alsatia. Yes—'

They plunged into an enormous and eager conversation, first about books, then about shooting, in which the girl seemed to have an interest and about which she persuaded Flory to talk. She was quite thrilled when he described the murder of an elephant which he had perpetrated some years earlier. Flory scarcely noticed, and perhaps the girl did not either, that it was he who did all the talking. He could not stop himself, the joy of chattering was so great. And the girl was in a mood to listen. After all, he had saved her from the buffalo, and she did not yet believe that those monstrous brutes could be harmless; for the moment he was almost a hero in her eyes. When one does get any credit in this life, it is usually for something that one has not done. It was one of those times when the conversation flows so easily, so naturally, that one could go on talking forever. But suddenly, their pleasure evaporated, they started and fell silent. They had noticed that they were no longer alone.

At the other end of the veranda, between the rails, a coal-black moustachioed face was peeping with enormous curiosity. It belonged to old Sammy, the 'Mug' cook. Behind him stood Ma Pu, Ma Yi, Ko S'la's four eldest children, an unclaimed naked child, and two old women who had come down from the village upon the news that an 'Ingaleikma' was on view. Like carved teak statues with footlong cigars stuck in their wooden faces, the two old creatures gazed at the 'Ingaleikma' as English yokels might gaze at a Zulu warrior in full regalia.

'Those people . . .' the girl said uncomfortably, looking towards them.

Sammy, seeing himself detected, looked very guilty and pretended to be rearranging his pagri. The rest of the audience were a little abashed, except for the two wooden-faced old women.

'Dash their cheek!' Flory said. A cold pang of disappointment went through him. After all, it would not do for the girl to stay on his veranda any longer. Simultaneously both he and she had remembered that they were total strangers. Her face had turned a little pink. She began putting on her spectacles.

'I'm afraid an English girl is rather a novelty to these people,' he said. 'They don't mean any harm. Go away!' he added angrily, waving his hand at the audience, whereupon they vanished.

'Do you know, if you don't mind, I think I ought to be going,' the girl said. She had stood up. 'I've been out quite a long time. They may be wondering where I've got to.' 'Must you really? It's quite early. I'll see that you don't have to go home bareheaded in the sun.'

'I ought really—' she began again.

She stopped, looking at the doorway. Ma Hla May was emerging on to the veranda.

Ma Hla May came forward with her hand on her hip. She had come from within the house, with a calm air that asserted her right to be there. The two girls stood face to face, less than six feet apart.

No contrast could have been stranger; the one faintly coloured as an apple-blossom, the other dark and garish, with a gleam almost metallic on her cylinder of ebony hair and the salmon-pink silk of her longyi. Flory thought he had never noticed before how dark Ma Hla May's face was, and how outlandish her tiny, stiff body, straight as a soldier's, with not a curve in it except the vase-like curve of her hips. He stood against the veranda rail and watched the two girls, quite disregarded. For the best part of a minute neither of them could take her eyes from the other; but which found the spectacle more grotesque, more incredible, there is no saying.

Ma Hla May turned her face round to Flory, with her black brows, thin as pencil lines, drawn together. 'Who is this woman?' she demanded sullenly.

He answered casually, as though giving an order to a servant:

'Go away this instant. If you make any trouble I will afterwards take a bamboo and beat you till not one of your ribs is whole.'

Ma Hla May hesitated, shrugged her small shoulders and disappeared. And the other, gazing after her, said curiously:

'Was that a man or a woman?'

'A woman,' he said. 'One of the servants' wives, I believe. She came to ask about the laundry, that was all.'

'Oh, is THAT what Burmese women are like? They ARE queer little creatures! I saw a lot of them on my way up here in the train, but do you know, I thought they were all boys. They're just like a kind of Dutch doll, aren't they?'

She had begun to move towards the veranda steps, having lost interest in Ma Hla May now that she had disappeared. He did not stop her, for he thought Ma Hla May quite capable of coming back and making a scene. Not that it mattered much, for neither girl knew a word of the other's language. He called to Ko S'la, and Ko S'la came running with a big oiled-silk umbrella with bamboo ribs. He opened it respectfully at the foot of the steps and held it over the girl's head as she came down. Flory went with them as far as the gate. They stopped to shake hands, he turning a little sideways in the strong sunlight, hiding his birthmark.

'My fellow here will see you home. It was ever so kind of you to come in. I can't tell you how glad I am to have met you. You'll make such a difference to us here in Kyauktada.'

'Good-bye, Mr—oh, how funny! I don't even know your name.'

'Flory, John Flory. And yours—Miss Lackersteen, is it?'

'Yes. Elizabeth. Good-bye, Mr Flory. And thank you EVER so much. That awful buffalo. You quite saved my life.'

'It was nothing. I hope I shall see you at the Club this evening? I expect your uncle and aunt will be coming down. Good-bye for the time being, then.'

He stood at the gate, watching them as they went. Elizabeth— lovely name, too rare nowadays. He hoped she spelt it with a Z. Ko S'la trotted after her at a queer uncomfortable gait, reaching the umbrella over her head and keeping his body as far away from her as possible. A cool breath of wind blew up the hill. It was one of those momentary winds that blow sometimes in the cold weather in Burma, coming from nowhere, filling one with thirst and with nostalgia for cold sea-pools, embraces of mermaids, waterfalls, caves of ice. It rustled through the wide domes of the gold mohur trees, and fluttered the fragments of the anonymous letter that Flory had thrown over the gate half an hour earlier.

Chapter 7

Elizabeth lay on the sofa in the Lackersteen's drawing-room, with her feet up and a cushion behind her head, reading Michael Arlen's These Charming People. In a general way Michael Arlen was her favourite author, but she was inclined to prefer William J. Locke when she wanted something serious.

The drawing-room was a cool, light-coloured room with lime-washed walls a yard thick; it was large, but seemed smaller than it was, because of a litter of occasional tables and Benares brassware ornaments. It smelt of chintz and dying flowers. Mrs Lackersteen was upstairs, sleeping. Outside, the servants lay silent in their quarters, their heads tethered to their wooden pillows by the death-like sleep of midday. Mr Lackersteen, in his small wooden office down the road, was probably sleeping too. No one stirred except Elizabeth, and the chokra who pulled the punkah outside Mrs Lackersteen's bedroom, lying on his back with one heel in the loop of the rope.

Elizabeth was just turned twenty-two, and was an orphan. Her father had been less of a drunkard than his brother Tom, but he was a man of similar stamp. He was a tea-broker, and his fortunes fluctuated greatly, but he was by nature too optimistic to put money aside in prosperous phases. Elizabeth's mother had been an incapable, half-baked, vapouring, self-pitying woman who shirked all the normal duties of life on the strength of sensibilities which she did not possess. After messing about for years with such things as Women's Suffrage and Higher Thought, and making many abortive attempts at literature, she had finally taken up with painting. Painting is the only art that can be practised without either talent or hard work. Mrs Lackersteen's pose was that of an artist exiled among 'the Philistines'—these, needless to say, included her husband—and it was a pose that gave her almost unlimited scope for making a nuisance of herself.

In the last year of the War Mr Lackersteen, who had managed to avoid service, made a great deal of money, and just after the Armistice they moved into a huge, new, rather bleak house in Highgate, with quantities of greenhouses, shrubberies, stables and tennis courts. Mr Lackersteen had engaged a horde of servants, even, so great was his optimism, a butler. Elizabeth was sent for two terms to a very expensive boarding-school. Oh, the joy, the joy, the unforgettable joy of those two terms! Four of the girls at the school were 'the Honourable'; nearly all of them had ponies of their own, on which they were allowed to go riding on Saturday afternoons. There is a short period in everyone's life when his character is fixed forever; with Elizabeth, it was those two terms during which she rubbed shoulders with the rich. Thereafter her whole code of living was summed up in one belief, and that a simple one. It was that the Good ('lovely' was her name for it) is synonymous with the expensive, the elegant, the aristocratic; and the Bad ('beastly') is the cheap, the low, the shabby, the laborious. Perhaps it is in order to teach this creed that expensive girls' schools exist. The feeling subtilized itself as Elizabeth grew older, diffused itself through all her thoughts. Everything from a pair of stockings to a human soul was classifiable as 'lovely' or 'beastly'. And unfortunately—for Mr Lackersteen's prosperity did not last—it was the 'beastly' that had predominated in her life.

The inevitable crash came late in 1919. Elizabeth was taken away from school, to continue her education at a succession of cheap, beastly schools, with gaps of a term or two when her father could not pay the fees. He died when she was twenty, of influenza. Mrs Lackersteen was left with an income of L150 a year, which was to die with her. The two women could not, under Mrs Lackersteen's management, live on three pounds a week in England. They moved to Paris, where life was cheaper and where Mrs Lackersteen intended to dedicate herself wholly to Art.

Paris! Living in Paris! Flory had been a little wide of the mark when he pictured those interminable conversations with bearded artists under the green plane trees. Elizabeth's life in Paris had not been quite like that.

Her mother had taken a studio in the Montparnasse quarter, and relapsed at once into a state of squalid, muddling idleness. She was so foolish with money that her income would not come near covering expenses, and for several months Elizabeth did not even have enough to eat. Then she found a job as visiting teacher of English to the family of a French bank manager. They called her 'notre mees Anglaise'. The banker lived in the twelfth arrondissement, a long way from Montparnasse, and Elizabeth had taken a room in a pension near by. It was a narrow, yellow-faced house in a side street, looking out on to a poulterer's shop, generally decorated with reeking carcasses of wild boars, which old gentlemen like decrepit satyrs would visit every morning and sniff long and lovingly. Next door to the poulterer's was a fly-blown cafe with the sign 'Cafe de l'Amitie.

Bock Formidable'. How Elizabeth had loathed that pension! The patroness was an old black-clad sneak who spent her life in tiptoeing up and down stairs in hopes of catching the boarders washing stockings in their hand-basins. The boarders, sharp-tongued bilious widows, pursued the only man in the establishment, a mild, bald creature who worked in La Samaritaine, like sparrows worrying a bread-crust. At meals all of them watched each others' plates to see who was given the biggest helping. The bathroom was a dark den with leprous walls and a rickety verdigrised geyser which would spit two inches of tepid water into the bath and then mulishly stop working. The bank manager whose children Elizabeth taught was a man of fifty, with a fat, worn face and a bald, dark yellow crown resembling an ostrich's egg. The second day after her arrival he came into the room where the children were at their lessons, sat down beside Elizabeth and immediately pinched her elbow. The third day he pinched her on the calf, the fourth day behind the knee, the fifth day above the knee. Thereafter, every evening, it was a silent battle between the two of them, her hand under the table, struggling and struggling to keep that ferret-like hand away from her.

It was a mean, beastly existence. In fact, it reached levels of 'beastliness' which Elizabeth had not previously known to exist. But the thing that most depressed her, most filled her with the sense of sinking into some horrible lower world, was her mother's studio. Mrs Lackersteen was one of those people who go utterly to pieces when they are deprived of servants. She lived in a restless nightmare between painting and housekeeping, and never worked at either. At irregular intervals she went to a 'school' where she produced greyish still-lifes under the guidance of a master whose technique was founded on dirty brushes; for the rest, she messed about miserably at home with teapots and frying-pans. The state of her studio was more than depressing to Elizabeth; it was evil, Satanic. It was a cold, dusty pigsty, with piles of books and papers littered all over the floor, generations of saucepans slumbering in their grease on the rusty gas-stove, the bed never made till afternoon, and everywhere—in every possible place where they could be stepped on or knocked over—tins of paint-fouled turpentine and pots half full of cold black tea. You would lift a cushion from a chair and find a plate holding the remains of a poached egg underneath it. As soon as Elizabeth entered the door she would burst out:

'Oh, Mother, Mother dearest, how CAN you? Look at the state of this room! It is so terrible to live like this!'

'The room, dearest? What's the matter? Is it untidy?'

'Untidy! Mother, NEED you leave that plate of porridge in the middle of your bed? And those saucepans! It does look so dreadful. Suppose anyone came in!'

The rapt, other-wordly look which Mrs Lackersteen assumed when anything like work presented itself, would come into her eyes.

'None of MY friends would mind, dear. We are such Bohemians, we artists. You don't understand how utterly wrapped up we all are in our painting. You haven't the artistic temperament, you see, dear.'

'I must try and clean some of those saucepans. I just can't bear to think of you living like this. What have you done with the scrubbing-brush?'

'The scrubbing-brush? Now, let me think, I know I saw it somewhere. Ah yes! I used it yesterday to clean my palette. But it'll be all right if you give it a good wash in turpentine.'

Mrs Lackersteen would sit down and continue smudging a sheet of sketching paper with a Conte crayon while Elizabeth worked.

'How wonderful you are, dear. So practical! I can't think whom you inherit it from. Now with me, Art is simply EVERYTHING. I seem to feel it like a great sea surging up inside me. It swamps everything mean and petty out of existence. Yesterday I ate my lunch off Nash's Magazine to save wasting time washing plates. Such a good idea! When you want a clean plate you just tear off a sheet,' etc., etc., etc.

Elizabeth had no friends in Paris. Her mother's friends were women of the same stamp as herself, or elderly ineffectual bachelors living on small incomes and practising contemptible half-arts such as wood-engraving or painting on porcelain. For the rest, Elizabeth saw only foreigners, and she disliked all foreigners en bloc; or at least all foreign men, with their cheap-looking clothes and their revolting table manners. She had one great solace at this time. It was to go to the American library in the rue de l'Elysee and look at the illustrated papers. Sometimes on a Sunday or her free afternoon she would sit there for hours at the big shiny table, dreaming, over the Sketch, the Tatter, the Graphic, the Sporting and Dramatic.

Ah, what joys were pictured there! 'Hounds meeting on the lawn of Charlton Hall, the lovely Warwickshire seat of Lord Burrowdean.' 'The Hon. Mrs Tyke-Bowlby in the Park with her splendid Alsatian, Kublai Khan, which took second prize at Cruft's this summer.' 'Sunbathing at Cannes. Left to right: Miss Barbara Pilbrick, Sir Edward Tuke, Lady Pamela Westrope, Captain "Tuppy" Benacre.'

Lovely, lovely, golden world! On two occasions the face of an old schoolfellow looked at Elizabeth from the page. It hurt her in her breast to see it. There they all were, her old schoolfellows, with their horses and their cars and their husbands in the cavalry; and here she, tied to that dreadful job, that dreadful pension, her dreadful mother! Was it possible that there was no escape? Could she be doomed forever to this sordid meanness, with no hope of ever getting back to the decent world again?

It was not unnatural, with the example of her mother before her eyes, that Elizabeth should have a healthy loathing of Art. In fact, any excess of intellect—'braininess' was her word for it— tended to belong, in her eyes, to the 'beastly'. Real people, she felt, decent people—people who shot grouse, went to Ascot, yachted at Cowes—were not brainy. They didn't go in for this nonsense of writing books and fooling with paintbrushes; and all these Highbrow ideas—Socialism and all that. 'Highbrow' was a bitter word in her vocabulary. And when it happened, as it did once or twice, that she met a veritable artist who was willing to work penniless all his life, rather than sell himself to a bank or an insurance company, she despised him far more than she despised the dabblers of her mother's circle. That a man should turn deliberately away from all that was good and decent, sacrifice himself for a futility that led nowhere, was shameful, degrading, evil. She dreaded spinsterhood, but she would have endured it a thousand lifetimes through rather than marry such a man.

When Elizabeth had been nearly two years in Paris her mother died abruptly of ptomaine poisoning. The wonder was that she had not died of it sooner. Elizabeth was left with rather less than a hundred pounds in the world. Her uncle and aunt cabled at once from Burma, asking her to come out and stay with them, and saying that a letter would follow.

Mrs Lackersteen had reflected for some time over the letter, her pen between her lips, looking down at the page with her delicate triangular face like a meditative snake.

'I suppose we must have her out here, at any rate for a year. WHAT a bore! However, they generally marry within a year if they've any looks at all. What am I to say to the girl, Tom?'

'Say? Oh, just say she'll pick up a husband out here a damn sight easier than at home. Something of that sort, y'know.'

'My DEAR Tom! What impossible things you say!'

Mrs Lackersteen wrote:

Of course, this is a very small station and we are in the jungle a great deal of the time. I'm afraid you will find it dreadfully dull after the DELIGHTS of Paris. But really in some ways these small stations have their advantages for a young girl. She finds herself quite a QUEEN in the local society. The unmarried men are so lonely that they appreciate a girl's society in a quite wonderful way, etc., etc.

Elizabeth spent thirty pounds on summer frocks and set sail immediately. The ship, heralded by rolling porpoises, ploughed across the Mediterranean and down the Canal into a sea of staring, enamel-like blue, then out into the green wastes of the Indian Ocean, where flocks of flying fish skimmed in terror from the approaching hull. At night the waters were phosphorescent, and the wash of the bow was like a moving arrowhead of green fire. Elizabeth 'loved' the life on board ship. She loved the dancing on deck at nights, the cocktails which every man on board seemed anxious to buy for her, the deck games, of which, however, she grew tired at about the same time as the other members of the younger set. It was nothing to her that her mother's death was only two months past. She had never cared greatly for her mother, and besides, the people here knew nothing of her affairs. It was so lovely after those two graceless years to breathe the air of wealth again. Not that most of the people here were rich; but on board ship everyone behaves as though he were rich. She was going to love India, she knew. She had formed quite a picture of India, from the other passengers' conversation; she had even learned some of the more necessary Hindustani phrases, such as 'idher ao', 'jaldi', 'sahiblog', etc. In anticipation she tasted the agreeable atmosphere of Clubs, with punkahs flapping and barefooted white-turbaned boys reverently salaaming; and maidans where bronzed Englishmen with little clipped moustaches galloped to and fro, whacking polo balls. It was almost as nice as being really rich, the way people lived in India.

They sailed into Colombo through green glassy waters, where turtles and black snakes floated basking. A fleet of sampans came racing out to meet the ship, propelled by coal-black men with lips stained redder than blood by betel juice. They yelled and struggled round the gangway while the passengers descended. As Elizabeth and her friends came down, two sampan-wallahs, their prows nosing against the gangway, besought them with yells.

'Don't you go with him, missie! Not with him! Bad wicked man he, not fit taking missie!'

'Don't you listen him lies, missie! Nasty low fellow! Nasty low tricks him playing. Nasty NATIVE tricks!'

'Ha, ha! He is not native himself! Oh no! Him European man, white skin all same, missie! Ha ha!'

'Stop your bat, you two, or I'll fetch one of you a kick,' said the husband of Elizabeth's friend—he was a planter. They stepped into one of the sampans and were rowed towards the sun-bright quays. And the successful sampan-wallah turned and discharged at his rival a mouthful of spittle which he must have been saving up for a very long time.

This was the Orient. Scents of coco-nut oil and sandalwood, cinnamon and turmeric, floated across the water on the hot, swimming air. Elizabeth's friends drove her out to Mount Lavinia, where they bathed in a lukewarm sea that foamed like Coca-Cola. She came back to the ship in the evening, and they reached Rangoon a week later.

North of Mandalay the train, fuelled with wood, crawled at twelve miles an hour across a vast, parched plain, bounded at its remote edges by blue rings of hills. White egrets stood poised, motionless, like herons, and piles of drying chilis gleamed crimson in the sun. Sometimes a white pagoda rose from the plain like the breast of a supine giantess. The early tropic night settled down, and the train jolted on, slowly, stopping at little stations where barbaric yells sounded from the darkness. Half-naked men with their long hair knotted behind their heads moved to and fro in torchlight, hideous as demons in Elizabeth's eyes. The train plunged into forest, and unseen branches brushed against the windows. It was about nine o'clock when they reached Kyauktada, where Elizabeth's uncle and aunt were waiting with Mr Macgregor's car, and with some servants carrying torches. Her aunt came forward and took Elizabeth's shoulders in her delicate, saurian hands.

'I suppose you are our niece Elizabeth? We are SO pleased to see you,' she said, and kissed her.

Mr Lackersteen peered over his wife's shoulder in the torchlight. He gave a half-whistle, exclaimed, 'Well, I'll be damned!' and then seized Elizabeth and kissed her, more warmly than he need have done, she thought. She had never seen either of them before.

After dinner, under the punkah in the drawing-room, Elizabeth and her aunt had a talk together. Mr Lackersteen was strolling in the garden, ostensibly to smell the frangipani, actually to have a surreptitious drink that one of the servants smuggled to him from the back of the house.

'My dear, how really lovely you are! Let me look at you again.' She took her by the shoulders. 'I DO think that Eton crop suits you. Did you have it done in Paris?'

‘Yes. Everyone was getting Eton-cropped. It suits you if you’ve got a fairly small head.’

‘Lovely! And those tortoise-shell spectacles—such a becoming fashion! I’m told that all the—er—demi-mondaines in South America have taken to wearing them. I’d no idea I had such a RAVISHING beauty for a niece. How old did you say you were, dear?’

‘Twenty-two.’

‘Twenty-two! How delighted all the men will be when we take you to the Club tomorrow! They get so lonely, poor things, never seeing a new face. And you were two whole years in Paris? I can’t think what the men there can have been about to let you leave unmarried.’

‘I’m afraid I didn’t meet many men, Aunt. Only foreigners. We had to live so quietly. And I was working,’ she added, thinking this rather a disgraceful admission.

‘Of course, of course,’ sighed Mrs Lackersteen. ‘One hears the same thing on every side. Lovely girls having to work for their living. It is such a shame! I think it’s so terribly selfish, don’t you, the way these men remain unmarried while there are so MANY poor girls looking for husbands?’ Elizabeth not answering this, Mrs Lackersteen added with another sigh, ‘I’m sure if I were a young girl I’d marry anybody, literally ANYBODY!’

The two women’s eyes met. There was a great deal that Mrs Lackersteen wanted to say, but she had no intention of doing more than hint at it obliquely. A great deal of her conversation was carried on by hints; she generally contrived, however, to make her meaning reasonably clear. She said in a tenderly impersonal tone, as though discussing a subject of general interest:

‘Of course, I must say this. There ARE cases when, if girls fail to get married it's THEIR OWN FAULT. It happens even out here sometimes. Only a short time ago I remember a case—a girl came out and stayed a whole year with her brother, and she had offers from all kinds of men—policemen, forest officers, men in timber firms with QUITE good prospects. And she refused them all; she wanted to marry into the I.C.S., I heard. Well, what do you expect? Of course her brother couldn't go on keeping her forever. And now I hear she's at home, poor thing, working as a kind of lady help, practically a SERVANT. And getting only fifteen shillings a week! Isn't it dreadful to think of such things?'

'Dreadful!' Elizabeth echoed.

No more was said on this subject. In the morning, after she came back from Flory's house, Elizabeth was describing her adventure to her aunt and uncle. They were at breakfast, at the flower-laden table, with the punkah flapping overhead and the tall stork-like Mohammedan butler in his white suit and pagri standing behind Mrs Lackersteen's chair, tray in hand.

'And oh, Aunt, such an interesting thing! A Burmese girl came on to the veranda. I'd never seen one before, at least, not knowing they were girls. Such a queer little thing— she was almost like a doll with her round yellow face and her black hair screwed up on top. She only looked about seventeen. Mr Flory said she was his laundress.'

The Indian butler's long body stiffened. He squinted down at the girl with his white eyeballs large in his black face. He spoke English well. Mr Lackersteen paused with a forkful of fish half-way from his plate and his crass mouth open.

'Laundress?' he said. 'Laundress! I say, dammit, some mistake there! No such thing as a laundress in this country, y'know. Laundering work's all done by men. If you ask me—'

And then he stopped very suddenly, almost as though someone had trodden on his toe under the table.

Chapter 8

That evening Flory told Ko S'la to send for the barber—he was the only barber in the town, an Indian, and he made a living by shaving the Indian coolies at the rate of eight annas a month for a dry shave every other day. The Europeans patronized him for lack of any other. The barber was waiting on the veranda when Flory came back from tennis, and Flory sterilized the scissors with boiling water and Condy's fluid and had his hair cut.

'Lay out my best Palm Beach suit,' he told Ko S'la, 'and a silk shirt and my sambhur-skin shoes. Also that new tie that came from Rangoon last week.'

'I have done so, thakin,' said Ko S'la, meaning that he would do so. When Flory came into the bedroom he found Ko S'la waiting beside the clothes he had laid out, with a faintly sulky air. It was immediately apparent that Ko S'la knew why Flory was dressing himself up (that is, in hopes of meeting Elizabeth) and that he disapproved of it.

'What are you waiting for?' Flory said.

'To help you dress, thakin.'

'I shall dress myself this evening. You can go.'

He was going to shave—the second time that day—and he did not want Ko S'la to see him take shaving things into the bathroom. It was several years since he had shaved twice in one day. What providential luck that he had sent for that new tie only last week, he thought. He dressed himself very carefully, and spent nearly a quarter of an hour in brushing his hair, which was stiff and would never lie down after it had been cut.

Almost the next moment, as it seemed, he was walking with Elizabeth down the bazaar road. He had found her alone in the Club 'library', and with a sudden burst of courage asked her to come out with him; and she had come with a readiness that surprised him; not even stopping to say anything to her uncle and aunt. He had lived so long in Burma, he had forgotten English ways. It was very dark under the peepul trees of the bazaar road, the foliage hiding the quarter moon, but the stars here and there in a gap blazed white and low, like lamps hanging on invisible threads. Successive waves of scent came rolling, first the cloying sweetness of frangipani, then a cold putrid stench of dung or decay from the huts opposite Dr Veraswami's bungalow. Drums were throbbing a little distance away.

As he heard the drums Flory remembered that a pwe was being acted a little farther down the road, opposite U Po Kyin's house; in fact, it was U Po Kyin who had made arrangements for the pwe, though someone else had paid for it. A daring thought occurred to Flory. He would take Elizabeth to the pwe! She would love it—she must; no one with eyes in his head could resist a pwe-dance. Probably there would be a scandal when they came back to the Club together after a long absence; but damn it! what did it matter? She was different from that herd of fools at the Club.

And it would be such fun to go to the pwe together! At this moment the music burst out with a fearful pandemonium—a strident squeal of pipes, a rattle like castanets and the hoarse thump of drums, above which a man's voice was brassily squalling.

'Whatever is that noise?' said Elizabeth, stopping. 'It sounds just like a jazz band!'

'Native music. They're having a pwe—that's a kind of Burmese play; a cross between a historical drama and a revue, if you can imagine that. It'll interest you, I think. Just round the bend of the road here.'

'Oh,' she said rather doubtfully.

They came round the bend into a glare of light. The whole road for thirty yards was blocked by the audience watching the pwe. At the back there was a raised stage, under humming petrol lamps, with the orchestra squalling and banging in front of it; on the stage two men dressed in clothes that reminded Elizabeth of Chinese pagodas were posturing with curved swords in their hands. All down the roadway it was a sea of white muslin backs of women, pink scarves flung round their shoulders and black hair-cylinders. A few sprawled on their mats, fast asleep. An old Chinese with a tray of peanuts was threading his way through the crowd, intoning mournfully, 'Myaype! Myaype!'

'We'll stop and watch a few minutes if you like,' Flory said.

The blaze of lights and the appalling din of the orchestra had almost dazed Elizabeth, but what startled her most of all was the sight of this crowd of people sitting in the road as though it had been the pit of a theatre.

'Do they always have their plays in the middle of the road?' she said.

'As a rule. They put up a rough stage and take it down in the morning. The show lasts all night.'

'But are they ALLOWED to—blocking up the whole roadway?'

'Oh yes. There are no traffic regulations here. No traffic to regulate, you see.'

It struck her as very queer. By this time almost the entire audience had turned round on their mats to stare at the 'Ingaleikma'. There were half a dozen chairs in the middle of the crowd, where some clerks and officials were sitting. U Po Kyin was among them, and he was making efforts to twist his elephantine body round and greet the Europeans. As the music stopped the pock-marked Ba Taik came hastening through the crowd and shikoed low to Flory, with his timorous air.

'Most holy one, my master U Po Kyin asks whether you and the young white lady will not come and watch our pwe for a few minutes. He has chairs ready for you.'

'They're asking us to come and sit down,' Flory said to Elizabeth. 'Would you like to? It's rather fun. Those two fellows will clear off in a moment and there'll be some dancing. If it wouldn't bore you for a few minutes?'

Elizabeth felt very doubtful. Somehow it did not seem right or even safe to go in among that smelly native crowd. However, she trusted Flory, who presumably knew what was proper, and allowed him to lead her to the chairs. The Burmans made way on their mats, gazing after her and chattering; her shins brushed against warm, muslin-clad bodies, there was a feral reek of sweat. U Po Kyin leaned over towards her, bowing as well as he could and saying nasally:

'Kindly to sit down, madam! I am most honoured to make your

acquaintance. Good evening. Good morning, Mr Flory, sir! A most unexpected pleasure. Had we known that you were to honour us with your company, we would have provided whiskies and other European refreshments. Ha ha!'

He laughed, and his betel-reddened teeth gleamed in the lamplight like red tinfoil. He was so vast and so hideous that Elizabeth could not help shrinking from him. A slender youth in a purple longyi was bowing to her and holding out a tray with two glasses of yellow sherbet, iced. U Po Kyin clapped his hands sharply, 'Hey haung galay!' he called to a boy beside him. He gave some instructions in Burmese, and the boy pushed his way to the edge of the stage.

'He's telling them to bring on their best dancer in our honour,' Flory said. 'Look, here she comes.'

A girl who had been squatting at the back of the stage, smoking, stepped forward into the lamplight. She was very young, slim-shouldered, breastless, dressed in a pale blue satin longyi that hid her feet. The skirts of her ingyi curved outwards above her hips in little panniers, according to the ancient Burmese fashion. They were like the petals of a downward-pointing flower. She threw her cigar languidly to one of the men in the orchestra, and then, holding out one slender arm, writhed it as though to shake the muscles loose.

The orchestra burst into a sudden loud squalling. There were pipes like bagpipes, a strange instrument consisting of plaques of bamboo which a man struck with a little hammer, and in the middle there was a man surrounded by twelve tall drums of different sizes. He reached rapidly from one to another, thumping them with the heel of his hand. In a moment the girl began to dance. But at first it was not a dance, it was a rhythmic nodding, posturing and twisting of the elbows, like the movements of one of those jointed wooden figures on an old-fashioned roundabout. The way her neck and elbows rotated was precisely like a jointed doll, and yet incredibly sinuous. Her hands, twisting like snakeheads with the fingers close together, could lie back until they were almost along her forearms. By degrees her movements quickened. She began to leap from side to side, flinging herself down in a kind of curtsy and springing up again with extraordinary agility, in spite of the long longyi that imprisoned her feet. Then she danced in a grotesque posture as though sitting down, knees bent, body leaned forward, with her arms extended and writhing, her head also moving to the beat of the drums. The music quickened to a climax. The girl rose upright and whirled round as swiftly as a top, the pannier of her ingyi flying out about her like the petals of a snowdrop. Then the music stopped as abruptly as it had begun, and the girl sank again into a curtsy, amid raucous shouting from the audience.

Elizabeth watched the dance with a mixture of amazement, boredom and something approaching horror. She had sipped her drink and found that it tasted like hair oil. On a mat by her feet three Burmese girls lay fast asleep with their heads on the same pillow, their small oval faces side by side like the faces of kittens. Under cover of the music Flory was speaking in a low voice into Elizabeth's ear commenting on the dance.

'I knew this would interest you; that's why I brought you here. You've read books and been in civilized places, you're not like the rest of us miserable savages here. Don't you think this is worth watching, in its queer way? Just look at that girl's movements— look at that strange, bent-forward pose like a marionette, and the way her arms twist from the elbow like a cobra rising to strike. It's grotesque, it's even ugly, with a sort of wilful ugliness. And there's something sinister in it too. There's a touch of the diabolical in all Mongols. And yet when you look closely, what art, what centuries of culture you can see behind it! Every movement that girl makes has been studied and handed down through innumerable generations. Whenever you look closely at the art of these Eastern peoples you can see that—a civilization stretching back and back, practically the same, into times when we were dressed in woad. In some way that I can't define to you, the whole life and spirit of Burma is summed up in the way that girl twists her arms. When you see her you can see the rice fields, the villages under the teak trees, the pagodas, the priests in their yellow robes, the buffaloes swimming the rivers in the early morning, Thibaw's palace— '

His voice stopped abruptly as the music stopped. There were certain things, and a pwe-dance was one of them, that pricked him to talk discursively and incautiously; but now he realized that he had only been talking like a character in a novel, and not a very good novel. He looked away. Elizabeth had listened to him with a chill of discomfort. What WAS the man talking about? was her first thought. Moreover, she had caught the hated word Art more than once. For the first time she remembered that Flory was a total stranger and that it had been unwise to come out with him alone. She looked round her, at the sea of dark faces and the lurid glare of the lamps; the strangeness of the scene almost frightened her. What was she doing in this place? Surely it was not right to be sitting among the black people like this, almost touching them, in the scent of their garlic and their sweat? Why was she not back at the Club with the other white people? Why had he brought her here, among this horde of natives, to watch this hideous and savage spectacle?

The music struck up, and the pwe girl began dancing again. Her face was powdered so thickly that it gleamed in the lamplight like a chalk mask with live eyes behind it. With that dead-white oval face and those wooden gestures she was monstrous, like a demon. The music changed its tempo, and the girl began to sing in a brassy voice. It was a song with a swift trochaic rhythm, gay yet fierce. The crowd took it up, a hundred voices chanting the harsh syllables in unison. Still in that strange bent posture the girl turned round and danced with her buttocks protruded towards the audience. Her silk longyi gleamed like metal. With hands and elbows still rotating she wagged her posterior from side to side. Then—astonishing feat, quite visible through the longyi—she began to wriggle her two buttocks independently in time with the music.

There was a shout of applause from the audience. The three girls asleep on the mat woke up at the same moment and began clapping their hands wildly. A clerk shouted nasally 'Bravo! Bravo!' in English for the Europeans' benefit. But U Po Kyin frowned and waved his hand. He knew all about European women. Elizabeth, however, had already stood up.

'I'm going. It's time we were back,' she said abruptly. She was looking away, but Flory could see that her face was pink.

He stood up beside her, dismayed. 'But, I say! Couldn't you stay a few minutes longer? I know it's late, but—they brought this girl on two hours before she was due, in our honour. Just a few minutes?'

'I can't help it, I ought to have been back ages ago. I don't know WHAT my uncle and aunt will be thinking.'

She began at once to pick her way through the crowd, and he followed her, with not even time to thank the pwe people for their trouble. The Burmans made way with a sulky air. How like these English people, to upset everything by sending for the best dancer and then go away almost before she had started! There was a fearful row as soon as Flory and Elizabeth had gone, the pwe girl refusing to go on with her dance and the audience demanding that she should continue. However, peace was restored when two clowns hurried on to the stage and began letting off crackers and making obscene jokes.

Flory followed the girl abjectly up the road. She was walking quickly, her head turned away, and for some moments she would not speak. What a thing to happen, when they had been getting on so well together! He kept trying to apologize.

'I'm so sorry! I'd no idea you'd mind—'

'It's nothing. What is there to be sorry about? I only said it was time to go back, that's all.'

'I ought to have thought. One gets not to notice that kind of thing in this country. These people's sense of decency isn't the same as ours—it's stricter in some ways—but—'

'It's not that! It's not that!' she exclaimed quite angrily.

He saw that he was only making it worse. They walked on in silence, he behind. He was miserable. What a bloody fool he had been! And yet all the while he had no inkling of the real reason why she was angry with him. It was not the pwe girl's behaviour, in itself, that had offended her; it had only brought things to a head. But the whole expedition— the very notion of WANTING to rub shoulders with all those smelly natives—had impressed her badly. She was perfectly certain that that was not how white men ought to behave. And that extraordinary rambling speech that he had begun, with all those long words—almost, she thought bitterly, as though he were quoting poetry! It was how those beastly artists that you met sometimes in Paris used to talk. She had thought him a manly man till this evening. Then her mind went back to the morning's adventure, and how he had faced the buffalo barehanded, and some of her anger evaporated. By the time they reached the Club gate she felt inclined to forgive him. Flory had by now plucked up courage to speak again. He stopped, and she stopped too, in a patch where the boughs let through some starlight and he could see her face dimly.

'I say. I say, I do hope you're not really angry about this?'

'No, of course I'm not. I told you I wasn't.'

'I oughtn't to have taken you there. Please forgive me. Do you know, I don't think I'd tell the others where you've been. Perhaps it would be better to say you've just been out for a stroll, out in the garden—something like that. They might think it queer, a white girl going to a pwe. I don't think I'd tell them.'

'Oh, of course I won't!' she agreed with a warmness that surprised him. After that he knew that he was forgiven. But what it was that he was forgiven, he had not yet grasped.

They went into the Club separately, by tacit consent. The expedition had been a failure, decidedly. There was a gala air about the Club lounge tonight. The entire European community were waiting to greet Elizabeth, and the butler and the six chokras, in their best starched white suits, were drawn up on either side of the door, smiling and salaaming. When the Europeans had finished their greetings the butler came forward with a vast garland of flowers that the servants had prepared for the 'missiesahib'. Mr Macgregor made a very humorous speech of welcome, introducing everybody. He introduced Maxwell as 'our local arboreal specialist', Westfield as 'the guardian of law and order and—ah—terror of the local banditti', and so on and so forth. There was much laughter. The sight of a pretty girl's face had put everyone in such a good humour that they could even enjoy Mr Macgregor's speech—which, to tell the truth, he had spent most of the evening in preparing.

At the first possible moment Ellis, with a sly air, took Flory and Westfield by the arm and drew them away into the card-room. He was in a much better mood than usual. He pinched Flory's arm with his small, hard fingers, painfully but quite amiably.

'Well, my lad, everyone's been looking for you. Where have you been all this time?'

'Oh, only for a stroll.'

'For a stroll! And who with?'

'With Miss Lackersteen.'

'I knew it! So YOU'RE the bloody fool who's fallen into the trap, are you? YOU swallowed the bait before anyone else had time to look at it. I thought you were too old a bird for that, by God I did!'

'What do you mean?'

'Mean! Look at him pretending he doesn't know what I mean! Why, I mean that Ma Lackersteen's marked you down for her beloved nephew-in-law, of course. That is, if you aren't bloody careful. Eh, Westfield?'

'Quite right, ol' boy. Eligible young bachelor. Marriage halter and all that. They've got their eye on him.'

'I don't know where you're getting this idea from. The girl's hardly been here twenty-four hours.'

'Long enough for you to take her up the garden path, anyway. You watch your step. Tom Lackersteen may be a drunken sot, but he's not such a bloody fool that he wants a niece hanging round his neck for the rest of his life. And of course SHE knows which side her bread's buttered. So you take care and don't go putting your head into the noose.'

'Damn it, you've no right to talk about people like that. After all, the girl's only a kid—'

'My dear old ass'—Ellis, almost affectionate now that he had a new subject for scandal, took Flory by the coat lapel—'my dear, dear old ass, don't you go filling yourself up with moonshine. You think that girl's easy fruit: she's not. These girls out from home are all the same. "Anything in trousers but nothing this side the altar"—that's their motto, every one of them. Why do you think the girl's come out here?'

'Why? I don't know. Because she wanted to, I suppose.'

'My good fool! She come out to lay her claws into a husband, of course. As if it wasn't well known! When a girl's failed everywhere else she tries India, where every man's pining for the sight of a white woman. The Indian marriage-market, they call it. Meat market it ought to be. Shiploads of 'em coming out every year like carcasses of frozen mutton, to be pawed over by nasty old bachelors like you. Cold storage. Juicy joints straight from the ice.'

'You do say some repulsive things.'

'Best pasture-fed English meat,' said Ellis with a pleased air. 'Fresh consignments. Warranted prime condition.'

He went through a pantomime of examining a joint of meat, with goatish sniffs. This joke was likely to last Ellis a long time; his jokes usually did; and there was nothing that gave him quite so keen a pleasure as dragging a woman's name through mud.

Flory did not see much more of Elizabeth that evening. Everyone was in the lounge together, and there was the silly clattering chatter about nothing that there is on these occasions. Flory could never keep up that kind of conversation for long. But as for Elizabeth, the civilized atmosphere of the Club, with the white faces all round her and the friendly look of the illustrated papers and the 'Bonzo' pictures, reassured her after that doubtful interlude at the pwe.

When the Lackersteens left the Club at nine, it was not Flory but Mr Macgregor who walked home with them, ambling beside Elizabeth like some friendly saurian monster, among the faint crooked shadows of the gold mohur stems. The Prome anecdote, and many another, found a new home. Any newcomer to Kyauktada was apt to come in for rather a large share of Mr Macgregor's conversation, for the others looked on him as an unparalleled bore, and it was a tradition at the Club to interrupt his stories. But Elizabeth was by nature a good listener. Mr Macgregor thought he had seldom met so intelligent a girl.

Flory stayed a little longer at the Club, drinking with the others. There was much smutty talk about Elizabeth. The quarrel about Dr Veraswami's election had been shelved for the time being. Also, the notice that Ellis had put up on the previous evening had been taken down. Mr Macgregor had seen it during his morning visit to the Club, and in his fair-minded way he had at once insisted on its removal. So the notice had been suppressed; not, however, before it had achieved its object.

Chapter 9

During the next fortnight a great deal happened.

The feud between U Po Kyin and Dr Veraswami was now in full swing. The whole town was divided into two factions, with every native soul from the magistrates down to the bazaar sweepers enrolled on one side or the other, and all ready for perjury when the time came. But of the two parties, the doctor's was much the smaller and less efficiently libellous. The editor of the Burmese Patriot had been put on trial for sedition and libel, bail being refused. His arrest had provoked a small riot in Rangoon, which was suppressed by the police with the death of only two rioters. In prison the editor went on hunger strike, but broke down after six hours.

In Kyauktada, too, things had been happening. A dacoit named Nga Shwe O had escaped from the jail in mysterious circumstances. And there had been a whole crop of rumours about a projected native rising in the district. The rumours—they were very vague ones as yet—centred round a village named Thongwa, not far from the camp where Maxwell was girdling teak. A weiksa, or magician, was said to have appeared from nowhere and to be prophesying the doom of the English power and distributing magic bullet-proof jackets. Mr Macgregor did not take the rumours very seriously, but he had asked for an extra force of Military Police. It was said that a company of Indian infantry with a British officer in command would be sent to Kyauktada shortly. Westfield, of course, had hurried to Thongwa at the first threat, or rather hope, of trouble.

'God, if they'd only break out and rebel properly for once!' he said to Ellis before starting. 'But it'll be a bloody washout as usual. Always the same story with these rebellions—peter out almost before they've begun. Would you believe it, I've never fired my gun at a fellow yet, not even a dacoit. Eleven years of it, not counting the War, and never killed a man. Depressing.'

'Oh, well,' said Ellis, 'if they won't come up to the scratch you can always get hold of the ringleaders and give them a good bambooing on the Q.T. That's better than coddling them up in our damned nursing homes of prisons.'

'H'm, probably. Can't do it though, nowadays. All these kid-glove laws—got to keep them, I suppose, if we're fools enough to make 'em.'

'Oh, rot the laws. Bambooing's the only thing that makes any impression on the Burman. Have you seen them after they've been flogged? I have. Brought out of the jail on bullock carts, yelling, with the women plastering mashed bananas on their backsides. That's something they do understand. If I had my way I'd give it 'em on the soles of the feet the same as the Turks do.'

'Ah well. Let's hope they'll have the guts to show a bit of fight for once. Then we'll call out the Military Police, rifles and all. Plug a few dozen of 'em—that'll clear the air.'

However, the hoped-for opportunity did not come. Westfield and the dozen constables he had taken with him to Thongwa—jolly round-faced Gurkha boys, pining to use their kukris on somebody—found the district depressingly peaceful. There seemed not the ghost of a rebellion anywhere; only the annual attempt, as regular as the monsoon, of the villagers to avoid paying the capitation tax.

The weather was growing hotter and hotter. Elizabeth had had her first attack of prickly heat. Tennis at the Club had practically ceased; people would play one languid set and then fall into chairs and swallow pints of tepid lime-juice—tepid, because the ice came only twice weekly from Mandalay and melted within twenty-four hours of arriving. The Flame of the Forest was in full bloom. The Burmese women, to protect their children from the sun, streaked their faces with yellow cosmetic until they looked like little African witch-doctors. Flocks of green pigeons, and imperial pigeons as large as ducks, came to eat the berries of the big peepul trees along the bazaar road.

Meanwhile, Flory had turned Ma Hla May out of his house.

A nasty, dirty job! There was a sufficient pretext—she had stolen his gold cigarette-case and pawned it at the house of Li Yeik, the Chinese grocer and illicit pawnbroker in the bazaar—but still, it was only a pretext. Flory knew perfectly well, and Ma Hla May knew, and all the servants knew, that he was getting rid of her because of Elizabeth. Because of 'the Ingaleikma with dyed hair', as Ma Hla May called her.

Ma Hla May made no violent scene at first. She stood sullenly listening while he wrote her a cheque for a hundred rupees—Li Yeik or the Indian chetty in the bazaar would cash cheques—and told her that she was dismissed. He was more ashamed than she; he could not look her in the face, and his voice went flat and guilty. When the bullock cart came for her belongings, he shut himself in the bedroom skulking till the scene should be over.

Cartwheels grated on the drive, there was the sound of men shouting; then suddenly there was a fearful uproar of screams. Flory went outside. They were all struggling round the gate in the sunlight. Ma Hla May was clinging to the gatepost and Ko S'la was trying to bundle her out. She turned a face full of fury and despair towards Flory, screaming over and over, 'Thakin! Thakin! Thakin! Thakin! Thakin!' It hurt him to the heart that she should still call him thakin after he had dismissed her.

'What is it?' he said.

It appeared that there was a switch of false hair that Ma Hla May and Ma Yi both claimed. Flory gave the switch to Ma Yi and gave Ma Hla May two rupees to compensate her. Then the cart jolted away, with Ma Hla May sitting beside her two wicker baskets, straight-backed and sullen, and nursing a kitten on her knees. It was only two months since he had given her the kitten as a present.

Ko S'la, who had long wished for Ma Hla May's removal, was not altogether pleased now that it had happened. He was even less pleased when he saw his master going to church—or as he called it, to the 'English pagoda'—for Flory was still in Kyauktada on the Sunday of the padre's arrival, and he went to church with the others. There was a congregation of twelve, including Mr Francis, Mr Samuel and six native Christians, with Mrs Lackersteen playing 'Abide with Me' on the tiny harmonium with one game pedal. It was the first time in ten years that Flory had been to church, except to funerals. Ko S'la's notions of what went on in the 'English pagoda' were vague in the extreme; but he did know that church-going signified respectability—a quality which, like all bachelors' servants, he hated in his bones.

'There is trouble coming,' he said despondently to the other servants. 'I have been watching him (he meant Flory) these ten days past. He has cut down his cigarettes to fifteen a day, he has stopped drinking gin before breakfast, he shaves himself every evening—though he thinks I do not know it, the fool. And he has ordered half a dozen new silk shirts! I had to stand over the dirzi calling him bahinchut to get them finished in time. Evil omens! I give him three months longer, and then good-bye to the peace in this house!'

'What, is he going to get married?' said Ba Pe.

'I am certain of it. When a white man begins going to the English pagoda, it is, as you might say, the beginning of the end.'

'I have had many masters in my life,' old Sammy said. 'The worst was Colonel Wimpole sahib, who used to make his orderly hold me down over the table while he came running from behind and kicked me with very thick boots for serving banana fritters too frequently. At other times, when he was drunk, he would fire his revolver through the roof of the servants' quarters, just above our heads. But I would sooner serve ten years under Colonel Wimpole sahib than a week under a memsahib with her kit-kit. If our master marries I shall leave the same day.'

'I shall not leave, for I have been his servant fifteen years. But I know what is in store for us when that woman comes. She will shout at us because of spots of dust on the furniture, and wake us up to bring cups of tea in the afternoon when we are asleep, and come poking into the cookhouse at all hours and complain over dirty saucepans and cockroaches in the flour bin. It is my belief that these women lie awake at nights thinking of new ways to torment their servants.'

'They keep a little red book,' said Sammy, 'in which they enter the bazaar-money, two annas for this, four annas for that, so that a man cannot earn a pice. They make more kit-kit over the price of an onion than a sahib over five rupees.'

'Ah, do I not know it! She will be worse than Ma Hla May. Women!' he added comprehensively, with a kind of sigh.

The sigh was echoed by the others, even by Ma Pu and Ma Yi. Neither took Ko S'la's remarks as a stricture upon her own sex, Englishwomen being considered a race apart, possibly not even human, and so dreadful that an Englishman's marriage is usually the signal for the flight of every servant in his house, even those who have been with him for years.

Chapter 10

But as a matter of fact, Ko S'la's alarm was premature. After knowing Elizabeth for ten days, Flory was scarcely more intimate with her than on the day when he had first met her.

As it happened, he had her almost to himself during these ten days, most of the Europeans being in the jungle. Flory himself had no right to be loitering in headquarters, for at this time of year the work of timber-extraction was in full swing, and in his absence everything went to pieces under the incompetent Eurasian overseer. But he had stayed— pretext, a touch of fever—while despairing letters came almost every day from the overseer, telling of disasters. One of the elephants was ill, the engine of the light railway that was used for carrying teak logs to the river had broken down, fifteen of the coolies had deserted. But Flory still lingered, unable to tear himself away from Kyauktada while Elizabeth was there, and continually seeking—never, as yet, to much purpose—to recapture that easy and delightful friendship of their first meeting.

They met every day, morning and evening, it was true. Each evening they played a single of tennis at the Club—Mrs Lackersteen was too limp and Mr Lackersteen too liverish for tennis at this time of year—and afterwards they would sit in the lounge, all four together, playing bridge and talking. But though Flory spent hours in Elizabeth's company, and often they were alone together, he was never for an instant at his ease with her. They talked—so long as they talked of trivialities—with the utmost freedom, yet they were distant, like strangers. He felt stiff in her presence, he could not forget his birthmark; his twice-scraped chin smarted, his body tortured him for whisky and tobacco—for he tried to cut down his drinking and smoking when he was with her. After ten days they seemed no nearer the relationship he wanted.

For somehow, he had never been able to talk to her as he longed to talk. To talk, simply to talk! It sounds so little, and how much it is! When you have existed to the brink of middle age in bitter loneliness, among people to whom your true opinion on every subject on earth is blasphemy, the need to talk is the greatest of all needs. Yet with Elizabeth serious talk seemed impossible. It was as though there had been a spell upon them that made all their conversation lapse into banality; gramophone records, dogs, tennis racquets—all that desolating Club-chatter. She seemed not to WANT to talk of anything but that. He had only to touch upon a subject of any conceivable interest to hear the evasion, the 'I shan't play', coming into her voice. Her taste in books appalled him when he discovered it. Yet she was young, he reminded himself, and had she not drunk white wine and talked of Marcel Proust under the Paris plane trees? Later, no doubt, she would understand him and give him the companionship he needed. Perhaps it was only that he had not won her confidence yet.

He was anything but tactful with her. Like all men who have lived much alone, he adjusted himself better to ideas than to people. And so, though all their talk was superficial, he began to irritate her sometimes; not by what he said but by what he implied. There was an uneasiness between them, ill-defined and yet often verging upon quarrels. When two people, one of whom has lived long in the country while the other is a newcomer, are thrown together, it is inevitable that the first should act as cicerone to the second. Elizabeth, during these days, was making her first acquaintance with Burma; it was Flory, naturally, who acted as her interpreter, explaining this, commenting upon that. And the things he said, or the way he said them, provoked in her a vague yet deep disagreement. For she perceived that Flory, when he spoke of the 'natives', spoke nearly always IN FAVOUR of them. He was forever praising Burmese customs and the Burmese character; he even went so far as to contrast them favourably with the English. It disquieted her. After all, natives were natives—interesting, no doubt, but finally only a 'subject' people, an inferior people with black faces. His attitude was a little TOO tolerant. Nor had he grasped, yet, in what way he was antagonizing her. He so wanted her to love Burma as he loved it, not to look at it with the dull, incurious eyes of a memsahib! He had forgotten that most people can be at ease in a foreign country only when they are disparaging the inhabitants.

He was too eager in his attempts to interest her in things Oriental. He tried to induce her, for instance, to learn Burmese, but it came to nothing. (Her aunt had explained to her that only missionary-women spoke Burmese; nice women found kitchen Urdu quite as much as they needed.) There were countless small disagreements like that. She was grasping, dimly, that his views were not the views an Englishman should hold. Much more clearly she grasped that he was asking her to be fond of the Burmese, even to admire them; to admire people with black faces, almost savages, whose appearance still made her shudder!

The subject cropped up in a hundred ways. A knot of Burmans would pass them on the road. She, with her still fresh eyes, would gaze after them, half curious and half repelled; and she would say to Flory, as she would have said to anybody:

'How REVOLTINGLY ugly these people are, aren't they?'

'ARE they? I always think they're rather charming-looking, the Burmese. They have such splendid bodies! Look at that fellow's shoulders—like a bronze statue. Just think what sights you'd see in England if people went about half naked as they do here!'

'But they have such hideous-shaped heads! Their skulls kind of slope up behind like a tom-cat's. And then the way their foreheads slant back—it makes them look so WICKED. I remember reading something in a magazine about the shape of people's heads; it said that a person with a sloping forehead is a CRIMINAL TYPE.'

'Oh, come, that's a bit sweeping! Round about half the people in the world have that kind of forehead.'

'Oh, well, if you count COLOURED people, of course—!'

Or perhaps a string of women would pass, going to the well: heavy-set peasant-girls, copper-brown, erect under their water-pots with strong marelike buttocks protruded. The Burmese women repelled Elizabeth more than the men; she felt her kinship with them, and the hatefulness of being kin to creatures with black faces.

'Aren't they too simply dreadful? So COARSE-LOOKING; like some kind of animal. Do you think ANYONE could think those women attractive?'

'Their own men do, I believe.'

'I suppose they would. But that black skin—I don't know how anyone could bear it!'

'But, you know, one gets used to the brown skin in time. In fact they say—I believe it's true—that after a few years in these countries a brown skin seems more natural than a white one. And after all, it IS more natural. Take the world as a whole, it's an eccentricity to be white.'

'You DO have some funny ideas!'

And so on and so on. She felt all the while an unsatisfactoriness, an unsoundness in the things he said. It was particularly so on the evening when Flory allowed Mr Francis and Mr Samuel, the two derelict Eurasians, to entrap him in conversation at the Club gate.

Elizabeth, as it happened, had reached the Club a few minutes before Flory, and when she heard his voice at the gate she came round the tennis-screen to meet him. The two Eurasians had sidled up to Flory and cornered him like a pair of dogs asking for a game. Francis was doing most of the talking. He was a meagre, excitable man, and as brown as a cigar-leaf, being the son of a South Indian woman; Samuel, whose mother had been a Karen, was pale yellow with dull red hair. Both were dressed in shabby drill suits, with vast topis beneath which their slender bodies looked like the stalks of toadstools.

Elizabeth came down the path in time to hear fragments of an enormous and complicated autobiography. Talking to white men—talking, for choice, about himself—was the great joy of Francis's life. When, at intervals of months, he found a European to listen to him, his life-history would pour out of him in unquenchable torrents. He was talking in a nasal, sing-song voice of incredible rapidity:

'Of my father, sir, I remember little, but he was very choleric man and many whackings with big bamboo stick all knobs on both for self, little half-brother and two mothers. Also how on occasion of bishop's visit little half-brother and I dress in longyis and sent among the Burmese children to preserve incognito. My father never rose to be bishop, sir. Four converts only in twenty-eight years, and also too great fondness for Chinese rice-spirit very fiery noised abroad and spoil sales of my father's booklet entitled The Scourge of Alcohol, published with the Rangoon Baptist Press, one rupee eight annas. My little half-brother die one hot weather, always coughing, coughing,' etc., etc.

The two Eurasians perceived the presence of Elizabeth. Both doffed their topis with bows and brilliant displays of teeth. It was probably several years since either of them had had a chance of talking to an Englishwoman. Francis burst out more effusively than ever. He was chattering in evident dread that he would be interrupted and the conversation cut short.

'Good evening to you, madam, good evening, good evening! Most honoured to make your acquaintance, madam! Very sweltering is the weather these days, is not? But seasonable for April. Not too much you are suffering from prickly heat, I trust? Pounded tamarind applied to the afflicted spot is infallible. Myself I suffer torments each night. Very prevalent disease among we Europeans.'

He pronounced it Europian, like Mr Chollop in Martin Chuzzlewit. Elizabeth did not answer. She was looking at the Eurasians somewhat coldly. She had only a dim idea as to who or what they were, and it struck her as impertinent that they should speak to her.

'Thanks, I'll remember about the tamarind,' Flory said.

'Specific of renowned Chinese doctor, sir. Also, sir-madam, may I advise to you, wearing only Terai hat is not judicious in April, sir. For the natives all well, their skulls are adamant. But for us sunstroke ever menaces. Very deadly is the sun upon European skull. But is it that I detain you, madam?'

This was said in a disappointed tone. Elizabeth had, in fact, decided to snub the Eurasians. She did not know why Flory was allowing them to hold him in conversation. As she turned away to stroll back to the tennis court, she made a practice stroke in the air with her racquet, to remind Flory that the game was overdue. He saw it and followed her, rather reluctantly, for he did not like snubbing the wretched Francis, bore though he was.

'I must be off,' he said. 'Good evening, Francis. Good evening, Samuel.'

'Good evening, sir! Good evening, madam! Good evening, good evening!' They receded with more hat flourishes.

'Who ARE those two?' said Elizabeth as Flory came up with her. 'Such extraordinary creatures! They were in church on Sunday. One of them looks almost white. Surely he isn't an Englishman?'

'No, they're Eurasians—sons of white fathers and native mothers. Yellow-bellies is our friendly nickname for them.'

'But what are they doing here? Where do they live? Do they do any work?'

'They exist somehow or other in the bazaar. I believe Francis acts as clerk to an Indian money-lender, and Samuel to some of the pleaders. But they'd probably starve now and then if it weren't for the charity of the natives.'

'The natives! Do you mean to say—sort of CADGE from the natives?'

'I fancy so. It would be a very easy thing to do, if one cared to. The Burmese won't let anyone starve.'

Elizabeth had never heard of anything of this kind before. The notion of men who were at least partly white living in poverty among 'natives' so shocked her that she stopped short on the path, and the game of tennis was postponed for a few minutes.

'But how awful! I mean, it's such a bad example! It's almost as bad as if one of US was like that. Couldn't something be done for those two? Get up a subscription and send them away from here, or something?'

'I'm afraid it wouldn't help much. Wherever they went they'd be in the same position.'

'But couldn't they get some proper work to do?'

'I doubt it. You see, Eurasians of that type—men who've been brought up in the bazaar and had no education—are done for from the start. The Europeans won't touch them with a stick, and they're cut off from entering the lower-grade Government services. There's nothing they can do except cadge, unless they chuck all pretension to being Europeans. And really you can't expect the poor devils to do that. Their drop of white blood is the sole asset they've got. Poor Francis, I never meet him but he begins telling me about his prickly heat. Natives, you see, are supposed not to suffer from prickly heat—bosh, of course, but people believe it. It's the same with sunstroke. They wear those huge topis to remind you that they've got European skulls. A kind of coat of arms. The bend sinister, you might say.'

This did not satisfy Elizabeth. She perceived that Flory, as usual, had a sneaking sympathy with the Eurasians. And the appearance of the two men had excited a peculiar dislike in her. She had placed their type now. They looked like dagoes. Like those Mexicans and Italians and other dago people who play the mauvais role in so many a film.

'They looked awfully degenerate types, didn't they? So thin and weedy and cringing; and they haven't got at all HONEST faces. I suppose these Eurasians ARE very degenerate? I've heard that half-castes always inherit what's worst in both races. Is that true?'

'I don't know that it's true. Most Eurasians aren't very good specimens, and it's hard to see how they could be, with their upbringing. But our attitude towards them is rather beastly. We always talk of them as though they'd sprung up from the ground like mushrooms, with all their faults ready-made. But when all's said and done, we're responsible for their existence.'

'Responsible for their existence?'

'Well, they've all got fathers, you see.'

'Oh . . . Of course there's that. . . . But after all, YOU aren't responsible. I mean, only a very low kind of man would—er—have anything to do with native women, wouldn't he?'

'Oh, quite. But the fathers of both those two were clergymen in holy orders, I believe.'

He thought of Rosa McFee, the Eurasian girl he had seduced in Mandalay in 1913. The way he used to sneak down to the house in a gharry with the shutters down; Rosa's corkscrew curls; her withered old Burmese mother, giving him tea in the dark living-room with the fern pots and the wicker divan. And afterwards, when he had chucked Rosa, those dreadful, imploring letters on scented note-paper, which, in the end, he had ceased opening.

Elizabeth reverted to the subject of Francis and Samuel after tennis.

'Those two Eurasians—does anyone here have anything to do with them? Invite them to their houses or anything?'

'Good gracious, no. They're complete outcasts. It's not considered quite the thing to talk to them, in fact. Most of us say good morning to them—Ellis won't even do that.'

'But YOU talked to them.'

'Oh well, I break the rules occasionally. I meant that a pukka sahib probably wouldn't be seen talking to them. But you see, I try—just sometimes, when I have the pluck—NOT to be a pukka sahib.'

It was an unwise remark. She knew very well by this time the meaning of the phrase 'pukka sahib' and all it stood for. His remark had made the difference in their viewpoint a little clearer. The glance she gave him was almost hostile, and curiously hard; for her face could look hard sometimes, in spite of its youth and its flower-like skin. Those modish tortoise-shell spectacles gave her a very self-possessed look. Spectacles are queerly expressive things—almost more expressive, indeed, than eyes.

As yet he had neither understood her nor quite won her trust. Yet on the surface, at least, things had not gone ill between them. He had fretted her sometimes, but the good impression that he had made that first morning was not yet effaced. It was a curious fact that she scarcely noticed his birthmark at this time. And there were some subjects on which she was glad to hear him talk. Shooting, for example—she seemed to have an enthusiasm for shooting that was remarkable in a girl. Horses, also; but he was less knowledgeable about horses. He had arranged to take her out for a day's shooting, later, when he could make preparations. Both of them were looking forward to the expedition with some eagerness, though not entirely for the same reason.

Chapter 11

Flory and Elizabeth walked down the bazaar road. It was morning, but the air was so hot that to walk in it was like wading through a torrid sea. Strings of Burmans passed, coming from the bazaar, on scraping sandals, and knots of girls who hurried by four and five abreast, with short quick steps, chattering, their burnished hair gleaming. By the roadside, just before you got to the jail, the fragments of a stone pagoda were littered, cracked and overthrown by the strong roots of a peepul tree. The angry carved faces of demons looked up from the grass where they had fallen. Near by another peepul tree had twined itself round a palm, uprooting it and bending it backwards in a wrestle that had lasted a decade.

They walked on and came to the jail, a vast square block, two hundred yards each way, with shiny concrete walls twenty feet high. A peacock, pet of the jail, was mincing pigeon-toed along the parapet. Six convicts came by, head down, dragging two heavy handcarts piled with earth, under the guard of Indian warders. They were long-sentence men, with heavy limbs, dressed in uniforms of coarse white cloth with small dunces' caps perched on their shaven crowns. Their faces were greyish, cowed and curiously flattened. Their leg-irons jingled with a clear ring. A woman came past carrying a basket of fish on her head. Two crows were circling round it and making darts at it, and the woman was flapping one hand negligently to keep them away.

There was a din of voices a little distance away. 'The bazaar's just round the corner,' Flory said. 'I think this is a market morning. It's rather fun to watch.'

He had asked her to come down to the bazaar with him, telling her it would amuse her to see it. They rounded the bend. The bazaar was an enclosure like a very large cattle pen, with low stalls, mostly palm-thatched, round its edge. In the enclosure, a mob of people seethed, shouting and jostling; the confusion of their multi-coloured clothes was like a cascade of hundreds-and-thousands poured out of a jar. Beyond the bazaar one could see the huge, miry river. Tree branches and long streaks of scum raced down it at seven miles an hour. By the bank a fleet of sampans, with sharp beak-like bows on which eyes were painted, rocked at their mooring-poles.

Flory and Elizabeth stood watching for a moment. Files of women passed balancing vegetable baskets on their heads, and pop-eyed children who stared at the Europeans. An old Chinese in dungarees faded to sky-blue hurried by, nursing some unrecognizable, bloody fragment of a pig's intestines.

'Let's go and poke around the stalls a bit, shall we?' Flory said.

'Is it all right going in among the crowd? Everything's so horribly dirty.'

'Oh, it's all right, they'll make way for us. It'll interest you.'

Elizabeth followed him doubtfully and even unwillingly. Why was it that he always brought her to these places? Why was he forever dragging her in among the 'natives', trying to get her to take an interest in them and watch their filthy, disgusting habits? It was all wrong, somehow. However, she followed, not feeling able to explain her reluctance. A wave of stifling air met them; there was a reek of garlic, dried fish, sweat, dust, anise, cloves and turmeric. The crowd surged round them, swarms of stocky peasants with cigar-brown faces, withered elders with their grey hair tied in a bun behind, young mothers carrying naked babies astride the hip. Flo was trodden on and yelped. Low, strong shoulders bumped against Elizabeth, as the peasants, too busy bargaining even to stare at a white woman, struggled round the stalls.

'Look!' Flory was pointing with his stick to a stall, and saying something, but it was drowned by the yells of two women who were shaking their fists at each other over a basket of pineapples. Elizabeth had recoiled from the stench and din, but he did not notice it, and led her deeper into the crowd, pointing to this stall and that. The merchandise was foreign-looking, queer and poor. There were vast pomelos hanging on strings like green moons, red bananas, baskets of heliotrope-coloured prawns the size of lobsters, brittle dried fish tied in bundles, crimson chilis, ducks split open and cured like hams, green coco-nuts, the larvae of the rhinoceros beetle, sections of sugar-cane, dahs, lacquered sandals, check silk longyis, aphrodisiacs in the form of large, soap-like pills, glazed earthenware jars four feet high, Chinese sweetmeats made of garlic and sugar, green and white cigars, purple prinjals, persimmon-seed necklaces, chickens cheeping in wicker cages, brass Buddhas, heart-shaped betel leaves, bottles of Kruschen salts, switches of false hair, red clay cooking-pots, steel shoes for bullocks, papier-mache marionettes, strips of alligator hide with magical properties. Elizabeth's head was beginning to swim. At the other end of the bazaar the sun gleamed through a priest's umbrella, blood-red, as though through the ear of a giant. In front of a stall four Dravidian women were pounding turmeric with heavy stakes in a large wooden mortar. The hot-scented yellow powder flew up and tickled Elizabeth's nostrils, making her sneeze. She felt that she could not endure this place a moment longer. She touched Flory's arm.

'This crowd—the heat is so dreadful. Do you think we could get into the shade?'

He turned round. To tell the truth, he had been too busy talking—mostly inaudibly, because of the din—to notice how the heat and stench were affecting her.

'Oh, I say, I am sorry. Let's get out of it at once. I tell you what, we'll go along to old Li Yeik's shop—he's the Chinese grocer—and he'll get us a drink of something. It is rather stifling here.'

'All these spices—they kind of take your breath away. And what is that dreadful smell like fish?'

'Oh, only a kind of sauce they make out of prawns. They bury them and then dig them up several weeks afterwards.'

'How absolutely horrible!'

'Quite wholesome, I believe. Come away from that!' he added to Flo, who was nosing at a basket of small gudgeon-like fish with spines on their gills.

Li Yeik's shop faced the farther end of the bazaar. What Elizabeth had really wanted was to go straight back to the Club, but the European look of Li Yeik's shop-front—it was piled with Lancashire-made cotton shirts and almost incredibly cheap German clocks— comforted her somewhat after the barbarity of the bazaar. They were about to climb the steps when a slim youth of twenty, damnably dressed in a longyi, blue cricket blazer and bright yellow shoes, with his hair parted and greased 'Ingaleik fashion', detached himself from the crowd and came after them. He greeted Flory with a small awkward movement as though restraining himself from shikoing.

'What is it?' Flory said.

'Letter, sir.' He produced a grubby envelope.

'Would you excuse me?' Flory said to Elizabeth, opening the letter. It was from Ma Hla May—or rather, it had been written for her and she had signed it with a cross—and it demanded fifty rupees, in a vaguely menacing manner.

Flory pulled the youth aside. 'You speak English? Tell Ma Hla May I'll see about this later. And tell her that if she tries blackmailing me she won't get another pice. Do you understand?'

'Yes, sir.'

'And now go away. Don't follow me about, or there'll be trouble.'

'Yes, sir.'

'A clerk wanting a job,' Flory explained to Elizabeth as they went up the steps. 'They come bothering one at all hours.' And he reflected that the tone of the letter was curious, for he had not expected Ma Hla May to begin blackmailing him so soon; however, he had not time at the moment to wonder what it might mean.

They went into the shop, which seemed dark after the outer air. Li Yeik, who was sitting smoking among his baskets of merchandise— there was no counter—hobbled eagerly forward when he saw who had come in. Flory was a friend of his. He was an old bent-kneed man dressed in blue, wearing a pigtail, with a chinless yellow face, all cheekbones, like a benevolent skull. He greeted Flory with nasal honking noises which he intended for Burmese, and at once hobbled to the back of the shop to call for refreshments. There was a cool sweetish smell of opium. Long strips of red paper with black lettering were pasted on the walls, and at one side there was a little altar with a portrait of two large, serene-looking people in embroidered robes, and two sticks of incense smouldering in front of it. Two Chinese women, one old, and a girl were sitting on a mat rolling cigarettes with maize straw and tobacco like chopped horsehair. They wore black silk trousers, and their feet, with bulging, swollen insteps, were crammed into red-heeled wooden slippers no bigger than a doll's. A naked child was crawling slowly about the floor like a large yellow frog.

'Do look at those women's feet!' Elizabeth whispered as soon as Li Yeik's back was turned. 'Isn't it simply dreadful! How do they get them like that? Surely it isn't natural?'

'No, they deform them artificially. It's going out in China, I believe, but the people here are behind the times. Old Li Yeik's pigtail is another anachronism. Those small feet are beautiful according to Chinese ideas.'

'Beautiful! They're so horrible I can hardly look at them. These people must be absolute savages!'

'Oh no! They're highly civilized; more civilized than we are, in my opinion. Beauty's all a matter of taste. There are a people in this country called the Palaungs who admire long necks in women. The girls wear broad brass rings to stretch their necks, and they put on more and more of them until in the end they have necks like giraffes. It's no queerer than bustles or crinolines.'

At this moment Li Yeik came back with two fat, round-faced Burmese girls, evidently sisters, giggling and carrying between them two chairs and a blue Chinese teapot holding half a gallon. The two girls were or had been Li Yeik's concubines. The old man had produced a tin of chocolates and was prising off the lid and smiling in a fatherly way, exposing three long, tobacco-blackened teeth. Elizabeth sat down in a very uncomfortable frame of mind. She was perfectly certain that it could not be right to accept these people's hospitality. One of the Burmese girls had at once gone behind the chairs and begun fanning Flory and Elizabeth, while the other knelt at their feet and poured out cups of tea. Elizabeth felt very foolish with the girl fanning the back of her neck and the Chinaman grinning in front of her. Flory always seemed to get her into these uncomfortable situations. She took a chocolate from the tin Li Yeik offered her, but she could not bring herself to say 'thank you'.

'Is this ALL RIGHT?' she whispered to Flory.

'All right?'

'I mean, ought we to be sitting down in these people's house? Isn't it sort of—sort of infra dig?'

'It's all right with a Chinaman. They're a favoured race in this country. And they're very democratic in their ideas. It's best to treat them more or less as equals.'

'This tea looks absolutely beastly. It's quite green. You'd think they'd have the sense to put milk in it, wouldn't you?'

'It's not bad. It's a special kind of tea old Li Yeik gets from China. It has orange blossoms in it, I believe.'

'Ugh! It tastes exactly like earth,' she said, having tasted it.

Li Yeik stood holding his pipe, which was two feet long with a metal bowl the size of an acorn, and watching the Europeans to see whether they enjoyed his tea. The girl behind the chair said something in Burmese, at which both of them burst out giggling again. The one kneeling on the floor looked up and gazed in a naive admiring way at Elizabeth. Then she turned to Flory and asked him whether the English lady wore stays. She pronounced it s'tays.

'Ch!' said Li Yeik in a scandalized manner, stirring the girl with his toe to silence her.

'I should hardly care to ask her,' Flory said.

'Oh, thakin, please do ask her! We are so anxious to know!'

There was an argument, and the girl behind the chair forgot fanning and joined in. Both of them, it appeared, had been pining all their lives to see a veritable pair of s'tays. They had heard so many tales about them; they were made of steel on the principle of a strait waistcoat, and they compressed a woman so tightly that she had no breasts, absolutely no breasts at all! The girls pressed their hands against their fat ribs in illustration. Would not Flory be so kind as to ask the English lady? There was a room behind the shop where she could come with them and undress. They had been so hoping to see a pair of s'tays.

Then the conversation lapsed suddenly. Elizabeth was sitting stiffly, holding her tiny cup of tea, which she could not bring herself to taste again, and wearing a rather hard smile. A chill fell upon the Orientals; they realized that the English girl, who could not join in their conversation, was not at her ease. Her elegance and her foreign beauty, which had charmed them a moment earlier, began to awe them a little. Even Flory was conscious of the same feeling. There came one of those dreadful moments that one has with Orientals, when everyone avoids everyone else's eyes, trying vainly to think of something to say. Then the naked child, which had been exploring some baskets at the back of the shop, crawled across to where the European sat. It examined their shoes and stockings with great curiosity, and then, looking up, saw their white faces and was seized with terror. It let out a desolate wail, and began making water on the floor.

The old Chinese woman looked up, clicked her tongue and went on rolling cigarettes. No one else took the smallest notice. A pool began to form on the floor. Elizabeth was so horrified that she set her cup down hastily, and spilled the tea. She plucked at Flory's arm.

'That child! Do look what it's doing! Really, can't someone—it's too awful!' For a moment everyone gazed in astonishment, and then they all grasped what was the matter. There was a flurry and a general clicking of tongues. No one had paid any attention to the child—the incident was too normal to be noticed—and now they all felt horribly ashamed. Everyone began putting the blame on the child. There were exclamations of 'What a disgraceful child! What a disgusting child!' The old Chinese woman carried the child, still howling, to the door, and held it out over the step as though wringing out a bath sponge. And in the same moment, as it seemed, Flory and Elizabeth were outside the shop, and he was following her back to the road with Li Yeik and the others looking after them in dismay.

'If THAT'S what you call civilized people—!' she was exclaiming.

'I'm sorry,' he said feebly. 'I never expected—'

'What absolutely DISGUSTING people!'

She was bitterly angry. Her face had flushed a wonderful delicate pink, like a poppy bud opened a day too soon. It was the deepest colour of which it was capable. He followed her past the bazaar and back to the main road, and they had gone fifty yards before he ventured to speak again.

'I'm so sorry that this should have happened! Li Yeik is such a decent old chap. He'd hate to think that he'd offended you. Really it would have been better to stay a few minutes. Just to thank him for the tea.'

'Thank him! After THAT!'

'But honestly, you oughtn't to mind that sort of thing. Not in this country. These people's whole outlook is so different from ours. One has to adjust oneself. Suppose, for instance, you were back in the Middle Ages—'

'I think I'd rather not discuss it any longer.'

It was the first time they had definitely quarrelled. He was too miserable even to ask himself how it was that he offended her. He did not realize that this constant striving to interest her in Oriental things struck her only as perverse, ungentlemanly, a deliberate seeking after the squalid and the 'beastly'. He had not grasped even now with what eyes she saw the 'natives'. He only knew that at each attempt to make her share his life, his thoughts, his sense of beauty, she shied away from him like a frightened horse.

They walked up the road, he to the left of her and a little behind. He watched her averted cheek and the tiny gold hairs on her nape beneath the brim of her Terai hat. How he loved her, how he loved her! It was as though he had never truly loved her till this moment, when he walked behind her in disgrace, not even daring to show his disfigured face. He made to speak several times, and stopped himself. His voice was not quite ready, and he did not know what he could say that did not risk offending her somehow. At last he said, flatly, with a feeble pretence that nothing was the matter:

'It's getting beastly hot, isn't it?'

With the temperature at 90 degrees in the shade it was not a brilliant remark. To his surprise she seized on it with a kind of eagerness. She turned to face him, and she was smiling again.

'Isn't it simply BAKING!'

With that they were at peace. The silly, banal remark, bringing with it the reassuring atmosphere of Club-chatter, had soothed her like a charm. Flo, who had lagged behind, came puffing up to them dribbling saliva; in an instant they were talking, quite as usual, about dogs. They talked about dogs for the rest of the way home, almost without a pause. Dogs are an inexhaustible subject. Dogs, dogs! thought Flory as they climbed the hot hillside, with the mounting sun scorching their shoulders through their thin clothes, like the breath of fire—were they never to talk of anything except dogs? Or failing dogs, gramophone records and tennis racquets? And yet, when they kept to trash like this, how easily, how amicably they could talk!

They passed the glittering white wall of the cemetery and came to the Lackersteens' gate. Old mohur trees grew round it, and a clump of hollyhocks eight feet high, with round red flowers like blowsy girls' faces. Flory took off his hat in the shade and fanned his face.

'Well, we're back before the worst of the heat comes. I'm afraid our trip to the bazaar wasn't altogether a success.'

'Oh, not at all! I enjoyed it, really I did.'

'No—I don't know, something unfortunate always seems to happen.—Oh, by the way! You haven't forgotten that we're going out shooting the day after tomorrow? I hope that day will be all right for you?'

'Yes, and my uncle's going to lend me his gun. Such awful fun! You'll have to teach me all about shooting. I AM so looking forward to it.'

‘So am I. It’s a rotten time of year for shooting, but we’ll do our best. Goodbye for the present, then.’

‘Good-bye, Mr Flory.’

She still called him Mr Flory though he called her Elizabeth. They parted and went their ways, each thinking of the shooting trip, which, both of them felt, would in some way put things right between them.

Chapter 12

In the sticky, sleepy heat of the living-room, almost dark because of the beaded curtain, U Po Kyin was marching slowly up and down, boasting. From time to time he would put a hand under his singlet and scratch his sweating breasts, huge as a woman's with fat. Ma Kin was sitting on her mat, smoking slender white cigars. Through the open door of the bedroom one could see the corner of U Po Kyin's huge square bed, with carved teak posts, like a catafalque, on which he had committed many and many a rape.

Ma Kin was now hearing for the first time of the 'other affair' which underlay U Po Kyin's attack on Dr Veraswami. Much as he despised her intelligence, U Po Kyin usually let Ma Kin into his secrets sooner or later. She was the only person in his immediate circle who was not afraid of him, and there was therefore a pleasure in impressing her.

'Well, Kin Kin,' he said, 'you see how it has all gone according to plan! Eighteen anonymous letters already, and every one of them a masterpiece. I would repeat some of them to you if I thought you were capable of appreciating them.'

'But supposing the Europeans take no notice of your anonymous letters? What then?'

'Take no notice? Aha, no fear of that! I think I know something about the European mentality. Let me tell you, Kin Kin, that if there is one thing I CAN do, it is to write an anonymous letter.'

This was true. U Po Kyin's letters had already taken effect, and especially on their chief target, Mr Macgregor.

Only two days earlier than this, Mr Macgregor had spent a very troubled evening in trying to make up his mind whether Dr Veraswami was or was not guilty of disloyalty to the Government. Of course, it was not a question of any overt act of disloyalty—that was quite irrelevant. The point was, was the doctor the KIND of man who would hold seditious opinions? In India you are not judged for what you do, but for what you ARE. The merest breath of suspicion against his loyalty can ruin an Oriental official. Mr Macgregor had too just a nature to condemn even an Oriental out of hand. He had puzzled as late as midnight over a whole pile of confidential papers, including the five anonymous letters he had received, besides two others that had been forwarded to him by Westfield, pinned together with a cactus thorn.

It was not only the letters. Rumours about the doctor had been pouring in from every side. U Po Kyin fully grasped that to call the doctor a traitor was not enough in itself; it was necessary to attack his reputation from every possible angle. The doctor was charged not only with sedition, but also with extortion, rape, torture, performing illegal operations, performing operations while blind drunk, murder by poison, murder by sympathetic magic, eating beef, selling death certificates to murderers, wearing his shoes in the precincts of the pagoda and making homosexual attempts on the Military Police drummer boy. To hear what was said of him, anyone would have imagined the doctor a compound of Machiavelli, Sweeny Todd and the Marquis de Sade. Mr Macgregor had not paid much attention at first. He was too accustomed to this kind of thing. But with the last of the anonymous letters U Po Kyin had brought off a stroke that was brilliant even for him.

It concerned the escape of Nga Shwe O, the dacoit, from Kyauktada jail. Nga Shwe O, who was in the middle of a well-earned seven years, had been preparing his escape for several months past, and as a start his friends outside had bribed one of the Indian warders. The warder received his hundred rupees in advance, applied for leave to visit the death-bed of a relative and spent several busy days in the Mandalay brothels. Time passed, and the day of the escape was postponed several times—the warder, meanwhile, growing more and more homesick for the brothels. Finally he decided to earn a further reward by betraying the plot to U Po Kyin. But U Po Kyin, as usual, saw his chance. He told the warder on dire penalties to hold his tongue, and then, on the very night of the escape, when it was too late to do anything, sent another anonymous letter to Mr Macgregor, warning him that an escape was being attempted. The letter added, needless to say, that Dr Veraswami, the superintendent of the jail, had been bribed for his connivance.

In the morning there was a hullabaloo and a rushing to and fro of warders and, policemen at the jail, for Nga Shwe O had escaped. (He was a long way down the river, in a sampan provided by U Po Kyin.) This time Mr Macgregor was taken aback. Whoever had written the letter must have been privy to the plot, and was probably telling the truth about the doctor's connivance. It was a very serious matter. A jail superintendent who will take bribes to let a prisoner escape is capable of anything. And therefore— perhaps the logical sequence was not quite clear, but it was clear enough to Mr Macgregor—therefore the charge of sedition, which was the main charge against the doctor, became much more credible.

U Po Kyin had attacked the other Europeans at the same time. Flory, who was the doctor's friend and his chief source of prestige, had been scared easily enough into deserting him. With Westfield it was a little harder. Westfield, as a policeman, knew a great deal about U Po Kyin and might conceivably upset his plans. Policemen and magistrates are natural enemies. But U Po Kyin had known how to turn even this fact to advantage. He had accused the doctor, anonymously of course, of being in league with the notorious scoundrel and bribe-taker U Po Kyin. That settled Westfield. As for Ellis, no anonymous letters were needed in his case; nothing could possibly make him think worse of the doctor than he did already.

U Po Kyin had even sent one of his anonymous letters to Mrs Lackersteen, for he knew the power of European women. Dr Veraswami, the letter said, was inciting the natives to abduct and rape the European women—no details were given, nor were they needed. U Po Kyin had touched Mrs Lackersteen's weak spot. To her mind the words 'sedition', 'Nationalism,', 'rebellion', 'Home Rule', conveyed one thing and one only, and that was a picture of herself being raped by a procession of jet-black coolies with rolling white eyeballs. It was a thought that kept her awake at night sometimes. Whatever good regard the Europeans might once have had for the doctor was crumbling rapidly.

'So you see,' said U Po Kyin with a pleased air, 'you see how I have undermined him. He is like a tree sawn through at the base. One tap and down he comes. In three weeks or less I shall deliver that tap.'

'How?'

'I am just coming to that. I think it is time for you to hear about it. You have no sense in these matters, but you know how to hold your tongue.

You have heard talk of this rebellion that is brewing near Thongwa village?'

'Yes. They are very foolish, those villagers. What can they do with their dahs and spears against the Indian soldiers? They will be shot down like wild animals.'

'Of course. If there is any fighting it will be a massacre. But they are only a pack of superstitious peasants. They have put their faith in these absurd bullet-proof jackets that are being distributed to them. I despise such ignorance.'

'Poor men! Why do you not stop them, Ko Po Kyin? There is no need to arrest anybody. You have only to go to the village and tell them that you know their plans, and they will never dare to go on.'

'Ah well, I could stop them if I chose, of course. But then I do not choose. I have my reasons. You see, Kin Kin—you will please keep silent about this—this is, so to speak, my own rebellion. I arranged it myself.'

'What!'

Ma Kin dropped her cigar. Her eyes had opened so wide that the pale blue white showed all round the pupil. She was horrified. She burst out:

'Ko Po Kyin, what are you saying? You do not mean it! You, raising a rebellion—it cannot be true!'

'Certainly it is true. And a very good job we are making of it. That magician whom I brought from Rangoon is a clever fellow. He has toured all over India as a circus conjurer. The bullet-proof jackets were bought at Whiteaway & Laidlaw's stores, one rupee eight annas each. They are costing me a pretty penny, I can tell you.'

'But, Ko Po Kyin! A rebellion! The terrible fighting and shooting, and all the poor men who will be killed! Surely you have not gone mad? Are you not afraid of being shot yourself?'

U Po Kyin halted in his stride. He was astonished. 'Good gracious, woman, what idea have you got hold of now? You do not suppose that *I* am rebelling against the Government? I—a Government servant of thirty years' standing! Good heavens, no! I said that I had STARTED the rebellion, not that I was taking part in it. It is these fools of villagers who are going to risk their skins, not I. No one dreams that I have anything to do with it, or ever will, except Ba Sein and one or two others.'

'But you said it was you who were persuading them to rebel?'

'Of course. I have accused Veraswami of raising a rebellion against the Government. Well, I must have a rebellion to show, must I not?'

'Ah, I see. And when the rebellion breaks out, you are going to say that Dr Veraswami is to blame for it. Is that it?'

'How slow you are! I should have thought even a fool would have seen that I am raising the rebellion merely in order to crush it. I am—what is that expression Mr Macgregor uses? Agent provocateur— Latin, you would not understand. I am agent provocateur. First I persuade these fools at Thongwa to rebel, and then I arrest them as rebels. At the very moment when it is due to start, I shall pounce on the ringleaders and clap every one of them in jail. After that, I dare say there may possibly be some fighting. A few men may be killed and a few more sent to the Andamans. But, meanwhile, I shall be first in the field. U Po Kyin, the man who quelled a most dangerous rising in the nick of time! I shall be the hero of the district.'

U Po Kyin, justly proud of his plan, began to pace up and down the room again with his hands behind his back, smiling. Ma Kin considered the plan in silence for some time. Finally she said:

'I still do not see why you are doing this, Ko Po Kyin. Where is it all leading? And what has it got to do with Dr Veraswami?'

'I shall never teach you wisdom, Kin Kin! Did I not tell you at the beginning that Veraswami stands in my way? This rebellion is the very thing to get rid of him. Of course we shall never prove that he is responsible for it; but what does that matter? All the

Europeans will take it for granted that he is mixed up in it somehow. That is how their minds work. He will be ruined for life. And his fall is my rise. The blacker I can paint him, the more glorious my own conduct will appear. Now do you understand?'

'Yes, I do understand. And I think it is a base, evil plan. I wonder you are not ashamed to tell it me.'

'Now, Kin Kin! Surely you are not going to start that nonsense over again?'

'Ko Po Kyin, why is it that you are only happy when you are being wicked? Why is it that everything you do must bring evil to others? Think of that poor doctor who will be dismissed from his post, and those villagers who will be shot or flogged with bamboos or imprisoned for life. Is it necessary to do such things? What can you want with more money when you are rich already?'

'Money! Who is talking about money? Some day, woman, you will realize that there are other things in the world besides money. Fame, for example. Greatness. Do you realize that the Governor of Burma will very probably pin an Order on my breast for my loyal action in this affair? Would not even you be proud of such an honour as that?'

Ma Kin shook her head, unimpressed. 'When will you remember, Ko Po Kyin, that you are not going to live a thousand years? Consider what happens to those who have lived wickedly. There is such a thing, for instance, as being turned into a rat or a frog. There is even hell. I remember what a priest said to me once about hell, something that he had translated from the Pali scriptures, and it was very terrible. He said, "Once in a thousand centuries two red-hot spears will meet in your heart, and you will say to yourself, 'Another thousand centuries of my torment are ended, and there is as much to come as there has been before.'" Is it not very dreadful to think of such things, Ko Po Kyin?'

U Po Kyin laughed and gave a careless wave of his hand that meant 'pagodas'.

'Well, I hope you may still laugh when it comes to the end. But for myself, I should not care to look back upon such a life.'

She relighted her cigar with her thin shoulder turned disapprovingly on U Po Kyin while he took several more turns up and down the room. When he spoke, it was more seriously than before, and even with a touch of diffidence.

'You know, Kin Kin, there is another matter behind all this. Something that I have not told to you or to anyone else. Even Ba Sein does not know. But I believe I will tell it you now.'

'I do not want to hear it, if it is more wickedness.'

'No, no. You were asking just now what is my real object in this affair. You think, I suppose, that I am ruining Veraswami merely because I dislike him and his ideas about bribes as a nuisance. It is not only that. There is something else that is far more important, and it concerns you as well as me.'

'What is it?'

'Have you never felt in you, Kin Kin, a desire for higher things? Has it never struck you that after all our successes—all my successes, I should say—we are almost in the same position as when we started? I am worth, I dare say, two lakhs of rupees, and yet look at the style in which we live! Look at this room! Positively it is no better than that of a peasant. I am tired of eating with my fingers and associating only with Burmans—poor, inferior people—and living, as you might say, like a miserable Township Officer. Money is not enough; I should like to feel that I have risen in the world as well. Do you not wish sometimes for a way of life that is a little more—how shall I say—elevated?'

'I do not know how we could want more than what we have already. When I was a girl in my village I never thought that I should live in such a house as this. Look at those English chairs—I have never sat in one of them in my life. But I am very proud to look at them and think that I own them.'

'Ch! Why did you ever leave that village of yours, Kin Kin? You are only fit to stand gossiping by the well with a stone water-pot on your head. But I am more ambitious, God be praised. And now I will tell you the real reason why I am intriguing against Veraswami. It is in my mind to do something that is really magnificent. Something noble, glorious! Something that is the very highest honour an Oriental can attain to. You know what I mean, of course?'

'No. What do you mean?'

'Come, now! The greatest achievement of my life! Surely you can guess?'

'Ah, I know! You are going to buy a motor-car. But oh, Ko Po Kyin, please do not expect me to ride in it!'

U Po Kyin threw up his hands in disgust. 'A motor-car! You have the mind of a bazaar peanut-seller! I could buy twenty motor-cars if I wanted them. And what use would a motor-car be in this place? No, it is something far grander than that.'

'What, then?'

'It is this. I happen to know that in a month's time the Europeans are going to elect one native member to their Club. They do not want to do it, but they will have orders from the Commissioner, and they will obey. Naturally, they would elect Veraswami, who is the highest native official in the district. But I have disgraced Veraswami. And so—'

'What?'

U Po Kyin did not answer for a moment. He looked at Ma Kin, and his vast yellow face, with its broad jaw and numberless teeth, was so softened that it was almost child-like. There might even have been tears in his tawny eyes. He said in a small, almost awed voice, as though the greatness of what he was saying overcame him:

'Do you not see, woman? Do you not see that if Veraswami is disgraced I shall be elected to the Club myself?'

The effect of it was crushing. There was not another word of argument on Ma Kin's part.

The magnificence of U Po Kyin's project had struck her dumb.

And not without reason, for all the achievements of U Po Kyin's life were as nothing beside this. It is a real triumph—it would be doubly so in Kyauktada—for an official of the lower ranks to worm his way into the European Club. The European Club, that remote, mysterious temple, that holy of holies far harder of entry than Nirvana! Po Kyin, the naked gutter-boy of Mandalay, the thieving clerk and obscure official, would enter that sacred place, call Europeans 'old chap', drink whisky and soda and knock white balls to and fro on the green table! Ma Kin, the village woman, who had first seen the light through the chinks of a bamboo hut thatched with palm-leaves, would sit on a high chair with her feet imprisoned in silk stockings and high-heeled shoes (yes, she would actually wear shoes in that place!) talking to English ladies in Hindustani about baby-linen! It was a prospect that would have dazzled anybody.

For a long time Ma Kin remained silent, her lips parted, thinking of the European Club and the splendours that it might contain. For the first time in her life she surveyed U Po Kyin's intrigues without disapproval. Perhaps it was a feat greater even than the storming of the Club to have planted a grain of ambition in Ma Kin's gentle heart.

Chapter 13

As Flory came through the gate of the hospital compound four ragged sweepers passed him, carrying some dead coolie, wrapped in sackcloth, to a foot-deep grave in the jungle. Flory crossed the brick-like earth of the yard between the hospital sheds. All down the wide verandas, on sheetless charpoys, rows of grey-faced men lay silent and moveless. Some filthy-looking curs, which were said to devour amputated limbs, dozed or snapped at their fleas among the piles of the buildings. The whole place wore a sluttish and decaying air. Dr Veraswami struggled hard to keep it clean, but there was no coping with the dust and the bad water-supply, and the inertia of sweepers and half-trained Assistant Surgeons.

Flory was told that the doctor was in the out-patients' department. It was a plaster-walled room furnished only with a table and two chairs, and a dusty portrait of Queen Victoria, much awry. A procession of Burmans, peasants with gnarled muscles beneath their faded rags, were filing into the room and queueing up at the table. The doctor was in shirt-sleeves and sweating profusely. He sprang to his feet with an exclamation of pleasure, and in his usual fussy haste thrust Flory into the vacant chair and produced a tin of cigarettes from the drawer of the table.

'What a delightful visit, Mr Flory! Please to make yourself comfortable—that iss, if one can possibly be comfortable in such a place ass this, ha, ha! Afterwards, at my house, we will talk with beer and amenities. Kindly excuse me while I attend to the populace.'

Flory sat down, and the hot sweat immediately burst out and drenched his shirt. The heat of the room was stifling. The peasants steamed garlic from all their pores. As each man came to the table the doctor would bounce from his chair, prod the patient in the back, lay a black ear to his chest, fire off several questions in villainous Burmese, then bounce back to the table and scribble a prescription. The patients took the prescriptions across the yard to the Compounder, who gave them bottles filled with water and various vegetable dyes. The Compounder supported himself largely by the sale of drugs, for the Government paid him only twenty-five rupees a month. However, the doctor knew nothing of this.

On most mornings the doctor had not time to attend to the out-patients himself, and left them to one of the Assistant Surgeons. The Assistant Surgeon's methods of diagnosis were brief. He would simply ask each patient, 'Where is your pain? Head, back or belly?' and at the reply hand out a prescription from one of three piles that he had prepared beforehand. The patients much preferred this method to the doctor's. The doctor had a way of asking them whether they had suffered from venereal diseases—an ungentlemanly, pointless question—and sometimes he horrified them still more by suggesting operations. 'Belly-cutting' was their phrase for it. The majority of them would have died a dozen times over rather than submit to 'belly-cutting'.

As the last patient disappeared the doctor sank into his chair, fanning his face with the prescription-pad.

'Ach, this heat! Some mornings I think that never will I get the smell of garlic out of my nose! It iss amazing to me how their very blood becomes impregnated with it. Are you not suffocated, Mr Flory? You English have the sense of smell almost too highly developed. What torments you must all suffer in our filthy East!'

'Abandon your noses, all ye who enter here, what? They might write that up over the Suez Canal. You seem busy this morning?'

'Ass ever. Ah but, my friend, how discouraging iss the work of a doctor in this country! These villagers—dirty, ignorant savages! Even to get them to come to hospital iss all we can do, and they will die of gangrene or carry a tumour ass large ass a melon for ten years rather than face the knife. And such medicines ass their own so-called doctors give to them! Herbs gathered under the new moon, tigers' whiskers, rhinoceros horn, urine, menstrual blood! How men can drink such compounds iss disgusting.'

'Rather picturesque, all the same. You ought to compile a Burmese pharmacopoeia, doctor. It would be almost as good as Culpeper.'

'Barbarous cattle, barbarous cattle,' said the doctor, beginning to struggle into his white coat. 'Shall we go back to my house? There iss beer and I trust a few fragments of ice left. I have an operation at ten, strangulated hernia, very urgent. Till then I am free.'

'Yes. As a matter of fact there's something I rather wanted to talk to you about.'

They recrossed the yard and climbed the steps of the doctor's veranda. The doctor, having felt in the ice-chest and found that the ice was all melted to tepid water, opened a bottle of beer and called fussily to the servants to set some more bottles swinging in a cradle of wet straw. Flory was standing looking over the veranda rail, with his hat still on. The fact was that he had come here to utter an apology. He had been avoiding the doctor for nearly a fortnight—since the day, in fact, when he had set his name to the insulting notice at the Club. But the apology had got to be uttered. U Po Kyin was a very good judge of men, but he had erred in supposing that two anonymous letters were enough to scare Flory permanently away from his friend.

'Look here, doctor, you know what I wanted to say?'

'I? No.'

'Yes, you do. It's about that beastly trick I played on you the other week. When Ellis put that notice on the Club board and I signed my name to it. You must have heard about it. I want to try and explain—'

'No, no, my friend, no, no!' The doctor was so distressed that he sprang across the veranda and seized Flory by the arm. 'You shall NOT explain! Please never mention it! I understand perfectly—but most perfectly.'

'No, you don't understand. You couldn't. You don't realize just what KIND of pressure is put on one to make one do things like that. There was nothing to make me sign the notice. Nothing could have happened if I'd refused. There's no law telling us to be beastly to Orientals—quite the contrary. But—it's just that one daren't be loyal to an Oriental when it means going against the others. It doesn't DO. If I'd stuck out against signing the notice I'd have been in disgrace at the Club for a week or two. So I funked it, as usual.'

'Please, Mr Flory, please! Possitively you will make me uncomfortable if you continue. Ass though I could not make all allowances for your position!'

'Our motto, you know is, "In India, do as the English do".'

'Of course, of course. And a most noble motto. "Hanging together", ass you call it. It iss the secret of your superiority to we Orientals.'

'Well, it's never much use saying one's sorry. But what I did come here to say was that it shan't happen again. In fact—'

'Now, now, Mr Flory, you will oblige me by saying no more upon this subject. It iss all over and forgotten. Please to drink up your beer before it becomes ass hot ass tea. Also, I have a thing to tell you. You have not asked for my news yet.'

'Ah, your news. What is your news, by the way? How's everything been going all this time? How's Ma Britannia? Still moribund?'

'Aha, very low, very low! But not so low ass I. I am in deep waters, my friend.'

'What? U Po Kyin again? Is he still libelling you?'

'If he iss libelling me! This time it iss—well, it iss something diabolical. My friend, you have heard of this rebellion that is supposed to be on the point of breaking out in the district?'

'I've heard a lot of talk. Westfield's been out bent on slaughter, but I hear he can't find any rebels. Only the usual village Hampdens who won't pay their taxes.'

'Ah yes. Wretched fools! Do you know how much iss the tax that most of them have refused to pay? Five rupees! They will get tired of it and pay up presently. We have this trouble every year. But ass for the rebellion—the SO-CALLED rebellion, Mr Flory—I wish you to know that there iss more in it than meets the eye.'

'Oh? What?'

To Flory's surprise the doctor made such a violent gesture of anger that he spilled most of his beer. He put his glass down on the veranda rail and burst out:

'It iss U Po Kyin again! That unutterable scoundrel! That crocodile deprived of natural feeling! That—that—'

'Go on. "That obscene trunk of humors, that swol'n parcel of dropsies, that bolting-hutch of beastliness"—go on. What's he been up to now?'

'A villainy unparalleled'—and here the doctor outlined the plot for a sham rebellion, very much as U Po Kyin had explained it to Ma Kin. The only detail not known to him was U Po Kyin's intention of getting himself elected to the European Club. The doctor's face could not accurately be said to flush, but it grew several shades blacker in his anger. Flory was so astonished that he remained standing up.

'The cunning old devil! Who'd have thought he had it in him? But how did you manage to find all this out?'

'Ah, I have a few friends left. But now do you see, my friend, what ruin he iss preparing for me? Already he hass calumniated me right and left. When this absurd rebellion breaks out, he will do everything in his power to connect my name with it. And I tell you that the slightest suspicion of my loyalty could be ruin for me, ruin! If it were ever breathed that I were even a sympathizer with this rebellion, there iss an end of me.'

'But, damn it, this is ridiculous! Surely you can defend yourself somehow?'

'How can I defend myself when I can prove nothing? I know that all this iss true, but what use iss that? If I demand a public inquiry, for every witness I produce U Po Kyin would produce fifty. You do not realize the influence of that man in the district. No one dare speak against him.'

'But why need you prove anything? Why not go to old Macgregor and tell him about it? He's a very fair-minded old chap in his way. He'd hear you out.'

'Useless, useless. You have not the mind of an intriguer, Mr Flory. Qui s'excuse, s'accuse, iss it not? It does not pay to cry that there iss a conspiracy against one.'

'Well, what are you going to do, then?'

'There iss nothing I can do. Simply I must wait and hope that my prestige will carry me through. In affairs like this, where a native official's reputation iss at stake, there iss no question of proof, of evidence. All depends upon one's standing with the Europeans. If my standing iss good, they will not believe it of me; if bad, they will believe it. Prestige iss all.'

They were silent for a moment. Flory understood well enough that 'prestige iss all'. He was used to these nebulous conflicts, in which suspicion counts for more than proof, and reputation for more than a thousand witnesses. A thought came into his head, an uncomfortable, chilling thought which would never have occurred to him three weeks earlier. It was one of those moments when one sees quite clearly what is one's duty, and, with all the will in the world to shirk it, feels certain that one must carry it out. He said:

'Suppose, for instance, you were elected to the Club? Would that do your prestige any good?'

'If I were elected to the Club! Ah, indeed, yes! The Club! It iss a fortress impregnable. Once there, and no one would listen to these tales about me any more than if it were about you, or Mr Macgregor, or any other European gentleman. But what hope have I that they will elect me after their minds have been poisoned against me?'

'Well now, look here, doctor, I tell you what. I'll propose your name at the next general meeting. I know the question's got to come up then, and if someone comes forward with the name of a candidate, I dare say no one except Ellis will blackball him. And in the meantime—'

'Ah, my friend, my dear friend!' The doctor's emotion caused him almost to choke. He seized Flory by the hand. 'Ah, my friend, that iss noble! Truly it iss noble! But it iss too much. I fear that you will be in trouble with your European friends again. Mr Ellis, for example—would he tolerate it that you propose my name?'

'Oh, bother Ellis. But you must understand that I can't promise to get you elected. It depends on what Macgregor says and what mood the others are in. It may all come to nothing.'

The doctor was still holding Flory's hand between his own, which were plump and damp. The tears had actually started into his eyes, and these, magnified by his spectacles, beamed upon Flory like the liquid eyes of a dog.

'Ah, my friend! If I should but be elected! What an end to all my troubles! But, my friend, ass I said before, do not be too rash in this matter. Beware of U Po Kyin! By now he will have numbered you among hiss enemies. And even for you hiss enmity can be a danger.'

'Oh, good Lord, he can't touch me. He's done nothing so far—only a few silly anonymous letters.'

'I would not be too sure. He hass subtle ways to strike. And for sure he will raise heaven and earth to keep me from being elected to the Club. If you have a weak spot, guard it, my friend. He will find it out. He strikes always at the weakest spot.'

'Like the crocodile,' Flory suggested.

'Like the crocodile,' agreed the doctor gravely. 'Ah but, my friend, how gratifying to me if I should become a member of your European Club! What an honour, to be the associate of European gentlemen! But there iss one other matter, Mr Flory, that I did not care to mention before. It iss—I hope this iss clearly understood—that I have no intention of USING the Club in any way. Membership is all I desire. Even if I were elected, I should not, of course, ever presume to COME to the Club.'

'Not come to the Club?'

'No, no! Heaven forbid that I should force my society upon the European gentlemen! Simply I should pay my subscriptions. That, for me, iss a privilege high enough. You understand that, I trust?'

'Perfectly, doctor, perfectly.'

Flory could not help laughing as he walked up the hill. He was definitely committed now to proposing the doctor's election. And there would be such a row when the others heard of it—oh, such a devil of a row! But the astonishing thing was that it only made him laugh. The prospect that would have appalled him a month back now almost exhilarated him.

Why? And why had he given his promise at all? It was a small thing, a small risk to take—nothing heroic about it—and yet it was unlike him. Why, after all these years—the circumspect, pukka sahib-like years—break all the rules so suddenly?

He knew why. It was because Elizabeth, by coming into his life, had so changed it and renewed it that all the dirty, miserable years might never have passed. Her presence had changed the whole orbit of his mind. She had brought back to him the air of England— dear England, where thought is free and one is not condemned forever to dance the danse du pukka sahib for the edification of the lower races. Where is the life that late I led? he thought. Just by existing she had made it possible for him, she had even made it natural to him, to act decently.

Where is the life that late I led? he thought again as he came through the garden gate. He was happy, happy. For he had perceived that the pious ones are right when they say that there is salvation and life can begin anew. He came up the path, and it seemed to him that his house, his flowers, his servants, all the life that so short a time ago had been drenched in ennui and homesickness, were somehow made new, significant, beautiful inexhaustibly. What fun it could all be, if only you had someone to share it with you! How you could love this country, if only you were not alone! Nero was out on the path, braving the sun for some grains of paddy that the mali had dropped, taking food to his goats. Flo made a dash at him, panting, and Nero sprang into the air with a flurry and lighted on Flory's shoulder. Flory walked into the house with the little red cock in his arms, stroking his silky ruff and the smooth, diamond-shaped feathers of his back.

He had not set foot on the veranda before he knew that Ma Hla May was in the house. It did not need Ko S'la to come hurrying from within with a face of evil tidings. Flory had smelled her scent of sandalwood, garlic, coco-nut oil and the jasmine in her hair. He dropped Nero over the veranda rail.

'THE WOMAN has come back,' said Ko S'la.

Flory had turned very pale. When he turned pale the birthmark made him hideously ugly. A pang like a blade of ice had gone through his entrails. Ma Hla May had appeared in the doorway of the bedroom. She stood with her face downcast, looking at him from beneath lowered brows.

'Thakin,' she said in a low voice, half sullen, half urgent.

'Go away!' said Flory angrily to Ko S'la, venting his fear and anger upon him.

'Thakin,' she said, 'come into the bedroom here. I have a thing to say to you.'

He followed her into the bedroom. In a week—it was only a week—her appearance had degenerated extraordinarily. Her hair looked greasy. All her lockets were gone, and she was wearing a Manchester longyi of flowered cotton, costing two rupees eight annas. She had coated her face so thick with powder that it was like a clown's mask, and at the roots of her hair, where the powder ended, there was a ribbon of natural-coloured brown skin. She looked a drab. Flory would not face her, but stood looking sullenly through the open doorway to the veranda.

'What do you mean by coming back like this? Why did you not go home to your village?'

'I am staying in Kyauktada, at my cousin's house. How can I go back to my village after what has happened?'

'And what do you mean by sending men to demand money from me? How can you want more money already, when I gave you a hundred rupees only a week ago?'

'How can I go back?' she repeated, ignoring what he had said. Her voice rose so sharply that he turned round. She was standing very upright, sullen, with her black brows drawn together and her lips pouted.

'Why cannot you go back?'

'After that! After what you have done to me!'

Suddenly she burst into a furious tirade. Her voice had risen to the hysterical graceless scream of the bazaar women when they quarrel.

'How can I go back, to be jeered at and pointed at by those low, stupid peasants whom I despise? I who have been a bo-kadaw, a white man's wife, to go home to my father's house, and shake the paddy basket with old hags and women who are too ugly to find husbands! Ah, what shame, what shame! Two years I was your wife, you loved me and cared for me, and then without warning, without reason, you drove me from your door like a dog. And I must go back to my village, with no money, with all my jewels and silk longyis gone, and the people will point and say, "There is Ma Hla May who thought herself cleverer than the rest of us. And behold! her white man has treated her as they always do." I am ruined, ruined! What man will marry me after I have lived two years in your house? You have taken my youth from me. Ah, what shame, what shame!'

He could not look at her; he stood helpless, pale, hang-dog. Every word she said was justified, and how tell her that he could do no other than he had done? How tell her that it would have been an outrage, a sin, to continue as her lover? He almost cringed from her, and the birthmark stood on his yellow face like a splash of ink. He said flatly, turning instinctively to money—for money had never failed with Ma Hla May:

'I will give you money. You shall have the fifty rupees you asked me for—more later. I have no more till next month.'

This was true. The hundred rupees he had given her, and what he had spent on clothes, had taken most of his ready money. To his dismay she burst into a loud wail. Her white mask puckered up and the tears sprang quickly out and coursed down her cheeks. Before he could stop her she had fallen on her knees in front of him, and she was bowing, touching the floor with her forehead in the 'full' shiko of utter abasement.

‘Get up, get up!’ he exclaimed. The shameful, abject shiko, neck bent, body doubled up as though inviting a blow, always horrified him. ‘I can’t bear that. Get up this instant.’

She wailed again, and made an attempt to clasp his ankles. He stepped backwards hurriedly.

‘Get up, now, and stop that dreadful noise. I don’t know what you are crying about.’

She did not get up, but only rose to her knees and wailed at him anew. ‘Why do you offer me money? Do you think it is only for money that I have come back? Do you think that when you have driven me from your door like a dog it is only because of money that I care?’

‘Get up,’ he repeated. He had moved several paces away, lest she should seize him. ‘What do you want if it is not money?’

‘Why do you hate me?’ she wailed. ‘What harm have I done you? I stole your cigarette-case, but you were not angry at that. You are going to marry this white woman, I know it, everyone knows it. But what does it matter, why must you turn me away? Why do you hate me?’

‘I don’t hate you. I can’t explain. Get up, please get up.’

She was weeping quite shamelessly now. After all, she was hardly more than a child. She looked at him through her tears, anxiously, studying him for a sign of mercy. Then, a dreadful thing, she stretched herself at full length, flat on her face.

‘Get up, get up!’ he cried out in English. ‘I can’t bear that— it’s too abominable!’

She did not get up, but crept, wormlike, right across the floor to his feet. Her body made a broad ribbon on the dusty floor. She lay prostrate in front of him, face hidden, arms extended, as though before a god's altar.

'Master, master,' she whimpered, 'will you not forgive me? This once, only this once! Take Ma Hla May back. I will be your slave, lower than your slave. Anything sooner than turn me away.'

She had wound her arms round his ankles, actually was kissing his toes. He stood looking down at her with his hands in his pockets, helpless. Flo came ambling into the room, walked to where Ma Hla May lay and sniffed at her longyi. She wagged her tail vaguely, recognizing the smell. Flory could not endure it. He bent down and took Ma Hla May by the shoulders, lifting her to her knees.

'Stand up, now,' he said. 'It hurts me to see you like this. I will do what I can for you. What is the use of crying?'

Instantly she cried out in renewed hope: 'Then you will take me back? Oh, master, take Ma Hla May back! No one need ever know. I will stay here when that white woman comes, she will think I am one of the servants' wives. Will you not take me back?'

'I cannot. It's impossible,' he said, turning away again.

She heard finality in his tone, and uttered a harsh, ugly cry. She bent forward again in a shiko, beating her forehead against the floor. It was dreadful. And what was more dreadful than all, what hurt in his breast, was the utter gracelessness, the lowness of the emotion beneath those entreaties. For in all this there was not a spark of love for him. If she wept and grovelled it was only for the position she had once had as his mistress, the idle life, the rich clothes and dominion over servants. There was something pitiful beyond words in that. Had she loved him he could have driven her from his door with far less compunction. No sorrows are so bitter as those that are without a trace of nobility. He bent down and picked her up in his arms.

'Listen, Ma Hla May,' he said; 'I do not hate you, you have done me no evil. It is I who have wronged you. But there is no help for it now. You must go home, and later I will send you money. If you like you shall start a shop in the bazaar. You are young. This will not matter to you when you have money and can find yourself a husband.'

'I am ruined!' she wailed again. 'I shall kill myself. I shall jump off the jetty into the river. How can I live after this disgrace?'

He was holding her in his arms, almost caressing her. She was clinging close to him, her face hidden against his shirt, her body shaking with sobs. The scent of sandalwood floated into his nostrils. Perhaps even now she thought that with her arms around him and her body against his she could renew her power over him. He disentangled himself gently, and then, seeing that she did not fall on her knees again, stood apart from her.

'That is enough. You must go now. And look, I will give you the fifty rupees I promised you.'

He dragged his tin uniform case from under the bed and took out five ten-rupee notes. She stowed them silently in the bosom of her ingyi. Her tears had ceased flowing quite suddenly. Without speaking she went into the bathroom for a moment, and came out with her face washed to its natural brown, and her hair and dress rearranged. She looked sullen, but not hysterical any longer.

'For the last time, thakin: you will not take me back? That is your last word?'

'Yes. I cannot help it.'

'Then I am going, thakin.'

'Very well. God go with you.'

Leaning against the wooden pillar of the veranda, he watched her walk down the path in the strong sunlight. She walked very upright, with bitter offence in the carriage of her back and head. It was true what she had said, he had robbed her of her youth. His knees were trembling uncontrollably. Ko S'la came behind him, silent-footed. He gave a little deprecating cough to attract Flory's attention.

'What's the matter now?'

'The holy one's breakfast is getting cold.'

'I don't want any breakfast. Get me something to drink—gin.'

Where is the life that late I led?

Chapter 14

Like long curved needles threading through embroidery, the two canoes that carried Flory and Elizabeth threaded their way up the creek that led inland from the eastern bank of the Irrawaddy. It was the day of the shooting trip—a short afternoon trip, for they could not stay a night in the jungle together. They were to shoot for a couple of hours in the comparative cool of the evening, and be back at Kyauktada in time for dinner.

The canoes, each hollowed out of a single tree-trunk, glided swiftly, hardly rippling the dark brown water. Water hyacinth with profuse spongy foliage and blue flowers had choked the stream so that the channel was only a winding ribbon four feet wide. The light filtered, greenish, through interlacing boughs. Sometimes one could hear parrots scream overhead, but no wild creatures showed themselves, except once a snake that swam hurriedly away and disappeared among the water hyacinth.

'How long before we get to the village?' Elizabeth called back to Flory. He was in a larger canoe behind, together with Flo and Ko S'la, paddled by a wrinkly old woman dressed in rags.

‘How far, grandmama?’ Flory asked the canoe-woman.

The old woman took her cigar out of her mouth and rested her paddle on her knees to think. ‘The distance a man can shout,’ she said after reflection.

‘About half a mile,’ Flory translated.

They had come two miles. Elizabeth’s back was aching. The canoes were liable to upset at a careless moment, and you had to sit bolt upright on the narrow backless seat, keeping your feet as well as possible out of the bilge, with dead prawns in it, that sagged to and fro at the bottom. The Burman who paddled Elizabeth was sixty years old, half naked, leaf-brown, with a body as perfect as that of a young man. His face was battered, gentle and humorous. His black cloud of hair, finer than that of most Burmans, was knotted loosely over one ear, with a wisp or two tumbling across his cheek. Elizabeth was nursing her uncle’s gun across her knees. Flory had offered to take it, but she had refused; in reality, the feel of it delighted her so much that she could not bring herself to give it up. She had never had a gun in her hand until today. She was wearing a rough skirt with brogue shoes and a silk shirt like a man’s, and she knew that with her Terai hat they looked well on her. She was very happy, in spite of her aching back and the hot sweat that tickled her face, and the large, speckled mosquitoes that hummed round her ankles.

The stream narrowed and the beds of water hyacinth gave place to steep banks of glistening mud, like chocolate. Rickety thatched huts leaned far out over the stream, their piles driven into its bed. A naked boy was standing between two of the huts, flying a green beetle on a piece of thread like a kite. He yelled at the sight of the Europeans, whereat more children appeared from nowhere. The old Burman guided the canoe to a jetty made of a single palm-trunk laid in the mud—it was covered with barnacles and so gave foothold—and sprang out and helped Elizabeth ashore. The others followed with the bags and cartridges, and Flo, as she always did on these occasions, fell into the mud and sank as deep as the shoulder. A skinny old gentleman wearing a magenta paso, with a mole on his cheek from which four yard-long grey hairs sprouted, came forward shikoing and cuffing the heads of the children who had gathered round the jetty.

'The village headman,' Flory said.

The old man led the way to his house, walking ahead with an extraordinary crouching gait, like a letter L upside down—the result of rheumatism combined with the constant shikoing needed in a minor Government official. A mob of children marched rapidly after the Europeans, and more and more dogs, all yapping and causing Flo to shrink against Flory's heels. In the doorway of every hut clusters of moonlike, rustic faces gaped at the 'Ingaleikma'. The village was darkish under the shade of broad leaves. In the rains the creek would flood, turning the lower parts of the village into a squalid wooden Venice where the villagers stepped from their front doors into their canoes.

The headman's house was a little bigger than the others, and it had a corrugated iron roof, which, in spite of the intolerable din it made during the rains, was the pride of the headman's life. He had foregone the building of a pagoda, and appreciably lessened his chances of Nirvana, to pay for it. He hastened up the steps and gently kicked in the ribs a youth who was lying asleep on the veranda. Then he turned and shikoed again to the Europeans, asking them to come inside.

'Shall we go in?' Flory said. 'I expect we shall have to wait half an hour.'

'Couldn't you tell him to bring some chairs out on the veranda?' Elizabeth said. After her experience in Li Yeik's house she had privately decided that she would never go inside a native house again, if she could help it.

There was a fuss inside the house, and the headman, the youth and some women dragged forth two chairs decorated in an extraordinary manner with red hibiscus flowers, and also some begonias growing in kerosene tins. It was evident that a sort of double throne had been prepared within for the Europeans. When Elizabeth had sat down the headman reappeared with a teapot, a bunch of very long, bright green bananas, and six coal-black cheroots. But when he had poured her out a cup of tea Elizabeth shook her head, for the tea looked, if possible, worse even than Li Yeik's.

The headman looked abashed and rubbed his nose. He turned to Flory and asked him whether the young thakin-ma would like some milk in her tea. He had heard that Europeans drank milk in their tea. The villages should, if it were desired, catch a cow and milk it. However, Elizabeth still refused the tea; but she was thirsty, and she asked Flory to send for one of the bottles of soda-water that Ko S'la had brought in his bag. Seeing this, the headman retired, feeling guiltily that his preparations had been insufficient, and left the veranda to the Europeans.

Elizabeth was still nursing her gun on her knees, while Flory leaned against the veranda rail pretending to smoke one of the headman's cheroots. Elizabeth was pining for the shooting to begin. She plied Flory with innumerable questions.

'How soon can we start out? Do you think we've got enough cartridges? How many beaters shall we take? Oh, I do so hope we have some luck! You do think we'll get something, don't you?'

'Nothing wonderful, probably. We're bound to get a few pigeons, and perhaps jungle fowl. They're out of season, but it doesn't matter shooting the cocks. They say there's a leopard round here, that killed a bullock almost in the village last week.'

'Oh, a leopard! How lovely if we could shoot it!'

'It's very unlikely, I'm afraid. The only rule with this shooting in Burma is to hope for nothing. It's invariably disappointing. The jungles teem with game, but as often as not you don't even get a chance to fire your gun.'

'Why is that?'

'The jungle is so thick. An animal may be five yards away and quite invisible, and half the time they manage to dodge back past the beaters. Even when you see them it's only for a flash of a second. And again, there's water everywhere, so that no animal is tied down to one particular spot. A tiger, for instance, will roam hundreds of miles if it suits him. And with all the game there is, they need never come back to a kill if there's anything suspicious about it. Night after night, when I was a boy, I've sat up over horrible stinking dead cows, waiting for tigers that never came.'

Elizabeth wriggled her shoulder-blades against the chair. It was a movement that she made sometimes when she was deeply pleased. She loved Flory, really loved him, when he talked like this. The most trivial scrap of information about shooting thrilled her. If only he would always talk about shooting, instead of about books and Art and that mucky poetry! In a sudden burst of admiration she decided that Flory was really quite a handsome man, in his way. He looked so splendidly manly, with his pagri-cloth shirt open at the throat, and his shorts and puttees and shooting boots! And his face, lined, sunburned, like a soldier's face. He was standing with his birthmarked cheek away from her. She pressed him to go on talking.

'DO tell me some more about tiger-shooting. It's so awfully interesting!'

He described the shooting, years ago, of a mangy old man-eater who had killed one of his coolies. The wait in the mosquito-ridden machan; the tiger's eyes approaching through the dark jungle, like great green lanterns; the panting, slobbering noise as he devoured the coolie's body, tied to a stake below. Flory told it all perfunctorily enough—did not the proverbial Anglo Indian bore always talk about tiger-shooting?—but Elizabeth wriggled her shoulders delightedly once more. He did not realize how such talk as this reassured her and made up for all the times when he had bored her and disquieted her. Six shock-headed youths came down the path, carrying dahs over their shoulders, and headed by a stringy but active old man with grey hair. They halted in front of the headman's house, and one of them uttered a hoarse whoop, whereat the headman appeared and explained that these were the beaters. They were ready to start now, if the young thakin-ma did not find it too hot.

They set out. The side of the village away from the creek was protected by a hedge of cactus six feet high and twelve thick. One went up a narrow lane of cactus, then along a rutted, dusty bullock-cart track, with bamboos as tall as flagstaffs growing densely on either side. The beaters marched rapidly ahead in single file, each with his broad dah laid along his forearm. The old hunter was marching just in front of Elizabeth. His longyi was hitched up like a loin-cloth, and his meagre thighs were tattooed with dark blue patterns, so intricate that he might have been wearing drawers of blue lace. A bamboo the thickness of a man's wrist had fallen and hung across the path. The leading beater severed it with an upward flick of his dah; the prisoned water gushed out of it with a diamond-flash. After half a mile they reached the open fields, and everyone was sweating, for they had walked fast and the sun was savage.

'That's where we're going to shoot, over there,' Flory said.

He pointed across the stubble, a wide dust-coloured plain, cut up into patches of an acre or two by mud boundaries. It was horribly flat, and lifeless save for the snowy egrets. At the far edge a jungle of great trees rose abruptly, like a dark green cliff. The beaters had gone across to a small tree like a hawthorn twenty yards away. One of them was on his knees, shikoing to the tree and gabbling, while the old hunter poured a bottle of some cloudy liquid on to the ground. The others stood looking on with serious, bored faces, like men in church.

'What ARE those men doing?' Elizabeth said.

'Only sacrificing to the local gods. Nats, they call them—a kind of dryad. They're praying to him to bring us good luck.'

The hunter came back and in a cracked voice explained that they were to beat a small patch of scrub over to the right before proceeding to the main jungle. Apparently the Nat had counselled this. The hunter directed Flory and Elizabeth where to stand, pointing with his dah. The six beaters, plunged into the scrub; they would make a detour and beat back towards the paddy-fields. There were some bushes of the wild rose thirty yards from the jungle's edge, and Flory and Elizabeth took cover behind one of these, while Ko S'la squatted down behind another bush a little distance away, holding Flo's collar and stroking her to keep her quiet. Flory always sent Ko S'la to a distance when he was shooting, for he had an irritating trick of clicking his tongue if a shot was missed. Presently there was a far-off echoing sound—a sound of tapping and strange hollow cries; the beat had started. Elizabeth at once began trembling so uncontrollably that she could not keep her gun-barrel still. A wonderful bird, a little bigger than a thrush, with grey wings and body of blazing scarlet, broke from the trees and came towards them with a dipping flight. The tapping and the cries came nearer. One of the bushes at the jungle's edge waved violently—some large animal was emerging. Elizabeth raised her gun and tried to steady it. But it was only a naked yellow beater, dah in hand. He saw that he had emerged and shouted to the others to join him.

Elizabeth lowered her gun. 'What's happened?'

'Nothing. The beat's over.'

'So there was nothing there!' she cried in bitter disappointment.

'Never mind, one never gets anything the first beat. We'll have better luck next time.'

They crossed the lumpy stubble, climbing over the mud boundaries that divided the fields, and took up their position opposite the high green wall of the jungle. Elizabeth had already learned how to load her gun. This time the beat had hardly started when Ko S'la whistled sharply.

'Look out!' Flory cried. 'Quick, here they come!'

A flight of green pigeons were dashing towards them at incredible speed, forty yards up. They were like a handful of catapulted stones whirling through the sky. Elizabeth was helpless with excitement. For a moment she could not move, then she flung her barrel into the air, somewhere in the direction of the birds, and tugged violently at the trigger. Nothing happened—she was pulling at the trigger-guard. Just as the birds passed overhead she found the triggers and pulled both of them simultaneously. There was a deafening roar and she was thrown backwards a pace with her collar-bone almost broken. She had fired thirty yards behind the birds. At the same moment she saw Flory turn and level his gun. Two of the pigeons, suddenly checked in their flight, swirled over and dropped to the ground like arrows. Ko S'la yelled, and he and Flo raced after them.

'Look out!' said Flory, 'here's an imperial pigeon. Let's have him!'

A large heavy bird, with flight much slower than the others, was flapping overhead. Elizabeth did not care to fire after her previous failure. She watched Flory thrust a cartridge into the breech and raise his gun, and the white plume of smoke leapt up from the muzzle. The bird planed heavily down, his wing broken. Flo and Ko S'la came running excitedly up, Flo with the big imperial pigeon in her mouth, and Ko S'la grinning and producing two green pigeons from his Kachin bag.

Flory took one of the little green corpses to show to Elizabeth. 'Look at it. Aren't they lovely things? The most beautiful bird in Asia.'

Elizabeth touched its smooth feathers with her finger-tip. It filled her with bitter envy, because she had not shot it. And yet it was curious, but she felt almost an adoration for Flory now that she had seen how he could shoot.

'Just look at its breast-feathers; like a jewel. It's murder to shoot them. The Burmese say that when you kill one of these birds they vomit, meaning to say, "Look, here is all I possess, and I've taken nothing of yours. Why do you kill me?" I've never seen one do it, I must admit.'

'Are they good to eat?'

'Very. Even so, I always feel it's a shame to kill them.'

'I wish I could do it like you do!' she said enviously.

'It's only a knack, you'll soon pick it up. You know how to hold your gun, and that's more than most people do when they start.'

However, at the next two beats, Elizabeth could hit nothing. She had learned not to fire both barrels at once, but she was too paralysed with excitement ever to take aim. Flory shot several more pigeons, and a small bronze-wing dove with back as green as verdigris. The jungle fowl were too cunning to show themselves, though one could hear them cluck-clucking all round, and once or twice the sharp trumpet-call of a cock. They were getting deeper into the jungle now. The light was greyish, with dazzling patches of sunlight. Whichever way one looked one's view was shut in by the multitudinous ranks of trees, and the tangled bushes and creepers that struggled round their bases like the sea round the piles of a pier. It was so dense, like a bramble bush extending mile after mile, that one's eyes were oppressed by it. Some of the creepers were huge, like serpents. Flory and Elizabeth struggled along narrow game-tracks, up slippery banks, thorns tearing at their clothes. Both their shirts were drenched with sweat. It was stifling hot, with a scent of crushed leaves. Sometimes for minutes together invisible cidadas would keep up a shrill, metallic pinging like the twanging of a steel guitar, and then, by stopping, make a silence that startled one.

As they were walking to the fifth beat they came to a great peepul tree in which, high up, one could hear imperial pigeons cooing. It was a sound like the far-off lowing of cows. One bird fluttered out and perched alone on the topmost bough, a small greyish shape. 'Try a sitting shot,' Flory said to Elizabeth. 'Get your sight on him and pull off without waiting. Don't shut your left eye.'

Elizabeth raised her gun, which had begun trembling as usual. The beaters halted in a group to watch, and some of them could not refrain from clicking their tongues; they thought it queer and rather shocking to see a woman handle a gun. With a violent effort of will Elizabeth kept her gun still for a second, and pulled the trigger. She did not hear the shot; one never does when it has gone home. The bird seemed to jump upwards from the bough, then down it came, tumbling over and over, and stuck in a fork ten yards up. One of the beaters laid down his dah and glanced appraisingly at the tree; then he walked to a great creeper, thick as a man's thigh and twisted like a stick of barley sugar, that hung far out from a bough. He ran up the creeper as easily as though it had been a ladder, walked upright along the broad bough, and brought the pigeon to the ground. He put it limp and warm into Elizabeth's hand.

She could hardly give it up, the feel of it so ravished her. She could have kissed it, hugged it to her breast. All the men, Flory and Ko S'la and the beaters, smiled at one another to see her fondling the dead bird. Reluctantly, she gave it to Ko S'la to put in the bag. She was conscious of an extraordinary desire to fling her arms round Flory's neck and kiss him; and in some way it was the killing of the pigeon that made her feel this.

After the fifth beat the hunter explained to Flory that they must cross a clearing that was used for growing pineapples, and would beat another patch of jungle beyond. They came out into sunlight, dazzling after the jungle gloom. The clearing was an oblong of an acre or two hacked out of the jungle like a patch mown in long grass, with the pineapples, prickly cactus-like plants, growing in rows, almost smothered by weeds. A low hedge of thorns divided the field in the middle. They had nearly crossed the field when there was a sharp cock-a-doodle-doo from beyond the hedge.

'Oh, listen!' said Elizabeth, stopping. 'Was that a jungle cock?'

'Yes. They come out to feed about this time.'

'Couldn't we go and shoot him?'

'We'll have a try if you like. They're cunning beggars. Look, we'll stalk up the hedge until we get opposite where he is. We'll have to go without making a sound.'

He sent Ko S'la and the beaters on, and the two of them skirted the field and crept along the hedge. They had to bend double to keep themselves out of sight. Elizabeth was in front. The hot sweat trickled down her face, tickling her upper lip, and her heart was knocking violently. She felt Flory touch her heel from behind. Both of them stood upright and looked over the hedge together.

Ten yards away a little cock the size of a bantam, was pecking vigorously at the ground. He was beautiful, with his long silky neck-feathers, bunched comb and arching, laurel-green tail. There were six hens with him, smaller brown birds, with diamond-shaped feathers like snake-scales on their backs. All this Elizabeth and Flory saw in the space of a second, then with a squawk and a whirr the birds were up and flying like bullets for the jungle. Instantly, automatically as it seemed, Elizabeth raised her gun and fired. It was one of those shots where there is no aiming, no consciousness of the gun in one's hand, when one's mind seems to fly behind the charge and drive it to the mark. She knew the bird was doomed even before she pulled the trigger. He tumbled, showered feathers thirty yards away. 'Good shot, good shot!' cried Flory. In their excitement both of them dropped their guns, broke through the thorn hedge and raced side by side to where the bird lay.

'Good shot!' Flory repeated, as excited as she. 'By Jove, I've never seen anyone kill a flying bird their first day, never! You got your gun off like lightning. It's marvellous!'

They were kneeling face to face with the dead bird between them. With a shock they discovered that their hands, his right and her left, were clasped tightly together. They had run to the place hand-in-hand without noticing it.

A sudden stillness came on them both, a sense of something momentous that must happen. Flory reached across and took her other hand. It came yieldingly, willingly. For a moment they knelt with their hands clasped together. The sun blazed upon them and the warmth breathed out of their bodies; they seemed to be floating upon clouds of heat and joy. He took her by the upper arms to draw her towards him.

Then suddenly he turned his head away and stood up, pulling Elizabeth to her feet. He let go of her arms. He had remembered his birthmark. He dared not do it. Not here, not in daylight! The snub it invited was too terrible. To cover the awkwardness of the moment he bent down and picked up the jungle cock.

'It was splendid,' he said. 'You don't need any teaching. You can shoot already. We'd better get on to the next beat.'

They had just crossed the hedge and picked up their guns when there was a series of shouts from the edge of the jungle. Two of the beaters were running towards them with enormous leaps, waving their arms wildly in the air.

'What is it?' Elizabeth said.

'I don't know. They've seen some animal or other. Something good, by the look of them.'

'Oh, hurrah! Come on!'

They broke into a run and hurried across the field, breaking through the pineapples and the stiff prickly weeds. Ko S'la and five of the beaters were standing in a knot all talking at once, and the other two were beckoning excitedly to Flory and Elizabeth. As they came up they saw in the middle of the group an old woman who was holding up her ragged longyi with one hand and gesticulating with a big cigar in the other. Elizabeth could hear some word that sounded like 'Char' repeated over and over again.

'What is it they're saying?' she said.

The beaters came crowding round Flory, all talking eagerly and pointing into the jungle. After a few questions he waved his hand to silence them and turned to Elizabeth:

'I say, here's a bit of luck! This old girl was coming through the jungle, and she says that at the sound of the shot you fired just now, she saw a leopard run across the path. These fellows know where he's likely to hide. If we're quick they may be able to surround him before he sneaks away, and drive him out. Shall we try it?'

'Oh, do let's! Oh, what awful fun! How lovely, how lovely if we could get that leopard!'

'You understand it's dangerous? We'll keep close together and it'll probably be all right, but it's never absolutely safe on foot. Are you ready for that?'

'Oh, of course, of course! I'm not frightened. Oh, do let's be quick and start!'

'One of you come with us, and show us the way,' he said to the beaters. 'Ko S'la, put Flo on the leash and go with the others. She'll never keep quiet with us. We'll have to hurry,' he added to Elizabeth.

Ko S'la and the beaters hurried off along the edge of the jungle. They would strike in and begin beating farther up. The other beater, the same youth who had climbed the tree after the pigeon, dived into the jungle, Flory and Elizabeth following. With short rapid steps, almost running, he led them through a labyrinth of game-tracks. The bushes trailed so low that sometimes one had almost to crawl, and creepers hung across the path like trip-wires. The ground was dusty and silent underfoot. At some landmark in the jungle the beater halted, pointed to the ground as a sign that this spot would do, and put his finger on his lips to enjoin silence. Flory took four SG cartridges from his pockets and took Elizabeth's gun to load it silently.

There was a faint rustling behind them, and they all started. A nearly naked youth with a pellet-bow, come goodness knows whence, had parted the bushes. He looked at the beater, shook his head and pointed up the path. There was a dialogue of signs between the two youths, then the beater seemed to agree. Without speaking all four stole forty yards along the path, round a bend, and halted again. At the same moment a frightful pandemonium of yells, punctuated by barks from Flo, broke out a few hundred yards away.

Elizabeth felt the beater's hand on her shoulder, pushing her downwards. They all four squatted down under cover of a prickly bush, the Europeans in front, the Burmans behind. In the distance there was such a tumult of yells and the rattle of dahs against tree-trunks that one could hardly believe six men could make so much noise. The beaters were taking good care that the leopard should not turn back upon them. Elizabeth watched some large, pale yellow ants marching like soldiers over the thorns of the bush. One fell on to her hand and crawled up her forearm. She dared not move to brush it away. She was praying silently, 'Please God, let the leopard come! Oh please, God, let the leopard come!'

There was a sudden loud pattering on the leaves. Elizabeth raised her gun, but Flory shook his head sharply and pushed the barrel down again. A jungle fowl scuttled across the path with long noisy strides.

The yells of the beaters seemed hardly to come any closer, and this end of the jungle the silence was like a pall. The ant on Elizabeth's arm bit her painfully and dropped to the ground. A dreadful despair had begun to form in her heart; the leopard was not coming, he had slipped away somewhere, they had lost him. She almost wished they had never heard of the leopard, the disappointment was so agonizing. Then she felt the beater pinch her elbow. He was craning his face forward, his smooth, dull yellow cheek only a few inches from her own; she could smell the coco-nut oil in his hair. His coarse lips were puckered as in a whistle; he had heard something. Then Flory and Elizabeth heard it too, the faintest whisper, as though some creature of air were gliding through the jungle, just brushing the ground with its foot. At the same moment the leopard's head and shoulders emerged from the undergrowth, fifteen yards down the path.

He stopped with his forepaws on the path. They could see his low, flat-eared head, his bare eye-tooth and his thick, terrible forearm. In the shadow he did not look yellow but grey. He was listening intently. Elizabeth saw Flory spring to his feet, raise his gun and pull the trigger instantly. The shot roared, and almost simultaneously there was a heavy crash as the brute dropped flat in the weeds. 'Look out!' Flory cried, 'he's not done for!' He fired again, and there was a fresh thump as the shot went home. The leopard gasped. Flory threw open his gun and felt in his pocket for a cartridge, then flung all his cartridges on to the path and fell on his knees, searching rapidly among them.

'Damn and blast it!' he cried. 'There isn't a single SG among them. Where in hell did I put them?'

The leopard had disappeared as he fell. He was thrashing about in the undergrowth like a great, wounded snake, and crying out with a snarling, sobbing noise, savage and pitiful. The noise seemed to be coming nearer. Every cartridge Flory turned up had 6 or 8 marked on the end. The rest of the large-shot cartridges had, in fact, been left with Ko S'la. The crashing and snarling were now hardly five yards away, but they could see nothing, the jungle was so thick.

The two Burmans were crying out 'Shoot! Shoot! Shoot!' The sound of 'Shoot! Shoot!' got farther away—they were skipping for the nearest climbable trees. There was a crash in the undergrowth so close that it shook the bush by which Elizabeth was standing.

'By God, he's almost on us!' Flory said. 'We must turn him somehow. Let fly at the sound.'

Elizabeth raised her gun. Her knees were knocking like castanets, but her hand was as steady as stone. She fired rapidly, once, twice. The crashing noise receded. The leopard was crawling away, crippled but swift, and still invisible.

'Well done! You've scared him,' Flory said.

'But he's getting away! He's getting away!' Elizabeth cried, dancing about in agitation. She made to follow him. Flory jumped to his feet and pulled her back.

'No fear! You stay here. Wait!'

He slipped two of the small-shot cartridges into his gun and ran after the sound of the leopard. For a moment Elizabeth could not see either beast or man, then they reappeared in a bare patch thirty yards away. The leopard was writhing along on his belly, sobbing as he went. Flory levelled his gun and fired at four yards' distance. The leopard jumped like a cushion when one hits it, then rolled over, curled up and lay still. Flory poked the body with his gun-barrel. It did not stir.

'It's all right, he's done for,' he called. 'Come and have a look at him.'

The two Burmans jumped down from their tree, and they and Elizabeth went across to where Flory was standing. The leopard—it was a male—was lying curled up with his head between his forepaws. He looked much smaller than he had looked alive; he looked rather pathetic, like a dead kitten. Elizabeth's knees were still quivering. She and Flory stood looking down at the leopard, close together, but not clasping hands this time.

It was only a moment before Ko S'la and the others came up, shouting with glee. Flo gave one sniff at the dead leopard, then down went her tail and she bolted fifty yards, whimpering. She could not be induced to come near him again. Everyone squatted down round the leopard and gazed at him. They stroked his beautiful white belly, soft as a hare's, and squeezed his broad pugs to bring out the claws, and pulled back his black lips to examine the fangs. Presently two of the beaters cut down a tall bamboo and slung the leopard upon it by his paws, with his long tail trailing down, and then they marched back to the village in triumph. There was no talk of further shooting, though the light still held. They were all, including the Europeans, too anxious to get home and boast of what they had done.

Flory and Elizabeth walked side by side across the stubble field. The others were thirty yards ahead with the guns and the leopard, and Flo was slinking after them a long way in the rear. The sun was going down beyond the Irrawaddy. The light shone level across the field, gilding the stubble stalks, and striking into their faces with a yellow, gentle beam. Elizabeth's shoulder was almost touching Flory's as they walked. The sweat that had drenched their shirts had dried again. They did not talk much. They were happy with that inordinate happiness that comes of exhaustion and achievement, and with which nothing else in life—no joy of either the body or the mind—is even able to be compared.

'The leopard skin is yours,' Flory said as they approached the village.

'Oh, but you shot him!'

'Never mind, you stick to the skin. By Jove, I wonder how many of the women in this country would have kept their heads like you did! I can just see them screaming and fainting. I'll get the skin cured for you in Kyauktada jail. There's a convict there who can cure skins as soft as velvet. He's doing a seven-year sentence, so he's had time to learn the job.'

'Oh well, thanks awfully.'

No more was said for the present. Later, when they had washed off the sweat and dirt, and were fed and rested, they would meet again at the Club. They made no rendezvous, but it was understood between them that they would meet. Also, it was understood that Flory would ask Elizabeth to marry him, though nothing was said about this either.

At the village Flory paid the beaters eight annas each, superintended the skinning of the leopard, and gave the headman a bottle of beer and two of the imperial pigeons. The skin and skull were packed into one of the canoes. All the whiskers had been stolen, in spite of Ko S'la's efforts to guard them. Some young men of the village carried off the carcass in order to eat the heart and various other organs, the eating of which they believed would make them strong and swift like the leopard.

Chapter 15

When Flory arrived at the Club he found the Lackersteens in an unusually morose mood. Mrs Lackersteen was sitting, as usual, in the best place under the punkah, and was reading the Civil List, the Debrett of Burma. She was in a bad temper with her husband, who had defied her by ordering a 'large peg' as soon as he reached the Club, and was further defying her by reading the Pink'un. Elizabeth was alone in the stuffy little library, turning over the pages of an old copy of Blackwood's.

Since parting with Flory, Elizabeth had had a very disagreeable adventure. She had come out of her bath and was half-way through dressing for dinner when her uncle had suddenly appeared in her room—pretext, to hear some more about the day's shooting— and begun pinching her leg in a way that simply could not be misunderstood. Elizabeth was horrified. This was her first introduction to the fact that some men are capable of making love to their nieces. We live and learn. Mr Lackersteen had tried to carry the thing off as a joke, but he was too clumsy and too nearly drunk to succeed. It was fortunate that his wife was out of hearing, or there might have been a first-rate scandal.

After this, dinner was an uncomfortable meal. Mr Lackersteen was sulking. What rot it was, the way these women put on airs and prevented you from having a good time! The girl was pretty enough to remind him of the Illustrations in La Vie Parisienne, and damn it! wasn't he paying for her keep? It was a shame. But for Elizabeth the position was very serious. She was penniless and had no home except her uncle's house. She had come eight thousand miles to stay here. It would be terrible if after only a fortnight her uncle's house were to be made uninhabitable for her.

Consequently, one thing was much surer in her mind than it had been: that if Flory asked her to marry him (and he would, there was little doubt of it), she would say yes. At another time it was just possible that she would have decided differently. This afternoon, under the spell of that glorious, exciting, altogether 'lovely' adventure, she had come near to loving Flory; as near as, in his particular case, she was able to come. Yet even after that, perhaps, her doubts would have returned. For there had always been something dubious about Flory; his age, his birthmark, his queer, perverse way of talking—that 'highbrow' talk that was at once unintelligible and disquieting. There had been days when she had even disliked him. But now her uncle's behaviour had turned the scale. Whatever happened she had got to escape from her uncle's house, and that soon. Yes, undoubtedly she would marry Flory when he asked her!

He could see her answer in her face as he came into the library. Her air was gentler, more yielding than he had known it. She was wearing the same lilac-coloured frock that she had worn that first morning when he met her, and the sight of the familiar frock gave him courage. It seemed to bring her nearer to him, taking away the strangeness and the elegance that had sometimes unnerved him.

He picked up the magazine she had been reading and made some remark; for a moment they chattered in the banal way they so seldom managed to avoid. It is strange how the drivelling habits of conversation will persist into almost all moments. Yet even as they chattered they found themselves drifting to the door and then outside, and presently to the big frangipani tree by the tennis court. It was the night of the full moon. Flaring like a white-hot coin, so brilliant that it hurt one's eyes, the moon swam rapidly upwards in a sky of smoky blue, across which drifted a few wisps of yellowish cloud. The stars were all invisible. The croton bushes, by day hideous things like jaundiced laurels, were changed by the moon into jagged black and white designs like fantastic wood-cuts. By the compound fence two Dravidian coolies were walking down the road, transfigured, their white rags gleaming. Through the tepid air the scent streamed from the frangipani trees like some intolerable compound out of a penny-in-the-slot machine.

'Look at the moon, just look at it!' Flory said. 'It's like a white sun. It's brighter than an English winter day.'

Elizabeth looked up into the branches of the frangipani tree, which the moon seemed to have changed into rods of silver. The light lay thick, as though palpable, on everything, crusting the earth and the rough bark of trees like some dazzling salt, and every leaf seemed to bear a freight of solid light, like snow. Even Elizabeth, indifferent to such things, was astonished.

'It's wonderful! You never see moonlight like that at Home. It's so—so—' No adjective except 'bright' presenting itself, she was silent. She had a habit of leaving her sentences unfinished, like Rosa Dartle, though for a different reason.

'Yes, the old moon does her best in this country. How that tree does stink, doesn't it? Beastly, tropical thing! I hate a tree that blooms all the year round, don't you?'

He was talking half abstractedly, to cover the time till the coolies should be out of sight. As they disappeared he put his arm round Elizabeth's shoulder, and then, when she did not start or speak, turned her round and drew her against him. Her head came against his breast, and her short hair grazed his lips. He put his hand under her chin and lifted her face up to meet his. She was not wearing her spectacles.

'You don't mind?'

'No.'

'I mean, you don't mind my—this thing of mine?' he shook his head slightly to indicate the birthmark. He could not kiss her without first asking this question.

'No, no. Of course not.'

A moment after their mouths met he felt her bare arms settle lightly round his neck. They stood pressed together, against the smooth trunk of the frangipani tree, body to body, mouth to mouth, for a minute or more. The sickly scent of the tree came mingling with the scent of Elizabeth's hair. And the scent gave him a feeling of stultification, of remoteness from Elizabeth, even though she was in his arms. All that that alien tree symbolized for him, his exile, the secret, wasted years—it was like an unbridgeable gulf between them. How should he ever make her understand what it was that he wanted of her? He disengaged himself and pressed her shoulders gently against the tree, looking down at her face, which he could see very clearly though the moon was behind her.

'It's useless trying to tell you what you mean to me,' he said. '"What you mean to me!" These blunted phrases! You don't know, you can't know, how much I love you. But I've got to try and tell you. There's so much I must tell you. Had we better go back to the Club? They may come looking for us. We can talk on the veranda.'

'Is my hair very untidy?' she said.

'It's beautiful.'

'But has it got untidy? Smooth it for me, would you, please?'

She bent her head towards him, and he smoothed the short, cool locks with his hand. The way she bent her head to him gave him a curious feeling of intimacy, far more intimate than the kiss, as though he had already been her husband. Ah, he must have her, that was certain! Only by marrying her could his life be salvaged. In a moment he would ask her. They walked slowly through the cotton bushes and back to the Club, his arm still round her shoulder.

'We can talk on the veranda,' he repeated. 'Somehow, we've never really talked, you and I. My God, how I've longed all these years for somebody to talk to! How I could talk to you, interminably, interminably! That sounds boring. I'm afraid it will be boring. I must ask you to put up with it for a little while.'

She made a sound of remonstrance at the word 'boring'.

'No, it is boring, I know that. We Anglo-Indians are always looked on as bores. And we ARE bores. But we can't help it. You see, there's—how shall I say?—a demon inside us driving us to talk. We walk about under a load of memories which we long to share and somehow never can. It's the price we pay for coming to this country.'

They were fairly safe from interruption on the side veranda, for there was no door opening directly upon it. Elizabeth had sat down with her arms on the little wicker table, but Flory remained strolling back and forth, with his hands in his coatpockets, stepping into the moonlight that streamed beneath the eastern eaves of the veranda, and back into the shadows.

'I said just now that I loved you. Love! The word's been used till it's meaningless. But let me try to explain. This afternoon when you were there shooting with me, I thought, my God! here at last is somebody who can share my life with me, but really share it, really LIVE it with me—do you see—'

He was going to ask her to marry him—indeed, he had intended to ask her without more delay. But the words were not spoken yet; instead, he found himself talking egoistically on and on. He could not help it. It was so important that she should understand something of what his life in this country had been; that she should grasp the nature of the loneliness that he wanted her to nullify. And it was so devilishly difficult to explain. It is devilish to suffer from a pain that is all but nameless. Blessed are they who are stricken only with classifiable diseases! Blessed are the poor, the sick, the crossed in love, for at least other people know what is the matter with them and will listen to their belly-achings with sympathy. But who that has not suffered it understands the pain of exile? Elizabeth watched him as he moved to and fro, in and out of the pool of moonlight that turned his silk coat to silver. Her heart was still knocking from the kiss, and yet her thoughts wandered as he talked. Was he going to ask her to marry him? He was being so slow about it! She was dimly aware that he was saying something about loneliness. Ah, of course! He was telling her about the loneliness she would have to put up with in the jungle, when they were married. He needn't have troubled. Perhaps you did get rather lonely in the jungle sometimes? Miles from anywhere, no cinemas, no dances, no one but each other to talk to, nothing to do in the evenings except read—rather a bore, that. Still, you could have a gramophone. What a difference it would make when those new portable radio sets got out to Burma! She was about to say this when he added:

'Have I made myself at all clear to you? Have you got some picture of the life we live here? The foreignness, the solitude, the melancholy! Foreign trees, foreign flowers, foreign landscapes, foreign faces. It's all as alien as a different planet. But do you see— and it's this that I so want you to understand—do you see, it mightn't be so bad living on a different planet, it might even be the most interesting thing imaginable, if you had even one person to share it with. One person who could see it with eyes something like your own. This country's been a kind of solitary hell to me—it's so to most of us—and yet I tell you it could be a paradise if one weren't alone. Does all this seem quite meaningless?'

He had stopped beside the table, and he picked up her hand. In the half-darkness he could see her face only as a pale oval, like a flower, but by the feeling of her hand he knew instantly that she had not understood a word of what he was saying. How should she, indeed? It was so futile, this meandering talk! He would say to her at once, Will you marry me? Was there not a lifetime to talk in? He took her other hand and drew her gently to her feet.

'Forgive me all this rot I've been talking.'

'It's all right,' she murmured indistinctly, expecting that he was about to kiss her.

'No, it's rot talking like that. Some things will go into words, some won't. Besides, it was an impertinence to go belly-aching on and on about myself. But I was trying to lead up to something. Look, this is what I wanted to say. Will—'

'Eliz-a-beth!'

It was Mrs Lackersteen's high-pitched, plaintive voice, calling from within the Club.

'Elizabeth? Where are you, Elizabeth?'

Evidently she was near the front door—would be on the veranda in a moment. Flory pulled Elizabeth against him. They kissed hurriedly. He released her, only holding her hands.

'Quickly, there's just time. Answer me this. Will you—'

But that sentence never got any further. At the same moment something extraordinary happened under his feet—the floor was surging and rolling like a sea—he was staggering, then dizzily falling, hitting his upper arm a thump as the floor rushed towards him. As he lay there he found himself jerked violently backwards and forwards as though some enormous beast below were rocking the whole building on its back.

The drunken floor righted itself very suddenly, and Flory sat up, dazed but not much hurt. He dimly noticed Elizabeth sprawling beside him, and screams coming from within the Club. Beyond the gate two Burmans were racing through the moonlight with their long hair streaming behind them. They were yelling at the top of their voices:

'Nga Yin is shaking himself! Nga Yin is shaking himself!'

Flory watched them unintelligently. Who was Nga Yin? Nga is the prefix given to criminals. Nga Yin must be a dacoit. Why was he shaking himself? Then he remembered. Nga Yin was a giant supposed by the Burmese to be buried, like Typhaeus, beneath the crust of the earth. Of course! It was an earthquake.

'An earthquake!' he exclaimed, and he remembered Elizabeth and moved to pick her up. But she was already sitting up, unhurt, and rubbing the back of her head.

'Was that an earthquake?' she said in a rather awed voice.

Mrs Lackersteen's tall form came creeping round the corner of the veranda, clinging to the wall like some elongated lizard. She was exclaiming hysterically:

'Oh dear, an earthquake! Oh, what a dreadful shock! I can't bear it—my heart won't stand it! Oh dear, oh dear! An earthquake!'

Mr Lackersteen tottered after her, with a strange ataxic step caused partly by earth-tremors and partly by gin.

'An earthquake, dammit!' he said.

Flory and Elizabeth slowly picked themselves up. They all went inside, with that queer feeling in the soles of the feet that one has when one steps from a rocking boat on to the shore. The old butler was hurrying from the servants' quarters, thrusting his pagri on his head as he came, and a troop of twittering chokras after him.

'Earthquake, sir, earthquake!' he bubbled eagerly.

'I should damn well think it was an earthquake,' said Mr Lackersteen as he lowered himself cautiously into a chair. 'Here, get some drinks, butler. By God, I could do with a nip of something after that.'

They all had a nip of something. The butler, shy yet beaming, stood on one leg beside the table, with the tray in his hand. 'Earthquake, sir, BIG earthquake!' he repeated enthusiastically. He was bursting with eagerness to talk; so, for that matter, was everyone else. An extraordinary joie de vivre had come over them all as soon as the shaky feeling departed from their legs. An earthquake is such fun when it is over. It is so exhilarating to reflect that you are not, as you well might be, lying dead under a heap of ruins. With one accord they all burst out talking: 'My dear, I've never

HAD such a shock—I fell absolutely FLAT on my back—I thought it was a dam' pariah dog scratching itself under the floor—I thought it must be an explosion somewhere—' and so on and so forth; the usual earthquake-chatter. Even the butler was included in the conversation.

'I expect you can remember ever so many earthquakes can't you butler?' said Mrs Lackersteen, quite graciously, for her.

'Oh yes, madam, many earthquakes! 1887, 1899, 1906, 1912—many, many I can remember, madam!'

'The 1912 one was a biggish one,' Flory said.

'Oh, sir, but 1906 was bigger! Very bad shock, sir! And big heathen idol in the temple fall down on top of the thathanabaing, that is Buddhist bishop, madam, which the Burmese say mean bad omen for failure of paddy crop and foot-and-mouth disease. Also in 1887 my first earthquake I remember, when I was a little chokra, and Major Maclagan sahib was lying under the table and promising he sign the teetotal pledge tomorrow morning. He not know it was an earthquake. Also two cows was killed by falling roofs,' etc., etc.

The Europeans stayed in the Club till midnight, and the butler popped into the room as many as half a dozen times, to relate a new anecdote. So far from snubbing him, the Europeans even encouraged him to talk. There is nothing like an earthquake for drawing people together. One more tremor, or perhaps two, and they would have asked the butler to sit down at table with them.

Meanwhile, Flory's proposal went no further. One cannot propose marriage immediately after an earthquake. In any case, he did not see Elizabeth alone for the rest of that evening. But it did not matter, he knew that she was his now. In the morning there would be time enough. On this thought, at peace in his mind, and dog-tired after the long day, he went to bed.

Chapter 16

The vultures in the big pyinkado trees by the cemetery flapped from their dung-whitened branches, steadied themselves on the wing, and climbed by vast spirals into the upper air. It was early, but Flory was out already. He was going down to the Club, to wait until Elizabeth came and then ask her formally to marry him. Some instinct, which he did not understand, prompted him to do it before the other Europeans returned from the jungle.

As he came out of the compound gate he saw that there was a new arrival at Kyauktada. A youth with a long spear like a needle in his hand was cantering across the maidan on a white pony. Some Sikhs, looking like sepoys, ran after him, leading two other ponies, a bay and a chestnut, by the bridle. When he came level with him Flory halted on the road and shouted good morning. He had not recognized the youth, but it is usual in small stations to make strangers welcome. The other saw that he was hailed, wheeled his pony negligently round and brought it to the side of the road. He was a youth of about twenty-live, lank but very straight, and manifestly a cavalry officer. He had one of those rabbit-like faces common among English soldiers, with pale blue eyes and a little triangle of fore-teeth visible between the lips; yet hard, fearless and even brutal in a careless fashion—a rabbit, perhaps, but a tough and martial rabbit. He sat his horse as though he were part of it, and he looked offensively young and fit. His fresh face was tanned to the exact shade that went with his light-coloured eyes, and he was as elegant as a picture with his white buckskin topi and his polo-boots that gleamed like an old meerschaum pipe. Flory felt uncomfortable in his presence from the start.

'How d'you do?' said Flory. 'Have you just arrived?'

'Last night, got in by the late train.' He had a surly, boyish voice. 'I've been sent up here with a company of men to stand by in case your local bad-mashes start any trouble. My name's Verrall—Military Police,' he added, not, however, inquiring Flory's name in return.

'Oh yes. We heard they were sending somebody. Where are you putting up?'

'Dak bungalow, for the time being. There was some black beggar staying there when I got in last night—Excise Officer or something. I booted him out. This is a filthy hole, isn't it?' he said with a backward movement of his head, indicating the whole of Kyauktada.

'I suppose it's like the rest of these small stations. Are you staying long?'

'Only a month or so, thank God. Till the rains break. What a rotten maidan you've got here, haven't you? Pity they can't keep this stuff cut,' he added, swishing the dried-up grass with the point of his spear. 'Makes it so hopeless for polo or anything.'

'I'm afraid you won't get any polo here,' Flory said. 'Tennis is the best we can manage. There are only eight of us all told, and most of us spend three-quarters of our time in the jungle.'

'Christ! What a hole!'

After this there was a silence. The tall, bearded Sikhs stood in a group round their horses' heads, eyeing Flory without much favour. It was perfectly clear that Verral was bored with the conversation and wanted to escape. Flory had never in his life felt so completely de trop, or so old and shabby. He noticed that Verrall's pony was a beautiful Arab, a mare, with proud neck and arching, plume-like tail; a lovely milk-white thing, worth several thousands of rupees. Verrall had already twitched the bridle to turn away, evidently feeling that he had talked enough for one morning.

'That's a wonderful pony of yours,' Flory said.

'She's not bad, better than these Burma scrubs. I've come out to do a bit of tent-pegging. It's hopeless trying to knock a polo ball about in this muck. Hey, Hira Singh!' he called, and turned his pony away.

The sepoy holding the bay pony handed his bridle to a companion, ran to a spot forty yards away, and fixed a narrow boxwood peg in the ground. Verral took no further notice of Flory. He raised his spear and poised himself as though taking aim at the peg, while the Indians backed their horses out of the way and stood watching critically. With a just perceptible movement Verrall dug his knees into the pony's sides. She bounded forward like a bullet from a catapult. As easily as a centaur the lank, straight youth leaned over in the saddle, lowered his spear and plunged it clean through the peg. One of the Indians muttered gruffly 'Shabash!' Verrall raised his spear behind him in the orthodox fashion, and then, pulling his horse to a canter, wheeled round and handed the transfixed peg to the sepoy.

Verrall rode twice more at the peg, and hit it each time. It was done with matchless grace and with extraordinary solemnity. The whole group of men, Englishman and Indians, were concentrated upon the business of hitting the peg as though it had been a religious ritual. Flory still stood watching, disregarded—Verrall's face was one of those that are specially constructed for ignoring unwelcome strangers—but from the very fact that he had been snubbed unable to tear himself away. Somehow, Verrall had filled him with a horrible sense of inferiority. He was trying to think of some pretext for renewing the conversation, when he looked up the hillside and saw Elizabeth, in pale blue, coming out of her uncle's gate. She must have seen the third transfixing of the peg. His heart stirred painfully. A thought occurred to him, one of those rash thoughts that usually lead to trouble. He called to Verrall, who was a few yards away from him, and pointed with his stick.

'Do these other two know how to do it?'

Verrall looked over his shoulder with a surly air. He had expected Flory to go away after being ignored.

'What?'

'Can these other two do it?' Flory repeated.

'The chestnut's not bad. Bolts if you let him, though.'

'Let me have a shot at the peg, would you?'

'All right,' said Verrall ungraciously. 'Don't go and cut his mouth to bits.'

A sepoy brought the pony, and Flory pretended to examine the curb-chain. In reality he was temporizing until Elizabeth should be thirty or forty yards away. He made up his mind that he would stick the peg exactly at the moment when she passed (it is easy enough on the small Burma ponies, provided that they will gallop straight), and then ride up to her with it on his point. That was obviously the right move. He did not want her to think that that pink-faced young whelp was the only person who could ride. He was wearing shorts, which are uncomfortable to ride in, but he knew that, like nearly everyone, he looked his best on horseback.

Elizabeth was approaching. Flory stepped into the saddle, took the spear from the Indian and waved it in greeting to Elizabeth. She made no response, however. Probably she was shy in front of Verrall. She was looking away, towards the cemetery, and her cheeks were pink.

'Chalo,' said Flory to the Indian, and then dug his knees into the horse's sides.

The very next instant, before the horse had taken to bounds, Flory found himself hurtling through the air, hitting the ground with a crack that wrenched his shoulder almost out of joint, and rolling over and over. Mercifully the spear fell clear of him. He lay supine, with a blurred vision of blue sky and floating vultures. Then his eyes focused on the khaki pagri and dark face of a Sikh, bearded to the eyes, bending over him.

'What's happened?' he said in English, and he raised himself painfully on his elbow. The Sikh made some gruff answer and pointed. Flory saw the chestnut pony careering away over the maidan, with the saddle under its belly. The girth had not been tightened, and had slipped round; hence his fall.

When Flory sat up he found that he was in extreme pain. The right shoulder of his shirt was torn open and already soaking with blood, and he could feel more blood oozing from his cheek. The hard earth had grazed him. His hat, too, was gone. With a deadly pang he remembered Elizabeth, and he saw her coming towards him, barely ten yards away, looking straight at him as he sprawled there so ignominiously. My God, my God! he thought, O my God, what a fool I must look! The thought of it even drove away the pain of the fall. He clapped a hand over his birth-mark, though the other cheek was the damaged one.

'Elizabeth! Hullo, Elizabeth! Good morning!'

He had called out eagerly, appealingly, as one does when one is conscious of looking a fool. She did not answer, and what was almost incredible, she walked on without pausing even for an instant, as though she had neither seen nor heard him.

'Elizabeth!' he called again, taken aback; 'did you see my fall? The saddle slipped. The fool of a sepoy hadn't—'

There was no question that she had heard him now. She turned her face full upon him for a moment, and looked at him and through him as though he had not existed. Then she gazed away into the distance beyond the cemetery. It was terrible. He called after her in dismay—

'Elizabeth! I say, Elizabeth!'

She passed on without a word, without a sign, without a look. She was walking sharply down the road, with a click of heels, her back turned upon him.

The sepoys had come round him now, and Verrall, too, had ridden across to where Flory lay. Some of the sepoys had saluted Elizabeth; Verrall had ignored her, perhaps not seeing her. Flory rose stiffly to his feet. He was badly bruised, but no bones were broken.

The Indians brought him his hat and stick, but they did not apologize for their carelessness. They looked faintly contemptuous, as though thinking that he had only got what he deserved. It was conceivable that they had loosened the girth on purpose.

'The saddle slipped,' said Flory in the weak, stupid way that one does at such moments.

'Why the devil couldn't you look at it before you got up?' said Verrall briefly. 'You ought to know these beggars aren't to be trusted.'

Having said which he twitched his bridle and rode away, feeling the incident closed. The sepoys followed him without saluting Flory. When Flory reached his gate he looked back and saw that the chestnut pony had already been caught and re-saddled, and Verrall was tent-pegging upon it.

The fall had so shaken him that even now he could hardly collect his thoughts. What could have made her behave like that? She had seen him lying bloody and in pain, and she had walked past him as though he had been a dead dog. How could it have happened? HAD it happened? It was incredible. Could she be angry with him? Could he have offended her in any way? All the servants were waiting at the compound fence. They had come out to watch the tent-pegging, and every one of them had seen his bitter humiliation. Ko S'la ran part of the way down the hill to meet him, with concerned face.

'The god has hurt himself? Shall I carry the god back to the house?'

'No,' said the god. 'Go and get me some whisky and a clean shirt.'

When they got back to the house Ko S'la made Flory sit down on the bed and peeled off his torn shirt which the blood had stuck to his body. Ko S'la clicked his tongue.

'Ah ma lay? These cuts are full of dirt. You ought not to play these children's games on strange ponies, thakin. Not at your age. It is too dangerous.'

'The saddle slipped,' Flory said.

'Such games,' pursued Ko S'la, 'are all very well for the young police officer. But you are no longer young, thakin. A fall hurts at your age. You should take more care of yourself.'

'Do you take me for an old man?' said Flory angrily. His shoulder was smarting abominably.

'You are thirty-five, thakin,' said Ko S'la politely but firmly.

It was all very humiliating. Ma Pu and Ma Yi, temporarily at peace, had brought a pot of some dreadful mess which they declared was good for cuts. Flory told Ko S'la privately to throw it out of the window and substitute boracic ointment. Then, while he sat in a tepid bath and Ko S'la sponged the dirt out of his grazes, he puzzled helplessly, and, as his head grew clearer, with a deeper and deeper dismay, over what had happened. He had offended her bitterly, that was clear. But, when he had not even seen her since last night, how COULD he have offended her? And there was no even plausible answer.

He explained to Ko S'la several times over that his fall was due to the saddle slipping. But Ko S'la, though sympathetic, clearly did not believe him. To the end of his days, Flory perceived, the fall would be attributed to his own bad horsemanship. On the other hand, a fortnight ago, he had won undeserved renown by putting to flight the harmless buffalo. Fate is even-handed, after a fashion.

Chapter 17

Flory did not see Elizabeth again until he went down to the Club after dinner. He had not, as he might have done, sought her out and demanded an explanation. His face unnerved him when he looked at it in the glass. With the birthmark on one side and the graze on the other it was so woebegone, so hideous, that he dared not show himself by daylight. As he entered the Club lounge he put his hand over his birthmark—pretext, a mosquito bite on the forehead. It would have been more than his nerve was equal to, not to cover his birthmark at such a moment. However, Elizabeth was not there.

Instead, he tumbled into an unexpected quarrel. Ellis and Westfield had just got back from the jungle, and they were sitting drinking, in a sour mood. News had come from Rangoon that the editor of the Burmese Patriot had been given only four months' imprisonment for his libel against Mr Macregor, and Ellis was working himself up into a rage over this light sentence. As soon as Flory came in Ellis began baiting him with remarks about 'that little nigger Very-slimy'. At the moment the very thought of quarrelling made Flory yawn, but he answered incautiously, and there was an argument. It grew heated, and after Ellis had called Flory a nigger's Nancy Boy and Flory had replied in kind, Westfield too lost his temper. He was a good-natured man, but Flory's Bolshie ideas sometimes annoyed him. He could never understand why, when there was so clearly a right and a wrong opinion about everything, Flory always seemed to delight in choosing the wrong one. He told Flory 'not to start talking like a damned Hyde Park agitator', and then read him a snappish little sermon, taking as his text the five chief beatitudes of the pukka sahib, namely:

Keeping up our prestige, The firm hand (without the velvet glove), We white men must hang together, Give them an inch and they'll take an ell, and Esprit de Corps.

All the while his anxiety to see Elizabeth was so gnawing at Flory's heart that he could hardly hear what was said to him. Besides, he had heard it all so often, so very often—a hundred times, a thousand times it might be, since his first week in Rangoon, when his burra sahib (an old Scotch gin-soaker and great breeder of racing ponies, afterwards warned off the turf for some dirty business of running the same horse under two different names) saw him take off his topi to pass a native funeral and said to him reprovingly: 'Remember laddie, always remember, we are sahiblog and they are dirrt!' It sickened him, now, to have to listen to such trash. So he cut Westfield short by saying blasphemously:

'Oh, shut up! I'm sick of the subject. Veraswami's a damned good fellow—a damned sight better than some white men I can think of. Anyway, I'm going to propose his name for the Club when the general meeting comes. Perhaps he'll liven this bloody place up a bit.'

Whereat the row would have become serious if it had not ended as most rows ended at the Club—with the appearance of the butler, who had heard the raised voices.

'Did master call, sir?'

'No. Go to hell,' said Ellis morosely.

The butler retired, but that was the end of the dispute for the time being. At this moment there were footsteps and voices outside; the Lackersteens were arriving at the Club.

When they entered the lounge, Flory could not even nerve himself to look directly at Elizabeth; but he noticed that all three of them were much more smartly dressed than usual. Mr Lackersteen was even wearing a dinner-jacket—white, because of the season— and was completely sober. The boiled shirt and pique waistcoat seemed to hold him upright and stiffen his moral fibre like a breastplate. Mrs Lackersteen looked handsome and serpentine in a red dress. In some indefinable way all three gave the impression that they were waiting to receive some distinguished guest.

When drinks had been called for, and Mrs Lackersteen had usurped the place under the punkah, Flory took a chair on the outside of the group. He dared not accost Elizabeth yet. Mrs Lackersteen had begun talking in an extraordinary, silly manner about the dear Prince of Wales, and putting on an accent like a temporarily promoted chorus-girl playing the part of a duchess in a musical comedy. The others wondered privately what the devil was the matter with her. Flory had stationed himself almost behind Elizabeth. She was wearing a yellow frock, cut very short as the fashion then was, with champagne-coloured stockings and slippers to match, and she carried a big ostrich-feather fan. She looked so modish, so adult, that he feared her more than he had ever done. It was unbelievable that he had ever kissed her. She was talking easily to all the others at once, and now and again he dared to put a word into the general conversation; but she never answered him directly, and whether or not she meant to ignore him, he could not tell.

'Well,' said Mrs Lackersteen presently, 'and who's for a rubbah?'

She said quite distinctly a 'rubbah'. Her accent was growing more aristocratic with every word she uttered. It was unaccountable. It appeared that Ellis, Westfield and Mr Lackersteen were for a 'rubbah'. Flory refused as soon as he saw that Elizabeth was not playing. Now or never was his chance to get her alone. When they all moved for the card-room, he saw with a mixture of fear and relief that Elizabeth came last. He stopped in the doorway, barring her path. He had turned dreadly pale. She shrank from him a little.

'Excuse me,' they both said simultaneously.

'One moment,' he said, and do what he would his voice trembled. 'May I speak to you? You don't mind—there's something I must say.'

'Will you please let me pass, Mr Flory?'

'Please! Please! We're alone now. You won't refuse just to let me speak?'

'What is it, then?'

'It's only this. Whatever I've done to offend you—please tell me what it is. Tell me and let me put it right. I'd sooner cut my hand off than offend you. Just tell me, don't let me go on not even knowing what it is.'

'I really don't know what you're talking about. "Tell you how you've offended me?" Why should you have OFFENDED me?'

'But I must have! After the way you behaved!'

'"After the way I behaved?" I don't know what you mean. I don't know why you're talking in this extraordinary way at all.'

'But you won't even speak to me! This morning you cut me absolutely dead.'

'Surely I can do as I like without being questioned?'

'But please, please! Don't you see, you must see, what it's like for me to be snubbed all of a sudden. After all, only last night you—'

She turned pink. 'I think it's absolutely—absolutely caddish of you to mention such things!'

'I know, I know. I know all that. But what else can I do? You walked past me this morning as though I'd been a stone. I know that I've offended you in some way. Can you blame me if I want to know what it is that I've done?'

He was, as usual, making it worse with every word he said. He perceived that whatever he had done, to be made to speak of it seemed to her worse than the thing itself. She was not going to explain. She was going to leave him in the dark—snub him and then pretend that nothing had happened; the natural feminine move. Nevertheless he urged her again:

'Please tell me. I can't let everything end between us like this.'

'"End between us"? There was nothing to end,' she said coldly.

The vulgarity of this remark wounded him, and he said quickly:

'That wasn't like you, Elizabeth! It's not generous to cut a man dead after you've been kind to him, and then refuse even to tell him the reason. You might be straightforward with me. Please tell me what it is that I've done.'

She gave him an oblique, bitter look, bitter not because of what he had done, but because he had made her speak of it. But perhaps she was anxious to end the scene, and she said:

'Well then, if you absolutely force me to speak of it—'

'Yes?'

'I'm told that at the very same time as you were pretending to— well, when you were . . . with me—oh, it's too beastly! I can't speak of it.'

'Go on.'

'I'm told that you're keeping a Burmese woman. And now, will you please let me pass?'

With that she sailed—there was no other possible word for it—she sailed past him with a swish of her short skirts, and vanished into the card-room. And he remained looking after her, too appalled to speak, and looking unutterably ridiculous.

It was dreadful. He could not face her after that. He turned to hurry out of the Club, and then dared not even pass the door of the card-room, lest she should see him. He went into the lounge, wondering how to escape, and finally climbed over the veranda rail and dropped on to the small square of lawn that ran down to the Irrawaddy. The sweat was running from his forehead. He could have shouted with anger and distress. The accursed luck of it! To be caught out over a thing like that. 'Keeping a Burmese woman'—and it was not even true! But much use it would ever be to deny it. Ah, what damned, evil chance could have brought it to her ears?

But as a matter of fact, it was no chance. It had a perfectly sound cause, which was also the cause of Mrs Lackersteen's curious behaviour at the Club this evening. On the previous night, just before the earthquake, Mrs Lackersteen had been reading the Civil List. The Civil List (which tells you the exact income of every official in Burma) was a source of inexhaustible interest to her. She was in the middle of adding up the pay and allowances of a Conservator of Forests whom she had once met in Mandalay, when it occurred to her to look up the name of Lieutenant Verrall, who, she had heard from Mr Macregor, was arriving at Kyauktada tomorrow with a hundred Military Policemen. When she found the name, she saw in front of it two words that startled her almost out of her wits.

The words were 'The Honourable'!

The HONOURABLE! Lieutenants the Honourable are rare anywhere, rare as diamonds in the Indian Army, rare as dodos in Burma. And when you are the aunt of the only marriageable young woman within fifty miles, and you hear that a lieutenant the Honourable is arriving no later than tomorrow—well! With dismay Mrs Lackersteen remembered that Elizabeth was out in the garden with Flory—that drunken wretch Flory, whose pay was barely seven hundred rupees a month, and who, it was only too probable, was already proposing to her! She hastened immediately to call Elizabeth inside, but at this moment the earthquake intervened. However, on the way home there was an opportunity to speak. Mrs Lackersteen laid her hand affectionately on Elizabeth's arm and said in the tenderest voice she had ever succeeded in producing:

'Of course you know, Elizabeth dear, that Flory is keeping a Burmese woman?'

For a moment this deadly charge actually failed to explode. Elizabeth was so new to the ways of the country that the remark made no impression on her. It sounded hardly more significant than 'keeping a parrot'.

'Keeping a Burmese woman? What for?'

'What FOR? My dear! what DOES a man keep a woman for?'

And, of course, that was that.

For a long time Flory remained standing by the river bank. The moon was up, mirrored in the water like a broad shield of electron. The coolness of the outer air had changed Flory's mood. He had not even the heart to be angry any longer. For he had perceived, with the deadly self-knowledge and self-loathing that come to one at such a time, that what had happened served him perfectly right. For a moment it seemed to him that an endless procession of Burmese women, a regiment of ghosts, were marching past him in the moonlight. Heavens, what numbers of them! A thousand—no, but a full hundred at the least. 'Eyes right!' he thought despondently. Their heads turned towards him, but they had no faces, only featureless discs. He remembered a blue longyi here, a pair of ruby ear-rings there, but hardly a face or a name. The gods are just and of our pleasant vices (pleasant, indeed!) make instruments to plague us. He had dirtied himself beyond redemption, and this was his just punishment.

He made his way slowly through the croton bushes and round the clubhouse. He was too saddened to feel the full pain of the disaster yet. It would begin hurting, as all deep wounds do, long afterwards. As he passed through the gate something stirred the leaves behind him. He started. There was a whisper of harsh Burmese syllables.

'Pike-san pay-like! Pike-san pay-like!'

He turned sharply. The 'pike-san pay-like' ('Give me the money') was repeated. He saw a woman standing under the shadow of the gold mohur tree. It was Ma Hla May. She stepped out into the moonlight warily, with a hostile air, keeping her distance as though afraid that he would strike her. Her face was coated with powder, sickly white in the moon, and it looked as ugly as a skull, and defiant.

She had given him a shock. 'What the devil are you doing here?' he said angrily in English.

'Pike-san pay-like!'

'What money? What do you mean? Why are you following me about like this?'

'Pike-san pay-like!' she repeated almost in a scream. 'The money you promised me, thakin. You said you would give me more money. I want it now, this instant!'

'How can I give it you now? You shall have it next month. I have given you a hundred and fifty rupees already.'

To his alarm she began shrieking 'Pike-san pay-like!' and a number of similar phrases almost at the top of her voice. She seemed on the verge of hysterics. The volume of noise that she produced was startling.

'Be quiet! They'll hear you in the Club!' he exclaimed, and was instantly sorry for putting the idea into her head.

'Aha! NOW I know what will frighten you! Give me the money this instant, or I will scream for help and bring them all out here. Quick, now, or I begin screaming!'

'You bitch!' he said, and took a step towards her. She sprang nimbly out of reach, whipped off her slipper, and stood defying him.

'Be quick! Fifty rupees now and the rest tomorrow. Out with it! Or I give a scream they can hear as far as the bazaar!'

Flory swore. This was not the time for such a scene. Finally he took out his pocket-book, found twenty-five rupees in it, and threw them on to the ground. Ma Hla May pounced on the notes and counted them.

'I said fifty rupees, thakin!'

'How can I give it you if I haven't got it? Do you think I carry hundreds of rupees about with me?'

'I said fifty rupees!'

'Oh, get out of my way!' he said in English, and pushed past her.

But the wretched woman would not leave him alone. She began to follow him up the road like a disobedient dog, screaming out 'Pike-san pay-like! Pike-san pay-like!' as though mere noise could bring the money into existence. He hurried, partly to draw her away from the Club, partly in hopes of shaking her off, but she seemed ready to follow him as far as the house if necessary. After a while he could not stand it any longer, and he turned to drive her back.

'Go away this instant! If you follow me any farther you shall never have another anna.'

'Pike-san pay-like!'

'You fool,' he said, 'what good is this doing? How can I give you the money when I have not another pice on me?'

'That is a likely story!'

He felt helplessly in his pockets. He was so wearied that he would have given her anything to be rid of her. His fingers encountered his cigarette-case, which was of gold. He took it out.

'Here, if I give you this will you go away? You can pawn it for thirty rupees.'

Ma Hla May seemed to consider, then said sulkily, 'Give it me.'

He threw the cigarette-case on to the grass beside the road. She grabbed it and immediately sprang back clutching it to her ingyi, as though afraid that he would take it away again. He turned and made for the house, thanking God to be out of the sound of her voice. The cigarette-case was the same one that she had stolen ten days ago.

At the gate he looked back. Ma Hla May was still standing at the bottom of the hill, a greyish figurine in the moonlight. She must have watched him up the hill like a dog watching a suspicious stranger out of sight. It was queer. The thought crossed his mind, as it had a few days earlier when she sent him the blackmailing letter, that her behaviour had been curious and unlike herself. She was showing a tenacity of which he would never have thought her capable—almost, indeed, as though someone else were egging her on.

Chapter 18

After the row overnight Ellis was looking forward to a week of baiting Flory. He had nicknamed him Nancy—short for nigger's Nancy Boy, but the women did not know that—and was already inventing wild scandals about him. Ellis always invented scandals about anyone with whom he had quarrelled—scandals which grew, by repeated embroideries, into a species of saga. Flory's incautious remark that Dr Veraswami was a 'damned good fellow' had swelled before long into a whole Daily Worker-ful of blasphemy and sedition.

'On my honour, Mrs Lackersteen,' said Ellis—Mrs Lackersteen had taken a sudden dislike to Flory after discovering the great secret about Verrall, and she was quite ready to listen to Ellis's tales— 'on my honour, if you'd been there last night and heard the things that man Flory was saying—well, it'd have made you shiver in your shoes!'

'Really! You know, I always thought he had such CURIOUS ideas. What has he been talking about now? Not SOCIALISM, I hope?'

'Worse.'

There were long recitals. However, to Ellis's disappointment, Flory had not stayed in Kyauktada to be baited. He had gone back to camp the day after his dismissal by Elizabeth. Elizabeth heard most of the scandalous tales about him. She understood his character perfectly now. She understood why it was that he had so often bored her and irritated her. He was a highbrow—her deadliest word—a highbrow, to be classed with Lenin, A. J. Cook and the dirty little poets in the Montparnasse cafes. She could have forgiven him even his Burmese mistress more easily than that. Flory wrote to her three days later; a weak, stilted letter, which he sent by hand—his camp was a day's march from Kyauktada. Elizabeth did not answer.

It was lucky for Flory that at present he was too busy to have time to think. The whole camp was at sixes and sevens since his long absence. Nearly thirty coolies were missing, the sick elephant was worse than ever, and a vast pile of teak logs which should have been sent off ten days earlier were still waiting because the engine would not work. Flory, a fool about machinery, struggled with the bowels of the engine until he was black with grease and Ko S'la told him sharply that white men ought not to do 'coolie-work'. The engine was finally persuaded to run, or at least to totter. The sick elephant was discovered to be suffering from tapeworms. As for the coolies, they had deserted because their supply of opium had been cut off—they would not stay in the jungle without opium, which they took as a prophylactic against fever. U Po Kyin, willing to do Flory a bad turn, had caused the Excise Officers to make a raid and seize the opium. Flory wrote to Dr Veraswami, asking for his help. The doctor sent back a quantity of opium, illegally procured, medicine for the elephant and a careful letter of instructions. A tapeworm measuring twenty-one feet was extracted. Flory was busy twelve hours a day. In the evening if there was no more to do he would plunge into the jungle and walk and walk until the sweat stung his eyes and his knees were bleeding from the briers. The nights were his bad time. The bitterness of what had happened was sinking into him, as it usually does, by slow degrees.

Meanwhile, several days had passed and Elizabeth had not yet seen Verrall at less than a hundred yards' distance. It had been a great disappointment when he had not appeared at the Club on the evening of his arrival. Mr Lackersteen was really quite angry when he discovered that he had been hounded into his dinner-jacket for nothing. Next morning Mrs Lackersteen made her husband send an officious note to the dakbungalow, inviting Verrall to the Club; there was no answer, however. More days passed, and Verrall made no move to join in the local society. He had even neglected his official calls, not even bothering to present himself at Mr Macgregor's office. The dakbungalow was at the other end of the town, near the station, and he had made himself quite comfortable there. There is a rule that one must vacate a dakbungalow after a stated number of days, but Verrall peaceably ignored it. The Europeans only saw him at morning and evening on the maidan. On the second day after his arrival fifty of his men turned out with sickles and cleared a large patch of the maidan, after which Verrall was to be seen galloping to and fro, practising polo strokes. He took not the smallest notice of any Europeans who passed down the road. Westfield and Ellis were furious, and even Mr Macgregor said that Verrall's behaviour was 'ungracious'. They would all have fallen at the feet of a lieutenant the Honourable if he had shown the smallest courtesy; as it was, everyone except the two women detested him from the start. It is always so with titled people, they are either adored or hated. If they accept one it is charming simplicity, if they ignore one it is loathsome snobbishness; there are no half-measures.

Verrall was the youngest son of a peer, and not at all rich, but by the method of seldom paying a bill until a writ was issued against him, he managed to keep himself in the only things he seriously cared about:

clothes and horses. He had come out to India in a British cavalry regiment, and exchanged into the Indian Army because it was cheaper and left him greater freedom for polo. After two years his debts were so enormous that he entered the Burma Military Police, in which it was notoriously possible to save money; however, he detested Burma—it is no country for a horseman— and he had already applied to go back to his regiment. He was the kind of soldier who can get exchanges when he wants them. Meanwhile, he was only to be in Kyauktada for a month, and he had no intention of mixing himself up with all the petty sahiblog of the district. He knew the society of those small Burma stations—a nasty, poodle-faking, horseless riffraff. He despised them.

They were not the only people whom Verrall despised, however. His various contempts would take a long time to catalogue in detail. He despised the entire non-military population of India, a few famous polo players excepted. He despised the entire Army as well, except the cavalry. He despised all Indian regiments, infantry and cavalry alike. It was true that he himself belonged to a native regiment, but that was only for his own convenience. He took no interest in Indians, and his Urdu consisted mainly of swear-words, with all the verbs in the third person singular. His Military Policemen he looked on as no better than coolies. 'Christ, what God-forsaken swine!' he was often heard to mutter as he moved down the ranks inspecting, with the old subahdar carrying his sword behind him. Verrall had even been in trouble once for his outspoken opinions on native troops. It was at a review, and Verrall was among the group of officers standing behind the general. An Indian infantry regiment approached for the march-past.

'The —— Rifles,' somebody said.

'AND look at it,' said Verrall in his surly boy's voice.

The white-haired colonel of the —— Rifles was standing near. He flushed to the neck, and reported Verrall to the general. Verrall was reprimanded, but the general, a British Army officer himself, did not rub it in very hard. Somehow, nothing very serious ever did happen to Verrall, however offensive he made himself. Up and down India, wherever he was stationed, he left behind him a trail of insulted people, neglected duties and unpaid bills. Yet the disgraces that ought to have fallen on him never did. He bore a charmed life, and it was not only the handle to his name that saved him. There was something in his eye before which duns, burra memsahibs and even colonels quailed.

It was a disconcerting eye, pale blue and a little protuberant, but exceedingly clear. It looked you over, weighed you in the balance and found you wanting, in a single cold scrutiny of perhaps five seconds. If you were the right kind of man—that is, if you were a cavalry officer and a polo player—Verrall took you for granted and even treated you with a surly respect; if you were any other type of man whatever, he despised you so utterly that he could not have hidden it even if he would. It did not even make any difference whether you were rich or poor, for in the social sense he was not more than normally a snob. Of course, like all sons of rich families, he thought poverty disgusting and that poor people are poor because they prefer disgusting habits. But he despised soft living. Spending, or rather owing, fabulous sums on clothes, he yet lived almost as ascetically as a monk. He exercised himself ceaselessly and brutally, rationed his drink and his cigarettes, slept on a camp bed (in silk pyjamas) and bathed in cold water in the bitterest winter. Horsemanship and physical fitness were the only gods he knew. The stamp of hoofs on the maidan, the strong, poised feeling of his body, wedded centaurlike to the saddle, the polo-stick springy in his hand—these were his religion, the breath of his life. The Europeans in Burma—boozing, womanizing, yellow-faced loafers—made him physically sick when he thought of their habits. As for social duties of all descriptions, he called them poodle-faking and ignored them. Women he abhorred. In his view they were a kind of siren whose one aim was to lure men away from polo and enmesh them in tea-fights and tennis-parties. He was not, however, quite proof against women. He was young, and women of nearly all kinds threw themselves at his head; now and again he succumbed. But his lapses soon disgusted him, and he was too callous when the pinch came to have any difficulty about escaping. He had had perhaps a dozen such escapes during his two years in India.

A whole week went by. Elizabeth had not even succeeded in making Verrall's acquaintance. It was so tantalizing! Every day, morning and evening, she and her aunt walked down to the Club and back again, past the maidan; and there was Verrall, hitting the polo-balls the sepoys threw for him, ignoring the two women utterly. So near and yet so far! What made it even worse was that neither woman would have considered it decent to speak of the matter directly. One evening the polo-ball, struck too hard, came swishing through the grass and rolled across the road in front of them. Elizabeth and her aunt stopped involuntarily. But it was only a sepoy who ran to fetch the ball. Verrall had seen the women and kept his distance.

Next morning Mrs Lackersteen paused as they came out of the gate. She had given up riding in her rickshaw lately. At the bottom of the maidan the Military Policemen were drawn up, a dust-coloured rank with bayonets glittering. Verrall was facing them, but not in uniform—he seldom put on his uniform for morning parade, not thinking it necessary with mere Military Policemen. The two women were looking at everything except Verrall, and at the same time, in some manner, were contriving to look at him.

'The wretched thing is,' said Mrs Lackersteen—this was a propos de bottes, but the subject needed no introduction—'the wretched thing is that I'm afraid your uncle simply MUST go back to camp before long.'

'Must he really?'

'I'm afraid so. It is so HATEFUL in camp at this time of year! Oh, those mosquitoes!'

'Couldn't he stay a bit longer? A week, perhaps?'

'I don't see how he can. He's been nearly a month in headquarters now. The firm would be furious if they heard of it. And of course both of us will have to go with him. SUCH a bore! The mosquitoes— simply terrible!'

Terrible indeed! To have to go away before Elizabeth had so much as said how-do-you-do to Verrall! But they would certainly have to go if Mr Lackersteen went. It would never do to leave him to himself. Satan finds some mischief still, even in the jungle. A ripple like fire ran down the line of sepoys; they were unfixing bayonets before marching away. The dusty rank turned left, saluted, and marched off in columns of fours. The orderlies were coming from the police lines with the ponies and polo-sticks. Mrs Lackersteen took a heroic decision.

'I think,' she said, 'we'll take a short-cut across the maidan. It's SO much quicker than going right round by the road.'

It WAS quicker by about fifty yards, but no one ever went that way on foot, because of the grass-seeds that got into one's stockings. Mrs Lackersteen plunged boldly into the grass, and then, dropping even the pretence of making for the Club, took a bee-line for Verrall, Elizabeth following. Either woman would have died on the rack rather than admit that she was doing anything but take a short-cut. Verrall saw them coming, swore, and reined in his pony. He could not very well cut them dead now that they were coming openly to accost him. The damned cheek of these women! He rode slowly towards them with a sulky expression on his face, chivvying the polo-ball with small strokes.

'Good morning, Mr Verrall!' Mrs Lackersteen called out in a voice of saccharine, twenty yards away.

'Morning!' he returned surlily, having seen her face and set her down as one of the usual scraggy old boiling-fowls of an Indian station.

The next moment Elizabeth came level with her aunt. She had taken off her spectacles and was swinging her Terai hat on her hand. What did she care for sunstroke? She was perfectly aware of the prettiness of her cropped hair. A puff of wind—oh, those blessed breaths of wind, coming from nowhere in the stifling hot-weather days!—had caught her cotton frock and blown it against her, showing the outline of her body, slender and strong like a tree. Her sudden appearance beside the older, sun-scorched woman was a revelation to Verrall. He started so that the Arab mare felt it and would have reared on her hind legs, and he had to tighten the rein. He had not known until this moment, not having bothered to inquire, that there were any YOUNG women in Kyauktada.

'My niece,' Mrs Lackersteen said.

He did not answer, but he had thrown away the polo-stick, and he took off his topi. For a moment he and Elizabeth remained gazing at one another. Their fresh faces were unmarred in the pitiless light. The grass-seeds were tickling Elizabeth's shins so that it was agony, and without her spectacles she could only see Verrall and his horse as a whitish blur. But she was happy, happy! Her heart bounded and the blood flowed into her face, dyeing it like a thin wash of aquarelle. The thought, 'A peach, by

Christ!' moved almost fiercely through Verrall's mind. The sullen Indians, holding the ponies' heads, gazed curiously at the scene, as though the beauty of the two young people had made its impression even on them.

Mrs Lackersteen broke the silence, which had lasted half a minute.

'You know, Mr Verrall,' she said somewhat archly, 'we think it RATHER unkind of you to have neglected us poor people all this time. When we're so PINING for a new face at the Club.'

He was still looking at Elizabeth when he answered, but the change in his voice was remarkable.

'I've been meaning to come for some days. Been so fearfully busy—getting my men into their quarters and all that. I'm sorry,' he added—he was not in the habit of apologizing, but really, he had decided, this girl was rather an exceptional bit of stuff—'I'm sorry about not answering your note.'

'Oh, not at all! We QUITE understood. But we do hope we shall see you at the Club this evening! Because, you know,' she concluded even more archly, 'if you disappoint us any longer, we shall begin to think you rather a NAUGHTY young man!'

'I'm sorry,' he repeated. 'I'll be there this evening.'

There was not much more to be said, and the two women walked on to the Club. But they stayed barely five minutes. The grass-seeds were causing their shins such torment that they were obliged to hurry home and change their stockings at once.

Verrall kept his promise and was at the Club that evening. He arrived a little earlier than the others, and he had made his presence thoroughly felt before being in the place five minutes. As Ellis entered the Club the old butler darted out of the card-room and waylaid him. He was in great distress, the tears rolling down his cheeks.

'Sir! Sir!'

'What the devil's the matter now!' said Ellis.

'Sir! Sir! New master been beating me, sir!'

'What?'

'BEATING me sir!' His voice rose on the 'beating' with a long tearful wail—'be-e-e-eating!'

'Beating you? Do you good. Who's been beating you?'

'New master, sir. Military Police sahib. Beating me with his foot, sir—HERE!' He rubbed himself behind.

'Hell!' said Ellis.

He went into the lounge. Verrall was reading the Field, and invisible except for Palm Beach trouser-ends and two lustrous sooty-brown shoes. He did not trouble to stir at hearing someone else come into the room. Ellis halted.

'Here, you—what's your name—Verrall!'

'What?'

'Have you been kicking our butler?'

Verrall's sulky blue eye appeared round the corner of the Field, like the eye of a crustacean peering round a rock.

'What?' he repeated shortly.

'I said, have you been kicking our bloody butler?'

'Yes.'

'Then what the hell do you mean by it?'

'Beggar gave me his lip. I sent him for a whisky and soda, and he brought it warm. I told him to put ice in it, and he wouldn't— talked some bloody rot about saving the last pieces of ice. So I kicked his bottom. Serve him right.'

Ellis turned quite grey. He was furious. The butler was a piece of Club property and not to be kicked by strangers. But what most angered Ellis was the thought that Verrall quite possibly suspected him of being SORRY for the butler—in fact, of disapproving of kicking AS SUCH.

'Serve him right? I dare say it bloody well did serve him right. But what in hell's that got to do with it? Who are YOU to come kicking our servants?'

'Bosh, my good chap. Needed kicking. You've let your servants get out of hand here.'

'You damned, insolent young tick, what's it got to do with YOU if he needed kicking? You're not even a member of this Club. It's our job to kick the servants, not yours.'

Verrall lowered the Field and brought his other eye into play. His surly voice did not change its tone. He never lost his temper with a European; it was never necessary.

'My good chap, if anyone gives me lip I kick his bottom. Do you want me to kick yours?'

All the fire went out of Ellis suddenly. He was not afraid, he had never been afraid in his life; only, Verrall's eye was too much for him. That eye could make you feel as though you were under Niagara! The oaths wilted on Ellis's lips; his voice almost deserted him. He said querulously and even plaintively:

'But damn it, he was quite right not to give you the last bit of ice. Do you think we only buy ice for you? We can only get the stuff twice a week in this place.'

'Rotten bad management on your part, then,' said Verrall, and retired behind the Field, content to let the matter drop.

Ellis was helpless. The calm way in which Verrall went back to his paper, quite genuinely forgetting Ellis's existence, was maddening. Should he not give the young swab a good, rousing kick?

But somehow, the kick was never given. Verrall had earned many kicks in his life, but he had never received one and probably never would. Ellis seeped helplessly back to the card-room, to work off his feelings on the butler, leaving Verrall in possession of the lounge.

As Mr Macgregor entered the Club gate he heard the sound of music. Yellow chinks of lantern-light showed through the creeper that covered the tennis-screen. Mr Macgregor was in a happy mood this evening. He had promised himself a good, long talk with Miss Lackersteen—such an exceptionally intelligent girl, that!—and he had a most interesting anecdote to tell her (as a matter of fact, it had already seen the light in one of those little articles of his in Blackwood's) about a dacoity that had happened in Sagaing in 1913. She would love to hear it, he knew. He rounded the tennis-screen expectantly. On the court, in the mingled light of the waning moon and of lanterns slung among the trees, Verrall and Elizabeth were dancing. The chokras had brought out chairs and a table for the gramophone, and round these the other Europeans were sitting or standing. As Mr Macgregor halted at the corner of the court, Verrall and Elizabeth circled round and glided past him, barely a yard away. They were dancing very close together, her body bent backwards under his. Neither noticed Mr Macgregor.

Mr Macgregor made his way round the court. A chilly, desolate feeling had taken possession of his entrails. Good-bye, then, to his talk with Miss Lackersteen! It was an effort to screw his face into its usual facetious good-humour as he came up to the table.

'A Terpsichorean evening!' he remarked in a voice that was doleful in spite of himself.

No one answered. They were all watching the pair on the tennis court. Utterly oblivious of the others, Elizabeth and Verrall glided round and round, round and round, their shoes sliding easily on the slippery concrete. Verrall danced as he rode, with matchless grace. The gramophone was playing 'Show Me the Way to Go Home,' which was then going round the world like a pestilence and had got as far as Burma:

'Show me the way to go home, I'm tired an' I wanna go to bed; I had a little drink 'bout an hour ago, An' it's gone right TO my head!' etc.

The dreary, depressing trash floated out among the shadowy trees and the streaming scents of flowers, over and over again, for Mrs Lackersteen was putting the gramophone needle back to the start when it neared the centre. The moon climbed higher, very yellow, looking, as she rose from the murk of dark clouds at the horizon, like a sick woman creeping out of bed. Verrall and Elizabeth danced on and on, indefatigably, a pale voluptuous shape in the gloom. They moved in perfect unison like some single animal. Mr Macgregor, Ellis, Westfield and Mr Lackersteen stood watching them, their hands in their pockets, finding nothing to say. The mosquitoes came nibbling at their ankles. Someone called for drinks, but the whisky was like ashes in their mouths. The bowels of all four older men were twisted with bitter envy.

Verrall did not ask Mrs Lackersteen for a dance, nor, when he and Elizabeth finally sat down, did he take any notice of the other Europeans. He merely monopolized Elizabeth for half an hour more, and then, with a brief good night to the Lackersteens and not a word to anyone else, left the Club. The long dance with Verrall had left Elizabeth in a kind of dream. He had asked her to come out riding with him! He was going to lend her one of his ponies! She never even noticed that Ellis, angered by her behaviour, was doing his best to be openly rude. It was late when the Lackersteens got home, but there was no sleep yet for Elizabeth or her aunt. They were feverishly at work till midnight, shortening a pair of Mrs Lackersteen's jodhpurs, and letting out the calves, to fit Elizabeth.

'I hope, dear, you CAN ride a horse?' said Mrs Lackersteen.

'Oh, of course! I've ridden ever such a lot, at home.'

She had ridden perhaps a dozen times in all, when she was sixteen. No matter, she would manage somehow! She would have ridden a tiger, if Verrall were to accompany her.

When at last the jodhpurs were finished and Elizabeth had tried them on, Mrs Lackersteen sighed to see her. She looked ravishing in jodhpurs, simply ravishing! And to think that in only a day or two they had got to go back to camp, for weeks, months perhaps, leaving Kyauktada and this most DESIRABLE young man! The pity of it! As they moved to go upstairs Mrs Lackersteen paused at the door. It had come into her head to make a great and painful sacrifice. She took Elizabeth by the shoulders and kissed her with a more real affection than she had ever shown.

'My dear, it would be such a SHAME for you to go away from Kyauktada just now!'

'It would, rather.'

‘Then I’ll tell you what, dear. We WON’T go back to that horrid jungle! Your uncle shall go alone. You and I shall stay in Kyauktada.’

Chapter 19

The heat was growing worse and worse. April was nearly over, but there was no hope of rain for another three weeks, five weeks it might be. Even the lovely transient dawns were spoiled by the thought of the long, blinding hours to come, when one's head would ache and the glare would penetrate through every covering and glue up one's eyelids with restless sleep. No one, Oriental or European, could keep awake in the heat of the day without a struggle; at night, on the other hand, with the howling dogs and the pools of sweat that collected and tormented one's prickly heat, no one could sleep. The mosquitoes at the Club were so bad that sticks of incense had to be kept burning in all the corners, and the women sat with their legs in pillowslips. Only Verrall and Elizabeth were indifferent to the heat. They were young and their blood was fresh, and Verrall was too stoical and Elizabeth too happy to pay any attention to the climate.

There was much bickering and scandal-mongering at the Club these days. Verrall had put everyone's nose out of joint. He had taken to coming to the Club for an hour or two in the evenings, but he ignored the other members, refused the drinks they offered him, and answered attempts at conversation with surly monosyllables. He would sit under the punkah in the chair that had once been sacred to Mrs Lackersteen, reading such of the papers as interested him, until Elizabeth came, when he would dance and talk with her for an hour or two and then make off without so much as a good-night to anybody. Meanwhile Mr Lackersteen was alone in his camp, and, according to the rumours which drifted back to Kyauktada, consoling loneliness with quite a miscellany of Burmese women.

Elizabeth and Verrall went out riding together almost every evening now. Verrall's mornings, after parade, were sacred to polo practice, but he had decided that it was worth while giving up the evenings to Elizabeth. She took naturally to riding, just as she had to shooting; she even had the assurance to tell Verrall that she had 'hunted quite a lot' at home. He saw at a glance that she was lying, but at least she did not ride so badly as to be a nuisance to him.

They used to ride up the red road into the jungle, ford the stream by the big pyinkado tree covered with orchids, and then follow the narrow cart-track, where the dust was soft and the horses could gallop. It was stifling hot in the dusty jungle, and there were always mutterings of faraway, rainless thunder. Small martins flitted round the horses, keeping pace with them, to hawk for the flies their hooves turned up. Elizabeth rode the bay pony, Verrall the white. On the way home they would walk their sweat-dark horses abreast, so close sometimes his knee brushed against hers, and talk. Verrall could drop his offensive manner and talk amicably enough when he chose, and he did choose with Elizabeth.

Ah, the joy of those rides together! The joy of being on horseback and in the world of horses—the world of hunting and racing, polo and pigsticking! If Elizabeth had loved Verrall for nothing else, she would have loved him for bringing horses into her life. She tormented him to talk about horses as once she had tormented Flory to talk about shooting. Verrall was no talker, it was true. A few gruff, jerky sentences about polo and pigsticking, and a catalogue of Indian stations and the names of regiments, were the best he could do. And yet somehow the little he said could thrill Elizabeth as all Flory's talk had never done. The mere sight of him on horseback was more evocative than any words. An aura of horsemanship and soldiering surrounded him. In his tanned face and his hard, straight body Elizabeth saw all the romance, the splendid panache of a cavalryman's life. She saw the North-West Frontier and the Cavalry Club—she saw the polo grounds and the parched barrack yards, and the brown squadrons of horsemen galloping with their long lances poised and the trains of their pagris streaming; she heard the bugle-calls and the jingle of spurs, and the regimental bands playing outside the messrooms while the officers sat at dinner in their stiff, gorgeous uniforms. How splendid it was, that equestrian world, how splendid! And it was HER world, she belonged to it, she had been born of it. These days, she lived, thought, dreamed horses, almost like Verrall himself. The time came when she not only TOLD her taradiddle about having 'hunted quite a lot', she even came near believing it.

In every possible way they got on so well together. He never bored her and fretted her as Flory had done. (As a matter of fact, she had almost forgotten Flory, these days; when she thought of him, it was for some reason always his birthmark that she remembered.) It was a bond between them that Verrall detested anything 'highbrow' even more than she did. He told her once that he had not read a book since he was eighteen, and that indeed he 'loathed' books; 'except, of course, Jorrocks and all that'. On the evening of their third or fourth ride they were parting at the Lackersteens' gate. Verrall had successfully resisted all Mrs Lackersteen's invitations to meals; he had not yet set foot inside the Lackersteens' house, and he did not intend to do so. As the syce was taking Elizabeth's pony, Verrall said:

‘I tell you what. Next time we come out you shall ride Belinda. I’ll ride the chestnut. I think you’ve got on well enough not to go and cut Belinda’s mouth up.’

Belinda was the Arab mare. Verrall had owned her two years, and till this moment he had never once allowed anyone else to mount her, not even the syce. It was the greatest favour that he could imagine. And so perfectly did Elizabeth appreciate Verrall’s point of view that she understood the greatness of the favour, and was thankful.

The next evening, as they rode home side by side, Verrall put his arm round Elizabeth’s shoulder, lifted her out of the saddle and pulled her against him. He was very strong. He dropped the bridle, and with his free hand, lifted her face up to meet his; their mouths met. For a moment he held her so, then lowered her to the ground and slipped from his horse. They stood embraced, their thin, drenched shirts pressed together, the two bridles held in the crook of his arm.

It was about the same time that Flory, twenty miles away, decided to come back to Kyauktada. He was standing at the jungle’s edge by the bank of a dried-up stream, where he had walked to tire himself, watching some tiny, nameless finches eating the seeds of the tall grasses. The cocks were chrome-yellow, the hens like hen sparrows. Too tiny to bend the stalks, they came whirring towards them, seized them in midflight and bore them to the ground by their own weight. Flory watched the birds incuriously, and almost hated them because they could light no spark of interest in him. In his idleness he flung his dah at them, scaring them away. If she were here, if she were here! Everything— birds, trees, flowers, everything—was deadly and meaningless because she was not here. As the days passed the knowledge that he had lost her had grown surer and more actual until it poisoned every moment.

He loitered a little way into the jungle, flicking at creepers with his dah. His limbs felt slack and leaden. He noticed a wild vanilla plant trailing over a bush, and bent down to sniff at its slender, fragrant pods. The scent brought him a feeling of staleness and deadly ennui. Alone, alone, in the sea of life enisled! The pain was so great that he struck his fist against a tree, jarring his arm and splitting two knuckles. He must go back to Kyauktada. It was folly, for barely a fortnight had passed since the scene between them, and his only chance was to give her time to forget it. Still, he must go back. He could not stay any longer in this deadly place, alone with his thoughts among the endless, mindless leaves.

A happy thought occurred to him. He could take Elizabeth the leopard-skin that was being cured for her in the jail. It would be a pretext for seeing her, and when one comes bearing gifts one is generally listened to. This time he would not let her cut him short without a word. He would explain, extenuate—make her realize that she had been unjust to him. It was not right that she should condemn him because of Ma Hla May, whom he had turned out of doors for Elizabeth's own sake. Surely she must forgive him when she heard the truth of the story? And this time she SHOULD hear it; he would force her to listen to him if he had to hold her by the arms while he did it.

He went back the same evening. It was a twenty-mile journey, by rutted cart-tracks, but Flory decided to march by night, giving the reason that it was cooler. The servants almost mutinied at the idea of a night-march, and at the very last moment old Sammy collapsed in a semi-genuine fit and had to be plied with gin before he could start. It was a moonless night. They made their way by the light of lanterns, in which Flo's eyes gleamed like emeralds and the bullocks' eyes like moonstones. When the sun was up the servants halted to gather sticks and cook breakfast, but Flory was in a fever to be at Kyauktada, and he hurried ahead. He had no feeling of tiredness. The thought of the leopard-skin had filled him with extravagant hopes. He crossed the glittering river by sampan and went straight to Dr Veraswami's bungalow, getting there about ten.

The doctor invited him to breakfast, and—having shooed the women into some suitable hiding-place—took him into his own bath-room so that he could wash and shave. At breakfast the doctor was very excited and full of denunciations of 'the crocodile'; for it appeared that the pseudo-rebellion was now on the point of breaking out. It was not till after breakfast that Flory had an opportunity to mention the leopard-skin.

'Oh, by the way, doctor. What about that skin I sent to the jail to be cured? Is it done yet?'

'Ah—' said the doctor in a slightly disconcerted manner, rubbing his nose. He went inside the house—they were breakfasting on the veranda, for the doctor's wife had protested violently against Flory being brought indoors—and came back in a moment with the skin rolled up in a bundle.

'Ass a matter of fact—' he began, unrolling it.

'Oh, doctor!'

The skin had been utterly ruined. It was as stiff as cardboard, with the leather cracked and the fur discoloured and even rubbed off in patches. It also stank abominably. Instead of being cured, it had been converted into a piece of rubbish.

'Oh, doctor! What a mess they've made of it! How the devil did it happen?'

'I am so sorry, my friend! I wass about to apologize. It wass the best we could do. There iss no one at the jail who knows how to cure skins now.'

'But, damn it, that convict used to cure them so beautifully!'

‘Ah, yes. But he iss gone from us these three weeks, alas.’

‘Gone? I thought he was doing seven years?’

‘What? Did you not hear, my friend? I thought you knew who it wass that used to cure the skins. It was Nga Shwe O.’

‘Nga Shwe O?’

‘The dacoit who escaped with U Po Kyin’s assistance.’

‘Oh, hell!’

The mishap had daunted him dreadfully. Nevertheless, in the afternoon, having bathed and put on a clean suit, he went up to the Lackersteens’ house, at about four. It was very early to call, but he wanted to make sure of catching Elizabeth before she went down to the Club. Mrs Lackersteen, who had been asleep and was not prepared for visitors, received him with an ill grace, not even asking him to sit down.

‘I’m afraid Elizabeth isn’t down yet. She’s dressing to go out riding. Wouldn’t it be better if you left a message?’

‘I’d like to see her, if you don’t mind. I’ve brought her the skin of that leopard we shot together.’

Mrs Lackersteen left him standing up in the drawing-room, feeling lumpish and abnormally large as one does at such times. However, she fetched Elizabeth, taking the opportunity of whispering to her outside the door: ‘Get rid of that dreadful man as soon as you can, dear. I can’t bear him about the house at this time of day.’

As Elizabeth entered the room Flory’s heart pounded so violently that a reddish mist passed behind his eyes. She was wearing a silk shirt and jodhpurs, and she was a little sunburned. Even in his memory she had never been so beautiful. He quailed; on the instant he was lost—every scrap of his screwed-up courage had fled. Instead of stepping forward to meet her he actually backed away. There was a fearful crash behind him; he had upset an occasional table and sent a bowl of zinnias hurtling across the floor.

'I'm so sorry!' he exclaimed in horror.

'Oh, not at ALL! PLEASE don't worry about it!'

She helped him to pick up the table, chattering all the while as gaily and easily as though nothing had happened: 'You HAVE been away a long time, Mr Flory! You're quite a STRANGER! We've SO missed you at the Club!' etc., etc. She was italicizing every other word, with that deadly, glittering brightness that a woman puts on when she is dodging a moral obligation. He was terrified of her. He could not even look her in the face. She took up a box of cigarettes and offered him one, but he refused it. His hand was shaking too much to take it.

'I've brought you that skin,' he said flatly.

He unrolled it on the table they had just picked up. It looked so shabby and miserable that he wished he had never brought it. She came close to him to examine the skin, so close that her flower-like cheek was not a foot from his own, and he could feel the warmth of her body. So great was his fear of her that he stepped hurriedly away. And in the same moment she too stepped back with a wince of disgust, having caught the foul odour of the skin. It shamed him terribly. It was almost as though it had been himself and not the skin that stank.

'Thank you EVER so much, Mr Flory!' She had put another yard between herself and the skin. 'Such a LOVELY big skin, isn't it?'

‘It was, but they’ve spoiled it, I’m afraid.’

‘Oh no! I shall love having it!—Are you back in Kyauktada for long? How dreadfully hot it must have been in camp!’

‘Yes, it’s been very hot.’

For three minutes they actually talked of the weather. He was helpless. All that he had promised himself to say, all his arguments and pleadings, had withered in his throat. ‘You fool, you fool,’ he thought, ‘what are you doing? Did you come twenty miles for this? Go on, say what you came to say! Seize her in your arms; make her listen, kick her, beat her—anything sooner than let her choke you with this drivel!’ But it was hopeless, hopeless. Not a word could his tongue utter except futile trivialities. How could he plead or argue, when that bright easy air of hers, that dragged every word to the level of Club-chatter silenced him before he spoke? Where do they learn it, that dreadful tee-heeing brightness? In these brisk modern girls’ schools, no doubt. The piece of carrion on the table made him more ashamed every moment. He stood there almost voiceless, lumpishly ugly with his face yellow and creased after the sleepless night, and his birthmark like a smear of dirt.

She got rid of him after a very few minutes. ‘And now, Mr Flory, if you DON’T mind, I ought really—’

He mumbled rather than said, ‘Won’t you come out with me again some time? Walking, shooting—something?’

‘I have so LITTLE time nowadays! ALL my evenings seem to be full. This evening I’m going out riding. With Mr Verrall,’ she added.

It was possible that she added that in order to wound him. This was the first that he had heard of her friendship with Verrall. He could not keep the dread, flat tone of envy out of his voice as he said:

'Do you go out riding much with Verrall?'

'Almost every evening. He's such a wonderful horseman! And he has absolute STRINGS of polo ponies!'

'Ah. And of course I have no polo ponies.'

It was the first thing he had said that even approached seriousness, and it did no more than offend her. However, she answered him with the same gay easy air as before, and then showed him out. Mrs Lackersteen came back to the drawing-room, sniffed the air, and immediately ordered the servants to take the reeking leopard-skin outside and burn it.

Flory lounged at his garden gate, pretending to feed the pigeons. He could not deny himself the pain of seeing Elizabeth and Verrall start on their ride. How vulgarly, how cruelly she had behaved to him! It is dreadful when people will not even have the decency to quarrel. Presently Verrall rode up to the Lackersteens' house on the white pony, with a syce riding the chestnut, then there was a pause, then they emerged together, Verrall on the chestnut pony, Elizabeth on the white, and trotted quickly up the hill. They were chattering and laughing, her silk-shirted shoulder very close to his. Neither looked towards Flory.

When they had disappeared into the jungle, Flory still loafed in the garden. The glare was waning to yellow. The mali was at work grubbing up the English flowers, most of which had died, slain by too much sunshine, and planting balsams, cockscombs, and more zinnias. An hour passed, and a melancholy, earth-coloured Indian loitered up the drive, dressed in a loin-cloth and a salmon-pink pagri on which a washing-basket was balanced. He laid down his basket and salaamed to Flory.

'Who are you?'

'Book-wallah, sahib.'

The book-wallah was an itinerant peddler of books who wandered from station to station throughout Upper Burma. His system of exchange was that for any book in his bundle you gave him four annas, and any other book. Not quite ANY book, however, for the book-wallah, though analphabetic, had learned to recognize and refuse a Bible.

'No, sahib,' he would say plaintively, 'no. This book (he would turn it over disapprovingly in his flat brown hands) this book with a black cover and gold letters—this one I cannot take. I know not how it is, but all sahibs are offering me this book, and none are taking it. What can it be that is in this black book? Some evil, undoubtedly.'

'Turn out your trash,' Flory said.

He hunted among them for a good thriller—Edgar Wallace or Agatha Christie or something; anything to still the deadly restlessness that was at his heart. As he bent over the books he saw that both Indians were exclaiming and pointing towards the edge of the jungle.

'Dekko!' said the mali in his plum-in-the-mouth voice.

The two ponies were emerging from the jungle. But they were riderless. They came trotting down the hill with the silly guilty air of a horse that has escaped from its master, with the stirrups swinging and clashing under their bellies.

Flory remained unconsciously clasping one of the books against his chest. Verrall and Elizabeth had dismounted. It was not an accident; by no effort of the mind could one imagine Verrall falling off his horse. They had dismounted, and the ponies had escaped.

They had dismounted—for what? Ah, but he knew for what! It was not a question of suspecting; he KNEW. He could see the whole thing happening, in one of those hallucinations that are so perfect in detail, so vilely obscene, that they are past bearing. He threw the book violently down and made for the house, leaving the book-wallah disappointed. The servants heard him moving about indoors, and presently he called for a bottle of whisky. He had a drink and it did him no good. Then he filled a tumbler two-thirds full, added enough water to make it drinkable, and swallowed it. The filthy, nauseous dose was no sooner down his throat than he repeated it. He had done the same thing in camp once, years ago, when he was tortured by toothache and three hundred miles from a dentist. At seven Ko S'la came in as usual to say that the bath-water was hot. Flory was lying in one of the long chairs, with his coat off and his shirt torn open at the throat.

'Your bath, thakin,' said Ko S'la.

Flory did not answer, and Ko S'la touched his arm, thinking him asleep. Flory was much too drunk to move. The empty bottle had rolled across the floor, leaving a trail of whisky-drops behind it. Ko S'la called for Ba Pe and picked up the bottle, clicking his tongue.

'Just look at this! He has drunk more than three-quarters of a bottle!'

'What, again? I thought he had given up drinking?'

'It is that accursed woman, I suppose. Now we must carry him carefully. You take his heels, I'll take his head. That's right. Hoist him up!'

They carried Flory into the other room and laid him gently on the bed.

'Is he really going to marry this "Ingaleikma"?' said Ba Pe.

'Heaven knows. She is the mistress of the young police officer at present, so I was told. Their ways are not our ways. I think I know what he will be wanting tonight,' he added as he undid Flory's braces—for Ko S'la had the art, so necessary in a bachelor's servant, of undressing his master without waking him.

The servants were rather more pleased than not to see this return to bachelor habits. Flory woke about midnight, naked in a pool of sweat. His head felt as though some large, sharp-cornered metal object were bumping about inside it. The mosquito net was up, and a young woman was sitting beside the bed fanning him with a wicker fan. She had an agreeable negroid face, bronze-gold in the candlelight. She explained that she was a prostitute, and that Ko S'la had engaged her on his own responsibility for a fee of ten rupees.

Flory's head was splitting. 'For God's sake get me something to drink,' he said feebly to the woman. She brought him some soda-water which Ko S'la had cooled in readiness and soaked a towel and put a wet compress round his forehead. She was a fat, good-tempered creature. She told him that her name was Ma Sein Galay, and that besides plying her other trade she sold paddy baskets in the bazaar near Li Yeik's shop. Flory's head felt better presently, and he asked for a cigarette; whereupon Ma Sein Galay, having fetched the cigarette, said naively, 'Shall I take my clothes off now, thakin?'

Why not? he thought dimly. He made room for her in the bed. But when he smelled the familiar scent of garlic and coco-nut oil, something painful happened within him, and with his head pillowed on Ma Sein Galay's fat shoulder he actually wept, a thing he had not done since he was fifteen years old.

Chapter 20

Next morning there was great excitement in Kyauktada, for the long-rumoured rebellion had at last broken out. Flory heard only a vague report of it at the time. He had gone back to camp as soon as he felt fit to march after the drunken night, and it was not until several days later that he learned the true history of the rebellion, in a long, indignant letter from Dr Veraswami.

The doctor's epistolary style was queer. His syntax was shaky and he was as free with capital letters as a seventeenth-century divine, while in the use of italics he rivalled Queen Victoria. There were eight pages of his small but sprawling handwriting.

MY DEAR FRIEND [the letter ran],—You will much regret to hear that the WILES OF THE CROCODILE have matured. The rebellion—the SO-CALLED rebellion—is all over and finished. And it has been, alas! a more Bloody affair than I had hoped should have been the case.

All has fallen out as I have prophesied to you it would be. On the day when you came back to Kyauktada U Po Kyin's SPIES have informed him that the poor unfortunate men whom he have Deluded are assembling in the jungle near Thongwa. The same night he sets out secretly with U Lugale, the Police Inspector, who is as great a Rogue as he, if that could be, and twelve constables. They make a swift raid upon Thongwa and surprise the rebels, of whom they are only Seven!! in a ruined field hut in the jungle. Also Mr Maxwell, who have heard rumours of the rebellion, came across from his camp bringing his Rifle and was in time to join U Po Kyin and the police in their attack on the hut. The next morning the clerk Ba Sein, who is U Po Kyin's JACKALL and DIRTY WORKER, have orders to raise the cry of rebellion as Sensationally as possible, which was done, and Mr Macgregor, Mr Westfield and Lieutenant Verrall all rush out to Thongwa carrying fifty sepoys armed with rifles besides Civil Police. But they arrive to find it is all over and U Po Kyin was sitting under a big teak tree in the middle of the village and PUTTING ON AIRS and lecturing the villages, whereat they are all bowing very frightened and touching the ground with their foreheads and swearing they will be forever loyal to the Government, and the rebellion is already at an end. The SO-CALLED weiksa, who is no other than a circus conjurer and the MINION of U Po Kyin, have vanished for parts unknown, but six rebels have been Caught. So there is an end.

Also I should inform you that there was most regrettably a Death. Mr Maxwell was I think TOO ANXIOUS to use his Rifle and when one of the rebels try to run away he fired and shoot him in the abdomen, at which he died. I think the villagers have some BAD FEELING towards Mr Maxwell because of it. But from the point of view legal all is well for Mr Maxwell, because the men were undoubtedly conspiring against the Government.

Ah, but, my Friend, I trust that you understand how disastrous may all this be for me! You will realise, I think, what is its bearing upon the Contest between U Po Kyin and myself, and the supreme LEG-UP it must give to him. It is the TRIUMPH OF THE CROCODILE. U Po Kyin is now the Hero of the district. He is the PET of the Europeans. I am told that even Mr Ellis has praised his conduct. If you could witness the abominable Conceitedness and the LIES he is now telling as to how there were not seven rebels but Two Hundred!! and how he crushed upon them revolver in hand—he who only directing operations from a SAFE DISTANCE while the police and Mr Maxwell creep up upon the hut—you would find is veritably Nauseous I assure you. He has had the effrontery to send in an official report of the matter which started, 'By my loyal promptitude and reckless daring', and I hear that positively he had had this Conglomeration of lies written out in readiness days BEFORE THE OCCURRENCE. It is Disgusting. And to think that now when he is at the Height of his triumph he will again begin to calumniate me with all the venom at his disposal etc. etc.

The rebels' entire stock of weapons had been captured. The armoury with which, when their followers were assembled, they had proposed to march upon Kyauktada, consisted of the following:

Item, one shotgun with a damaged left barrel, stolen from a Forest Officer three years earlier.

Item, six home-made guns with barrels of zinc piping stolen from the railway. These could be fired, after a fashion, by thrusting a nail through the touch-hole and striking it with a stone.

Item, thirty-nine twelve-bore cartridges.

Item, eleven dummy guns carved out of teakwood.

Item, some large Chinese crackers which were to have been fired in terrorem.

Later, two of the rebels were sentenced to fifteen years' transportation, three to three years' imprisonment and twenty-five lashes, and one to two years' imprisonment.

The whole miserable rebellion was so obviously at an end that the Europeans were not considered to be in any danger, and Maxwell had gone back to his camp unguarded. Flory intended to stay in camp until the rains broke, or at least until the general meeting at the Club. He had promised to be in for that, to propose the doctor's election; though now, with his own trouble to think of, the whole business of the intrigue between U Po Kyin and the doctor sickened him.

More weeks crawled by. The heat was dreadful now. The overdue rain seemed to have bred a fever in the air. Flory was out of health, and worked incessantly, worrying over petty jobs that should have been left to the overseer, and making the coolies and even the servants hate him. He drank gin at all hours, but not even drinking could distract him now. The vision of Elizabeth in Verrall's arms haunted him like a neuralgia or an earache. At any moment it would come upon him, vivid and disgusting, scattering his thoughts, wrenching him back from the brink of sleep, turning his food to dust in his mouth. At times he flew into savage rages, and once even struck Ko S'la. What was worse than all was the DETAIL—the always filthy detail—in which the imagined scene appeared. The very perfection of the detail seemed to prove that it was true.

Is there anything in the world more graceless, more dishonouring, than to desire a woman whom you will never have? Throughout all these weeks Flory's mind held hardly a thought which was not murderous or obscene. It is the common effect of jealousy. Once he had loved Elizabeth spiritually, sentimentally indeed, desiring her sympathy more than her caresses; now, when he had lost her, he was tormented by the basest physical longing. He did not even idealize her any longer. He saw her now almost as she was—silly, snobbish, heartless—and it made no difference to his longing for her. Does it ever make any difference? At nights when he lay awake, his bed dragged outside the tent for coolness, looking at the velvet dark from which the barking of a gyi sometimes sounded, he hated himself for the images that inhabited his mind. It was so base, this envying of the better man who had beaten him. For it was only envy—even jealousy was too good a name for it. What right had he to be jealous? He had offered himself to a girl who was too young and pretty for him, and she had turned him down— rightly. He had got the snub he deserved. Nor was there any appeal from that decision; nothing would ever make him young again, or take away his birthmark and his decade of lonely debaucheries. He could only stand and look on while the better man took her, and envy him, like—but the simile was not even mentionable. Envy is a horrible thing. It is unlike all other kinds of suffering in that there is no disguising it, no elevating it into tragedy. It is more than merely painful, it is disgusting.

But meanwhile, was it true, what he suspected? Had Verrall really become Elizabeth's lover? There is no knowing, but on the whole the chances were against it, for, had it been so, there would have been no concealing it in such a place as Kyauktada. Mrs Lackersteen would probably have guessed it, even if the others had not. One thing was certain, however, and that was that Verrall had as yet made no proposal of marriage. A week went by, two weeks, three weeks; three weeks is a very long time in a small Indian station. Verrall and Elizabeth rode together every evening, danced together every night; yet Verrall had never so much as entered the Lackersteens' house. There was endless scandal about Elizabeth, of course. All the Orientals of the town had taken it for granted that she was Verrall's mistress. U Po Kyin's version (he had a way of being essentially right even when he was wrong in detail) was that Elizabeth had been Flory's concubine and had deserted him for Verrall because Verrall paid her more. Ellis, too, was inventing tales about Elizabeth that made Mr Macgregor squirm. Mrs Lackersteen, as a relative, did not hear these scandals, but she was growing nervous. Every evening when Elizabeth came home from her ride she would meet her hopefully, expecting the 'Oh, aunt! What DO you think!'—and then the glorious news. But the news never came, and however carefully she studied Elizabeth's face, she could divine nothing.

When three weeks had passed Mrs Lackersteen became fretful and finally half angry. The thought of her husband, alone—or rather, not alone—in his camp, was troubling her. After all, she had sent him back to camp in order to give Elizabeth her chance with Verrall (not that Mrs Lackersteen would have put it so vulgarly as that). One evening she began lecturing and threatening Elizabeth in her oblique way. The conversation consisted of a sighing monologue with very long pauses—for Elizabeth made no answer whatever.

Mrs Lackersteen began with some general remarks, apropos of a photograph in the Tatler, about these fast MODERN girls who went about in beach pyjamas and all that and made themselves so dreadfully CHEAP with men. A girl, Mrs Lackersteen said, should NEVER make herself too cheap with a man; she should make herself— but the opposite of 'cheap' seemed to be 'expensive', and that did not sound at all right, so Mrs Lackersteen changed her tack. She went on to tell Elizabeth about a letter she had had from home with further news of that poor, POOR dear girl who was out in Burma for a while and had so foolishly neglected to get married. Her sufferings had been quite heartrending, and it just showed how glad a girl ought to be to marry anyone, literally ANYONE. It appeared that the poor, poor dear girl had lost her job and been practically STARVING for a long time, and now she had actually had to take a job as a common kitchen maid under a horrid, vulgar cook who bullied her most shockingly.

And it seemed that the black beetles in the kitchen were simply beyond belief! Didn't Elizabeth think it too absolutely dreadful? BLACK BEETLES!

Mrs Lackersteen remained silent for some time, to allow the black beetles to sink in, before adding:

'SUCH a pity that Mr Verrall will be leaving us when the rains break. Kyauktada will seem quite EMPTY without him!'

'When do the rains break, usually?' said Elizabeth as indifferently as she could manage.

'About the beginning of June, up here. Only a week or two now. . . . My dear, it seems absurd to mention it again, but I cannot get out of my head the thought of that poor, poor dear girl in the kitchen among the BLACK BEETLES!'

Black beetles recurred more than once in Mrs Lackersteen's conversation during the rest of the evening. It was not until the following day that she remarked in the tone of someone dropping an unimportant piece of gossip:

'By the way, I believe Flory is coming back to Kyauktada at the beginning of June. He said he was going to be in for the general meeting at the Club. Perhaps we might invite him to dinner some time.'

It was the first time that either of them had mentioned Flory since the day when he had brought Elizabeth the leopard-skin. After being virtually forgotten for several weeks, he had returned to each woman's mind, a depressing pis aller.

Three days later Mrs Lackersteen sent word to her husband to come back to Kyauktada. He had been in camp long enough to earn a short spell in headquarters. He came back, more florid than ever— sunburn, he explained—and having acquired such a trembling of the hands that he could barely light a cigarette. Nevertheless, that evening he celebrated his return by manoeuvring Mrs Lackersteen out of the house, coming into Elizabeth's bedroom and making a spirited attempt to rape her.

During all this time, unknown to anyone of importance, further sedition was afoot. The 'weiksa' (now far away, peddling the philosopher's stone to innocent villagers in Martaban) had perhaps done his job a little better than he intended. At any rate, there was a possibility of fresh trouble—some isolated, futile outrage, probably. Even U Po Kyin knew nothing of this yet. But as usual the gods were fighting on his side, for any further rebellion would make the first seem more serious than it had been, and so add to his glory.

Chapter 21

O western wind, when wilt thou blow, that the small rain down can rain? It was the first of June, the day of the general meeting, and there had not been a drop of rain yet. As Flory came up the Club path the sun of afternoon, slanting beneath his hat-brim, was still savage enough to scorch his neck uncomfortably. The mali staggered along the path, his breast-muscles slippery with sweat, carrying two kerosene-tins of water on a yoke. He dumped them down, slopping a little water over his lank brown feet, and salaamed to Flory.

'Well, mali, is the rain coming?'

The man gestured vaguely towards the west. 'The hills have captured it, sahib.'

Kyauktada was ringed almost round by hills, and these caught the earlier showers, so that sometimes no rain fell till almost the end of June. The earth of the flower-beds, hoed into large untidy lumps, looked grey and hard as concrete. Flory went into the lounge and found Westfield loafing by the veranda, looking out over the river, for the chicks had been rolled up. At the foot of the veranda a chokra lay on his back in the sun, pulling the punkah rope with his heel and shading his face with a broad strip of banana leaf.

'Hullo, Flory! You've got thin as a rake.'

'So've you.'

'H'm, yes. Bloody weather. No appetite except for booze. Christ, won't I be glad when I hear the frogs start croaking. Let's have a spot before the others come. Butler!'

'Do you know who's coming to the meeting?' Flory said, when the butler had brought whisky and tepid soda.

'Whole crowd, I believe. Lackersteen got back from camp three days ago. By God, that man's been having the time of his life away from his missus! My inspector was telling me about the goings-on at his camp. Tarts by the score. Must have imported 'em specially from Kyauktada. He'll catch it all right when the old woman sees his Club bill. Eleven bottles of whisky sent out to his camp in a fortnight.'

'Is young Verrall coming?'

'No, he's only a temporary member. Not that he'd trouble to come anyway, young tick. Maxwell won't be here either. Can't leave camp just yet, he says. He sent word Ellis was to speak for him if there's any voting to be done. Don't suppose there'll be anything to vote about, though eh?' he added, looking at Flory obliquely, for both of them remembered their previous quarrel on this subject.

'I suppose it lies with Macgregor.'

'What I mean is, Macgregor'll have dropped that bloody rot about electing a native member, eh? Not the moment for it just now. After the rebellion and all that.'

'What about the rebellion, by the way?' said Flory. He did not want to start wrangling about the doctor's election yet. There was going to be trouble and to spare in a few minutes. 'Any more news— are they going to have another try, do you think?'

'No. All over, I'm afraid. They caved in like the funks they are. The whole district's as quiet as a bloody girls' school. Most disappointing.'

Flory's heart missed a beat. He had heard Elizabeth's voice in the next room. Mr Macgregor came in at this moment, Ellis and Mr Lackersteen following. This made up the full quota, for the women members of the Club had no votes. Mr Macgregor was already dressed in a silk suit, and was carrying the Club account books under his arm. He managed to bring a sub-official air even into such petty business as a Club meeting.

'As we seem to be all here,' he said after the usual greetings, 'shall we—ah—proceed with our labours?'

'Lead on, Macduff,' said Westfield, sitting down.

'Call the butler, someone, for Christ's sake,' said Mr Lackersteen. 'I daren't let my missus hear me calling him.'

'Before we apply ourselves to the agenda,' said Mr Macgregor when he had refused a drink and the others had taken one, 'I expect you will want me to run through the accounts for the half-year?'

They did not want it particularly, but Mr Macgregor, who enjoyed this kind of thing, ran through the accounts with great thoroughness. Flory's thoughts were wandering. There was going to be such a row in a moment—oh, such a devil of a row! They would be furious when they found that he was proposing the doctor after all. And Elizabeth was in the next room. God send she didn't hear the noise of the row when it came. It would make her despise him all the more to see the others baiting him. Would he see her this evening? Would she speak to him? He gazed across the quarter-mile of gleaming river. By the far bank a knot of men, one of them wearing a green gaungbaung, were waiting beside a sampan. In the channel, by the nearer bank, a huge, clumsy Indian barge struggled with desperate slowness against the racing current. At each stroke the ten rowers, Dravidian starvelings, ran forward and plunged their long primitive oars, with heart-shaped blades, into the water. They braced their meagre bodies, then tugged, writhed, strained backwards like agonized creatures of black rubber, and the ponderous hull crept onwards a yard or two. Then the rowers sprang forward, panting, to plunge their oars again before the current should check her.

'And now,' said Mr Macgregor more gravely, 'we come to the main point of the agenda. That, of course, is this—ah—distasteful question, which I am afraid must be faced, of electing a native member to this Club. When we discussed the matter before—'

'What the hell!'

It was Ellis who had interrupted. He was so excited that he had sprung to his feet.

'What the hell! Surely we aren't starting THAT over again? Talk about electing a damned nigger so this Club, after everything that's happened! Good God, I thought even Flory had dropped it by this time!'

'Our friend Ellis appears surprised. The matter has been discussed before, I believe.'

'I should think it damned well was discussed before! And we all said what we thought of it. By God—'

'If our friend Ellis will sit down for a few moments—' said Mr Macgregor tolerantly.

Ellis threw himself into his chair again, exclaiming, 'Bloody rubbish!' Beyond the river Flory could see the group of Burmans embarking. They were lifting a long, awkward-shaped bundle into the sampan. Mr Macregor had produced a letter from his file of papers.

'Perhaps I had better explain how this question arose in the first place. The Commissioner tells me that a circular has been sent round by the Government, suggesting that in those Clubs where there are no native members, one at least shall be co-opted; that is, admitted automatically. The circular says—ah yes! here it is: "It is mistaken policy to offer social affronts to native officials of high standing." I may say that I disagree most emphatically. No doubt we all do. We who have to do the actual work of government see things very differently from these—ah—Paget M.P.s who interfere with us from above. The Commissioner quite agrees with me. However—'

'But it's all bloody rot!' broke in Ellis. 'What's it got to do with the Commissioner or anyone else? Surely we can do as we like in our own bloody Club? They've no right to dictate to us when we're off duty.'

'Quite,' said Westfield.

'You anticipate me. I told the Commissioner that I should have to put the matter before the other members. And the course he suggests is this. If the idea finds any support in the Club, he thinks it would be better if we co-opted our native member. On the other hand, if the entire Club is against it, it can be dropped. That is, if opinion is quite unanimous.'

'Well, it damned well is unanimous,' said Ellis.

'D'you mean,' said Westfield, 'that it depends on ourselves whether we have 'em in here or no?'

'I fancy we can take it as meaning that.'

'Well, then, let's say we're against it to a man.'

'And say it bloody firmly, by God. We want to put our foot down on this idea once and for all.'

'Hear, hear!' said Mr Lackersteen gruffly. 'Keep the black swabs out of it. Esprit de corps and all that.'

Mr Lackersteen could always be relied upon for sound sentiments in a case like this. In his heart he did not care and never had cared a damn for the British Raj, and he was as happy drinking with an Oriental as with a white man; but he was always ready with a loud 'Hear, hear!' when anyone suggested the bamboo for disrespectful servants or boiling oil for Nationalists. He prided himself that though he might booze a bit and all that, dammit, he WAS loyal. It was his form of respectability. Mr Macgregor was secretly rather relieved by the general agreement. If any Oriental member were co-opted, that member would have to be Dr Veraswami, and he had had the deepest distrust of the doctor ever since Nga Shwe O's suspicious escape from the jail.

'Then I take it that you are all agreed?' he said. 'If so, I will inform the Commissioner. Otherwise, we must begin discussing the candidate for election.'

Flory stood up. He had got to say his say. His heart seemed to have risen into his throat and to be choking him. From what Mr Macgregor had said, it was clear that it was in his power to secure the doctor's election by speaking the word. But oh, what a bore, what a nuisance it was! What an infernal uproar there would be! How he wished he had never given the doctor that promise! No matter, he had given it, and he could not break it. So short a time ago he would have broken it, en bon pukka sahib, how easily! But not now. He had got to see this thing through. He turned himself sidelong so that his birthmark was away from the others. Already he could feel his voice going flat and guilty.

'Our friend Flory has something to suggest?'

'Yes. I propose Dr Veraswami as a member of this Club.'

There was such a yell of dismay from three of the others that Mr Macgregor had to rap sharply on the table and remind them that the ladies were in the next room. Ellis took not the smallest notice. He had sprung to his feet again, and the skin round his nose had gone quite grey. He and Flory remained facing one another, as though on the point of blows.

'Now, you damned swab, will you take that back?'

'No, I will not.'

'You oily swine! You nigger's Nancy Boy! You crawling, sneaking,— bloody bastard!'

'Order!' exclaimed Mr Macgregor.

'But look at him, look at him!' cried Ellis almost tearfully. 'Letting us all down for the sake of a pot-bellied nigger! After all we've said to him! When we've only got to hang together and we can keep the stink of garlic out of this Club for ever. My God, wouldn't it make you spew your guts up to see anyone behaving like such a—?'

'Take it back, Flory, old man!' said Westfield. 'Don't be a bloody fool!'

'Downright Bolshevism, dammit!' said Mr Lackersteen.

'Do you think I care what you say? What business is it of yours? It's for Macgregor to decide.'

'Then do you—ah—adhere to your decision?' said Mr Macgregor gloomily.

'Yes.'

Mr Macgregor sighed. 'A pity! Well, in that case I suppose I have no choice—'

'No, no, no!' cried Ellis, dancing about in his rage. 'Don't give in to him! Put it to the vote. And if that son of a bitch doesn't put in a black ball like the rest of us, we'll first turf him out of the Club himself, and then—well! Butler!'

'Sahib!' said the butler, appearing.

'Bring the ballot box and the balls. Now clear out!' he added roughly when the butler had obeyed.

The air had gone very stagnant; for some reason the punkah had stopped working. Mr Macgregor stood up with a disapproving but judicial mien, taking the two drawers of black and white balls out of the ballot box.

'We must proceed in order. Mr Flory proposes Dr Veraswami, the Civil Surgeon, as a member of this Club. Mistaken, in my opinion, greatly mistaken; however—! Before putting the matter to the vote—'

'Oh, why make a song and dance about it?' said Ellis. 'Here's my contribution! And another for Maxwell.' He plumped two black balls into the box. Then one of his sudden spasms of rage seized him, and he took the drawer of white balls and pitched them across the floor. They went flying in all directions. 'There! Now pick one up if you want to use it!'

'You damned fool! What good do you think that does?'

'Sahib!'

They all started and looked round. The chokra was goggling at them over the veranda rail, having climbed up from below. With one skinny arm he clung to the rail and with the other gesticulated towards the river.

'Sahib! Sahib!'

'What's up?' said Westfield.

They all moved for the window. The sampan that Flory had seen across the river was lying under the bank at the foot of the lawn, one of the men clinging to a bush to steady it. The Burman in the green gaungbaung was climbing out.

'That's one of Maxwell's Forest Rangers!' said Ellis in quite a different voice. 'By God! something's happened!'

The Forest Ranger saw Mr Macgregor, shikoed in a hurried, preoccupied way and turned back to the sampan. Four other men, peasants, climbed out after him, and with difficulty lifted ashore the strange bundle that Flory had seen in the distance. It was six feet long, swathed in cloths, like a mummy. Something happened in everybody's entrails. The Forest Ranger glanced at the veranda, saw that there was no way up, and led the peasants round the path to the front of the Club. They had hoisted the bundle on to their shoulders as funeral bearers hoist a coffin. The butler had flitted into the lounge again, and even his face was pale after its fashion—that is, grey.

'Butler!' said Mr Macgregor sharply.

'Sir!'

'Go quickly and shut the door of the card-room. Keep it shut. Don't let the memsahibs see.'

‘Yes, sir!’

The Burmans, with their burden, came heavily down the passage. As they entered the leading man staggered and almost fell; he had trodden on one of the white balls that were scattered about the floor. The Burmans knelt down, lowered their burden to the floor and stood over it with a strange reverent air, slightly bowing, their hands together in a shiko. Westfield had fallen on his knees, and he pulled back the cloth.

‘Christ! Just look at him!’ he said, but without much surprise. ‘Just look at the poor little b—!’

Mr Lackersteen had retreated to the other end of the room, with a bleating noise. From the moment when the bundle was lifted ashore they had all known what it contained. It was the body of Maxwell, cut almost to pieces with dahs by two relatives of the man whom he had shot.

CHAPTER 22

Maxwell's death had caused a profound shock in Kyauktada. It would cause a shock throughout the whole of Burma, and the case—'the Kyauktada case, do you remember?'—would still be talked of years after the wretched youth's name was forgotten. But in a purely personal way no one was much distressed. Maxwell had been almost a nonentity—just a 'good fellow' like any other of the ten thousand ex colore good fellows of Burma—and with no close friends. No one among the Europeans genuinely mourned for him. But that is not to say that they were not angry. On the contrary, for the moment they were almost mad with rage. For the unforgivable had happened—A WHITE MAN had been killed. When that happens, a sort of shudder runs through the English of the East. Eight hundred people, possibly, are murdered every year in Burma; they matter nothing; but the murder of A WHITE MAN is a monstrosity, a sacrilege. Poor Maxwell would be avenged, that was certain. But only a servant or two, and the Forest Ranger who had brought in his body and who had been fond of him, shed any tears for his death.

On the other hand, no one was actually pleased, except U Po Kyin.

'This is a positive gift from heaven!' he told Ma Kin. 'I could not have arranged it better myself. The one thing I needed to make them take my rebellion seriously was a little bloodshed. And here it is! I tell you, Ma Kin, every day I grow more certain that some higher power is working on my behalf.'

'Ko Po Kyin, truly you are without shame! I do not know how you dare to say such things. Do you not shudder to have murder upon your soul?'

'What! I? Murder upon my soul? What are you talking about? I have never killed so much as a chicken in my life.'

'But you are profiting by this poor boy's death.'

'Profiting by it! Of course I am profiting by it! And why not, indeed? Am I to blame if somebody else choose to commit murder? The fisherman catches fish, and he is damned for it. But are we damned for eating the fish? Certainly not. Why NOT eat the fish, once it is dead? You should study the Scriptures more carefully, my dear Kin Kin.'

The funeral took place next morning, before breakfast. All the Europeans were present, except Verrall, who was careering about the maidan quite as usual, almost opposite the cemetery. Mr Macgregor read the burial service. The little group of Englishmen stood round the grave, their topis in their hands, sweating into the dark suits that they had dug out from the bottom of their boxes. The harsh morning light beat without mercy upon their faces, yellower than ever against the ugly, shabby clothes. Every face except Elizabeth's looked lined and old. Dr Veraswami and half a dozen other Orientals were present, but they kept themselves decently in the background. There were sixteen gravestones in the little cemetery; assistants of timber firms, officials, soldiers killed in forgotten skirmishes.

'Sacred to the memory of John Henry Spagnall, late of the Indian

Imperial Police, who was cut down by cholera while in the unremitting exercise of' etc., etc., etc.

Flory remembered Spagnall dimly. He had died very suddenly in camp after his second go of delirium tremens. In a corner there were some graves of Eurasians, with wooden crosses. The creeping jasmine, with tiny orange-hearted flowers, had overgrown everything. Among the jasmine, large rat-holes led down into the graves.

Mr Macgregor concluded the burial service in a ripe, reverent voice, and led the way out of the cemetery, holding his grey topi— the Eastern equivalent of a top hat—against his stomach. Flory lingered by the gate, hoping that Elizabeth would speak to him, but she passed him without a glance. Everyone had shunned him this morning. He was in disgrace; the murder had made his disloyalty of last night seem somehow horrible. Ellis had caught Westfield by the arm, and they halted at the grave-side, taking out their cigarette-cases. Flory could hear their slangy voices coming across the open grave.

'My God, Westfield, my God, when I think of that poor little b— lying down there—oh, my God, how my blood does boil! I couldn't sleep all night, I was so furious.'

'Pretty bloody, I grant. Never mind, promise you a couple of chaps shall swing for it. Two corpses against their one—best we can do.'

'Two! It ought to be fifty! We've got to raise heaven and hell to get these fellows hanged. Have you got their names yet?'

'Yes, rather!! Whole blooming district knows who did it. We always do know who's done it in these cases. Getting the bloody villagers to talk—that's the only trouble.'

'Well, for God's sake get them to talk this time. Never mind the bloody law. Whack it out of them. Torture them—anything. If you want to bribe any witnesses, I'm good for a couple of hundred chips.'

Westfield sighed. 'Can't do that sort of thing, I'm afraid. Wish we could. My chaps'd know how to put the screw on a witness if you gave 'em the word. Tie 'em down on an ant-hill. Red peppers. But that won't do nowadays. Got to keep our own bloody silly laws. But never mind, those fellows'll swing all right. We've got all the evidence we want.'

'Good! And when you've arrested them, if you aren't sure of getting a conviction, shoot them, jolly well shoot them! Fake up an escape or something. Anything sooner than let those b—s go free.'

'They won't go free, don't you fear. We'll get 'em. Get SOMEBODY, anyhow. Much better hang wrong fellow than no fellow,' he added, unconsciously quoting.

'That's the stuff! I'll never sleep easy again till I've seen them swinging,' said Ellis as they moved away from the grave. 'Christ! Let's get out of this sun! I'm about perishing with thirst.'

Everyone was perishing, more or less, but it seemed hardly decent to go down to the Club for drinks immediately after the funeral. The Europeans scattered for their houses, while four sweepers with mamooties flung the grey, cement-like earth back into the grave, and shaped it into a rough mound.

After breakfast, Ellis was walking down to his office, cane in hand. It was blinding hot. Ellis had bathed and changed back into shirt and shorts, but wearing a thick suit even for an hour had brought on his prickly heat abominably. Westfield had gone out already, in his motor launch, with an inspector and half a dozen men, to arrest the murderers. He had ordered Verrall to accompany him—not that Verrall was needed, but, as Westfield said, it would do the young swab good to have a spot of work.

Ellis wriggled his shoulders—his prickly heat was almost beyond bearing. The rage was stewing in his body like a bitter juice. He had brooded all night over what had happened. They had killed a white man, killed A WHITE MAN, the bloody sods, the sneaking, cowardly hounds! Oh, the swine, the swine, how they ought to be made to suffer for it! Why did we make these cursed kid-glove laws? Why did we take everything lying down? Just suppose this had happened in a German colony, before the War! The good old Germans! They knew how to treat the niggers. Reprisals! Rhinoceros hide whips! Raid their villages, kill their cattle, burn their crops, decimate them, blow them from the guns.

Ellis gazed into the horrible cascades of light that poured through the gaps in the trees. His greenish eyes were large and mournful. A mild, middle-aged Burman came by, balancing a huge bamboo, which he shifted from one shoulder to the other with a grunt as he passed Ellis. Ellis's grip tightened on his stick. If that swine, now, would only attack you! Or even insult you—anything, so that you had the right to smash him! If only these gutless curs would ever show fight in any conceivable way! Instead of just sneaking past you, keeping within the law so that you never had a chance to get back at them. Ah, for a real rebellion—martial law proclaimed and no quarter given! Lovely, sanguinary images moved through his mind. Shrieking mounds of natives, soldiers slaughtering them. Shoot them, ride them down, horses' hooves trample their guts out, whips cut their faces in slices!

Five High School boys came down the road abreast. Ellis saw them coming, a row of yellow, malicious faces—epicene faces, horribly smooth and young, grinning at him with deliberate insolence. It was in their minds to bait him, as a white man. Probably they had heard of the murder, and—being Nationalists, like all schoolboys— regarded it as a victory. They grinned full in Ellis's face as they passed him. They were trying openly to provoke him, and they knew that the law was on their side. Ellis felt his breast swell. The look of their faces, jeering at him like a row of yellow images, was maddening. He stopped short.

'Here! What are you laughing at, you young ticks?'

The boys turned.

'I said what the bloody hell are you laughing at?'

One of the boys answered, insolently—but perhaps his bad English made him seem more insolent than he intended.

'Not your business.'

There was about a second during which Ellis did not know what he was doing. In that second he had hit out with all his strength, and the cane landed, crack! right across the boy's eyes. The boy recoiled with a shriek, and in the same instant the other four had thrown themselves upon Ellis. But he was too strong for them. He flung them aside and sprang back, lashing out with his stick so furiously that none of them dared come near.

'Keep your distance, you —s! Keep off, or by God I'll smash another of you!' Though they were four to one he was so formidable that they surged back in fright. The boy who was hurt had fallen on his knees with his arms across his face, and was screaming 'I am blinded! I am blinded!' Suddenly the other four turned and darted for a pile of laterite, used for road-mending, which was twenty yards away. One of Ellis's clerks had appeared on the veranda of the office and was leaping up and down in agitation.

'Come up, sir come up at once. They will murder you!'

Ellis disdained to run, but he moved for the veranda steps. A lump of laterite came sailing through the air and shattered itself against a pillar, whereat the clerk scooted indoors. But Ellis turned on the veranda to face the boys, who were below, each carrying an armful of laterite. He was cackling with delight.

'You damned, dirty little niggers!' he shouted down at them. 'You got a surprise that time, didn't you? Come up on this veranda and fight me, all four of you! You daren't. Four to one and you daren't face me! Do you call yourselves men? You sneaking, mangy little rats!'

He broke into Burmese, calling them the incestuous children of pigs. All the while they were pelting him with lumps of laterite, but their arms were feeble and they threw ineptly. He dodged the stones, and as each one missed him he cackled in triumph. Presently there was a sound of shouts up the road, for the noise had been heard at the police station, and some constables were emerging to see what was the matter. The boys took fright and bolted, leaving Ellis a complete victor.

Ellis had heartily enjoyed the affray, but he was furiously angry as soon as it was over. He wrote a violent note to Mr Macgregor, telling him that he had been wantonly assaulted and demanding vengeance. Two clerks who had witnessed the scene, and a chaprassi, were sent along to Mr Macgregor's office to corroborate the story. They lied in perfect unison. 'The boys had attacked Mr Ellis without any provocation whatever, he had defended himself,' etc., etc. Ellis, to do him justice, probably believed this to be a truthful version of the story. Mr Macgregor was somewhat disturbed, and ordered the police to find the four schoolboys and interrogate them. The boys, however, had been expecting something of the kind, and were lying very low; the police searched the bazaar all day without finding them. In the evening the wounded boy was taken to a Burmese doctor, who, by applying some poisonous concoction of crushed leaves to his left eye, succeeded in blinding him.

The Europeans met at the Club as usual that evening, except for Westfield and Verrall, who had not yet returned. Everyone was in a bad mood. Coming on top of the murder, the unprovoked attack on Ellis (for that was the accepted description of it) had scared them as well as angered them. Mrs Lackersteen was twittering to the tune of 'We shall all be murdered in our beds'. Mr Macgregor, to reassure her, told her in cases of riot the European ladies were always locked inside the jail until everything was over; but she did not seem much comforted. Ellis was offensive to Flory, and Elizabeth cut him almost dead. He had come down to the Club in the insane hope of making up their quarrel, and her demeanour made him so miserable that for the greater part of the evening he skulked in the library. It was not till eight o'clock when everyone had swallowed a number of drinks, that the atmosphere grew a little more friendly, and Ellis said:

'What about sending a couple of chokras up to our houses and getting our dinners sent down here? We might as well have a few rubbers of bridge. Better than mooning about at home.'

Mrs Lackersteen, who was in dread of going home, jumped at the suggestion. The Europeans occasionally dined at the Club when they wanted to stay late. Two of the chokras were sent for, and on being told what was wanted of them, immediately burst into tears. It appeared that if they went up the hill they were certain of encountering Maxwell's ghost. The mali was sent instead. As the man set out Flory noticed that it was again the night of the full moon—four weeks to a day since that evening, now unutterably remote, when he had kissed Elizabeth under the frangipani tree.

They had just sat down at the bridge table, and Mrs Lackersteen had just revoked out of pure nervousness, when there was a heavy thump on the roof. Everyone started and look up.

'A coco-nut falling!' said Mr Macgregor.

'There aren't any coco-nut trees here,' said Ellis.

The next moment a number of things happened all together. There was another and much louder bang, one of the petrol lamps broke from its hook and crashed to the ground, narrowly missing Mr Lackersteen, who jumped aside with a yelp, Mrs Lackersteen began screaming, and the butler rushed into the room, bareheaded, his face the colour of bad coffee.

'Sir, sir! Bad men come! Going to murder us all, sir!'

'What? Bad men? What do you mean?'

'Sir, all the villagers are outside! Big stick and dah in their hands, and all dancing about! Going to cut master's throat, sir!'

Mrs Lackersteen threw herself backwards in her chair. She was setting up such a din of screams as to drown the butler's voice.

'Oh, be quiet!' said Ellis sharply, turning on her. 'Listen, all of you! Listen to that!'

There was a deep, murmurous, dangerous sound outside, like the humming of an angry giant. Mr Macgregor, who had stood up, stiffened as he heard it, and settled his spectacles pugnaciously on his nose.

'This is some kind of disturbance! Butler, pick that lamp up. Miss Lackersteen, look to your aunt. See if she is hurt. The rest of you come with me!'

They all made for the front door, which someone, presumably the butler, had closed. A fusillade of small pebbles was rattling against it like hail. Mr Lackersteen wavered at the sound and retreated behind the others.

'I say, dammit, bolt that bloody door, someone!' he said.

'No, no!' said Mr Macgregor. 'We must go outside. It's fatal not to face them!'

He opened the door and presented himself boldly at the top of the steps. There were about twenty Burmans on the path, with dahs or sticks in their hands. Outside the fence, stretching up the road in either direction and far out on to the maidan, was an enormous crowd of people. It was like a sea of people, two thousand at the least, black and white in the moon, with here and there a curved dah glittering. Ellis had coolly placed himself beside Mr Macgregor, with his hands in his pockets. Mr Lackersteen had disappeared.

Mr Macgregor raised his hand for silence. 'What is the meaning of this?' he shouted sternly.

There were yells, and some lumps of laterite the size of cricket balls came sailing from the road, but fortunately hit no one. One of the men on the path turned and waved his arms to the others, shouting that they were not to begin throwing yet. Then he stepped forward to address the Europeans. He was a strong debonair fellow of about thirty, with down-curving moustaches, wearing a singlet, with his longyi kilted to the knee.

'What is the meaning of this?' Mr Macgregor repeated.

The man spoke up with a cheerful grin, and not very insolently.

'We have no quarrel with you, min gyi. We have come for the timber merchant, Ellis.' (He pronounced it Ellit.) 'The boy whom he struck this morning has gone blind. You must send Ellit out to us here, so that we can punish him. The rest of you will not be hurt.'

‘Just remember that fellow’s face,’ said Ellis over his shoulder to Flory. ‘We’ll get him seven years for this afterwards.’

Mr Macgregor had turned temporarily quite purple. His rage was so great that it almost choked him. For several moments he could not speak, and when he did so it was in English.

‘Whom do you think you are speaking to? In twenty years I have never heard such insolence! Go away this instant, or I shall call out the Military Police!’

‘You’d better be quick, min gyi. We know that there is no justice for us in your courts, so we must punish Ellit ourselves. Send him out to us here. Otherwise, all of you will weep for it.’

Mr Macgregor made a furious motion with his fist, as though hammering in a nail, ‘Go away, son of a dog!’ he cried, using his first oath in many years.

There was a thunderous roar from the road, and such a shower of stones, that everyone was hit, including the Burmans on the path. One stone took Mr Macgregor full in the face, almost knocking him down. The Europeans bolted hastily inside and barred the door. Mr Macgregor’s spectacles were smashed and his nose streaming blood. They got back to the lounge to find Mrs Lackersteen looping about in one of the long chairs like a hysterical snake, Mr Lackersteen standing irresolutely in the middle of the room, holding an empty bottle, the butler on his knees in the corner, crossing himself (he was a Roman Catholic), the chokras crying, and only Elizabeth calm, though she was very pale.

‘What’s happened?’ she exclaimed.

‘We’re in the soup, that’s what’s happened!’ said Ellis angrily, feeling at the back of his neck where a stone had hit him. ‘The Burmans are all round, shying rocks. But keep calm! They haven’t the guts to break the doors in.’

'Call out the police at once!' said Mr Macgregor indistinctly, for he was stanching his nose with his handkerchief.

'Can't!' said Ellis. 'I was looking round while you were talking to them. They've cut us off, rot their damned souls! No one could possibly get to the police lines. Veraswami's compound is full of men.'

'Then we must wait. We can trust them to turn out of their own accord. Calm yourself, my dear Mrs Lackersteen, PLEASE calm yourself! The danger is very small.'

It did not sound small. There were no gaps in the noise now, and the Burmans seemed to be pouring into the compounds by hundreds. The din swelled suddenly to such a volume that no one could make himself heard except by shouting. All the windows in the lounge had been shut, and some perforated zinc shutters within, which were sometimes used for keeping out insects, pulled to and bolted. There was a series of crashes as the windows were broken, and then a ceaseless thudding of stones from all sides, that shook the thin wooden walls and seemed likely to split them. Ellis opened a shutter and flung a bottle viciously among the crowd, but a dozen stones came hurtling in and he had to close the shutter hurriedly. The Burmans seemed to have no plan beyond flinging stones, yelling and hammering at the walls, but the mere volume of noise was unnerving. The Europeans were half dazed by it at first. None of them thought to blame Ellis, the sole cause of this affair; their common peril seemed, indeed, to draw them closer together for the while. Mr Macgregor, half-blind without his spectacles, stood distractedly in the middle of the room, yielding his right hand to Mrs Lackersteen, who was caressing it, while a weeping chokra clung to his left leg. Mr Lackersteen had vanished again. Ellis was stamping furiously up and down, shaking his fist in the direction of the police lines.

'Where are the police, the f— cowardly sods?' he yelled, heedless of the women. 'Why don't they turn out? My God, we won't get another chance like this in a hundred years! If we'd only ten rifles here, how we could slosh these b—s!'

'They'll be here presently!' Mr Macgregor shouted back. 'It will take them some minutes to penetrate that crowd.'

'But why don't they use their rifles, the miserable sons of bitches? They could slaughter them in bloody heaps if they'd only open fire. Oh, God, to think of missing a chance like this!'

A lump of rock burst one of the zinc shutters. Another followed through the hole it had made, stove in a 'Bonzo' picture, bounced off, cut Elizabeth's elbow, and finally landed on the table. There was a roar of triumph from outside, and then a succession of tremendous thumps on the roof. Some children had climbed into the trees and were having the time of their lives sliding down the roof on their bottoms. Mrs Lackersteen outdid all previous efforts with a shriek that rose easily above the din outside.

'Choke that bloody hag, somebody!' cried Ellis. 'Anyone'd think a pig was being killed. We've got to do something. Flory, Macgregor, come here! Think of a way out of this mess, someone!'

Elizabeth had suddenly lost her nerve and begun crying. The blow from the stone had hurt her. To Flory's astonishment, he found her clinging tightly to his arm. Even in that moment it made his heart turn over. He had been watching the scene almost with detachment— dazed by the noise, indeed, but not much frightened. He always found it difficult to believe Orientals could be really dangerous. Only when he felt Elizabeth's hand on his arm did he grasp the seriousness of the situation.

'Oh, Mr Flory, please, please think of something! You can, you can!

Anything sooner than let those dreadful men get in here!'

'If only one of us could get to the police lines!' groaned Mr Macgregor. 'A British officer to lead them! At the worst I must try and go myself.'

'Don't be a fool! Only get your throat cut!' yelled Ellis. '*I*'ll go if they really look like breaking in. But, oh, to be killed by swine like that! How furious it'd make me! And to think we could murder the whole bloody crowd if only we could get the police here!'

'Couldn't someone get along the river bank?' Flory shouted despairingly.

'Hopeless! Hundreds of them prowling up and down. We're cut off—Burmans on three sides and the river on the other!'

'The river!'

One of those startling ideas that are overlooked simply because they are so obvious had sprung into Flory's mind.

'The river! Of course! We can get to the police lines as easy as winking. Don't you see?'

'How?'

'Why, down the river—in the water! Swim!'

'Oh, good man!' cried Ellis, and smacked Flory on the shoulder. Elizabeth squeezed his arm and actually danced a step or two in glee. 'I'll go if you like!' Ellis shouted, but Flory shook his head. He had already begun slipping his shoes off. There was obviously no time to be lost. The Burmans had behaved like fools hitherto, but there was no saying what might happen if they succeeded in breaking in. The butler, who had got over his first fright, prepared to open the window that gave on the lawn, and glanced obliquely out. There were barely a score of Burmans on the lawn. They had left the back of the Club unguarded, supposing that the river cut off retreat.

'Rush down the lawn like hell!' Ellis shouted in Flory's ear. 'They'll scatter all right when they see you.'

'Order the police to open fire at once!' shouted Mr Macgregor from the other side. 'You have my authority.'

'And tell them to aim low! No firing over their heads. Shoot to kill. In the guts for choice!'

Flory leapt down from the veranda, hurting his feet on the hard earth, and was at the river bank in six paces. As Ellis had said, the Burmans recoiled for a moment when they saw him leaping down. A few stones followed him, but no one pursued—they thought, no doubt, that he was only attempting to escape, and in the clear moonlight they could see that it was not Ellis. In another moment he had pushed his way through the bushes and was in the water.

He sank deep down, and the horrible river ooze received him, sucking him knee-deep so that it was several seconds before he could free himself. When he came to the surface a tepid froth, like the froth on stout, was lapping round his lips, and some spongy thing had floated into his throat and was choking him. It was a sprig of water hyacinth. He managed to spit it out, and found that the swift current had floated him twenty yards already. Burmans were rushing rather aimlessly up and down the bank, yelling. With his eye at the level of the water, Flory could not see the crowd besieging the Club; but he could hear their deep, devilish roaring, which sounded even louder than it had sounded on shore. By the time he was opposite the Military Police lines the bank seemed almost bare of men. He managed to struggle out of the current and flounder through the mud, which sucked off his left sock. A little way down the bank two old men were sitting beside a fence, sharpening fence-posts, as though there had not been a riot within a hundred miles of them. Flory crawled ashore, clambered over the fence and ran heavily across the moonwhite parade-ground, his wet trousers sagging. As far as he could tell in the noise, the lines were quite empty. In some stalls over to the right Verrall's horses were plunging about in a panic. Flory ran out on to the road, and saw what had happened.

The whole body of policemen, military and civil, about a hundred and fifty men in all, had attacked the crowd from the rear, armed only with sticks. They had been utterly engulfed. The crowd was so dense that it was like an enormous swarm of bees seething and rotating. Everywhere one could see policemen wedged helplessly among the hordes of Burmans, struggling furiously but uselessly, and too cramped even to use their sticks. Whole knots of men were tangled Laocoon-like in the folds of unrolled pagris. There was a terrific bellowing of oaths in three or four languages, clouds of dust, and a suffocating stench of sweat and marigolds—but no one seemed to have been seriously hurt. Probably the Burmans had not used their daks for fear of provoking rifle-fire. Flory pushed his way into the crowd and was immediately swallowed up like the others. A sea of bodies closed in upon him and flung him from side to side, bumping his ribs and choking him with their animal heat. He struggled onwards with an almost dreamlike feeling, so absurd and unreal was the situation. The whole riot had been ludicrous from the start, and what was most ludicrous of all was that the Burmans, who might have killed him, did not know what to do with him now he was among them. Some yelled insults in his face, some jostled him and stamped on his feet, some even tried to make way for him, as a white man. He was not certain whether he was fighting for his life, or merely pushing his way through the crowd. For quite a long time he was jammed, helpless, with his arms pinned against his sides, then he found himself wrestling with a stumpy Burman much stronger than himself, then a dozen men rolled against him like a wave and drove him deeper into the heart of the crowd. Suddenly he felt an agonizing pain in his right big toe—someone in boots had trodden on it. It was the Military Police subahdar, a Rajput, very fat, moustachioed, with his pagri gone. He was grasping a Burman by the throat and trying to hammer his face, while the sweat rolled off his bare, bald crown. Flory threw his arm round the subahdar's neck and managed to tear him away from his adversary and shout in his ear. His Urdu deserted him, and he bellowed in Burmese:

'Why did you not open fire?'

For a long time he could not hear the man's answer. Then he caught it:

'Hukm ne aya'—'I have had no order!'

'Idiot!'

At this moment another bunch of men drove against them, and for a minute or two they were pinned and quite unable to move. Flory realized that the subabdar had a whistle in his pocket and was trying to get at it. Finally he got it loose and blew piercing blasts, but there was no hope of rallying any men until they could get into a clear space. It was a fearful labour to struggle our of the crowd—it was like wading neck-deep through a viscous sea. At times the exhaustion of Flory's limbs was so complete that he stood passive, letting the crowd hold him and even drive him backwards. At last, more from the natural eddying of the crowd than by his own effort, he found himself flung out into the open. The subahdar had also emerged, ten or fifteen sepoys, and a Burmese Inspector of Police. Most of the sepoys collapsed on their haunches almost falling with fatigue, and limping, their feet having been trampled on.

'Come on, get up! Run like hell for the lines! Get some rifles and a clip of ammunition each.'

He was too overcome even to speak in Burmese, but the men understood him and lopped heavily towards the police lines. Flory followed them, to get away from the crowd before they turned on him again. When he reached the gate the sepoys were returning with their rifles and already preparing to fire.

'The sahib will give the order!' the subahdar panted.

'Here you!' cried Flory to the Inspector. 'Can you speak Hindustani?'

'Yes, sir.'

'Then tell them to fire high, right over the people's heads. And above all, to fire all together. Make them understand that.'

The fat Inspector, whose Hindustani was even worse than Flory's, explained what was wanted, chiefly by leaping up and down and gesticulating. The sepoys raised their rifles, there was a roar, and a rolling echo from the hillside. For a moment Flory thought that his order had been disregarded, for almost the entire section of the crowd nearest them had fallen like a swath of hay. However, they had only flung themselves down in panic. The sepoys fired a second volley, but it was not needed. The crowd had immediately begun to surge outwards from the Club like a river changing its course. They came pouring down the road, saw the armed men barring their way, and tried to recoil, whereupon there was a fresh battle between those in front and those behind; finally the whole crowd bulged outwards and began to roll slowly up the maidan. Flory and the sepoys moved slowly towards the Club on the heels of the retreating crowd. The policemen who had been engulfed were straggling back by ones and twos. Their pagris were gone and their puttees trailing yards behind them, but they had no damage worse than bruises. The Civil Policemen were dragging a very few prisoners among them. When they reached the Club compound the Burmans were still pouring out, an endless line of young men leaping gracefully through a gap in the hedge like a procession of gazelles. It seemed to Flory that it was getting very dark. A small white-clad figure extricated itself from the last of the crowd and tumbled limply into Flory's arms. It was Dr Veraswami, with his tie torn off but his spectacles miraculously unbroken.

'Doctor!'

'Ach, my friend! Ach, how I am exhausted!'

'What are you doing here? Were you right in the middle of that crowd?'

'I was trying to restrain them, my friend. It was hopeless until you came. But there is at least one man who bears the mark of this, I think!'

He held out a small fist for Flory to see the damaged knuckles. But it was certainly quite dark now. At the same moment Flory heard a nasal voice behind him.

'Well, Mr Flory, so it's all over already! A mere flash in the pan as usual. You and I together were a little too much for them— ha, ha!'

It was U Po Kyin. He came towards them with a martial air, carrying a huge stick, and with a revolver thrust into his belt. His dress was a studious negligee—singlet and Shan trousers—to give the impression that he had rushed out of his house post-haste. He had been lying low until the danger should be over, and was now hurrying forth to grab a share of any credit that might be going.

'A smart piece of work, sir!' he said enthusiastically. 'Look how they are flying up the hillside! We have routed them most satisfactory.'

'WE!' panted the doctor indignantly.

'Ah, my dear doctor! I did not perceive that you were there. It is possible that YOU also have been in the fighting? YOU—risking your most valuable life! Who would have believed such a thing?'

'You've taken your time getting here yourself!' said Flory angrily.

'Well, well sir, it is enough that we have dispersed them. Although,' he added with a touch of satisfaction, for he had noticed Flory's tone, 'they are going in the direction of the European houses, you will observe. I fancy that it will occur to them to do a little plundering on their way.'

One had to admire the man's impudence. He tucked his great stick under his arm and strolled beside Flory in an almost patronizing manner, while the doctor dropped behind, abashed in spite of himself. At the Club gate all three men halted. It was now extraordinarily dark, and the moon had vanished. Low overhead, just visible, black clouds were streaming eastward like a pack of hounds. A wind, almost cold, blew down the hillside and swept a cloud of dust and fine water-vapour before it. There was a sudden intensely rich scent of damp. The wind quickened, the trees rustled, then began beating themselves furiously together, the big frangipani tree by the tennis court flinging out a nebula of dimly seen blossom. All three men turned and hurried for shelter, the Orientals to their houses, Flory to the Club. It had begun raining.

Chapter 23

Next day the town was quieter than a cathedral city on Monday morning. It is usually the case after a riot. Except for the handful of prisoners, everyone who could possibly have been concerned in the attack on the Club had a watertight alibi. The Club garden looked as though a herd of bison had stampeded across it, but the houses had not been plundered, and there were no new casualties among the Europeans, except that after everything was over Mr Lackersteen had been found very drunk under the billiard-table, where he had retired with a bottle of whisky. Westfield and Verrall came back early in the morning, bringing Maxwell's murderers under arrest; or at any rate, bringing two people who would presently be hanged for Maxwell's murder. Westfield, when he heard the news of the riot, was gloomy but resigned. AGAIN it happened—a veritable riot, and he not there to quell it! It seemed fated that he should never kill a man. Depressing, depressing. Verrall's only comment was that it had been 'damned lip' on the part of Flory (a civilian) to give orders to the Military Police.

Meanwhile, it was raining almost without cease. As soon as he woke up and heard the rain hammering on the roof Flory dressed and hurried out, Flo following. Out of sight of the houses he took off his clothes and let the rain sluice down on his bare body. To his surprise, he found that he was covered with bruises from last night; but the rain had washed away every trace of his prickly heat within three minutes. It is wonderful, the healing power of rainwater. Flory walked down to Dr Veraswami's house, with his shoes squelching and periodical jets of water flowing down his neck from the brim of his Terai hat. The sky was leaden, and innumerable whirling storms chased one another across the maidan like squadrons of cavalry. Burmans passed, under vast wooden hats in spite of which their bodies streamed water like the bronze gods in the fountains. A network of rivulets was already washing the stones of the road bare. The doctor had just got home when Flory arrived, and was shaking a wet umbrella over the veranda rail. He hailed Flory excitedly.

'Come up, Mr Flory, come up at once! You are just apropos. I was on the point of opening a bottle of Old Tommy Gin. Come up and let me drink to your health, ass the saviour of Kyauktada!'

They had a long talk together. The doctor was in a triumphant mood. It appeared that what had happened last night had righted his troubles almost miraculously. U Po Kyin's schemes were undone. The doctor was no longer at his mercy—in fact, it was the other way about. The doctor explained to Flory:

'You see, my friend, this riot—or rather, your most noble behaviour in it—wass quite outside U Po Kyin's programme. He had started the SO-CALLED rebellion and had the glory of crushing it, and he calculated that any further outbreak would simply mean more glory still. I am told that when he heard of Mr Maxwell's death, hiss joy was positively'—the doctor nipped his thumb and forefinger together—'what iss the word I want?'

'Obscene?'

'Ah yes. Obscene. It iss said that actually he attempted to dance—can you imagine such a disgusting spectacle?—and exclaimed, "Now at least they will take my rebellion seriously!" Such iss his regard for human life. But now hiss triumph iss at an end. The riot hass tripped up in mid-career.'

'How?'

'Because, do you not see, the honours of the riot are not hiss, but yours! And I am known to be your friend. I stand, so to speak, in the reflection of your glory. Are you not the hero of the hour? Did not your European friends receive you with open arms when you returned to the Club last night?'

'They did, I must admit. It was quite a new experience for me. Mrs Lackersteen was all over me. "DEAR Mr Flory", she calls me now. And she's got her knife properly in Ellis. She hasn't forgotten that he called her a bloody hag and told her to stop squealing like a pig.'

'Ah, Mr Ellis iss sometimes over-emphatic in hiss expressions. I have noticed it.'

'The only fly in the ointment is that I told the police to fire over the crowd's heads instead of straight at them. It seems that's against all the Government regulations. Ellis was a little vexed about it. "Why didn't you plug some of the b—s when you had the chance?" he said. I pointed out that it would have meant hitting the police who were in the middle of the crowd; but as he said, they were only niggers anyway. However, all my sins are forgiven me. And Macgregor quoted something in Latin—Horace, I believe.'

It was half an hour later when Flory walked along to the Club. He had promised to see Mr Macgregor and settle the business of the doctor's election. But there would be no difficulty about it now. The others would eat out of his hand until the absurd riot was forgotten; he could have gone into the Club and made a speech in favour of Lenin, and they would have put up with it. The lovely rain streamed down, drenching him from head to foot, and filling his nostrils with the scent of earth, forgotten during the bitter months of drought. He walked up the wrecked garden, where the mali, bending down with the rain splashing on his bare back, was trowelling holes for zinnias. Nearly all the flowers had been trampled out of existence. Elizabeth was there, on the side veranda, almost as though she were waiting for him. He took off his hat, spilling a pool of water from the brim, and went round to join her.

'Good morning!' he said, raising his voice because of the rain that beat noisily on the low roof.

'Good morning! ISN'T it coming down? Simply PELTING!'

'Oh, this isn't real rain. You wait till July. The whole Bay of Bengal is going to pour itself on us, by instalments.'

It seemed that they must never meet without talking of the weather. Nevertheless, her face said something very different from the banal words. Her demeanour had changed utterly since last night. He took courage.

'How is the place where that stone hit you?'

She held her arm out to him and let him take it. Her air was gentle, even submissive. He realized that his exploit of last night had made him almost a hero in her eyes. She could not know how small the danger had really been, and she forgave him everything, even Ma Hla May, because he had shown courage at the right moment. It was the buffalo and the leopard over again. His heart thumped in his breast. He slipped his hand down her arm and clasped her fingers in his own.

'Elizabeth—'

'Someone will see us!' she said, and she withdrew her hand, but not angrily.

'Elizabeth, I've something I want to say to you. Do you remember a letter I wrote you from the jungle, after our—some weeks ago?'

'Yes.'

'You remember what I said in it?'

'Yes. I'm sorry I didn't answer it. Only—'

'I couldn't expect you to answer it, then. But I just wanted to remind you of what I said.'

In the letter, of course, he had only said, and feebly enough, that he loved her—would always love her, no matter what happened. They were standing face to face, very close together. On an impulse— and it was so swiftly done that afterwards he had difficulty in believing that it had ever happened—he took her in his arms and drew her towards him. For a moment she yielded and let him lift up her face and kiss her; then suddenly she recoiled and shook her head. Perhaps she was frightened that someone would see them, perhaps it was only because his moustache was so wet from the rain. Without saying anything more she broke from him and hurried away into the Club. There was a look of distress or compunction in her face; but she did not seem angry.

He followed her more slowly into the Club, and ran into Mr Macgregor, who was in a very good humour. As soon as he saw Flory he boomed genially, 'Aha! The conquering hero comes!' and then, in a more serious vein, offered him fresh congratulations. Flory improved the occasion by saying a few words on behalf of the doctor. He painted quite a lively picture of the doctor's heroism in the riot. 'He was right in the middle of the crowd, fighting like a tiger,' etc., etc. It was not too much exaggerated—for the doctor had certainly risked his life. Mr Macgregor was impressed, and so were the others when they heard of it. At all times the testimony of one European can do an Oriental more good than that of a thousand of his fellow countrymen; and at this moment Flory's opinion carried weight. Practically, the doctor's good name was restored. His election to the Club could be taken as assured.

However, it was not finally agreed upon yet, because Flory was returning to camp. He set out the same evening, marching by night, and he did not see Elizabeth again before leaving. It was quite safe to travel in the jungle now, for the futile rebellion was obviously finished. There is seldom any talk of rebellion after the rains have started—the Burmans are too busy ploughing, and in any case the waterlogged fields are impassable for large bodies of men. Flory was to return to Kyauktada in ten days, when the padre's six-weekly visit fell due. The truth was that he did not care to be in Kyauktada while both Elizabeth and Verrall were there. And yet, it was strange, but all the bitterness—all the obscene, crawling envy that had tormented him before—was gone now that he knew she had forgiven him. It was only Verrall who stood between them now. And even the thought of her in Verrall's arms could hardly move him, because he knew that at the worst the affair must have an end. Verrall, it was quite certain, would never marry Elizabeth; young men of Verrall's stamp do not marry penniless girls met casually at obscure Indian stations. He was only amusing himself with Elizabeth. Presently he would desert her, and she would return to him—to Flory. It was enough—it was far better than he had hoped. There is a humility about genuine love that is rather horrible in some ways.

U Po Kyin was furiously angry. The miserable riot had taken him unawares, so far as anything ever took him unawares, and it was like a handful of grit thrown into the machinery of his plans. The business of disgracing the doctor had got to be begun all over again. Begun it was, sure enough, with such a spate of anonymous letters that Hla Pe had to absent himself from office for two whole days—it was bronchitis this time—to get them written. The doctor was accused of every crime from pederasty to stealing Government postage stamps. The prison warder who had let Nga Shwe O escape had now come up for trial. He was triumphantly acquitted, U Po Kyin having spent as much as two hundred rupees in bribing the witnesses. More letters showered up on Mr Macgregor, proving in detail that Dr Veraswami, the real author of the escape, had tried to shift the blame on to a helpless subordinate. Nevertheless, the results were disappointing. The confidential letter which Mr Macgregor wrote to the Commissioner, reporting on the riot, was steamed open, and its tone was so alarming—Mr Macgregor had spoken of the doctor as 'behaving most creditably' on the night of the riot—that U Po Kyin called a council of war.

'The time has come for a vigorous move,' he said to the others— they were in conclave on the front veranda, before breakfast. Ma Kin was there, and Ba Sein and Hla Pe—the latter a bright-faced, promising boy of eighteen, with the manner of one who will certainly succeed in life.

'We are hammering against a brick wall,' U Po Kyin continued; 'and that wall is Flory. Who could have foreseen that that miserable coward would stand by his friend? However, there it is. So long as Veraswami has his backing, we are helpless.'

'I have been talking to the Club butler, sir,' said Ba Sein. 'He tells me that Mr Ellis and Mr Westfield still do not want the doctor to be elected to the Club. Do you not think they will quarrel with Flory again as soon as this business of the riot is forgotten?'

'Of course they will quarrel, they always quarrel. But in the meantime the harm is done. Just suppose that man WERE elected! I believe I should die of rage if it happened. No, there is only one move left. We must strike at Flory himself!'

'At Flory, sir! But he is a white man!'

'What do I care? I have ruined white men before now. Once let Flory be disgraced, and there is an end of the doctor. And he shall be disgraced! I will shame him so that he will never dare show his face in that Club again!'

'But, sir! A white man! What are we to accuse him of? Who would believe anything against a white man?'

'You have no strategy, Ko Ba Sein. One does not ACCUSE a white man; one has got to catch him in the act. Public disgrace, in flagrante delicto. I shall know how to set about it. Now be silent while I think.'

There was a pause. U Po Kyin stood gazing out into the rain with his small hands clasped behind him and resting on the natural plateau of his posterior. The other three watched him from the end of the veranda, almost frightened by this talk of attacking a white man, and waiting for some masterstroke to cope with a situation that was beyond them. It was a little like the familiar picture (is it Meissonier's?) of Napoleon at Moscow, poring over his maps while his marshals wait in silence, with their cocked hats in their hands. But of course U Po Kyin was more equal to the situation than Napoleon. His plan was ready within two minutes. When he turned round his vast face was suffused with excessive joy. The doctor had been mistaken when he described U Po Kyin as attempting to dance; U Po Kyin's figure was not designed for dancing; but, had it been so designed, he would have danced at this moment. He beckoned to Ba Sein and whispered in his ear for a few seconds.

'That is the correct move, I think?' he concluded.

A broad, unwilling, incredulous grin stole slowly across Ba Sein's face.

'Fifty rupees ought to cover all the expenses,' added U Po Kyin, beaming.

The plan was unfolded in detail. And when the others had taken it in, all of them, even Ba Sein, who seldom laughed, even Ma Kin, who disapproved from the bottom of her soul, burst into irrepressible peals of laughter. The plan was really too good to be resisted. It was genius.

All the while it was raining, raining. The day after Flory went back to camp it rained for thirty-eight hours at a stretch, sometimes slowing to the pace of English rain, sometimes pouring down in such cataracts that one thought the whole ocean must by now have been sucked up into the clouds. The rattling on the roof became maddening after a few hours. In the intervals between the rain the sun glared as fiercely as ever, the mud began to crack and steam, and patches of prickly heat sprang out all over one's body. Hordes of flying beetles had emerged from their cocoons as soon as the rain started; there was a plague of loathly creatures known as stink-bugs, which invaded the houses in incredible numbers, littered themselves over the dining-table and made one's food uneatable. Verrall and Elizabeth still went out riding in the evenings, when the rain was not too fierce. To Verrall, all climates were alike, but he did not like to see his ponies plastered with mud. Nearly a week went by. Nothing was changed between them—they were neither less nor more intimate than they had been before. The proposal of marriage, still confidently expected, was still unuttered. Then an alarming thing happened. The news filtered to the Club, through Mr Macgregor, that Verrall was leaving Kyauktada; the Military Police were to be kept at Kyauktada, but another officer was coming in Verrall's place, no one was certain when. Elizabeth was in horrible suspense. Surely, if he was going away, he must say something definite soon? She could not question him—dared not even ask him whether he was really going; she could only wait for him to speak. He said nothing. Then one evening, without warning, he failed to turn up at the Club. And two whole days passed during which Elizabeth did not see him at all.

It was dreadful, but there was nothing that could be done. Verrall and Elizabeth had been inseparable for weeks, and yet in a way they were almost strangers. He had kept himself so aloof from them all— had never even seen the inside of the Lackersteens' house. They did not know him well enough to seek him out at the dakbungalow, or write to him; nor did he reappear at morning parade on the maidan. There was nothing to do except wait until he chose to present himself again. And when he did, would he ask her to marry him? Surely, surely he must! Both Elizabeth and her aunt (but neither of them had even spoken of it openly) held it as an article of faith that he must ask her. Elizabeth looked forward to their next meeting with a hope that was almost painful. Please God it would be a week at least before he went! If she rode with him four times more, or three times—even if it were only twice, all might yet be well. Please God he would come back to her soon! It was unthinkable that when he came, it would only be to say good-bye! The two women went down to the Club each evening and sat there until quite late, listening for Verrall's footsteps outside while seeming not to listen; but he never appeared. Ellis, who understood the situation perfectly, watched Elizabeth with spiteful amusement. What made it worst of all was that Mr Lackersteen was now pestering Elizabeth unceasingly. He had become quite reckless. Almost under the eyes of the servants he would waylay her, catch hold of her and begin pinching and fondling her in the most revolting way. Her sole defence was to threaten that she would tell her aunt; happily he was too stupid to realize that she would never dare do it.

On the third morning Elizabeth and her aunt arrived at the Club just in time to escape a violent storm of rain. They had been sitting in the lounge for a few minutes when they heard the sound of someone stamping the water off his shoes in the passage. Each woman's heart stirred, for this might be Verrall. Then a young man entered the lounge, unbuttoning a long raincoat as he came. He was a stout, rollicking, chuckle-headed youth of about twenty-five, with fat fresh cheeks, butter-coloured hair, no forehead, and, as it turned out afterwards, a deafening laugh.

Mrs Lackersteen made some inarticulate sound—it was jerked out of her by her disappointment. The youth, however, hailed them with immediate bonhomie, being one of those who are on terms of slangy intimacy with everyone from the moment of meeting them.

'Hullo, hullo!' he said 'Enter the fairy prince! Hope I don't sort of intrude and all that? Not shoving in on any family gatherings or anything?'

'Not at all!' said Mrs Lackersteen in surprise.

'What I mean to say—thought I'd just pop in at the Club and have a glance round, don't you know. Just to get acclimatized to the local brand of whisky. I only got here last night.'

'Are you STATIONED here?' said Mrs Lackersteen, mystified—for they had not been expecting any newcomers.

'Yes, rather. Pleasure's mine, entirely.'

'But we hadn't heard. . . . Oh, of course! I suppose you're from the Forest Department? In place of poor Mr Maxwell?'

'What? Forest Department? No fear! I'm the new Military Police bloke, you know.'

'The—what?'

‘New Military Police bloke. Taking over from dear ole Verrall. The dear ole chap got orders to go back to his regiment. Going off in a fearful hurry. And a nice mess he’s left everything in for yours truly, too.’

The Military Policeman was a crass youth, but even he noticed that Elizabeth’s face turned suddenly sickly. She found herself quite unable to speak. It was several seconds before Mrs Lackersteen managed to exclaim:

‘Mr Verrall—going? Surely he isn’t going away YET?’

‘Going? He’s gone!’

‘GONE?’

‘Well, what I mean to say—train’s due to start in about half an hour. He’ll be along at the station now. I sent a fatigue party to look after him. Got to get his ponies aboard and all that.’

There were probably further explanations, but neither Elizabeth nor her aunt heard a word of them. In any case, without even a good-bye to the Military Policeman, they were out on the front steps within fifteen seconds. Mrs Lackersteen called sharply for the butler.

‘Butler! Send my rickshaw round to the front at once! To the station, jaldi!’ she added as the rickshaw-man appeared, and, having settled herself in the rickshaw, poked him in the back with the ferrule of her umbrella to start him.

Elizabeth had put on her raincoat and Mrs Lackersteen was cowering in the rickshaw behind her umbrella, but neither was much use against the rain. It came driving towards them in such sheets that Elizabeth’s frock was soaked before they had reached the gate, and the rickshaw almost overturned in the wind. The rickshaw-wallah put his head down and struggled into it, groaning. Elizabeth was in agony. It was a mistake, SURELY it was a mistake. He had written to her and the letter had gone astray. That was it, that MUST be it! It could not be that he had meant to leave her without even saying good-bye! And if it were so—no, not even then would she give up hope! When he saw her on the platform, for the last time, he could not be so brutal as to forsake her! As they neared the station she fell behind the rickshaw and pinched her cheeks to bring the blood into them. A squad of Military Police sepoys shuffled hurriedly by, their thin uniforms sodden into rags, pushing a handcart among them. Those would be Verrall's fatigue party. Thank God, there was a quarter of an hour yet. The train was not due to leave for another quarter of an hour. Thank God, at least, for this last chance of seeing him!

They arrived on the platform just in time to see the train draw out of the station and gather speed with a series of deafening snorts. The stationmaster, a little round, black man, was standing on the line looking ruefully after the train, and holding his waterproof-covered topi on to his head with one hand, while with the other he fended off two clamorous Indians who were bobbing at him and trying to thrust something upon his attention. Mrs Lackersteen leaned out of the rickshaw and called agitatedly through the rain.

'Stationmaster!'

'Madam!'

'What train is that?'

'That is the Mandalay train, madam.'

'The Mandalay train! It can't be!'

'But I assure you, madam! It is precisely the Mandalay train.' He came towards them, removing his topi.

'But Mr Verrall—the Police officer? Surely he's not on it?'

'Yes, madam, he have departed.' He waved his hand towards the train, now receding rapidly in a cloud of rain and steam.

'But the train wasn't due to start yet!'

'No, madam. Not due to start for another ten minutes.'

'Then why has it gone?'

The stationmaster waved his topi apologetically from side to side. His dark, squabby face looked quite distressed.

'I know, madam, I know! MOST unprecedented! But the young Military Police officer have positively COMMANDED me to start the train! He declare that all is ready and he do not wish to be kept waiting. I point out the irregularity. He say he do not care about irregularity. I expostulate. He insist. And in short—'

He made another gesture. It meant that Verrall was the kind of man who would have his way, even when it came to starting a train ten minutes early. There was a pause. The two Indians, imagining that they saw their chance, suddenly rushed forward, wailing, and offered some grubby notebooks for Mrs Lackersteen's inspection.

'What DO these men want?' cried Mrs Lackersteen distractedly.

'They are grass-wallahs, madam. They say that Lieutenant Verrall have departed owing them large sums of money. One for hay, the other for corn. Of mine it is no affair.'

There was a hoot from the distant train. It rolled round the bend, like a black-behinded caterpillar that looks over its shoulder as it goes, and vanished. The stationmaster's wet white trousers flapped forlornly about his legs. Whether Verrall had started the train early to escape Elizabeth, or to escape the grass-wallahs, was an interesting question that was never cleared up.

They made their way back along the road, and then struggled up the hill in such a wind that sometimes they were driven several paces backwards. When they gained the veranda they were quite out of breath. The servants took their streaming raincoats, and Elizabeth shook some of the water from her hair. Mrs Lackersteen broke her silence for the first time since they had left the station:

'WELL! Of all the unmannerly—of the simply ABOMINABLE. . . !'

Elizabeth looked pale and sickly, in spite of the rain and wind that had beaten into her face. But she would betray nothing.

'I think he might have waited to say good-bye to us,' she said coldly.

'Take my word for it, dear, you are thoroughly well rid of him! . . . As I said from the start, a most ODIOUS young man!'

Some time later, when they were sitting down to breakfast, having bathed and got into dry clothes, and feeling better, she remarked:

'Let me see, what day is this?'

'Saturday, Aunt.'

'Ah, Saturday. Then the dear padre will be arriving this evening. How many shall we be for the service tomorrow? Why, I think we shall ALL be here! How very nice! Mr Flory will be here too. I think he said he was coming back from the jungle tomorrow.' She added almost lovingly, 'DEAR Mr Flory!'

Chapter 24

It was nearly six o'clock in the evening, and the absurd bell in the six-foot tin steeple of the church went clank-clank, clank-clank! as old Mattu pulled the rope within. The rays of the setting sun, refracted by distant rainstorms, flooded the maidan with a beautiful, lurid light. It had been raining earlier in the day, and would rain again. The Christian community of Kyauktada, fifteen in number, were gathering at the church door for the evening service.

Flory was already there, and Mr Macgregor, grey topi and all, and Mr Francis and Mr Samuel, frisking about in freshly laundered drill suits—for the six-weekly church service was the great social event of their lives. The padre, a tall man with grey hair and a refined, discoloured face, wearing pince-nez, was standing on the church steps in his cassock and surplice, which he had put on in Mr Macgregor's house. He was smiling in an amiable but rather helpless way at four pink-cheeked Karen Christians who had come to make their bows to him; for he did not speak a word of their language nor they of his. There was one other Oriental Christian, a mournful, dark Indian of uncertain race, who stood humbly in the background. He was always present at the church services, but no one knew who he was or why he was a Christian. Doubtless he had been captured and baptized in infancy by the missionaries, for Indians who are converted when adults almost invariably lapse.

Flory could see Elizabeth coming down the hill, dressed in lilac-colour, with her aunt and uncle. He had seen her that morning at the Club—they had had just a minute alone together before the others came in. He had only asked her one question.

'Has Verrall gone—for good?'

'Yes.'

There had been no need to say any more. He had simply taken her by the arms and drawn her towards him. She came willingly, even gladly—there in the clear daylight, merciless to his disfigured face. For a moment she had clung to him almost like a child. It was a though he had saved her or protected her from something. He raised her face to kiss her, and found with surprise that she was crying. There had been no time to talk then, not even to say, 'Will you marry me?' No matter, after the service there would be time enough. Perhaps at his next visit, only six weeks hence, the padre would marry them.

Ellis and Westfield and the new Military Policeman were approaching from the Club, where they had been having a couple of quick ones to last them through the service. The Forest Officer who had been sent to take Maxwell's place, a sallow, tall man, completely bald except for two whisker-like tufts in front of his ears, was following them. Flory had not time to say more than 'Good evening' to Elizabeth when she arrived. Mattu, seeing that everyone was present, stopped ringing the bell, and the clergyman led the way inside, followed by Mr Macgregor, with his topi against his stomach, and the Lackersteens and the native Christians. Ellis pinched Flory's elbow and whispered boozily in his ear:

'Come on, line up. Time for the snivel-parade. Quick march!'

He and the Military Policeman went in behind the others, arm-in-arm, with a dancing step—the policeman, till they got inside, wagging his fat behind in imitation of a pwe-dancer. Flory sat down in the same pew as these two, opposite Elizabeth, on her right. It was the first time that he had ever risked sitting with his birthmark towards her. 'Shut your eyes and count twenty-five', whispered Ellis as they sat down, drawing a snigger from the policeman. Mrs Lackersteen had already taken her place at the harmonium, which was no bigger than a writing-desk. Mattu stationed himself by the door and began to pull the punkah—it was so arranged that it only flapped over the front pews, where the Europeans sat. Flo came nosing up the aisle, found Flory's pew and settled down underneath it. The service began.

Flory was only attending intermittently. He was dimly aware of standing and kneeling and muttering 'Amen' to interminable prayers, and of Ellis nudging him and whispering blasphemies behind his hymn book. But he was too happy to collect his thoughts. Hell was yielding up Eurydice. The yellow light flooded in through the open door, gilding the broad back of Mr Macgregor's silk coat like cloth-of-gold. Elizabeth, across the narrow aisle, was so close to Flory that he could hear every rustle of her dress and feel, as it seemed to him, the warmth of her body; yet he would not look at her even once, lest the others should notice it. The harmonium quavered bronchitically as Mrs Lackersteen struggled to pump sufficient air into it with the sole pedal that worked. The singing was a queer, ragged noise—an earnest booming from Mr Macgregor, a kind of shamefaced muttering from the other Europeans, and from the back a loud, wordless lowing, for the Karen Christians knew the tunes of the hymns but not the words.

They were kneeling down again. 'More bloody knee-drill,' Ellis whispered. The air darkened, and there was a light patter of rain on the roof; the trees outside rustled, and a cloud of yellow leaves whirled past the window. Flory watched them through the chinks of his fingers. Twenty years ago, on winter Sundays in his pew in the parish church at home, he used to watch the yellow leaves, as at this moment, drifting and fluttering against leaden skies. Was it not possible, now, to begin over again as though those grimy years had never touched him? Through his fingers he glanced sidelong at Elizabeth, kneeling with her head bent and her face hidden in her youthful, mottled hands. When they were married, when they were married! What fun they would have together in this alien yet kindly land! He saw Elizabeth in his camp, greeting him as he came home tired from work and Ko S'la hurried from the tent with a bottle of beer; he saw her walking in the forest with him, watching the hornbills in the peepul trees and picking nameless flowers, and in the marshy grazing-grounds, tramping through the cold-weather mist after snipe and teal. He saw his home as she would remake it. He saw his drawing-room, sluttish and bachelor-like no longer, with new furniture from Rangoon, and a bowl of pink balsams like rosebuds on the table, and books and water-colours and a black piano. Above all the piano! His mind lingered upon the piano—symbol, perhaps because he was unmusical, of civilized and settled life. He was delivered for ever from the sub-life of the past decade—the debaucheries, the lies, the pain of exile and solitude, the dealings with whores and moneylenders and pukka sahibs.

The clergyman stepped to the small wooden lectern that also served as a pulpit, slipped the band from a roll of sermon paper, coughed, and announced a text. 'In the name of the Father, the Son and the Holy Ghost. Amen.'

'Cut it short, for Christ's sake,' murmured Ellis.

Flory did not notice how many minutes passed. The words of the sermon flowed peacefully through his head, an indistinct burbling sound, almost unheard. When they were married, he was still thinking, when they were married—

Hullo! What was happening?

The clergyman had stopped short in the middle of a word. He had taken off his pince-nez and was shaking them with a distressed air at someone in the doorway. There was a fearful, raucous scream.

'Pike-san pay-like! Pike-san pay-like!'

Everyone jumped in their seats and turned round. It was Ma Hla May. As they turned she stepped inside the church and shoved old Mattu violently aside. She shook her fist at Flory.

'Pike-san pay-like! Pike-san pay-like! Yes, THAT'S the one I mean—Flory, Flory! (She pronounced it Porley.) That one sitting in front there, with the black hair! Turn round and face me, you coward! Where is the money you promised me?'

She was shrieking like a maniac. The people gaped at her, too astounded to move or speak. Her face was grey with powder, her greasy hair was tumbling down, her longyi was ragged at the bottom. She looked like a screaming hag of the bazaar. Flory's bowels seemed to have turned to ice. Oh God, God! Must they know—must Elizabeth know— that THAT was the woman who had been his mistress? But there was not a hope, not the vestige of a hope, of any mistake. She had screamed his name over and over again. Flo, hearing the familiar voice, wriggled from under the pew, walked down the aisle and wagged her tail at Ma Hla May. The wretched woman was yelling out a detailed account of what Flory had done to her.

'Look at me, you white men, and you women, too, look at me! Look how he has ruined me! Look at these rags I am wearing! And he is sitting there, the liar, the coward, pretending not to see me! He would let me starve at his gate like a pariah dog. Ah, but I will shame you! Turn round and look at me! Look at this body that you have kissed a thousand times—look—look—'

She began actually to tear her clothes open—the last insult of a base-born Burmese woman. The harmonium squeaked as Mrs Lackersteen made a convulsive movement. People had at last found their wits and began to stir. The clergyman, who had been bleating ineffectually, recovered his voice, 'Take that woman outside!' he said sharply.

Flory's face was ghastly. After the first moment he had turned his head away from the door and set his teeth in a desperate effort to look unconcerned. But it was useless, quite useless. His face was as yellow as bone, and the sweat glistened on his forehead. Francis and Samuel, doing perhaps the first useful deed of their lives, suddenly sprang from their pew, grabbed Ma Hla May by the arms and hauled her outside, still screaming.

It seemed very silent in the church when they had finally dragged her out of hearing. The scene had been so violent, so squalid, that everyone was upset by it. Even Ellis looked disgusted. Flory could neither speak nor stir. He sat staring fixedly at the altar, his face rigid and so bloodless that the birth-mark seemed to glow upon it like a streak of blue paint. Elizabeth glanced across the aisle at him, and her revulsion made her almost physically sick. She had not understood a word of what Ma Hla May was saying, but the meaning of the scene was perfectly clear. The thought that he had been the lover of that grey-faced, maniacal creature made her shudder in her bones. But worse than that, worse than anything, was his ugliness at this moment. His face appalled her, it was so ghastly, rigid and old. It was like a skull. Only the birthmark seemed alive in it. She hated him now for his birthmark. She had never known till this moment how dishonouring, how unforgivable a thing it was.

Like the crocodile, U Po Kyin had struck at the weakest spot. For, needless to say, this scene was U Po Kyin's doing. He had seen his chance, as usual, and tutored Ma Hla May for her part with considerable care. The clergyman brought his sermon to an end almost at once. As soon as it was over Flory hurried outside, not looking at any of the others. It was getting dark, thank God. At fifty yards from the church he halted, and watched the others making in couples for the Club. It seemed to him that they were hurrying. Ah, they would, of course! There would be something to talk about at the Club tonight! Flo rolled belly-upwards against his ankles, asking for a game. 'Get out, you bloody brute!' he said, and kicked her. Elizabeth had stopped at the church door. Mr Macgregor, happy chance, seemed to be introducing her to the clergyman. In a moment the two men went on in the direction of Mr Macgregor's house, where the clergyman was to stay for the night, and Elizabeth followed the others, thirty yards behind them. Flory ran after her and caught up with her almost at the Club gate.

'Elizabeth!'

She looked round, saw him, turned white, and would have hurried on without a word. But his anxiety was too great, and he caught her by the wrist.

'Elizabeth! I must—I've got to speak to you!'

'Let me go, will you!'

They began to struggle, and then stopped abruptly. Two of the Karens who had come out of the church were standing fifty yards away, gazing at them through the half-darkness with deep interest. Flory began again in a lower tone:

'Elizabeth, I know I've no right to stop you like this. But I must speak to you, I must! Please hear what I've got to say. Please don't run away from me!'

'What are you doing? Why are you holding on to my arm? Let me go this instant!'

'I'll let you go—there, look! But do listen to me, please! Answer me this one thing. After what's happened, can you ever forgive me?'

'Forgive you? What do you mean, FORGIVE you?'

'I know I'm disgraced. It was the vilest thing to happen! Only, in a sense it wasn't my fault. You'll see that when you're calmer. Do you think—not now, it was too bad, but later—do you think you can forget it?'

'I really don't know what you're talking about. Forget it? What has it got to do with ME? I thought it was very disgusting, but it's not MY business. I can't think why you're questioning me like this at all.'

He almost despaired at that. Her tone and even her words were the very ones she had used in that earlier quarrel of theirs. It was the same move over again. Instead of hearing him out she was going to evade him and put him off—snub him by pretending that he had no claim upon her.

'Elizabeth! Please answer me. Please be fair to me! It's serious this time. I don't expect you to take me back all at once. You couldn't, when I'm publicly disgraced like this. But, after all, you virtually promised to marry me—'

'What! Promised to marry you? WHEN did I promise to marry you?'

'Not in words, I know. But it was understood between us.'

'Nothing of the kind was understood between us! I think you are behaving in the most horrible way. I'm going along to the Club at once. Good evening!'

'Elizabeth! Elizabeth! Listen. It's not fair to condemn me unheard. You knew before what I'd done, and you knew that I'd lived a different life since I met you. What happened this evening was only an accident. That wretched woman, who, I admit, was once my—well—'

'I won't listen, I won't listen to such things! I'm going!'

He caught her by the wrists again, and this time held her. The Karens had disappeared, fortunately.

'No, no, you shall hear me! I'd rather offend you to the heart than have this uncertainty. It's gone on week after week, month after month, and I've never once been able to speak straight out to you. You don't seem to know or care how much you make me suffer. But this time you've got to answer me.'

She struggled in his grip, and she was surprisingly strong. Her face was more bitterly angry than he had ever seen or imagined it. She hated him so that she would have struck him if her hands were free.

'Let me go! Oh, you beast, you beast, let me go!'

'My God, my God, that we should fight like this! But what else can I do? I can't let you go without even hearing me. Elizabeth, you MUST listen to me!'

'I will not! I will not discuss it! What right have you to question me? Let me go!'

'Forgive me, forgive me! This one question. Will you—not now, but later, when this vile business is forgotten—will you marry me?'

'No, never, never!'

'Don't say it like that! Don't make it final. Say no for the present if you like—but in a month, a year, five years—'

'Haven't I said no? Why must you keep on and on?'

'Elizabeth, listen to me. I've tried again and again to tell you what you mean to me—oh, it's so useless talking about it! But do try and understand. Haven't I told you something of the life we live here? The sort of horrible death-in-life! The decay, the loneliness, the self-pity? Try and realize what it means, and that you're the sole person on earth who could save me from it.'

'Will you let me go? Why do you have to make this dreadful scene?'

'Does it mean nothing to you when I say that I love you? I don't believe you've ever realized what it is that I want from you. If you like, I'd marry you and promise never even touch you with my finger. I wouldn't mind even that, so long as you were with me. But I can't go on with my life alone, always alone. Can't you bring yourself ever to forgive me?'

'Never, never! I wouldn't marry you if you were the last man on earth. I'd as soon marry the—the sweeper!'

She had begun crying now. He saw that she meant what she said. The tears came into his own eyes. He said again:

'For the last time. Remember that it's something to have one person in the world who loves you. Remember that though you'll find men who are richer, and younger, and better in every way than I, you'll never find one who cares for you so much. And though I'm not rich, at least I could make you a home. There's a way of living—civilized, decent—'

'Haven't we said enough?' she said more calmly. 'Will you let me go before somebody comes?'

He relaxed his grip on her wrists. He had lost her, that was certain. Like a hallucination, painfully clear, he saw again their home as he had imagined it; he saw their garden, and Elizabeth feeding Nero and the pigeons on the drive by the sulphur-yellow phloxes that grew as high as her shoulder; and the drawing-room, with the water-colours on the walls, and the balsams in the china bowl mirrored by the table, and the book-shelves, and the black piano. The impossible, mythical piano—symbol of everything that that futile accident had wrecked!

'You should have a piano,' he said despairingly.

'I don't play the piano.'

He let her go. It was no use continuing. She was no sooner free of him than she took to her heels and actually ran into the Club garden, so hateful was his presence to her. Among the trees she stopped to take off her spectacles and remove the signs of tears from her face. Oh, the beast, the beast! He had hurt her wrists abominably. Oh, what an unspeakable beast he was! When she thought of his face as it had looked in church, yellow and glistening with the hideous birthmark upon it, she could have wished him dead. It was not what he had done that horrified her. He might have committed a thousand abominations and she could have forgiven him. But not after that shameful, squalid scene, and the devilish ugliness of his disfigured face in that moment. It was, finally, the birthmark that had damned him.

Her aunt would be furious when she heard that she had refused Flory. And there was her uncle and his leg-pinching—between the two of them, life here would become impossible. Perhaps she would have to go Home unmarried after all. Black beetles! No matter. Anything—spinsterhood, drudgery, anything—sooner than the alternative. Never, never, would she yield to a man who had been so disgraced! Death sooner, far sooner. If there had been mercenary thoughts in her mind an hour ago, she had forgotten them. She did not even remember that Verrall had jilted her and that to have married Flory would have saved her face. She knew only that he was dishonoured and less than a man, and that she hated him as she would have hated a leper or a lunatic. The instinct was deeper than reason or even self-interest, and she could no more have disobeyed it than she could have stopped breathing.

Flory, as he turned up the hill, did not run, but he walked as fast as he could. What he had to do must be done quickly. It was getting very dark. The wretched Flo, who even now had not grasped that anything serious was the matter, trotted close to his heels, whimpering in a self-pitying manner to reproach him for the kick he had given her. As he came up the path a wind blew through the plaintain trees, rattling the tattered leaves and bringing a scent of damp. It was going to rain again. Ko S'la had laid the dinner-table and was removing some flying beetles that had committed suicide against the petrol-lamp. Evidently he had not heard about the scene in church yet.

'The holy one's dinner is ready. Will the holy one dine now?'

'No, not yet. Give me that lamp.'

He took the lamp, went into the bedroom and shut the door, The stale scent of dust and cigarette-smoke met him, and in the white, unsteady glare of the lamp he could see the mildewed books and the lizards on the wall. So he was back again to this—to the old, secret life—after everything, back where he had been before.

Was it not possible to endure it! He had endured it before. There were palliatives—books, his garden, drink, work, whoring, shooting, conversations with the doctor.

No, it was not endurable any longer. Since Elizabeth's coming the power to suffer and above all to hope, which he had thought dead in him, had sprung to new life. The half-comfortable lethargy in which he had lived was broken. And if he suffered now, there was far worse to come. In a little while someone else would marry her. How he could picture it—the moment when he heard the news!—'Did you hear the Lackersteen kid's got off at last? Poor old So-and-so—booked for the altar, God help him,' etc., etc. And the casual question—'Oh, really? When is it to be?'—stiffening one's face, pretending to be uninterested. And then her wedding day approaching, her bridal night—ah, not that! Obscene, obscene. Keep your eyes fixed on that. Obscene. He dragged his tin uniform-case from under the bed, took out his automatic pistol, slid a clip of cartridges into the magazine, and pulled one into the breech.

Ko S'la was remembered in his will. There remained Flo. He laid his pistol on the table and went outside. Flo was playing with Ba Shin, Ko S'la's youngest son, under the lee of the cookhouse, where the servants had left the remains of a woodfire. She was dancing round him with her small teeth bared, pretending to bite him, while the tiny boy, his belly red in the glow of the embers, smacked weakly at her, laughing, and yet half frightened.

'Flo! Come here, Flo!'

She heard him and came obediently, and then stopped short at the bedroom door. She seemed to have grasped now that there was something wrong. She backed a little and stood looking timorously up at him, unwilling to enter the bedroom.

'Come in here!'

She wagged her tail, but did not move.

'Come on, Flo! Good old Flo! Come on!'

Flo was suddenly stricken with terror. She whined, her tail went down, and she shrank back. 'Come here, blast you!' he cried, and he took her by the collar and flung her into the room, shutting the door behind her. He went to the table for the pistol.

'No come here! Do as you're told!'

She crouched down and whined for forgiveness. It hurt him to hear it. 'Come on, old girl! Dear old Flo! Master wouldn't hurt you. Come here!' She crawled very slowly towards his feet, flat on her belly, whining, her head down as though afraid to look at him. When she was a yard away he fired, blowing her skull to fragments.

Her shattered brain looked like red velvet. Was that what he would look like? The heart, then, not the head. He could hear the servants running out of their quarters and shouting—they must have heard the sound of the shot. He hurriedly tore open his coat and pressed the muzzle of the pistol against his shirt. A tiny lizard, translucent like a creature of gelatine, was stalking a white moth along the edge of the table. Flory pulled the trigger with his thumb.

As Ko S'la burst into the room, for a moment he saw nothing but the dead body of the dog. Then he saw his master's feet, heels upwards, projecting from beyond the bed. He yelled to the others to keep the children out of the room, and all of them surged back from the doorway with screams. Ko S'la fell on his knees behind Flory's body, at the same moment as Ba Pe came running through the veranda.

'Has he shot himself?'

'I think so. Turn him over on his back. Ah, look at that! Run for the Indian doctor! Run for your life!'

There was a neat hole, no bigger than that made by a pencil passing through a sheet of blotting-paper, in Flory's shirt. He was obviously quite dead. With great difficulty Ko S'la managed to drag him on to the bed, for the other servants refused to touch the body. It was only twenty minutes before the doctor arrived. He had heard only a vague report that Flory was hurt, and had bicycled up the hill at top speed through a storm of rain. He threw his bicycle down in the flower-bed and hurried in through the veranda. He was out of breath, and could not see through his spectacles. He took them off, peering myopically at the bed. 'What iss it, my friend?' he said anxiously. 'Where are you hurt?' Then, coming closer, he saw what was on the bed, and uttered a harsh sound.

'Ach, what is this? What has happened to him?'

The doctor fell on his knees, tore Flory's shirt open and put his ear to his chest. An expression of agony came into his face, and he seized the dead man by the shoulders and shook him as though mere violence could bring him to life. One arm fell limply over the edge of the bed. The doctor lifted it back again, and then, with the dead hand between his own, suddenly burst into tears. Ko S'la was standing at the foot of the bed, his brown face full of lines. The doctor stood up, and then losing control of himself for a moment, leaned against the bedpost and wept noisily and grotesquely his back turned on Ko S'la. His fat shoulders were quivering. Presently he recovered himself and turned round again.

'How did this happen?'

'We heard two shots. He did it himself, that is certain. I do not know why.'

'How did you know that he did it on purpose? How do you know that it was not an accident?'

For answer, Ko S'la pointed silently to Flo's corpse. The doctor thought for a moment, and then, with gentle, practised hands, swathed the dead man in the sheet and knotted it at foot and head. With death, the birthmark had faded immediately, so that it was no more than a faint grey stain.

'Bury the dog at once. I will tell Mr Macgregor that this happened accidentally while he was cleaning his revolver. Be sure that you bury the dog. Your master was my friend. It shall not be written on his tombstone that he committed suicide.'

Chapter 25

It was lucky that the padre should have been at Kyauktada, for he was able, before catching the train on the following evening, to read the burial service in due form and even to deliver a short address on the virtues of the dead man. All Englishmen are virtuous when they are dead. 'Accidental death' was the official verdict (Dr Veraswami had proved with all his medico-legal skill that the circumstances pointed to accident) and it was duly inscribed upon the tombstone. Not that anyone believed it, of course. Flory's real epitaph was the remark, very occasionally uttered—for an Englishman who dies in Burma is so soon forgotten— 'Flory? Oh yes, he was a dark chap, with a birthmark. He shot himself in Kyauktada in 1926. Over a girl, people said. Bloody fool.' Probably no one, except Elizabeth, was much surprised at what had happened. There is a rather large number of suicides among the Europeans in Burma, and they occasion very little surprise.

Flory's death had several results. The first and most important of them was that Dr Veraswami was ruined, even as he had foreseen. The glory of being a white man's friend—the one thing that had saved him before—had vanished. Flory's standing with the other Europeans had never been good, it is true; but he was after all a white man, and his friendship conferred a certain prestige. Once he was dead, the doctor's ruin was assured. U Po Kyin waited the necessary time, and then struck again, harder than ever. It was barely three months before he had fixed it in the head of every European in Kyauktada that the doctor was an unmitigated scoundrel. No public accusation was ever made against him—U Po Kyin was most careful of that. Even Ellis would have been puzzled to say just what scoundrelism the doctor had been guilty of; but still, it was agreed that he was a scoundrel. By degrees, the general suspicion of him crystallized in a single Burmese phrase—'shok de'. Veraswami, it was said, was quite a clever little chap in his way— quite a good doctor for a native—but he was THOROUGHLY shok de. Shok de means, approximately, untrustworthy, and when a 'native' official comes to be known as shok de, there is an end of him.

The dreaded nod and wink passed somewhere in high places, and the doctor was reverted to the rank of Assistant Surgeon and transferred to Mandalay General Hospital. He is still there, and is likely to remain. Mandalay is rather a disagreeable town—it is dusty and intolerably hot, and it is said to have five main products all beginning with P, namely, pagodas, pariahs, pigs, priests and prostitutes—and the routine-work of the hospital is a dreary business. The doctor lives just outside the hospital grounds in a little bake-house of a bungalow with a corrugated iron fence round its tiny compound, and in the evenings he runs a private clinic to supplement his reduced pay. He has joined a second-rate club frequented by Indian pleaders. Its chief glory is a single European member—a Glasgow electrician named Macdougall, sacked from the Irrawaddy Flotilla Company for drunkenness, and now making a precarious living out of a garage. Macdougall is a dull lout, only interested in whisky and magnetos. The doctor, who will never believe that a white man can be a fool, tries almost every night to engage him in what he still calls 'cultured conversation'; but the results are very unsatisfying.

Ko S'la inherited four hundred rupees under Flory's will, and with his family he set up a tea-shop in the bazaar. But the shop failed, as it was bound to do with the two women fighting in it at all hours, and Ko S'la and Ba Pe were obliged to go back to service. Ko S'la was an accomplished servant. Besides the useful arts of pimping, dealing with money-lenders, carrying master to bed when drunk and making pick-me-ups known as prairie oysters on the following morning, he could sew, darn, refill cartridges, attend to a horse, press a suit, and decorate a dinner-table with wonderful, intricate patterns of chopped leaves and dyed rice-grains. He was worth fifty rupees a month. But he and Ba Pe had fallen into lazy ways in Flory's service, and, they were sacked from one job after another. They had a bad year of poverty, and little Ba Shin developed a cough, and finally coughed himself to death one stifling hot-weather night. Ko S'la is now a second boy to a Rangoon rice-broker with a neurotic wife who makes unending kit-kit, and Ba Pe is pani-wallah in the same house at sixteen rupees a month. Ma Hla May is in a brothel in Mandalay. Her good looks are all but gone, and her clients pay her only four annas and sometimes kick her and beat her. Perhaps more bitterly than any of the others, she regrets the good time when Flory was alive, and when she had not the wisdom to put aside any of the money she extracted from him.

U Po Kyin realized all his dreams except one. After the doctor's disgrace, it was inevitable that U Po Kyin should be elected to the Club, and elected he was, in spite of bitter protests from Ellis. In the end the other Europeans came to be rather glad that they had elected him, for he was a bearable addition to the Club. He did not come too often, was ingratiating in his manner, stood drinks freely, and developed almost at once into a brilliant bridge-player. A few months later he was transferred from Kyauktada and promoted. For a whole year, before his retirement, he officiated as Deputy Commissioner, and during that year alone he made twenty thousand rupees in bribes. A month after his retirement he was summoned to a durbar in Rangoon, to receive the decoration that had been awarded to him by the Indian Government.

It was an impressive scene, that durbar. On the platform, hung with flags and flowers, sat the Governor, frock-coated, upon a species of throne, with a bevy of aides-de-camp and secretaries behind him. All round the hall, like glittering waxworks, stood the tall, bearded sowars of the Governor's bodyguard, with pennoned lances in their hands. Outside, a band was blaring at intervals. The gallery was gay with the white ingyis and pink scarves of Burmese ladies, and in the body of the hall a hundred men or more were waiting to receive their decorations. There were Burmese officials in blazing Mandalay pasos, and Indians in cloth-of-gold pagris, and British officers in full-dress uniform with clanking sword-scabbards, and old thugyis with their grey hair knotted behind their heads and silver-hilted dahs slung from their shoulders. In a high, clear voice a secretary was reading out the list of awards, which varied from the C.I.E. to certificates of honour in embossed silver cases. Presently U Po Kyin's turn came and the secretary read from his scroll:

'To U Po Kyin, Deputy Assistant Commissioner, retired, for long and loyal service and especially for his timely aid in crushing a most dangerous rebellion in Kyauktada district'—and so on and so on.

Then two henchmen, placed there for the purpose hoisted U Po Kyin upright, and he waddled to the platform, bowed as low as his belly would permit, and was duly decorated and felicitated, while Ma Kin and other supporters clapped wildly and fluttered their scarves from the gallery.

U Po Kyin had done all that mortal man could do. It was time now to be making ready for the next world—in short, to begin building pagodas. But unfortunately, this was the very point at which his plans went wrong. Only three days after the Governor's durbar, before so much as a brick of those atoning pagodas had been laid, U Po Kyin was stricken with apoplexy and died without speaking again. There is no armour against fate. Ma Kin was heartbroken at the disaster. Even if she had built the pagodas herself, it would have availed U Po Kyin nothing; no merit can be acquired save by one's own act. She suffers greatly to think of U Po Kyin where he must be now—wandering in God knows what dreadful subterranean hell of fire, and darkness, and serpents, and genii. Or even if he has escaped the worst, his other fear has been realized, and he has returned to the earth in the shape of a rat or a frog. Perhaps at this very moment a snake is devouring him.

As to Elizabeth, things fell out better than she had expected. After Flory's death Mrs Lackersteen, dropping all pretences for once, said openly that there were no men in this dreadful place and the only hope was to go and stay several months in Rangoon or Maymyo. But she could not very well send Elizabeth to Rangoon or Maymyo alone, and to go with her practically meant condemning Mr Lackersteen to death from delirium tremens. Months passed, and the rains reached their climax, and Elizabeth had just made up her mind that she must go home after all, penniless and unmarried, when—Mr Macgregor proposed to her. He had had it in his mind for a long time; indeed, he had only been waiting for a decent interval to elapse after Flory's death.

Elizabeth accepted him gladly. He was rather old, perhaps, but a Deputy Commissioner is not to be despised—certainly he was a far better match than Flory. They are very happy. Mr Macgregor was always a good-hearted man, but he has grown more human and likeable since his marriage. His voice booms less, and he has given up his morning exercises. Elizabeth has grown mature surprisingly quickly, and a certain hardness of manner that always belonged to her has become accentuated. Her servants live in terror of her, though she speaks no Burmese. She has an exhaustive knowledge of the Civil List, gives charming little dinner-parties and knows how to put the wives of subordinate officials in their places—in short, she fills with complete success the position for which Nature had designed her from the first, that of a burra memsahib.

THE END

LIST OF TITLES WITH ISBN NO.

ISBN	TITLE
9788194914129	1984
9789390575220	1984 & Animal Farm (2In1)
9789390575572	1984 & Animal Farm (2In1): The International Best-Selling Classics
9789390575848	35 Sonnets
9789390575329	A Clergyman's Daughter
9789390575923	A Study In Scarlet
9789390896097	A Tale Of Two Cities
9789390896837	Abide in Christ
9789390896202	Abraham Lincoln
9789390896912	Absolute Surrender
9789390896608	African American Classic Collection
9789390575305	Aldous Huxley: The Collected Works
9789390896141	An Autobiography of M. K. Gandhi
9789390575886	Animal Farm
9789390575619	Animal Farm & The Great Gatsby (2In1)
9789390575626	Animal Farm & We
9789390896158	Anna Karenina
9789390575534	Antic Hay
9789390896165	Antony & Cleopatra
9789390896172	As I Lay Dying
9789390896226	As You like it
9789390575671	At Your Command
9789390575350	Awakened Imagination
9789390575114	Be What You Wish
9789390896233	Believe In yourself
9789390896998	Best of Charles Darwin: The Origin of Species & Autobiography
9789390896684	Best Of Horror : Dracula And Frankenstein
9789390575503	Best Of Mark Twain (The Adventures of Tom Sawyer AND The Adventures of Huckleberry Finn)
9789390896769	Black History Collection
9789390575756	Brave New World, Animal Farm & 1984 (3in1)
9789390896240	Brother Karamzov
9789390575053	Bulleh Shah Poetry
9789390575725	Burmese Days

9789390896257	Bushido
9789390896066	Can't Hurt Me
9788194914112	Chanakya Neeti: With The Complete Sutras
9789390896042	Crime and Punishment
9789390575527	Crome Yellow
9789390575046	Down and Out in Paris and London
9789390896844	Dracula
9789390575442	Emersons Essays: The Complete First & Second Series (Self-Reliance & Other Essays)
9789390575749	Emma
9789390575817	Essential Tozer Collection - The Pursuit of God & The Purpose of Man
9789390896578	Fascism What It Is and How to Fight It
9789390575688	Feeling is the Secret
9789390575190	Five Lessons
9789390575954	Frankenstein
9789390575237	Franz Kafka: Collected Works
9789390575282	Franz Kafka: Short Stories
9789390575060	George Orwell Collected Works
9789390575077	George Orwell Essays
9789390575213	George Orwell Poems
9788194914150	Greatest Poetry Ever Written Vol 1
9788194914143	Greatest Poetry Ever Written Vol 1
9789390896301	Gulliver's Travel
9789390575961	Gunaho Ka Devta
9789390575893	H. P. Lovecraft Selected Stories Vol 1
9789390575978	H. P. Lovecraft Selected Stories Vol 2
9789390896059	Hamlet
9789390575022	His Last Bow: Some Reminiscences of Sherlock Holmes
9789390896134	History of Western Philosophy
9789390575121	Homage To Catalonia
9789390896219	How to develop self-confidence and Improve public Speaking
9789390896295	How to enjoy your life and your Job
9789390575633	How to own your own mind
9789390896318	How to read Human Nature
9789390896325	How to sell your way through the life
9789390896370	How to use the laws of mind
9789390896387	How to use the power of prayer

9789390896028	How to win friends & Influence People
9788194824176	How To Win Friends and Influence People
9789390896103	Humility The Beauty of Holiness
9789390896653	Imperialism the Highest Stage of Capitalism
9789390575084	In Our Time
9789390575169	In Our Time & Three Stories and Ten poems
9789390575145	James Allen: The Collected Works
9789390896189	Jesus Himself
9789390575480	Jo's Boys
9789390896394	Julius Caesar
9789390575404	Keep the Aspidistra Flying
9789390896400	Kidnapped
9789390896424	King Lear
9789390575824	Lady Susan
9789390896455	Law of Success
9789390896264	Lincoln The Unknown
9789390575565	Little Men
9789390575640	Little Women
9788194914174	Lost Horizon
9789390896462	Macbeth
9789390896929	Man Eaters of Kumaon
9789390896523	Man The Dwelling Place of God
9789390896349	Man The Dwelling Place of God
9789390575909	Mansfield Park
9788194914136	Manto Ki 25 Sarvshreshth Kahaniya
9789390896509	Marxism, Anarchism, Communism
9789390575664	Mathematical Principles of Natural Philosophy
9788194914198	Meditations
9789390575800	Mein Kampf
9789390575794	Memory How To Develop, Train, And Use It
9789390896486	Mind Power
9789390896585	Money
9789390575039	Mortal Coils
9789390575770	My Life and Work
9789390896035	Narrative of the Life of Frederick Douglass
9789390575152	Neville Goddard: The Collected Works
9789390575985	Northanger Abbey
9789390896530	Notes From Underground

9789390896547	Oliver Twist
9789390575459	On War
9789390575541	One, None and a Hundred Thousand
9789390896554	Othelo
9789390575435	Out Of This World
9789390575015	Persuasion
9789390575510	Prayer The Art Of Believing
9789390575091	Pride and Prejudice
9789390896561	Psychic Perception
9789390575381	Rabindranath Tagore - 5 Best Short Stories Vol 2
9789390575367	Rabindranath Tagore - Short Stories (Masters Collections Including The Childs Return)
9789390575374	Rabindranath Tagore 5 Best Short Stories Vol 1 (Including The Childs Return
9789390896622	Romeo & Juliet
9789390896127	Sanatana Dharma
9789390575596	Seedtime & Harvest
9789390896639	Selected Stories of Guy De Maupassant
9789390575206	Self-Reliance & Other Essays
9789390575176	Sense and Sensibility
9789390575299	Shyamchi Aai
9789390896738	Socialism Utopian and Scientific
9789390896646	Success Through a Positive Mental Attitude
9789390575428	The Adventures of Huckleberry Finn
9789390575183	The Adventures of Sherlock Holmes
9789390575343	The Adventures of Tom Sawyer
9789390896691	The Alchemy Of Happiness
9789390575862	The Art Of Public Speaking
9789390896288	The Autobiography Of Charles Darwin
9788194914181	The Best of Franz Kafka: The Metamorphosis & The Trial
9789390575008	The Call Of Cthulhu and Other Weird Tales
9789390575107	The Case-Book of Sherlock Holmes
9789390896110	The Castle Of Otranto
9789390896745	The Communist Manifesto
9789390575589	The Complete Fiction of H. P. Lovecraft
9789390575497	The Complete Works of Florence Scovel Shinn
9789390896820	The Conquest of Breard
9789390896813	The Diary of a Young Girl

9789390896332	The Diary of a Young Girl The Definitive Edition of the Worlds Most Famous Diary
9789390575701	The Great Gatsby, Animal Farm & 1984 (3In1)
9789390575312	The Greatest Works Of George Orwell (5 Books) Including 1984 & Non-Fiction
9789390575992	The Hound of Baskervilles
9789390896707	The Idiot
9789390896714	The Invisible Man
9789390575657	The Knowledge of the holy
9789390575558	The Law & the Promise
9789390896721	The Law Of Attraction
9789390896776	The Leader in you
9789390896363	The Life of Christ
9789390896196	The Man-Eating Leopard of Rudraprayag
9789390896783	The Master Key to Riches
9789390575268	The Memoirs Of Sherlock Holmes
9789390896479	The Midsummer Night's Dream
9789390575466	The Mill On The Floss
9789390896790	The Miracles of your mind
9789390896660	The Mutual Aid A Factor in Evolution
9789390896448	The Origin of Species
9789390896905	The Peter Kropotkin Anthology The Conquest of Bread & Mutual Aid A Factor of Evolution
9789390896806	The Picture of Dorian Gray
9789390896271	The Picture of Dorian Gray
9789390575275	The Power Of Awareness
9789390896356	The Power of Concentration
9788194824169	The Power of Positive Thinking
9789390575411	The Power of the Spoken Word
9788194914105	The Power Of Your Subconscious Mind
9789390896899	The Power of Your Subconscious Mind
9789390896417	The Principles of Communism
9789390575787	The Psychology Of Mans Possible Evolution
9789390896615	The Psychology of Salesmanship
9789390575732	The Pursuit of God
9789390575398	The Pursuit of Happiness
9789390896851	The Quick and Easy Way to effective Speaking
9789390575947	The Return Of Sherlock Holmes

9789390575138	The Road To Wigan Pier
9789390896981	The Root of the Righteous
9789390575855	The Science Of Being Well
9788194914167	The Science Of Getting Rich, The Science Of Being Great & The Science Of Being Well (3In1)
9789390896011	The Screwtape Letters
9789390896073	The Screwtape Letters
9789390575336	The Secret Door to Success
9789390575695	The Secret Of Imagining
9789390896868	The Secret Of Success
9789390896431	The Seven Last Words
9789390575930	The Sign of the Four
9789390896004	The Sonnets
9789390896516	The Souls of Black Folk
9789390896875	The Sound and The Fury
9789390575244	The State and Revolution
9789390896882	The Story of My Life
9789390896936	The Story Of Oriental Philosophy
9789390896752	The Strange Case of Dr. Jekyll and Mr. Hyde
9789390896943	The Tempest
9789390575916	The Valley Of Fear
9789390575879	The Wind in the willows
9789390896080	The Wind in the willows
9789390575763	Their eyes were watching gofd
9789390575831	Three Stories
9789390896950	Twelfth Night
9789390896592	Twelve Years a Slave
9789390896677	Up from Slavery
9789390896974	Value Price and Profit
9789390896967	Wake Up and Live
9789390896493	With Christ in the School of Prayer
9789390575602	Your Faith is Your Fortune
9789390575473	Your Infinite Power To Be Rich
9789390575251	Your Word is Your Wand
9789390575718	Youth
9789391316099	A Christmas Carol
9789391316105	A Doll's House
9789391316501	A Passage to India

9789391316709	A Portrait of the Artist as a Young Man
9789391316112	A Tale of Two Cities
9789391316747	A Tear and a Smile
9789391316167	Agnes Gray
9789391316174	Alice's Adventures in Wonderland
9789391316136	Anandamath
9789391316181	Anne Of Green Gables
9789391316754	Anthem
9789391316198	Around The World in 80 Days
9789391316013	As A Man Thinketh
9789391316242	Autobiography of a Yogi
9789391316266	Beyond Good and Evil
9789391316761	Bleak House
9789391316778	Chitra, a Play in One Act
9789391316310	David Copperfield
9789391316075	Demian
9789391316785	Dubliners
9789391316051	Favourite Tales from the Arabian Nights
9789391316235	Gitanjali
9789391316068	Gravity
9789391316150	Great Speeches of Abraham Lincoln
9789391316662	Guerilla Warfare
9789391316839	Kim
9789391316822	Mother
9789391316211	My Childhood
9789391316846	Nationalism
9789391316327	Oliver Twist
9789391316853	Pygmalion
9789391316334	Relativity: The Special and the General Theory
9789391316389	Scientific Healing Affirmation
9789391316341	Sons and Lovers
9789391316587	Tales from India
9789391316372	Tess of The D'Urbervilles
9789391316396	The Awakening and Selected Stories
9789391316402	The Bhagvad Gita
9789391316303	The Book of Enoch
9789391316228	The Canterville Ghost
9789391316907	The Dynamic Laws of Prosperity

9789391316006	The Great Gatsby
9789391316860	The Hungry Stones and Other Stories
9789391316433	The Idiot
9789391316440	The Importance of Being Earnest
9789391316297	The Light of Asia
9789391316914	The Madman His Parables and Poems
9789391316457	The Odyssey
9789391316921	The Picture of Dorian Gray
9789391316464	The Prince
9789391316938	The Prophet
9789391316945	The Republic
9789391316518	The Scarlet Letter
9789391316143	The Seven Laws of Teaching
9789391316525	The Story of My Experiments with Truth
9789391316532	The Tales of the Mother Goose
9789391316549	The Thirty Nine Steps
9789391316594	The Time Machine
9789391316600	The Turn of the Screw
9789391316983	The Upanishads
9789391316617	The Yellow Wallpaper
9789391316426	The Yoga Sutras of Patanjali
9789391316990	Ulysses
9789391316624	Utopia
9789391316679	Vanity Fair
9789391316020	What Is To Be Done
9789391316686	Within A Budding Grove
9789391316693	Women in Love